STATESIDE—AND UNDER FIRE AGAIN

Slater tried to get up. Something slippery took his feet out from under him. His hand came up in front of his face, wet, warm, and dark. Not again, dear God, not again . . .

He crawled on his hands and knees. He pulled the body from the wall, ripping his shirt, trying to plug the holes. But there were too many, too many holes oozing life.

Freddy's mouth was full of blood. Each breath in was followed by a warm trickle out. Again and again he blew life in. Again and again it seeped out. *Breathe, goddamn you, breathe.* . . .

HALF A KLICK FROM HOME

C.T. WESTCOTT

CHARTER BOOKS, NEW YORK

HALF A KLICK FROM HOME

A Charter Book / published by arrangement with
the author

PRINTING HISTORY
Charter edition / April 1990

ISBN: 1-55773-336-8

Charter Books are published by The Berkley Publishing Group,
200 Madison Avenue, New York, New York 10016.
The name "CHARTER" and the "C" logo
are trademarks belonging to Charter Communications, Inc.

PRINTED IN THE UNITED STATES OF AMERICA

10   9   8   7   6   5   4   3   2   1

This book is dedicated to the memory of Lieutenant Colonel Charles T. Westcott, USMC (1874–1927), who took the 3rd Battalion, 5th Marines to France in the War to End All Wars. The faces have changed, Grampa, but the Corps is still pulling guard. *Semper Fi.*

"Men, I now knew, do not fight for flag or country, for the Marine Corps or glory or any other abstraction. They fight for one another."

—William Manchester
Goodbye, Darkness

Chapter One

July 1972

THE sentry's eyelids fluttered weakly as a hot phantom breeze drifted up from the south carrying the stink of the sea into the sentry shack. His nap disturbed, he muttered some unintelligible curse, then, groping like a blind man, cranked shut the louvered glass panels of the window facing the painfully brilliant waters of the bight. The heat and glare he could handle, but there was no sleeping with dragon's breath blowing damp and putrid in his nostrils.

Satisfied, Lance Corporal Freddy Claybourne, United States Marine Corps, drifted back into dreams of premium weed, air-conditioned motel rooms, and naked brown-skinned girls.

Down by the Shrimp Docks a rusty silver-gray Camaro made a screeching left turn through the shimmering heat and headed north on the blacktop road leading to the back gate of the Naval Annex. As it neared the gate and the sentry shack, the car slowed, then came to a stop opposite the shack's open doorway.

The Camaro's driver, a bearded young man dressed in filthy dungarees and a faded blue short-sleeved work shirt, drummed his fingers on the steering wheel while his foot played little games with the accelerator. On the seat beside him was a greasy, stained baseball hat with the words USS SIBLEY DD 592 stitched on the crown.

Whatever the driver was waiting for did not materialize. Impatiently he hit his horn. Still nothing. He hollered at the empty darkness of the shack's doorway.

"Hey, come on, man, quit fuckin' around."

Long seconds passed. Then, slowly, the doorframe was filled by a lean-looking black man wearing opaque wrap-around sunglasses and a tropical khaki uniform. A white barracks cover was cocked on his head so that the visor nearly sat on the bridge of his nose—a real hardass look.

Resting his right hand on the butt of the holstered .45 automatic at his hip, Freddy Claybourne spoke, the words coming sleepily and low, directed not so much at the driver as to the universe in general.

"You best be the Admir'l, mutha fucka, else I'm gonna cut your mutha fuckin' dick off an' feed it to the fish."

"Yeah, right," the driver answered. "Come on, I ain't got all day. I'm late for muster. Don't need no hassle, 'kay?"

Claybourne scowled down on the intruder. "Don't want no hassle, huh? What you blowin' your mutha fuckin' horn for? You think I'm deaf or somethin'? Don't be blowin' your mutha fuckin' horn at me, man, not ever. You got that, squid? Let's see some ID."

The driver squeezed the steering wheel until his knuckles turned white. His boyish face, only partially hidden by the scraggly beard, boiled crimson. "What the fuck for?" he growled between clenched teeth. "I got a goddamn base sticker, man, all you gotta do is look. On the bumper."

"You gonna give *me* the hassle, man?" Claybourne answered, his voice still velvety from his snooze. "You want me ta have ta call the SPs over at Main Side? Take 'em maybe half an hour ta get their fat butts out here. Let's see some ID."

"Aw shit!" The angry driver rolled in his seat and reached for his wallet. After a short search he pulled out his military ID and handed it over.

Claybourne pretended to examine the laminated card in great detail, pretty sure that the card's owner was getting ready to blow. He welcomed the diversion. His tour, as always, had been a long boring stand in the sun, and he would not be relieved for another two hours. Besides, the horn had disturbed a very choice dream and for that the sailor deserved a lesson in manners.

When he was positive he'd milked the ID for all the time it was worth, he tossed it back at the driver as if flipping a playing card. The move caught the driver unaware, and he fumbled for the card as it bounced off his forehead onto the floor at his feet.

While the sailor awkwardly scrambled for the ID, Claybourne walked over to the car window, casually placed his hands on each side of the doorframe, and leaned forward. He waited until the driver put the card back in his wallet.

"Now dig this, Crabtree," Freddy said, starting softly and then letting things grow. "See? I know your name now, Crab-fucking-tree, I got a picture of you in my brain, I know your name and I ain't gonna forget it. You ever blow your horn at me again, mutha fuck, and I be lookin' for you on the street. You dig, man? Some night on libs you maybe lose your fuckin' faggoty ass to my boot!"

The sailor stared back into the black face now dominating his world—thick maroon lips, flat pock-marked nose, wrap-around sunglasses reflecting pinpoints of sunlight— the face like some almost-forgotten boogieman from childhood nightmares. Suddenly the sailor named Crabtree wanted to destroy this thing, this thing that had spit on his manhood and insulted his life. This thing, this face, this black face, this *nigger* face, this nigger *Marine* face was all the harassment, pettiness, and chickenshit the military dished out. If he'd known a way, the sailor would have gladly ripped the face to shreds with his bare hands. Instead, he gunned the rusty Camaro's engine and croaked out a response, guarding his words carefully—a splash of colored ribbon on the sentry's chest advertised a part in a war half-a-world away. No telling what these crazy fucking Nam guys would do if you pushed 'em too far.

"You gonna let me through now?" the sailor managed. "You gonna let me through? 'Cause if you don't, my CO's gonna hear about this shit, asshole. You can't harass me, man, I ain't done nothing."

Claybourne's upper lip twitched, almost a smile. "Yeah you has, mutha fuck," he whispered calmly, "you pissed me off. You go ahead and cry to your CO, man, go ahead. Ain't gonna do you no good, though. See, Crab-fucking-tree, I am detainin' you for violatin' base regs. You tell your raggedy-assed CO that!"

"Bullshit!" the sailor nearly screamed, his face boiling like a big red blood blister. "That's bullshit! I didn't break any base regs! It's bullshit!"

"Says you."

"Yeah, says me." The sailor could taste the salty sweat dripping down his face.

"I oughta write you up, Crab-fucking-tree," Claybourne sighed, as if tiring of the game. "Oughta write your ass up. I was gonna leave you go, but I oughta write you up."

"What for? Just tell me that!" The sailor was barely able to catch his breath. "You don't know, do ya? 'Cause it's all bullshit! Fuckin' asshole!"

Claybourne's lips curled upward. He was enjoying himself, a big ol' tomcat toying with a half-dead sparrow. He leaned closer, making sure his breath blew hot on the other man's face.

"You uncovered, fuckhead," Freddy said. "Regs say you gotta be covered to enter this gate, and you ain't covered. Now you go tell *that* to your bad-ass CO, mister squid."

The sailor's faced paled. He glanced down at the baseball cap on the seat beside him. A small vein in his temple began to throb, the fuse to a keg of dynamite lit and burning. He had been had, the sailor realized, pure and simple. All this harassment by the nigger sentry would go unpunished by higher authority. He had failed to put on his hat before entering the base, a stupid regulation, but still a regulation. No matter how much he claimed harassment, the sentry could fall back on that simple fact.

With shaking hands, the sailor picked up the dirty

baseball cap and violently pulled it down on his head. Somebody was going to pay for this. No way for a man to be treated. NO WAY!

Claybourne pushed himself back from the doorframe and, with a minimum of exertion, waved the car through the gate onto the Annex. He had suddenly grown bored of the sailor's silly face.

The Camaro's clutch popped and the car took off in a howl of burnt rubber, headed in the direction of the Navy's destroyer berths a quarter mile away. Claybourne watched it disappear with a satisfied grin. Another fuckin' squid had bit the dust. Man, someday they would start rememberin' to put their hats on, then he'd have to look for some other little red-ass reg to nail their butts on. Till then, this "hat" bullshit would do just fine.

The roar of the car's engine faded. Freddy yawned and glanced down the road toward the Shrimp Docks. The emptiness he saw assured him of resumed peace and quiet. Slowly and deliberately, so as not to let the tropical fire of the afternoon sun sap any more of his strength, he turned and walked back into the shack where he could continue his nap. If there was one thing Post Six was good for, it was providing shade for catching some Z's.

By quarter after three the phantom breeze had died and the July heat lay thick around the sentry shack like a heavy woolen quilt. The waters of Key West Bight sat like turquoise chowder at a dead calm. The shrieking gulls, their bellies finally taking a back seat to the searching rays of the sun, had sought shade inside the deserted government apartment buildings that looked down on the sentry shack with the sightless eyes of empty windowpanes.

Claybourne had resisted the climbing temperature as long as he could, but the cement slab under his feet had become uncomfortably hot. Still in a hazy gray world of half-sleep, he slipped out of his shoes and into a pair of rubber-thonged shower clogs he'd smuggled on post, then let his chin drop back down to his chest. Back to dreamland, baby.

The air-conditioned motel room was just as he'd left it, the slightly stale odor of recycled air covered by some sweet perfume. The bed had been stripped of all but the bottom sheet and pillows, and the room was in darkness except for the glow of a lamp throwing a spotlight on center stage.

The naked woman with the skin like melted milk chocolate lay back on the pillows and moaned softly, then called his name with a faraway voice filled with honey, soft and warm and awe-filled. She wore some sort of Halloween mask over her face. Why she wore it, he didn't know or care. He only knew that in a few moments he would be continuing the legend. When word got out about this, they'd be lined up at his door, taking numbers for a chance to feel his magic. He watched as she extended her arms to him, beckoning. He felt himself float toward her, heard himself laugh, saw himself reflected in golden eyes. Yeah, definitely a legend here.

"Hey, honey, what's the matter with ma man?"

The voice, syrup-dipped and lilting, did not come from the dream but from the shack's doorway. It startled him, but from long practice, he hid the fact. Sleeping on duty, even in this backwater post of the Corps, was still a court-martial offense. Experience had taught him that as long as he had on the shades and didn't act like he'd been surprised, he could usually bluff his way out of any confrontation. In this case though, there wasn't any.

Claybourne opened his eyes. She was leaning against the doorframe with her hands behind her back so that her heavy breasts were thrust in his direction. The blouse was almost transparent; he had no trouble seeing that she wasn't wearing a bra. For a moment he was hypnotized as she moved her shoulders ever so slowly, causing a swaying motion that made him suck in his breath. Only when she spoke again did he look at her face.

"Why, Freddy Claybourne, ain't you glad to see me?"

She wore a shy little-girl smile edged in passion pink. There was nothing little-girl in her eyes, though, they spoke of pure, smoky sex. As if reinforcing that promise, she ran her hand seductively along the curve of a hip covered with a tight orange skirt ending just above mid-thigh. Claybourne swallowed hard. He couldn't remember her name.

Uninvited, she came closer. She smelled of soap, clean and fresh. Still smiling, she placed the fingers of one hand on the heavy rectangular brass plate that served as an ornamental buckle for his white web belt.

Freddy cleared his throat and tried to disguise the stammer in his voice. "B-b-ba-by. Thought I told ya. You ain't suppose to visit me on post. They catch you out here, my butt'll be in a sling."

Her fingers traced their way up from the buckle to the first button on his shirt. She began playing with it.

"I'm sorry, honey," she said, still not looking at him, "just that I ain't seen you in so long. Don't be mad at me. I couldn't stand that, baby, couldn't stand you bein' mad with me. Just want ta hear you say you love me again."

"Sure, baby, sure I love ya. What makes you think any diff'rent?"

Shandy, that was her name, Shandy. He'd gone out with her a couple of times and they'd had some fun. That was before he'd met Carlene. But Carlene was up north visiting relatives, or some such shit. Maybe he could get something going here for tomorrow night. Little Shandy had a nice bod, and hell, he had to consider the legend. Only one way to make it grow.

Visions from his daydream returned and Claybourne felt himself responding. Shandy moved closer and he could smell her heat and fire. Yes, definitely had to get reacquainted with this stuff, no question about it.

"But you said you'd call me, Freddy," Shandy sang. "It's been over a month, baby. Why didn't you call?"

Claybourne brought a hand up to her thigh and began a gentle caress through the fabric of the skirt. "Needed ta rest, baby. You just 'bout wore me out last time. Didn't wanna give you nothin' but my best." He chuckled. "Finally feelin' kinda strong again, though."

He could count the delicate corn rows in her hair, and by glancing straight down he saw the swelling of flesh beneath her blouse.

"You coulda called me." She sounded like a child whose birthday had been forgotten.

"Wanted to, damn straight. But we been hurtin' for people over to the Barracks. Almost on a runnin' guard. Gotta do my patriotic duty and all. I ain't had any town liberty since I went out with you last."

"Is that true?" the girl asked, finally looking up into his face. Her eyes were wide, glowing almost, "Oh, I wish I'da known, 'cause I thought you was lyin' ta me. 'Bout lovin' me an' all. But now I feel better. Now I know for sure. You my lover man . . . Ain't you my lover man, Freddy, ain't you?"

Something in the tone of her voice had changed, something that set off an alarm in Claybourne's mind. Hell, she almost sounded pissed.

"Course, you only my lover man when Carlene's out of town, like she is now. Ain't that right?" The song had gone completely out of Shandy's voice, replaced with barbed fishhooks, the big muthas. "Ain't that right?" she screamed. "Ain't that right, you son of a bitch!"

"Who's Carlene, baby?" Claybourne stepped back and felt the wall of the shack pressing against him. "I don't know no Carlene. You my only—"

Suddenly he couldn't speak. His belly muscles hadn't been ready for the blow, and he found himself bent nearly double by the pain. Shit! Shandy knew how ta throw one hell of a punch. Shit! His mind and his body were both paralyzed; all that registered was the lack of air and a flash of orange skirt exiting the shack. A long string of high-pitched curses rolled off down the road toward town. Then nothing.

Lord Jesus, God Almighty! The pain! What had she hit him with, a sledgehammer? With his back to the wall, he slowly slid down to a sitting position, the polished visor of his barracks cover pushing down on the bridge of his nose, knocking the sunglasses off his face. Clenching his hands to his stomach, he continued to gasp for a breath.

God damn, it hurt!

And as Freddy Claybourne sat there, as he sat like a puppet with its strings cut, he became aware of warm, wet fingers of moisture trickling down his left hip and buttock. Only then did he look down. Protruding from his lower left side was the bone handle of a knife.

CHAPTER TWO

THE bus from Miami turned into a darkened parking lot and eased to a stop. The hissing of the big Greyhound's brakes and the movement of the other passengers signaled Slater that his journey was over. Key West. End of the line.

He waited a minute or two for the aisle to clear, then got to his feet and headed for the door, stretching tired muscles and wiping away eye grit. It had been a long goddamn three days.

By the time he'd pulled his seabag from the belly of the bus, the handful of fellow travelers had already disappeared and the parking lot was deserted. He was about to ask for directions from the whipped-looking bus driver when he felt a second pair of hands grappling with the canvas strap on the bag.

Instinctively he yanked the strap away and squared to find himself almost eyeball-to-eyeball with a short heavyset man in a ratty-looking tee shirt who was grinning at him through a row of gold teeth. The man's skin reminded Slater of his old catcher's mitt, all dark brown leather and oil. An unlit cigarette dangled from the man's lower lip, and while one eye bore into him, the other seemed to be wandering all over the parking lot.

"Hey, Marine, be cool," the man said with a sing-song Latin accent, the cigarette bobbing in time with the music. "Jou lookin' for the Barracks, right?" Slater nodded. "Yeah, I could tell by that short hair jou got. Listen, Hector Manallo take jou there, OK? My cab, she's out in the street." He eased the bag out of Slater's hands and slung it over his shoulder. "Jeez! Dis bag is heavy, Bubba. What jou got inside, torpedoes or something'?"

Without waiting for an answer, the dark-skinned guy in baggy trousers began walking toward the small building with BUS TERMINAL lettered on a darkened window.

What the hell, Slater decided, must be getting on to two in the A.M. and I'm on new ground. God only knows how far I'll have to hump to get to where I'm going. What the hell?

"Hey! How much?" he shouted to the cabby.

"Regular fare is two-fifty, Bubba. Come on, let's go."

Slater shrugged and followed. Just thinking made him tired.

The cab driver turned the corner of the terminal and dove into the darkness of an alley hardly wider than a man's shoulders. Slater plunged in after him and immediately flinched—almost cried out—as the coolness of some broad-leafed plant brushed against his bare arm. He felt sweat bead on his forehead; the night was steaming hot and the heavy foliage on both sides of him gave off the same suffocating smell as the jungle. Shit! Just a touch of a leaf and his guts had flipped. Man, you are really strung-out, Jack.

For a second he thought about doing an about-face, find some other way out to the street. Only the sounds of rock music and the sight of light coming from the end of the short alley in front of him kept him from turning back.

When he got to the sidewalk, the cab driver was already stowing the seabag in the back seat of a low-riding, rust-eaten old Caddy. As he waited near the car's open door, Slater glanced up and down the street. For as far as he could see, the buildings were all painted brick or weathered clapboard, none more than three or four stories tall, darkened store fronts and neon bar signs, your basic fleet town. Diagonally across the street from him, the throbbing metallic sound of live rock music drifted from an open doorway. In the air he could smell the sea mixed with the odor of beer and piss and rotting garbage. Christ, it coulda been downtown Da Nang if you gave your brain half a chance.

"OK, let's go, Bubba."

The driver was holding the door for him, the unlit cigarette still twitching in his lips. Slater slipped into the roomy back seat and felt the car sway under him as the door slammed.

The driver climbed behind the wheel and a moment later started up in a roar of unmuffled internal combustion. Only after he'd pulled away from the curb did he light up the dangling cigarette. Then, with one arm stretched across the top of the seat, the other cocked on the window frame with only the tops of two fingers holding the beast's steering wheel on course, he began to shout over the grumbling thunder of the Caddy's engine.

"Dis here is Doo-val Street, Bubba. Main drag, jou know? Over there, dat the Coo-ban sandwich shop. Jou ever had a Coo-ban sandwich? Bubba, jou ain't lived 'til jou eat one of them fuckers. Better'n pussy, heh?"

Slater was just too damned tired to answer.

The car lurched to a stop at a red light and the engine gave signs of dying on the spot. The driver revved it; the whole chassis vibrated. At the same time, he flicked the ash from his cigarette into a tin can on the dashboard. The cab turned left on green.

"Now this is Southard Street," the cabby continued to jabber. "Straight shot to the base. Guys take their clothes to that laundromat, jou see there? Open all night. And up here, over to jou right, that the USO. Jou can tell by the sign. Gotta pretty gal runnin' it, but I hear she's cold fish. I dunno, maybe jou get lucky, eh?" The driver laughed and looked back over the seat, the gold in his teeth reflecting the street light as the Caddy rolled up onto the sidewalk and took out a metal trash can before bumping back down off the curb. The driver didn't seem the least bit worried. "Big tits, jou know? Hey, Bubba, jou wanna buy some shit?"

Slater had tuned the guy out pretty well. He wasn't sure if he'd heard the question right. "What'd you say, man?"

"Jou wanna buy some grass? Hector got some supremo stuff. Blow jou head off."

"No thanks, man. Just keep this heap on the road, will ya?"

Should have humped it, Slater thought. Jesus, trying to sell him dope not five minutes after he'd gotten off the bus. Jesus.

The cab continued its swaying voyage up the street, the driver still babbling. Ahead through the windshield Slater caught sight of a floodlit sign arched across the road. Below it, in the middle of the street, was a small building that looked like the top of an airport control tower. He could see the shape of two figures moving around inside in the greenish glow of tinted glass.

As the cab got closer, he could make out the gold letters on the crescent sign: US NAVAL BASE, KEY WEST.

"This here the main gate, Bubba," the cabby said as he began pumping his brakes. "After one o'clock, it be the only way in or outa this place. Jou find out. See there? Some a jou buddies."

Complying with a stop-for-the-sentry sign, the Caddy lurched to a halt opposite the concrete island that supported the small glass and yellow stucco building. One of the uniformed Marines inside looked up and then moved through an open doorway onto the island. He stopped a few feet from the driver's window, the visor of his cover pulled low over his forehead so that his face was in shadow. He was a young man, raw-boned and hard-looking with a chin that jutted out like an extra shelf.

"What ya got this time, Manallo," the sentry growled, "a drunk squid or your mother's boyfriend?"

The sentry's words were not spoken in a friendly tone, but the driver answered as if the two of them were old friends.

"Hey, Corporal Tollster, how jou doin'? They put jou back on Post One, huh? Good to see jou again."

"Cut the bullshit, Hector. What's your business?"

"Just helpin' out jou brudda Marine. Takin' him over to the Barracks where he wanna go."

The sentry named Tollster stepped down and leaned into the rear window. Slater raised a hand in greeting but the man made no sign in return.

"Never seen this guy before," Tollster said. "He ain't with the Barracks."

The words were spoken to the cabby, but Slater figured they were for him. He was wearing civvies—jeans and a button-down shirt—even though he'd had to eat the bus company's discount fare for service personnel traveling in uniform. "Just reporting in, man," he said. "Name's Slater. Sergeant. On PCS orders."

The sentry stared at him for a few seconds, then pointed at his levis. "If you're on PCS, how come you're travelin' in civvies?"

Slater shrugged. He didn't feel like going through all the bullshit of explaining that he'd gotten real tired of people looking at him like he was a cold-blooded hit man for Uncle Sam.

The sentry's lips remained tight. He wanted proof. "Let's see your ID."

Slater got out his ID card and handed it through the window. The sentry stood back from the car and tilted the card toward the light over his shoulder. The second sentry, a shorter man with jug-ears and the single stripe above crossed rifles on his sleeve that showed he was a lance corporal, stepped out onto the island. He too recognized the driver.

"Hector Manallo—what's happenin', pud-lick?"

The cabby ignored the question as he ran a comb through his hair. The second sentry peered over the corporal's shoulder to get a look at the ID. "Whatja got, Bone?" he asked.

Without answering, the other man finished reading and stepped back to the car. This time when he leaned into Slater's window, there was a big gap-toothed grin on his face. He tilted back the visor on his cover and extended a hand in Slater's direction.

"Welcome aboard, man. We can sure use your bod around here, believe it. Thought we was gonna have ta go to a running guard. Name's Tollster, Bone Tollster."

Slater took the man's hand. "Hey, man, how ya doin'? Never thought I'd make it. My butt is really draggin'."

Tollster remained leaning into the back seat, elbows on the window frame. "Come in on the midnight 'hound, huh?" He waved a thumb back over his shoulder at the lance corporal hovering behind him. "That fuckhead there is Narvel LeFey. We call him fuckhead 'cause he got the tip of his dick bit off down at Captain Willy's." Tollster turned his head. "Ain't that right, Nar-vel?"

"Fuck you, man," the other sentry laughed. "Howdy, Sarge," he said, leaning down and flicking a little two-finger salute in Slater's direction. "Good ta see ya."

A set of headlights approached from the opposite direction and LeFey passed back through the gatehouse to wave the vehicle off-base.

"Where you from, Slater?" Tollster seemed in no hurry for the cab to move along.

"First Marines."

"Oh yeah? Where abouts?"

"Down in some paddies, few klicks south of Marble Mountain. You?" Slater had noticed the ribbons on Tollster's chest. There was a Bronze Star and a Purple Heart along with the usual geedunk.

"Two-Eleven," the sentry answered. "Rockpile for awhile. Then the Hoi Van pass."

"Cannon-cocker, huh?"

"That's me," Tollster grinned. "How long you been back in the World?"

Slater pretended to do calculations in his head. "Oh,

about two weeks, two days, and sixteen hours. Right now I feel like I've been awake the whole goddamn time."

"Well, listen, man," Tollster said as he removed his cover and scratched at a thatch of short blond hair. "I'll let you dee-dee on out of here then. Get you some Z's. I'll call the Corporal of the Guard and let 'em know you're coming." He reached forward and roughly messed the driver's hair. "And don't let ol' Hector here rip ya off."

Manallo squirmed out of reach but the damage had already been done. "Hey, man! What the fuck jou doin?" the cabby fussed.

Tollster laughed and stepped over to the driver's window. He reached in and wiped his hands on the back of the cabby's tee shirt. Manallo went ape-shit.

"Hell, Hector," the sentry said as he backed away from the thrashing driver, "you're about due for an oil change, my man." He looked over at Slater. "Take it easy, man. You'll most likely be in Starboard Section 'cause we're the most short, so I'll be seeing ya."

Tollster readjusted his cover so that the visor once again covered most of his face with shadow, then stepped forward and gave the driver's door a whack. "Come on, Manallo. Get this fuckin' hemorrhoid moving, and make sure the sergeant here don't get lost. We need his ass."

Whatever Latin curse Manallo answered with was drowned out by the loud rumbling of the Caddy's engine as the accelerator was floored. For all the noise, the Caddy responded like an old man with bad knees. As it grumbled away from the main gate, Slater leaned back in the musty seat cushion. He felt relieved somehow, as though he was through the wire; an imaginary M-16 was clicked on safe.

A few minutes later the car hung a hard U turn and Slater was shoved roughly against the car door, then had to throw his arms out in front of him to keep his head from slamming into the back of the seat as the Caddy came to an abrupt stop. Manallo was out opening the rear door before Slater had a chance to take a deep breath. Didn't take a genius to figure the ride was over, though. He pushed his seabag out onto the sidewalk and followed it.

The Barracks stood in front of him behind a shoulder-high concrete wall topped with fancy wrought iron fencing. The building itself was pretty plain, three stories of cracked stucco with a peaked roof. It probably looked taller than it really was since it rested on a slope rising sharply from street level. The row of windows on the top and second deck were all dark except at the far left end; their darkness contrasted eerily with the yellow stucco facing that reflected the moonlight in a ghostly paleness.

He was standing at the bottom of steps that led to a portico and glass-louvered double doors. The portico was lighted by floodlights hidden behind two palm trees growing on each side of the walkway. About half the windows on the ground floor showed a dim light coming from inside, but there was no sign of activity.

"OK, Bubba," the cabby said, extending an open palm. "That be ten bucks."

Slater felt the hair on the back of his neck bristle. "Sorry," he said uneasily, sure he hadn't heard this character right. "What'd you say?"

"Jou owe me ten bucks."

The tingling on his neck got worse. He smelled ripoff. "Ten bucks, my ass. You said two-fifty."

"Hey, Bubba, I say two-fifty for the ride. It's seven-fifty extra for the tour."

"What tour?" The adrenaline started to pump. Suddenly the fatigue of the last three days and nights on the Greyhound were gone. Danger here.

"I give jou a tour a downtown, man. Don't jou remember? Come on, ten bucks. I ain't got all night."

This guy was unreal. "Kiss my ass," Slater said as he hoisted the seabag to his shoulder and turned. Just walk away, he decided, just walk away. No trouble.

It wasn't going to happen that way, though.

He was almost to the first step when he felt a hand pulling

on his arm. He wheeled slowly; the seabag was heavy. At first all he saw was the nasty scowl on Manallo's face. Then he spotted the snub-nosed revolver pointed at his midsection. He felt a molten jolt rise from his belly to his brain. Well now, Jack, looks like you might have to kill this son of a bitch.

"Jou give me ten bucks else I put a hole in jou guts," the cabby snarled. "Hector give jou the tour and jou gonna pay for the tour, jou fuckin' jarhead!"

The words had barely cleared Manallo's lips when the flying seabag, weighing close to fifty pounds, caught him full force in the middle of the chest. He staggered, then fell over backward to the pavement, the gun clattering across the cement. The Marine walked over to the weapon, paused, then crushed it under his foot, the plastic snapping loudly. He returned to where the cabby still lay and lifted the seabag from the man's chest.

A voice somewhere told Slater to step on the guy's throat and crush it like he'd crushed the cap gun. But he shoved the savage back in his padded cell. No big deal.

"How jou know?" Manallo gasped.

"Know what?"

"How jou know it's only a toy?"

"I didn't."

Slater dug into the pocket of his jeans, then dropped two crumpled dollar bills on Manallo's face. Without another word, he hoisted the bag to his shoulder again and began walking toward the brightly lit entranceway.

"Hey, Bubba!" Manallo called.

Slater stopped and looked back over his shoulder. The cabby had pushed himself to his knees.

"Yeah?"

"Jou owe me another fifty cents!"

Slater did a double take, made a kind of hiccuping sound that might've been a try at a laugh, then turned and climbed the last set of steps leading to the portico. When he reached the doorway, he looked back one more time.

Manallo was running a comb through his oily hair, standing next to the driver's door of the Caddy.

"Fuckin' jarhead!" the cabby shouted. "Maybe next time we meet up, I got a *real* piece."

Slater shook his head, managed a smile that said he didn't believe the cabby could have such balls, then pulled open the door and walked into the Barracks.

For the first time since leaving his father's house back in Detroit, Jack Slater felt as though he was finally on friendly ground.

CHAPTER THREE

THE air inside the Barracks felt frigid compared to the steaming heat outside. From somewhere deep in the building he heard the hum of a big compressor pumping out the cool. He was in a wide, high-ceilinged hallway that ended thirty yards away with another set of double doors leading outside again. There was a rec-room to his left. Nobody there so he moved off down another corridor extending to his right. He didn't call out to announce himself; it would have been like shouting in church.

The corridor opened onto a large empty room, dark except for a shaft of light coming from under a doorway off in the far corner. Slater headed for the light.

Suddenly he was down on the deck, the seabag flying out of his hands. He knew he'd tripped over something, something soft and alive, something that had turned into a cyclone of motion, entangling his legs and forcing him off balance. The sounds of the assault were like nothing he'd ever heard before, though—a clatter of claws followed by a coughing rasp and then a whole series of hard, rattling wheezes.

What the hell was it? Slater searched his mind for a clue. Nothing. Only an icy churning of fear in his gut. He hated the dark! Goddamn hated it!

His ear was suddenly filled with a blast of hot breath, then with a wet, slimy, fleshy-feeling something that got his attention like a swift kick in the tail. He rolled away from the awfulness and pushed himself to a sitting position.

"Jesus H. Christ!" he bellowed.

The face in front of him, caught in the light from the now

opened doorway, was a vision from hell. A jaw full of jagged teeth protruded over pink gums and pointed in a dozen different directions at once. The nose was crushed back into the face, nostrils flared and spouting snot. The eyes were widely spaced, dripping some kind of muck in long trails which were lost in heavy, meaty jowls. A hot rotting smell of bad meat blew from the creature's jaws into Slater's face and he almost gagged. A beast from hell, no doubt about it.

"Jesus H. Christ!" he shouted again. Whatever this thing was, it was coming right at him.

"Jiggs, you damn fool," a voice from the doorway sounded, "what the hell you doin'?"

Slater rolled on a hip and saw a short black man dressed in tropical khaki silhouetted by the light.

"Damn dog," the man continued, "gonna wake up the whole Barracks. Here there! Get off the man."

While Slater's attention had been drawn by the man's voice, the beast had locked on to one of his thighs with its two front legs and was now pumping its lower body at him with a great dripping hardon. The animal's tongue lolled out of its mouth like some thick pink snake, and its black eyes, fixed on Slater's face, were filled with a glassy, faraway look that spoke of take-no-prisoners lust.

"Looks like Jiggs is in love again," the Marine in the doorway said. "Just give him a whack 'cross his ugly nose, man. He'll give up."

Slater cautiously slapped the dog across the snout with the back of his hand, half expecting to lose at least a finger to those god-awful teeth. The dog snorted, stopped its humping, and gave Slater an almost human look of disbelief. But it still didn't let go of his leg.

"I think you got his attention," the other man said. "Slap him again; he'll let go."

Guy was right. Another backhand and the animal stepped back. It began shivering violently, its huge head drooping, the rasping sound of heavy breathing letting on that the dog was not real happy at getting shut down like that.

Slater's throat felt like he'd caught a chicken bone in there somewhere. He tried to speak. "What's with him, he queer or somethin'?"

The other man chuckled. "Could be, man, but ol' Jiggs there don't care what sex it is. If it moves, he'll fuck it. Should see him go after the vacuum cleaner. Shit, you wave a mop in front of his face and he'll either eat it or try ta get it pregnant. You're lucky he didn't chomp on your butt, man. Before the Sergeant Major got him, belonged ta some old lady up the Keys. One night some dude tried ta rip off her pad, and this fucker got his teeth into him and wouldn't let go. Cops had ta go 'round the dog's head with billy clubs before he'd quit. Think it did a number on his brain."

"I didn't see him," Slater said, suddenly feeling a little self-conscious about what had happened, about being so goddamned scared. "I was walking back here, tripped over him. Shit! Didn't know *what* the hell it was."

"Yeah, he sleeps out here . . . alone. Troops won't have him up topside 'cause he's always tryin' ta diddle 'em while they asleep. You must be the new dude. Tollster said you was comin' in. He should've told you ta come round back to the Guard Shack. We the only people workin' this time of night. Name's Benjamin. Sergeant of the Guard."

The man extended his hand and helped Slater to his feet. Despite the man's short height and slender frame, there was a wiry strength in his arms. Like many young black Marines Slater had met, he had cultivated a pencil-line moustache that did little to disguise his youth.

"Slater. Jack Slater. Glad to see you, man, in more ways than one. For a minute there I figured that dipshit cab driver had dropped me off at the wrong place."

Benjamin reached for the seabag, then moved back into the lighted room, motioning with his head for Slater to follow. The dog had collapsed in a heap and was already snoring, the tip of its tongue sticking out from between clenched teeth.

"Lemme guess," Benjamin said over his shoulder, "Hector Manallo, right?"

"Yeah, that's what Tollster called him."

"Man's a mutha fuck. Everybody knows Hector. A real mutha fuck."

The sign on the open door said GUARD OFFICE. The room was bare except for two desks and five or six chairs haphazardly scattered around as if they'd been used in some informal bull session. One wall was completely covered with an organizational chart displaying names written in with smudged grease pencil on acetate. Through a side door Slater could see a rack of .45 automatics on a high counter. Behind the counter was another Marine talking quietly on the phone.

"Yeah, Hector's a real bag of shit," Benjamin continued, dropping the seabag in a corner, then turning. "Always tryin' ta rip people off or fuck 'em up."

"Tell me about it," Slater said. "Crazy asshole tried to hold me up for ten bucks—with a goddamn toy gun! Damn thing had a plug in the barrel and the cylinders were empty. Real dumb-fuck."

"You got that right. Take a load off, man. I gotta go get the CDO up. He's gonna be happy ta see you. We're short personnel."

Benjamin disappeared back out the door they'd just entered. Slater pulled his seabag over to one of the folding chairs and sat down. From the bag he took out a brown file folder and began thumbing through its pages. He'd already read the orders a hundred times; they always boiled down to the same thing: his last two years in the Corps would be spent here at the Marine Barracks, Key West. Then what? Pump gas?

A few minutes later muffled voices came from the big room where he'd tripped over the dog. Benjamin came in with another man following in his footsteps. The new man was half dressed in a tee shirt and tropical trousers, the belt buckle hanging unfastened. His hair was close-cropped except for a small clump on top and a cowlick that stuck up in back like that kid on the Little Rascals. He was medium height and built with the kind of long-muscled leaness you saw in a lot of young Marines, but he also carried himself in a manner that Slater immediately recognized as authority. After almost two years in the Crotch, he could tell an officer from a mile away, and he instinctively got to his feet, not quite coming to attention, but standing straight with his arms held loosely at his sides.

"Any coffee left, Sergeant Benjamin?" The officer's voice sounded hoarse and brittle, the sound of a man pulled from sleep.

"Brewed fresh yesterday morning, sir."

"Anything." The officer blinked as his eyes grew accustomed to the light. He turned to Slater. "How about you, Marine. Want a cup?"

"Uh, no, sir," Slater answered. "I'm wired enough. Did a gallon of the stuff up in Miami waiting for the 'hound."

"You're not missing anything. Guard Shack coffee walks. Welcome aboard. I'm Lieutenant Kargo. Tonight I'm Command Duty Officer, but my usual job is Guard Officer. And since you'll be in the Guard . . ." Kargo held out his hand. "Welcome aboard."

"Slater, sir. Sorry about rousting you out of the rack. Coulda waited till morning."

"No sweat," Kargo said. "Had to get up to check posts anyway. Got your orders? Give 'em over and I'll endorse them right now."

Slater did as he was told and Kargo went over to one of the desks. He glanced at the first page as Benjamin returned from the Guard Shack with a mug in his hand and placed it on the desktop.

"Thanks," Kargo said. "Have Corporal Norwick log Sergeant Slater here reporting aboard for duty at whatever time it is."

"Zero two-forty, sir," Benjamin answered. "You want me to put Jiggs on report?"

"Yeah, rape and assault. Give it to the sergeant major in the morning. We didn't expect you for another two weeks or so, Slater."

"Sir?" He was surprised to learn he'd been expected.

"Headquarters sent us your SRB and an advanced copy of your orders. Didn't expect you for at least another fifteen days."

"Cut my leave short, sir. Things were getting . . . well, kinda dull back home. I decided what the hell, might as well—"

Kargo cut him off. "Sounds like you're trying to apologize for saving us a lot of problems. If you hadn't shown up, we'd have been shit out of luck. As of yesterday afternoon the Starboard Section is one man short so you've done us a big favor." Kargo opened the drawer in front of him and pulled out a pen. He scratched something at the bottom of the first page of orders, then pushed himself to his feet. "Sergeant Benjamin will get you bedded down. I'll hang on to your orders and give 'em to the Admin Chief in the morning. Once you're all squared away, Gunny Brownell or I will fill you in on what goes on around here. See you tomorrow."

The lieutenant got up and left the office. Benjamin motioned Slater to follow him with his gear. They passed through the Guard Shack, and after a few words with Norwick—a red-headed corporal with an accent straight out of the Arkansas hill country—they went outside onto a concrete porch that ran the length of the rear of the Barracks. A narrow street paralleled the porch, separating the building from a low row of Butler Buildings and a small parking lot where an old pickup truck with a camper in its cargo bed was sitting.

The camper's door hung open and soft strains of Latin music drifted from inside through the still night air. A few feet to the left of the vehicle was a body slumped in a lawn chair.

"What's the story over there?" Slater asked as Benjamin led him up a wide stairway with metal deckplates for steps.

Benjamin seemed to know right away what he was talking about. "That's Zamora's family. Been here more'n a month now. Followed him all the way from Arizona or somewhere—gramma, mother, sister'n law, and the ol' man there, his uncle who is constantly shit-faced. XO tried ta run the bunch of 'em off half a dozen times but they keep comin' back. Only time Zamora sees 'em is on payday, otherwise he leaves 'em alone like most everybody else. The ol' granny's a witch. Nobody wants ta mess with her shit."

"Mexican?"

"I dunno. Mexicans, Indians, Zamora don't say what. Myself, I figure they're gypsies or somethin'. Ain't hurt nobody yet."

The two men reached the top of the stairway and Slater found himself on a wide veranda looking out over the parking lot and the row of warehouses. He followed Benjamin to the far end of the deck where they entered another door, this one with a red light bulb glowing above the frame.

Except for a few low wattage nightlights, this part of the Barracks was dark. Wall lockers and bunkbeds loomed in the shadows, the sounds of snores and the creak of springs left no doubt that these were the living spaces. Place reeked of sweat and shoe polish and a dozen other smells of garrison life.

Benjamin led him down the middle of the bay, down a wide aisle formed by the lockers and bunks. They stopped at one rack with a bare mattress in the upper bunk and Benjamin handed him two folded sheets and a pillow case that had come from a cabinet back in the Guard Shack.

"You can sign for this stuff in the morning down to Supply," Benjamin whispered. "Don't worry about no blanket, won't need one 'til probably January. Reveille's at 0630. Company formation's at 0730." Benjamin gestured toward the empty bottom bunk of Slater's rack. "You might wanna know," he said matter-of-factly, "your bunkmate is Freddy Claybourne. He's out at the hospital. Got himself knifed on post yesterday by some ginch in town."

"Bad?" Slater was thinking too much about sleep to get interested.

"He'll live. But like the lieutenant said, we can sure use your butt right about now. I'll be talkin' to ya in the mornin' . . . be cool, man."

"Right. See ya."

Benjamin's footsteps gradually grew fainter until the crash of the door silenced them entirely. Slater heard a few groans in response to the noise, and somewhere at the end of the bay someone sleepily cursed the intrusion. Then there were only snores again.

Fumbling a little in the dark, he found an empty locker and tossed in his seabag. Benjamin had been right. Despite the air conditioner below, the bay was warm and humid; he would not need a blanket.

Later, as he lay in the fuzzy world between sleep and wakefulness, Slater's dream returned, the same dream he'd had over and over again since coming home. It was not a nightmare—though he guessed nightmares should've been expected—as much as it was a strange jerky collection of images, sights, and sounds.

Tonight he was back in the company area, safely inside the wire, behind the sandbags, back in the squad hooch. They were playing poker on the Hunchback's rack, all of them in a circle, Chaffey, Frankie, Banana Dick, the rest. And outside the circle was Choo Choo, trying to join in. But no one would deal him a card, no one would move over and make a place for him, no one called his name.

And even when Choo Choo tried to scream, no one heard. Not surprising for a dead man.

CHAPTER FOUR

MORNING formation. Slater stood loosely with about sixty other Marines in three ranks facing the rear of the Barracks. Up on the first deck veranda, the short black sergeant—Benjamin—was taking muster. To Slater's left the jug-eared kid named LeFey grumbled about missing chow. On Slater's right Bone Tollster continued a running commentary on Barracks life.

"Suck suck suck suck suck suck suck . . ."

Behind them, across the company street in the parking lot, Zamora's People were cooking breakfast in one of those big round cast-iron pots that reminded Slater of cartoons about cannibals and missionaries. A woman who looked about as old as rock stirred the steaming pot with a big wooden spoon while the rest of the family—two other women dressed like the cook in peasant skirts and shawls and an old man in sneakers and sagging trousers—sat around the pot in lawn chairs. The music he'd heard last night was still floating around, only now it was more up-tempo, a Latin shit-kicker.

"Uh-oh," he heard Tollster whisper loudly. "Stand the fuck by, girls. Screamin' Don is on the prowl."

There was, Slater could see right away, a tightening in the ranks. Nobody besides Tollster said anything, but all of a sudden the Marines around him were standing-to a little more, bringing heels together, dropping their hands to the seams of their trousers, squeezing butt muscles, rolling back shoulders. Fucking Wyatt Earp had arrived in Dodge City.

And the marshal was standing at the far end of the

company street. Slater spotted him out of the corner of his eye. A tall son of a bitch, six-four or -five maybe, with a long flat square build like an NFL tight end, one-ninety, two hundred pounds. Even from where he was standing, Slater caught the morning sunlight glinting off the railroad tracks of a Marine captain on the man's tropical khaki shirt, and on the pisscutter cocked so far down on the bridge of the man's nose that the hat looked for a minute like it was growing from his forehead.

"Who the hell is that?" Slater muttered to Tollster. "CO?"

"Naw, Executive Officer. Capt'n Brule. But the Major's TAD to some fuckin' school for generals so Screamin' Don's got the conn for the next few months—actin' CO. Too bad they ain't sending us grunts ta Nam anymore. I'd volunteer."

"Hardass, huh?"

"You got that right. . . . Aw shit, here he comes!"

Don Brule was steaming. The baby had had him and Peg up all night coughing and spitting phlegm. God damn it! Now these gypsies were *cooking* again! *Cooking* in his backyard. How many times had he run them off? How many times had he threatened Zamora with everything from fines to court-martial? How many times had he complained to that lard-gutted master chief over at Base Security? Nothing did any good. Zamora's people themselves pretended they didn't understand English, so they just stood there and stared when he jumped them. Zamora kept claiming he didn't know who these people were. As for the fat chief, well, Don Brule had been around long enough to know when the Navy was pulling his chain. He'd run Zamora's people off base a dozen times, and every time that fat fucking chief would turn right around and issue them another fourteen-day visitor's pass. The thing that really galled him was there wasn't a damn thing he—the Acting Commanding Officer of this lash-up for Christ's sakes—

could do about it. The parking lot where Zamora's people hung out was technically Navy property. It did not belong to the Barracks.

Just another sign of the Great Slack, the Great Huge Slack that grew in the heat of Key West like fertilized crabgrass. He'd already seen what the Great Slack had done to the Navy—long hair and beards and liberty in dungarees. Christ, even the officers looked like fucking hippies! No discipline. No pride. No leadership. Might as well have cancer.

Well, the Great Slack was not going to take over this outfit while he was in charge—no damn way. Thank God Major Brocksneider had been able to wangle those TAD orders. Now he had a chance to whip this crew into shape.

As far as he was concerned, Brocksneider was too easy-going, too pre-occupied with socializing with the local civilian big-shots. A motor transport officer for Christ's sakes, already selected for Lieutenant Colonel. Brocksneider wouldn't have recognized the Great Slack if it'd reared up and bit him on the ass. Don Brule could see it getting a toehold at the Barracks, though, little things like unshined brass and spots on uniforms and a slow, draggy response to orders. Worst of all, he'd begun to see improper haircuts—the surest sign of all that the Great Slack was infecting the men.

Let a little hair grow and the next thing you knew they'd be dealing with drugs and faggotry and all the other shit. Well, by God, he was now the acting CO and in a position to bring the Great Slack to a screaming halt. Might as well start with this abortion they called a formation.

From his position up on the porch, Sergeant Benjamin shouted them to attention and then double-timed down to follow the tall captain through the ranks. A deathlike stillness fell over the formation. Slater wisely locked his eyes "in-the-boat" while wondering what would come next. For a while all he heard was some muffled talk coming from far down the ranks. Then the tall captain, with Benjamin at his side, was stopping in front of a bent-shouldered little lance corporal directly in front of Slater, and he was able to get a closer look at the man Tollster had called Screamin' Don.

The officer was even bigger than he'd first figured. Not fat or anything, just big, with a long pale face and regulation glasses sitting just under that cocked pisscutter.

"They let your wife outta the hospital yet, Lesmon?" he heard the captain ask the droopy lance corporal.

"Yes, sir," the man answered meekly.

"The next time she decides to slit her wrists," the captain boomed so that everybody and his brother could hear, "you tell her to do it right. Quit scratching herself with a fingernail file. Open them suckers up with something heavy, like a butcher's knife. No, no. Belay that. Tell her to cut her fucking head off and be done with it. But I'll let you in on a little secret, stud. There is no way you'll be relieved from post again just 'cause she decides she's lonely and wants her hubby back. She'll just have to fucking bleed to death by herself 'cause you, stud, are not gonna be relieved. *You* will stay on post! You getting all this or you want me to write her a memo?"

"Got it sir," the man named Lesmon gulped.

"Good. Benjamin, this man is on report for not wearing a tee shirt."

Fuckin' amazing! Slater was so caught up with what the captain was saying that he'd let his eyes drift to watch. Some kind of built-in radar must've picked this up; the captain glanced over Lesmon's shoulder and caught him looking. Oh shit.

"What have we here?" he heard Brule say.

A few seconds later and the tall captain was standing front and center, close enough for Slater to get a whiff of aftershave.

"My my my my," the captain said, "what *have* we here?" Slater wasn't sure if he was supposed to answer the question or not. He decided maybe he'd better keep his mouth shut.

"You must be the new trooper came aboard last night."

"Yes, sir."

"You got a name, stud?"

"Slater, sir."

"From WestPac, right?"

"Yes, sir."

"Well, you're just about the saltiest thing I've seen in a long time . . . is it 'sergeant'?"

"Yes, sir."

"Good guess, huh? Your rank insignia is so damned fucked up I can barely tell."

Brule reached out and tugged at the small metal sergeant's chevrons on Slater's collar. Slater kept his eyes locked straight ahead, at about the level of the vee of the captain's shirt. He was aware of the man's ribbons: a Bronze Star with a combat "V" was first in line. Christ, Slater thought, was everybody in this outfit a hero?

"You sleep in that uniform, Marine?" Brule continued.

"No, sir."

"Looks like you did. You wear utilities around here, you get 'em starched and pressed, you got that?"

"Yes, sir."

The captain paused. Slater felt eyeballs giving him the once-over.

"How old are you, stud?"

"Twenty, sir."

"You ever hear of shoe polish?"

"Yes, sir."

"Coulda fooled me. Around here, we use it on our boots, more'n once a year, too. Where'd you get those boots, stud?"

"Seabag, sir."

"Oh, shit. All that mold and mildew, thought maybe you got 'em off a Salvation Army truck, maybe a dead dink. My mistake. You married?"

"No, sir."

"Good. Another candidate for suicide we don't need. When's the last time you had a haircut?"

Slater felt his ears burn. He couldn't remember.

"Well?"

"Ah, I think, about five or six weeks—"

"Let me tell you something, Slater," Brule interrupted. "We're up to our asses around here in salty E-5s from WestPac. You think you're gonna slide just because you've seen some action, you can forget it. This is the Marine Corps, stud. Now, before this day is out, you will get yourself a haircut. Not some fucking razor trim around the ears either, but a goddamn haircut just like mine."

Brule flexed his knees and dropped down far enough for Slater to look him in the eyes. The captain took off his pisscutter. Except for a quarter-inch of hair on top, the officer's head had been skinned.

Bloodshot eyes stared at him from behind the lenses of the glasses. There was nothing on the captain's face except a cold blank expression that said pretty damn clearly: "Don't fuck with me."

"You understand, stud?" Brule asked, running a hand over the stubble on his head. "Just like mine."

"I understand, sir," Slater answered.

Oh, he understood all right, he understood only too goddamn well.

Even with the hatch shut, Slater could hear Captain Brule screaming at some poor bastard in the office next door, but the shouting was only a muffled background noise as the Barracks' sergeant major handed out his own brand of discipline.

"Stand at attention when I talk ta you, ape-shit. And quit droolin' on my rug."

The sergeant major's words sounded like steel wool across slate. His name, Slater read from the red and gold desk plate, was J.G. Hollihan, a big lantern-jawed Irishman in his fifties with enough lines and creases in his face to qualify as a relief map.

Still waiting for an answer to his question, Hollihan jammed a cigar into the corner of his mouth and lit up.

"So what ya got ta say for yerself, turd," he continued. "And quit lickin' yer balls in fronta other enlisted personnel! Gawl damn moose-fuck! You cocksuckers is all the same. Well, ya ain't gettin' away with it this time. We got witnesses. You read him his rights yet, Delkirt?"

The only other person in the office was a tall skinny kid who reminded Slater of that Disney character who'd gotten wasted by the Headless Horseman. Delkirt stood off to one side of Hollihan's desk, a Service Record Book open in his hands.

"Yes I did, Sergeant Major," he said.

"And?"

"He refused to make a statement, and gave no indication that he desired legal counsel."

"Don't make no difference if he had. Like I said, turd, we got witnesses. Read the charges, Delkirt."

The skinny Marine cleared his throat and read from the SRB. "Charge One, Violation of Article 128 of the Uniformed Code of Military Justice. That at or about 0200, on or about 20 July, 1972, Private First Class U.S. Jiggs, USMC, did commit an assault on a non-commissioned officer. . . . Charge Two, Violation of Article 120, UCMJ, in that aforementioned individual did then attempt an act of rape on a non-commissioned officer."

The sergeant major pulled the cigar from his mouth and leaned over his desk to stare at the bulldog sprawled out on the carpet.

"How do ya plead, duck-brain?"

There was a pause, then the dog loudly broke wind. "Holy shit!" Hollihan roared as he fell back into the chair, mock astonishment on his face. "Add gross insubordination to the charges, Delkirt, and get them papers ready for the

XO to sign. Unless I miss my guess, the captain's gonna bust this turd ta buck private again."

"Aye, aye, Sergeant Major. You want his dress blues?"

"Yeah, give 'em over. Save some time."

Slater watched as Delkirt removed a small piece of navy blue material from the wall where it hung beneath a Smokey the Bear campaign hat. The blue cloth had red piping on its border and a gold PFC chevron sewn on one side. Delkirt placed the dog's uniform in front of the sergeant major who had taken a pen knife from his pocket. Methodically, Hollihan cut the stitches around the chevron and removed the rank insignia from the material.

"That's all, Delkirt," the sergeant major said. "Make sure you got a squared-away uniform for tomorrow night. You'll be standing Post Six."

A look of pure pain replaced the amusement on Delkirt's face. "Aw geez, Sergeant Major, not again! Captain Brule didn't say anything about—"

"Stow it, Marine," Hollihan interrupted. "Skipper ain't had a chance ta tell ya yet. I'm just tryin' ta give ya some extra time so's you can get yer shit together. Don't wanna hear no bitchin'. You know the score around here. Sometimes even us office poags gotta face extra duties when the Guard Roster is thin. Be a man and face yer duties with the proper attitude. Just be glad yer not getting Eleven like the sergeant here. Now get back to work."

Hollihan chuckled as the unhappy Delkirt left the office. Without looking at Slater, he yanked open a bottom drawer of his desk. The drawer rebelled loudly; the response to it was instantaneous.

First there was the sound of great panting, then the massive head and dripping jowls of now Buck Private Jiggs appeared around the corner of the desk. The dog locked eyeballs with Hollihan and let its tongue dangle.

"What the hell you want, Marine?" Hollihan asked as he lifted a can of Dinty Moore stew from the drawer. He glanced over at Slater for a moment, his eyes twinkling.

"How many times I gotta tell ya, turd, that ya don't screw around with yer own men?" Hollihan began to open the can with an old C-ration opener. "Gotta tell ya," he continued, "I'm disappointed as hell with ya, Private. I bust my butt to get you promoted and this is how ya pay me back. Next time it's a court-martial, ya understand? Assault and rape is serious charges."

The dog yawned in a pop of jaw ligaments, its bulging eyes riveted on the can of stew. "Oh that's the way it is, huh?" Hollihan asked. "Well, put this in yer seabag, Private—I just might eat this stuff my ownself."

With a plastic spoon he lifted a large chunk of meat from the can. Smacking his lips, he held the spoon up to his face, pausing to glance down at the dog who was beginning to shiver and shake. Slowly, ever so slowly, Hollihan slipped the spoon between his own lips and sucked the chunk of meat into his mouth with a loud, long slurp. As he began to chew, the dog started to bark furiously, a harsh, strained bark that sounded as though the animal was fighting through a lungful of dirt.

Hollihan pointed the empty spoon at the beast. "Glad ta hear yer repentin' on yer sins, Private, that yer gonna walk the straight and narrow from now on. Just don't let this perversion of yers become a habit. Bad for morale, tarnishes the image. Hell, if yer that horny, go screw the admiral's bitch. But leave these here fellow Marines alone!"

The next spoonful of stew disappeared into the quivering jaws of Private Jiggs, who rolled his eyes and waited greedily for more.

The meal was quickly done.

"Welcome home, Sergeant." The sergeant major spoke as he tossed the empty stew can into the trash and looked up. Slater watched the cracked, suntanned face break into a wide, nicotine-stained smile. "Only demand one thing around here, and that's harmony 'mongst the ranks." The man's voice sounded like a cement mixer. Slater thought if the dog could speak, he'd sound like this man.

"Now, you and this asshole had a little altercation last night," the sergeant major continued, "so the turd lost a stripe—it's that simple. I back my NCOs. But now I think it's time you two called a truce. It ain't easy bein' a grunt these days. Gotta have harmony 'mongst ourselves. Understand what I'm sayin', Sergeant?"

Hollihan didn't wait for an answer. Instead, he tossed Slater a dog biscuit.

Slater looked over at the dog and grinned. "I think I do. What's his name again?"

"Jiggs, but you can call him Shithead, he answers to both."

"Here ya go, Jiggs," Slater called. "Come and get it."

The dog hesitated for a moment, shifting its gaze from the biscuit to Hollihan and back again. Slowly, with an asthmatic wheeze, he ambled over to Slater and gently took the biscuit out of the Marine's hand.

In Supply Slater drew seven-eighty-two and white gear, and signed for his bedding. At the armory he was issued an M-14. The Education Office tried to get him to sign up for a correspondence course; Admin typed him a chow pass; the mail clerk put his name on a pigeon hole; the Training NCO scheduled him for a FAM fire with the .45 pistol. By eleven-thirty he was sitting in the Guard Office, listening to the Guard Chief tell him how his life would be run for the next two years.

"So that's basically our set-up here, Slater. Three reliefs twice a day on a Port and Starboard watch, liberty every other weekend from Friday afternoon till Guard Mount Monday morning. When you finish reading the orders, I'll answer any questions you've got on the duty. It's basic—we're here to insure that only authorized personnel come aboard this base."

Gunnery Sergeant Ed Brownell was every inch a recruiting poster. Slater pegged him at about thirty-five. He wore the same basic uniform as the rest of the Guard, but his tropical khaki short-sleeved shirt and trousers had been specially tailored to conform to his wide shoulders and slim waist so that there was not the hint of a wrinkle or fold to flaw sculptured lines. It was as if the uniform had been poured on, a tropical khaki skin all knife-edge creased, barely containing the powerful brown body beneath it.

Brownell's appearance and ramrod bearing alone were enough to get Slater's attention, but the four rows of ribbons above his left pocket inspired nothing but awe. There was a statement there, Slater knew, a story without words that even the most fucked-up Marine could read at a glance: Silver Star, two Bronze Stars, three Purple Hearts. You didn't need a high school diploma to know this man had paid some heavy dues for the three chevrons with a double rocker on his sleeve.

"When do I start?" Slater asked.

"Tomorrow night. Post Eleven. That's out here, on Fleming Key." Brownell pointed to a spot on a large map hanging on the wall behind him. His finger rested on a two-mile-long finger of land jutting out due north of the town and the Naval Annex. The island was connected to Key West by a short single-lane bridge.

"The whole area is restricted," Brownell continued. "That includes the waters around it out to fifty meters. Ammo dump for the Navy, mostly old stuff—five-inch and three-inch shells, a few torpedoes, some mines, and a lot of small arms. We're only out there at night; Navy has a gunnery chief there during the day. It's a two-man post when we can afford it. You ride in a Gray Ghost if one's available, otherwise you hump it."

The Gunny stared at him for a moment, then went over and sat down behind his desk. Slater suspected the man could read the disappointment on his face. Brownell spoke with understanding.

"I know. According to your SRB, you were a platoon sergeant your last two months in I Corps. Kind of a come-down, isn't it?"

"Kind of, yeah."

"There are reasons. First, maybe you've noticed by now, we're top-heavy with NCOs. We've got four times what the T/O calls for. Hell, half the Barracks is NCO."

"Yeah, I noticed."

"We've got more than a dozen E-5s alone, only rate six. You've got to start at the bottom like everybody else. Keep your nose clean and you'll be standing Corporal of the Guard and probably Sergeant of the Guard in no time, because people are always screwing up around here. I say again, *constantly* screwing up.

"Second, you haven't FAM fired with the .45 yet—can't put you on a post other than Fleming until we take care of that. On Fleming you'll carry your rifle.

"Third, the man you're replacing, the man who was scheduled to stand Eleven, got himself knifed on post yesterday. Maybe you heard."

"Yeah. My bunkmate. How's he doing?"

"He'll survive. You might want to remember that while the duty around here is pretty boring stuff, you can still get your crank in a wringer if you—"

Slater heard a crash of something heavy hitting the deck behind him. Startled, he jumped to his feet and went into a crouch. A rusted-out muffler rolled to a stop in front of Brownell's desk.

"Jesus fuckin' Christ, Gunny!" a funny high-pitched voice yelled. "Look at that shit! How'm I suppose ta keep them fuckin' trucks runnin' when those assholes at Public Works keep sendin' me shit like that?"

With a wrench in one hand, an oily rag in the other, the grease-stained kid doing the talking reminded Slater of Louie Malzone, the mechanic in his dad's gas station back home. Only Louie Malzone was a lot bigger. The guy in the doorway was barely five feet tall, a runt.

The gunny pushed his chair back from the desk but didn't get up. "Get that junk out of here right now, Van Groot," he ordered quietly. "Who told you life was easy?"

"What the fuck ya want me ta do with it?" the little man shouted. "Damn thing'll fall apart first time somebody drives over a bump."

"Take it back to your friends at the garage. I'm sure you can talk them into giving you a new one. You've got such a way with words."

"Shove it up their asses, that's what I'll do," the little man mumbled as he retrieved the muffler and huffed back out of the office, leaving in his wake the smell of motor oil, gasoline, and ground-in dirt. Only the filthy utility uniform and cap had given Slater a clue that this was a fellow Marine.

"As I was saying," Brownell said like nothing had happened, "Claybourne is going to be all right. Blade barely got through his white gear. Superficial wound—only took ten stitches. But he's down for a while. That leaves us a man short so we're going to have to put you on the roster right away."

"They know who did it?"

"Freddy wouldn't say."

Slater gestured at the empty doorway. "What was that all about?"

The gunny scowled, then laughed. "Haven't met Corporal Van Groot yet, huh? Best damn mechanic in the Corps. If it wasn't for his magic we'd be sending out reliefs in private vehicles. You'll be riding shotgun with him tomorrow night."

Another crash, more distant this time, brought Brownell to his feet. He walked over to the office window, then motioned Slater to join him. Out in a small parking area where three gray Navy pickup trucks stood in various stages of disassembly, the man named Van Groot was beating the rusted-out muffler with a sledgehammer.

"He takes some getting used to," the gunny finally said as they watched Van Groot toss the battered and flattened muffler into the bed of one of the trucks and climb behind the wheel. "But he gets the job done extremely well. That muffler will never be reissued to anyone, much less to this outfit. You all checked in?"

"Yeah, except for my medical records."

"You can drop 'em off at the dispensary on the way to chow."

"Thanks, Gunny," Slater said. He picked up his cap, and got ready to leave. "Anything else?" he asked.

"That's all," the gunny said. "Except, well, be advised that the Dutchman—Van Groot—is a little dinky-dow sometimes. I suggest you pretend to go along with him and you'll be all right. Good experience."

Slater was savvy enough to recognize a warning when he heard it.

Chapter Five

Bugle notes echoed through the twilight, and all over the base men turned toward the sound and came to attention. The "Colors" in front of the base Admin building were being hauled down the flagpole by a four-man detail from the Barracks. The detail of Marines included Corporal Howard Gurtzer, who played the bugle as few others could.

Over on the second deck, Freddy Claybourne rolled the pillow around his head and waited for the sound to stop. Somebody had to put that mutha fuckin' Gurtzer out of his misery, he decided. The shit the man played was unreal. Sometimes when folks heard Gurtzer play "Retreat" they didn't know whether to salute or shit in their covers.

The sound of the bugle came to an end and Claybourne unrolled the pillow. The squad cubical was empty; everybody was out on liberty or scarfing up twenty-five-cent near-beer at the EM Club. He was grounded, though; the no-duty medical chit canceling his date on Fleming with the crazy-fuck Dutchman had also confined him to bedrest in the Barracks.

Sheee-it! Didn't need no bed rest 'less it was in the line of doing his thing, Freddy snickered to himself.

The snicker became a grimace as a finger of fire shot up his side. The knife wound was still sore as hell. He worked his fingers under the bandage and traced the stitches. A few inches lower and to the right, he thought again, and the legend would've been doing his lovin' with a plastic tube.

The safety of his shooter was all there was to console him. The wild-eyed bitch with the great body who had almost sliced it off couldn't be touched. Shandy was only seventeen; one word from her and he'd be up on statutory rape charges, not to mention having her forty or so Conch brothers, cousins, and uncles looking him up with machetes, meat hooks, and anchor flukes. Better to leave things be.

He reached up and turned on the radio dangling from the bed springs above his rack. The new dude did not have a lock on his locker yet and Freddy had decided it was time to get acquainted. Stiffly, he rolled from the bunk. The wound throbbed when he straightened, but the pain dulled as he hobbled over to the locker where the new man had stored his gear. The metal door opened with a rasp, nicely covered by the licks of B.B. King. Claybourne alerted himself for the sounds of footsteps as he began going through the seabag.

Uniforms, ugly-as-shit civilian clothes, dress shoes, some photographs: a girl, not bad but no tits; a long-haired kid in granny glasses; a friendly-looking older man and woman grinning out from a front porch somewhere. Shoe polish, brasso, belt buckles, extra stripes, a sewing kit— what's with this dude, Claybourne thought. Wasn't shit in the bag. Hold on, what's this?

Freddy pulled a plain white envelope from the seabag and opened it. Strange, man—a cashier's check for fifteen hundred dollars made out to somebody named Martin Slater. The check was torn in two. He thumbed over the pieces for a few seconds, then stuffed them in the envelope and back into the bag. Nothing there for him.

He continued the search but didn't find anything else worth a shit. He put all the stuff back and was about to close the locker door when he felt a hand grab his shoulder. The hand came with an unfamiliar voice.

"Think that's my locker, man."

Damn! Being snuck-up on was getting to be a bad habit. He swung around to face the voice. The quick movement sent a spasm of pain up his side and made him cry out. Instinctively, he placed a protective hand over the bandage.

"Sheee-it! What you wanna be sneakin' up on me for, man? Sheee-it! Bet I busted a stitch!"

Freddy staggered over to his bunk and sat down, face stretched taut in a mask of agony. It didn't hurt all that bad but hell, he needed some cover-time to regroup.

Through a forced scowl of pain he saw that the new man was about his own height, five-ten or so, a little skinny but tight, like one of those damn "hippies" out on the street who lived on pills and sunflower seeds. Dude had a bad case of white walls that screamed PX barbershop, a real butcher job. But it was the eyes that attracted Claybourne's attention the most, for the eyes held the hollow look of a man recently back from the Nam.

"What were you doin' in my locker, man?" the new man asked. There seemed to be no anger in his voice, only question.

Freddy's mind raced. "Since when that your locker?" he gasped. "I keep my extra gear in there, man. Just checkin' it is all."

"Wasn't anything in there last night," the man said. He reached into the large brown paper bag he was carrying and pulled out a new combination lock. After attaching it to the locker, he looked back over at Claybourne. "It's mine now officially, OK? You got extra gear, stow it someplace else."

Freddy lay back on his pillow; the crisis had passed. "You walk mighty soft for a white dude," he said.

"Yeah," the new man said off-handedly as he unpacked the paper bag and put the stuff on top of a footlocker. "Next time I'll knock . . . want a Coke?" He held out a red can dripping with condensation.

"How much?"

"On the house."

"Yeah, I take one."

The man lifted a church key from the junk on the locker and punched holes in two cans of soda. He walked over and handed one to Claybourne.

"Name's Slater," he said.

"New dude, huh?" Freddy took a sip of the soft drink. It dribbled out of the corner of his mouth, forcing him to sit up.

"Right. You must be Claybourne."

"You got it."

"Heard you got knifed."

"You got it."

"That happen a lot, does it?"

Freddy grinned slyly. "Only when you got serious pussy trouble. So where they puttin' you, man?"

"Fleming Key?" Slater's eyebrows rose as though he wasn't quite sure he'd gotten the name right.

"Sheee-it. Dutchman gonna be happy. He digs new blood."

Slater looked puzzled. "What's with this Dutchman guy? Everybody keeps telling me to make out a will."

"Dutchman crazier'n shit, man."

"How so?"

"You find out, Jack. You find out." Freddy giggled and tilted the can back for another swallow. He remembered the torn check in the seabag. There was a story there someplace.

"The lieutenant and gunny seem like good people," Slater continued.

"They all right. Least they don't fuck with ya all the time. Brule, the XO, he's the one ta watch out for. Real mutha fucka. Call him Screamin' Don."

"Yeah, met him this morning. What's the duty like?"

"Can you say 'sucks'?"

"What I guessed. Heard I was comin' down here, thought I was gettin' a good deal. Don't look that way."

"Good deal? From the Crotch? You gotta be shittin' me, man. Onliest good deal they got is free coffins!"

A strange look came over Slater's face. Claybourne felt his skin crawl for a second. It was like the new dude was staring at something on the "other side."

The look passed.

"You ever run across a brother named Choo Choo Wilkes?" Slater asked as he rolled the Coke can in his hands.

Claybourne thought for a moment. "No. Never heard of no Choo Choo dude."

"He used ta say that, too—about the coffin. You kinda remind me of him."

"Like I said, don't know no Choo Choo. Knowed a Night Train once. 'Sides, we all look alike—right, white boy?"

"Your ass, man." Slater drained his Coke and began unbuttoning his utility blouse. "Anyway, he was always going through new guys' gear, thought the narcs were after him, thought the Crotch wanted to hang his butt so bad for blowin' a little weed that they'd stick some agent out in the bush so they could nail his ass."

Claybourne dropped his empty can on the deck and lay back down. "Told ya, man, I was lookin' for my extra gear."

Slater had his utility shirt off and was working on the laces of a pair of boots that looked brand new. "Tell me more about this Dutchman."

"Dude, ain't wrapped tight, dig? Always playin' these mutha fuckin' war games with ya. Dude wants ta go RECON so bad his mind turned ta shit."

"So why not just ignore him?"

Claybourne pushed himself to his elbows, his expression filled with disgust. "Man, the Dutchman eats bugs!"

Slater laughed. "So? That don't answer my question. Why don't you just ignore him?"

Freddy shook his head as if annoyed the new man wasn't getting it. "Man, you ignore that fucka, he put the evil eye on you. Follow you everywhere—the head, chowhall, libs. Everybody starts stayin' away from you, afraid of getting some of that eye, too. Pretty soon you start seein' him in your sleep, just starin'. Then, out there on Fleming, he just takes off inta the night. You don't know where he is till you start hearin' him whisperin' your name, 'cept you don't know whether it's him or just the wind. Next thing you know, man, he's got you in one of his booby traps, or he's blowin' on the back of your neck, or somethin'." Claybourne shivered. "Dude is fucked up, man, real fucked up."

"Booby traps? The honchos let him get away with it?"

"You shittin' me, man? Lieutenant and gunny love his ass. You make one false move, man, one little fuck-up, and they put you out with that dude for punishment. Saves 'em all the paperwork for Office Hours, dig? After a few weeks with the Dutchman, man, you are walkin' straight!" Claybourne chuckled softly. "But like I say, man, you find out."

Slater nodded at Freddy's bandaged side. "And I guess I owe it all to you," he said. "You and your girlfriend."

Freddy ran his fingertips over the middle of his bare chest and heaved a heavy sigh. "Yeah, I guess. That's the breaks, ain't they?"

The squadbay door crashed open and a voice bellowed from that direction. "Hey, Slater!" It was Tollster.

"Yo! Bone!" Slater answered as he slid off his trousers and reached for one of the summer-weight shirts he'd dumped on the footlocker with the other PX booty.

Moments later, his face flushed, Bone Tollster ambled into the cubicle. Claybourne pretended to shield his eyes from the glare of lavender jeans and a navy blue tank top.

"Come on, man," Tollster said to Slater, ignoring Claybourne, "we're heading for the Bamboo. The Crack always gives new dudes a free brew."

"Say, Tollster, where you get them trou?" Freddy asked. He didn't kill himself trying to make like he was impressed. "You been rollin' winos for their threads again?"

Tollster glanced over at the bunk. "Shit no. Got 'em from your mama's pimp."

"Suck ma dick, man."

Tollster looked over at Slater. "You met Freddy? How do ya like this guy? Pays some ginch to cut him just so's he don't have ta stand any doots."

"Hey, Tollster," Claybourne said, "your mama wipe her ass real good after she drop you?"

"Yeah, but least I didn't get farted out after a night a ribs and beer. Come on, Slater. Nar-vel is waitin' out in his ride downstairs. What do ya say?"

"Sounds good," Slater answered.

"That's right, that's right," Claybourne whined. "Leave me here all alone. Go on an' have a good time. Don't mind ol' Freddy. I'll just stay here an' bleed ta death."

"Aw, quit cryin' Fred," Tollster said. "I'll bring a brew back for ya. You can still piss, can't ya?"

"You find out. Middle of the night I mistake your face for a commode."

"Tool drool, Fred. You ain't never hit what you was aimin' at in your life."

"Shit," Claybourne grunted. He reached overhead and turned up his radio. The volume drowned out Tollster in a wave of heavy rhythm and blues.

Fuck this, Freddy thought. Wasting my time with Tollster. Tollster always played the game too damn good. Besides, he was getting tired. The new dude was clean, that was all he'd wanted to find out. Just never knew when the Green Machine'd put some weird dude or psycho or narc in the rack over your head. New dude seemed all right, except for the funny look that'd come over him when they started talking about coffins and dudes named after trains.

He rolled over on his good side, his back to the other two men, and thought about Shandy. Maybe he'd give her a call in a few weeks, after she'd had some time to cool down. Girl was definitely prime stuff. Course, that would come after he got even with the honky named Bronar.

By the time Tollster and Slater left, Freddy had dozed off, dreaming of swaying breasts, warm thighs, and revenge.

CHAPTER SIX

"How many times I gotta tell you boys—keep that damn animal off my pool table!"

The woman glared out over the bar at Jiggs who stood on a field of green felt watching Narvel LeFey try a difficult combination shot to the corner pocket.

The shot was unsuccessful, and as if to show his disappointment with LeFey's lack of skill, the dog picked up the cue ball in his jaws and began gnawing on it.

"Dang it!" the woman shrieked. "Get that ball away from him, LeFey, right damn now!"

The woman slid two drafts across the bar to Tollster and Slater. Her wrists were heavy with what looked to be several dozen silver bracelets, each delicately etched with its own design. They jangled as she reached for a burning cigarette in the ashtray in front of her.

"Come on, Rose," Tollster said. "What's the big deal? Jiggs can't hurt it none."

"Maybe not," she answered, "but his breath's so bad ain't nobody gonna wanna put their hands on that ball once he's done gummin' it ta death. . . . Wash it up real good, Narvel. I wanna check for teeth marks."

She had a kindly face, a face framed with rust-colored hair streaked with gray, a face full of a warmth Slater felt the moment Tollster introduced her. Even as she hollered at LeFey, Slater was aware of the kindness in her eyes. He took a liking to her immediately.

The way Tollster told it, this woman, Rose McCracken—"The Crack" as she was known to the Marines—had made her bar, The Bamboo Room, their unofficial home away from the Barracks. She was, in Slater's eyes, the original earth mother—late forties, overweight, jowly, and as familiar with cuss words as she seemed to be with the contents of dark bottles of Canadian whiskey.

He still had the lipstick smudge on his forehead where she'd planted a big kiss, welcoming him to her fold.

"Don't know why I let that mutt in here, anyway," Rose muttered as she knocked the ash from her cigarette. "I could lose my license."

"Aw, Jiggs needs some libs just like the rest of us, Rose," Tollster said. "You think he likes hangin' around the Barracks all the time? Look at him. He's havin' a ball!"

The other Marines at the bar, a half a dozen men Slater had met earlier, groaned or looked as though they'd just gotten a whiff of week-old fish heads.

Rose turned sad eyes on Slater while jerking her thumb at Tollster. "Poor shit," she said. "Some of that VC metal in his back has made its way to his brain. He used ta be such a smart boy. Now look at him—ready for the funny farm for Christopher's sake. Do me a favor, will ya, Slater? Someday when he ain't lookin', put a round in his ear. Thing like that ought not ta have ta suffer so."

Slater grinned and took another sip of his beer. While Tollster and Rose argued, he swung around on the bar stool and scoped-out the Bamboo Room.

The walls of the joint were lined with strips of smoke-stained bamboo. The bar itself ran down one side of the room; on the other were a few beat-up tables and chairs. Sawdust—dirty and mildewed—covered the floor, and the odors of hamburger grease, stale beer, and old piss lay heavily in the air. The jukebox over in a corner offered a selection of country and rock hits all at least six months old. A huge jar of pickled pigs' feet sat at one end of the bar, a gut-heaving mess of gristle and bone and God-only-knew what.

The Bamboo Room resembled its owner, Slater decided—crude, a little worn by life, maybe even a little over the hill. But it was the kind of joint he felt comfortable in, the kind of place where there was no need to worry about a few spilled suds or whether you'd wiped your feet on the welcome mat outside. The brew was cold and cheap.

LeFey slammed home the eight ball and Jiggs collapsed in a heap, his pool table now empty and safe for sleep. Slater turned back to the bar.

"So how ya like Key West so far, Jack?" Rose asked.

"Dunno. OK, I guess."

She produced a bowl from under the bar and pushed it in front of him. "Have a hard-boiled egg. Made 'em fresh this evenin'. Keys is a great place, you'll find. Get Bone here ta take ya out fishin'."

"Pap is the one who oughta do that," Tollster said, reaching for an egg. "Got himself a hundred-pound grouper the other day."

"The hell you say! He didn't offer me none." Rose poured herself another shot of whiskey.

"Yeah, well he sold it ta the cook over to the Outrigger. Got twenty cents a pound."

"Off season. Coupla months he could get fifty." She downed the contents of the shot glass in one gulp, then smacked her lips. "Hey! I forgot to tell ya. Got a letter from my sister's little girl. She's gonna come down for a visit." Rose beamed. "If you're real nice and pay your tab, Bone, I might introduce her to ya."

"Speakin' a tabs," Tollster belched, "you wanna give us two more? Slater here's gotta ride shotgun with the Dutchman tomorrow night."

"Where is that little pecker?" Rose asked as she drew two more beers from the tap. "He told me he was gonna come in tonight and settle up."

"Got me," Tollster said.

"Hey, Rose," one of the Marines at the end of the bar, a kid named Rodriguez, shouted. " 'Nuther brew down here, OK?"

The Crack waved. "Well, if you see him, tell him he

owes me some dough. Excuse me boys, gotta tend ta profits."

She walked away, wobbling slightly, a distinct thunk-ker-thunk sounding on the planking behind the bar. Tollster pointed to his thigh and made a sawing motion with his hand. He'd told Slater on the way over about the Crack's wooden leg. Slater nodded, visions of a female Long John Silver coming to mind. All Rose needed was a parrot on her shoulder.

By quarter to ten the other Marines had shoved off for a club on Duval Street that featured a live band and bar hogs who waited on tables. Tollster claimed the beer was too expensive there, and watered down to boot, so he, LeFey, and Slater had stayed at the Bamboo, listening to old Stones on the juke and watching Jiggs snore and slobber on the pool table. They sat at a table with a pitcher of beer and three bowls of stale popcorn.

Rose was off talking to a couple of shrimpers when the sailors came in. Slater knew they were sailors despite their silly-ass hippie clothes and long hair because he heard Tollster growl something about "fuckin' squids." There were seven of them, all with beards, moustaches, and hair over collars and ears. Slater rubbed a spot on the back of his neck where the PX barber had gouged him with the clippers. He felt naked.

The sailors clustered around the bar, pounding on it, demanding service. None were feeling any pain. Slater heard somebody yell to Rose that they'd come to celebrate the birthday of their ship. The announcement brought cheers from the other men. They roared even louder as Rose began lining up schooners of beer.

"Ain't that sweet," LeFey said disgustedly as he shoved a handful of popcorn into his mouth.

"Don't get inta heat, Nar-vel," Tollster said quietly. "They got us outnumbered." He picked up the pitcher. "Give us yer glass, Slater. Yer fallin' behind, man."

Slater pushed his glass across the table. He was feeling a little numb. "How'd she lose it?" he asked. The words seemed to take forever forming on his lips.

"Who lost what?" Tollster kept a careful eye on the pouring suds as he spoke.

"The Crack. How'd she lose the log, I mean leg?"

"Beats the hell outta me. It ain't somethin' she ever talks about."

"I hear she got run over by a train," LeFey said as his elbow slipped off the edge of the table.

"Shit. Heard it from who, Nar-vel?" Tollster wanted to know. "Yer mother, maybe?"

"How should I know? Just heard it is all. You think I remember everybody I ever heard anything from who it was?"

"I do not understand a thing you just said." Tollster reached over and tweaked LeFey's nose.

Slater rocked back in his chair. He saw one of the sailors at the bar staring at him. The man turned to another guy standing next to him and whispered something. The other man turned, glanced at Slater, then began to chuckle.

"Don't pay 'em no mind, Slater," Tollster said. "They think they're hot shit just 'cause they get to let their hair grow."

"Don't bother me," Slater heard himself lie. The beer felt cool going down his throat; it soothed the anger at being laughed at by the sailors.

"You jars want ta move that thing?" The voice came from behind them.

They turned to see two sailors, pool sticks in hand. One of them, a kid with inflamed pock marks on his face, pointed at Jiggs, who still snored contentedly on the pool table.

"Ain't ours," Tollster said with a grin. Slater was close enough to see that the grin was faked.

The kid with the pock marks looked at his buddy, a tall angular man with a moustache that drooped down the sides of his chin. The kid extended his stick and began poking Jiggs in the ribs.

"Wouldn't do that if I was you," LeFey cautioned.

The pock-marked kid ignored him and began thrusting the stick a little harder.

"Better count yer fingers, buddy," Tollster said as he gently kicked Slater's leg under the table.

The pock-marked kid looked over at them and smiled wickedly. His eyes stayed glued on Tollster as he rammed the stick harder at Jiggs' belly.

Slater blinked and missed most of the action. He was aware only of a blur of motion and the sound of wood being crushed, followed by a deep, guttural growl. He saw the pock-marked kid's jaw drop, his mouth forming a silent "O." The kid stared at the pool stick in his hand, the stick that now was a full foot shorter than it had been a second before. Where the cue tip had been, there was only jagged splintered wood.

Jiggs coughed, shook himself, then collapsed back down on the green felt. Without saying a word, the sailor with the moustache walked over to the walk rack, replaced his stick, and headed for the bar, leaving the pock-marked kid to stare at the dog alone.

Slater happily watched the kid just kind of slump into a chair. . . .

Tollster was pouring another round when they heard a voice bellowing from the direction of the Bamboo Room's front door.

"Make a hole, squid shit, make a hole!"

"Oh, no," Tollster moaned, "he's here."

The crowd of sailors parted as Van Groot stormed into the room, his jaw set, his eyes glaring straight ahead. He looked even shorter than he had in the Guard Office, and just as dirty. He wore a faded USMC sweatshirt without sleeves, some cut-off chinos, and a pair of scarred and ripped jungle boots. Except for a few hairs in front, greased up like a flat-top, his head was skinned. Slater half expected to see some automobile part come bouncing across the sawdust.

"What's happenin', Dutch," LeFey said as Van Groot grabbed a chair and sat down at the table.

"What are these fuckers doin' here?" he grumbled loudly, his eyes riveted on a chubby, pink-faced sailor, who peered at him with a sneer on his lips.

"Free country," Tollster said.

"Free, my ass. Since when did this place open its doors to squid scum?" Without waiting for an answer, the Dutchman pointed a finger at the chubby sailor and barked a challenge. "Hey, boy! I don't like them little squid eyes undressin' me. If yer that queer, there's a place down the street where you'll feel right at home. Fuckin' douche kit."

"Fuck you!" the chubby sailor answered angrily.

The Dutchman sprang to his feet, his fists clenched. One of Tollster's huge hands grabbed his sweatshirt and pulled him back down into his seat.

"Have a brew, Dutch," Tollster said. "We don't want no trouble, man. Have a brew."

Van Groot seemed to relax. He glared one last time at the chubby sailor, then picked up the beer pitcher with both hands and began to drink from the spout. Little trickles of suds dribbled off his chin into his lap.

"What are you so pissed about, man?" Tollster asked when Van Groot finally put the pitcher down and contentedly wiped his mouth with the back of his hand. "Swabbies been in here before."

"Had ta put a muffler out of its misery today," Van Groot answered. "Then the gunny clued me in that I gotta break in some new dude tomorrow night. New guys are *always* a pain in the ass."

"Yeah, but some of us learn fast." Slater didn't look at the man; he spoke to the glass in front of him.

"Meet your new shotgun, Dutch." Tollster pointed at

Slater while LeFey hid his smile behind another handful of popcorn. "Sergeant Slater here came aboard last night."

Van Groot did not sound impressed. "E-5, huh? You one of them pansy Airedale types?"

Slater looked up and studied the man for a few seconds. For all his cockiness and tough talk, the Dutchman had a little boy's face. There was more mischief there than meanness. Slater spoke as menacingly as he could.

"The last guy called me that died of missing gonads. Kinda messy, but they sure did taste good. You ever eat human balls, man?"

The Dutchman blinked, then began to laugh. "Nope, but I'll try anything once. Just ask Bone." He looked over at Tollster. "I think I'm gonna like this dude. We think the same sick shit." He looked back at Slater. "Only one thing though, I drive . . . least ways until I know if you can handle one of my girls without fuckin' up. I spend too damn much time workin' on them trucks ta have some E-5 who don't know Fleming Key screw up."

"Suits me fine," Slater answered.

LeFey burped. "God damn, Slater. You really ate somebody's balls?"

Later, after the Dutchman had disappeared into the back of the Bamboo for a head call, and while LeFey rested his forehead on the table, the sailors began to sing "Happy Birthday." They sang to a large sheet cake on the bar in front of them, all white icing and pink candles. The song came to an end just as Van Groot reappeared, zipping his fly and grinning.

Slater was three sheets to the wind. If it hadn't been for the fact that his chair was facing the bar, he would have missed what happened next; it only took a few seconds.

First, he was aware of the chubby sailor saying something about "midget jarheads jacking off in the head." Then he laughed as he watched the Dutchman vault up onto the bar and force march his way through the birthday cake,

making sure to put one of his boots in the exact middle of
the prize.

He saw the Dutchman go down at that point, down in a
sea of clutching hands and arms. Then everything got a little
hazy.

*It was like one of the dreams he'd been having—the same
surreal quality, the same fragmented transitions of mind
and body, the same foggy light surrounding shapes with
halos of white brilliance. He was floating, floating toward
the bar, Tollster's curses along with LeFey's blood-curdling
yell in his ear. The chubby sailor's face came into view, it
was spitting out a bloody tooth. From the fog he felt a fist
drive into his midsection, forcing the air from his body.*

*He swung wildly with a big roundhouse right, feeling
very proud of himself when it collided with flesh.*

*Something caught him between the shoulder blades and
he was suddenly face to face with the sawdust. There
seemed to be feet everywhere, all around his head, some of
them kicking at him, some landing, but he felt nothing. With
no conscious thought, he rolled out of the forest of legs, at
last coming to a clear space where he could push himself to
his knees. The Bamboo Room seemed to be part of a
merry-go-round; the walls were spinning around him. The
music blasting from the juke was right on, he decided. "Bad
Moon Rising." He looked up to see the fat end of a cue stick
coming right at his eyes. He marveled at the smooth
swing—the bat of Al Kaline about to lay some rope. At the
last possible instant the stick's path changed. Instead of
hitting him flush, it only glanced off an ear. Bright motes
danced in front of his eyes, little explosions of white energy.
He saw the sailor with the pock-marked face fall next to
him. The squid's mouth was wide, his eyes full of fear and
pain. He was screaming about his leg.*

Slater looked down and saw what the kid was yelling
about. Poor bastard. The pock-marked kid's leg was in the
grip of ferocious jaws and teeth. Looked like Jiggs was
pissed.

• • •

Two hours later, Gunny Brownell was pissed, too. He stalked up and down in front of the four men sitting in the Guard Office. Slater was reminded of a caged panther at feeding time.

"Will someone please explain to me why this crap always goes down when I've got the duty?" the gunny asked evenly. "Can't you schedule your shit for Staff Sergeant Hernandez or Salaski or Toliver? Why all the time when I'm CDO?"

Slater gingerly touched the bandage over his ear as the gunny spoke. The corpsman at the dispensary had given him a few stitches without any local. The booze was wearing off and the wound was beginning to throb.

"You think I enjoy having to run over to Shore Patrol headquarters in the middle of the night to sign out four shit-faced maniacs who get their jollies taking on the entire Seventh Fleet?" The gunny was beginning to sound a tad angry.

"Second Fleet, Gunny," the Dutchman cracked. "Seventh Fleet's in the Pacific. And don't forget Jiggs. He was in on it too, ya know."

The Dutchman's words sounded muffled and indistinct. Slater didn't know whether that was because of his own mangled ear or because of the Dutchman's swollen upper lip that had the color and shape of a small eggplant.

"I'm not forgetting anybody, wiseass," the gunny said. "Jiggs will be in quarantine for two weeks. Even longer if that sailor comes down with an infection." Brownell stopped his pacing and crossed his arms over his chest. "Now, would someone mind telling me what the hell happened?"

"Damn if we know, Gunny," Tollster offered, a fat colorful plum residing where his right eye should have been. "We were mindin' our own business, havin' a few brews, when these squids just went crazy. Ask the Crack, she'll tell ya."

"Miss McCracken's statement, to put it bluntly, is a crock of shit. She claims you were all defending her from rape. One of your victims, one who could still talk, said something about a 'cake' being destroyed. He claims one of you—the little shit—walked through the birthday cake of the USS *Blowfish*." Brownell moved a step closer to the Dutchman and focused on the man's boots. "What do you say to that, Van Groot?"

"No disrespect, Gunny," the Dutchman answered, "but that's bullshit. I was out takin' a head call when this ruckus started. I come back to see my buddies gettin' attacked by a buncha squids. What ya want me ta do, let 'em all get killed?"

Brownell showed no reaction except to move down the line a few steps. Slater was aware that the gunny had stopped in front of him.

"What about you, Slater? You were the senior man there. What the hell happened?"

Slater looked up. Brownell's eyes were bloodshot. He wondered how the man kept his uniform so fresh, even after midnight. "Not sure, Gunny," he managed. "It all happened pretty damn fast. I think those squids just had too much to drink."

"And I suppose you gents were sipping soda pop all night. Great start to your tour, Sergeant. Second night aboard and you've already got a file started with the Shore Patrol."

"Sorry, Gunny." Slater was starting to feel a little embarrassed.

"Too late for that." Brownell paused, then stepped back and addressed all of them. "If you think any of these injuries you've suffered are going to prevent you from standing post, forget it. Roster stands as is. That includes you, LeFey, you'll just have to salute left handed. You can thank your lucky stars that nobody is pressing charges or you'd all be in the county jail right now for assault and battery.

"Don't be surprised if you find your names on the 'police' detail for the next few years. Sergeant Major's got a lot of rocks that need a fresh coat of paint."

"Excuse me, Gunny." The duty Corporal of the Guard, a man Slater had not yet met, spoke from the Guard Shack. "Key West police on the line. Lesmon's wife slit her wrists again. Want me to relieve him?"

"Oh, hell," Brownell groaned. "OK, I'll be right there." He turned to the four of them again. "As for you turds—hit the sack and don't let me see you again until morning formation."

"Does this mean our liberty is canceled?" the Dutchman chirped.

Brownell squinted. "Yes, Corporal Van Groot, that's exactly what it means." He paused for dramatic effect. "Which will allow you time to get your salty non-reg boots cleaned up. Better run a toothbrush along the seams there, you know how the XO loves catching people sneaking chow on post." Brownell hooked on the CDO duty belt and headed for the door. "Good night, assholes."

They waited until they heard the CDO truck crank over out in the parking lot. Tollster was the first to rise. "Don't know about you," he said, "but I'm gonna grab some Z's. I got First Relief tomorra."

"Me, too," LeFey chimed in, tenderly holding his right arm in its sling. Sprained elbow, the doc had said.

Slater shook out the cobwebs, then looked up. The Dutchman was standing over him and offering a hand.

"What ya say there, Sarge?" the little man said. "Things could be worse. Ya coulda lost yer pecker."

Slater took the hand and pulled himself up. "Damn, Van Groot," he said. "Thought this place was gonna suck. But tonight has changed my thinking. I'm beginning to like it here. I'm beginning to like it a lot."

"Yeah," the Dutchman said with a distorted grin. "Tends ta grow on ya, don't it? Wait till we get on post."

CHAPTER SEVEN

THREE weeks after he'd had a bait knife shoved into his belly, Freddy Claybourne crouched in the darkness of a Key West alley outside the Dun-Rite transmission shop.

He'd been there a while. Bronar usually locked up around ten, but tonight the old man was burning the midnight oil. Freddy was in no hurry; the Section had liberty and he wasn't due back at the Barracks till seven-thirty the next morning. He could fuckin' wait all night if he had to; if the Crotch had taught him one thing, it was how to wait. He readjusted his position behind the garbage cans and tried not to think of the stink. . . .

When he'd first started having his *troubles* at the Barracks—about two months after reporting aboard— Kargo had sat down with him and they'd had a long rap. He'd clued in the lieutenant that he'd had his fill of the Green Machine and only wanted to be a civilian again. Kargo had told him "tough shit" but had also arranged for him to go to work during his off-duty hours at the Dun-Rite.

Like the lieutenant had laid it out, the job was part of a government program where small businesses agreed to train veterans still in the service in exchange for VA funds. It was supposed to be a two-way street: the vet got a wage and a skill to fall back on when he got out; the businessman got paid to train him.

Only it hadn't worked out that way.

Oh sure, mutha fuckin' Bronar got the federal money all right, and Claybourne got two bucks an hour. But the only "skills" he'd learned were how to push a broom and clean up grease and oil spills. Your basic "nigger" work—that's what Freddy called it when he bitched to the old Conch. Bronar made a face like somebody had pinched him on the ass. Then the old shit ordered him back to the broom, using that word, the word that finally let Freddy in on the joke, the word that told him the whole thing was just another honky ripoff.

"Git back ta work, *boy*," Bronar had said in that cracker drawl of his. "Ah'll be decidin' when yah ready ta learn a white man's job."

Claybourne had quit on the spot. Only problem was, he didn't bother to let Kargo or the VA know about his decision. So Bronar kept collecting from the VA for another six months with no one being the wiser. When some pencil-pusher finally wised up that Freddy hadn't been attending "classes," it was the Marine, not Bronar, who was penalized.

One ripoff deserved another, at least that was how Freddy saw it. The old honky bastard was going to repay him for about six months worth of GI Bill benefits he'd lost . . . and maybe a little bit more.

The light went out in the office window, followed shortly by the sounds of the alley door opening and closing. As Bronar busied himself with the padlock, it would have been easy for the man hiding in the darkness to creep up behind him and bash in his head. But that was not Freddy's style. He had seen death before, violent death, and it held no awe for him.

The NVA soldier had hung in the wire for three days. They had used the body to clear their weapons on coming in off patrol. Although he had quickly grown to hate every-thing about Vietnam, including his enemy, the sight of this riddled and torn mass of flesh, rotting and stinking in the heat and dust, had given him little sense of revenge. The sight of the corpse could never make up for the terror, the filth, the boredom that had taken over his life. The corpse was only a lifeless slab of meat, unable to see or feel the hatred of the Marines who spat on it twice a day. Claybourne had felt only relief when the company commander ordered the body removed.

He'd finally tasted sweet revenge, though, and had discovered that he loved every minute of it. The company had been running a routine sweep when they stumbled over a gook cache. It was a big one, buried underground in a layrbinth of tunnels—twenty tons of rice, dried fish, and US-issued powdered milk, along with a couple tons of small arms ammo and medical supplies, even several hundred new uniforms. The Marines had burned it all in an inferno provided by a Phantom's napalm. From a nearby hilltop Freddy had screamed in hysterical joy as the ammo went off like an endless string of firecrackers. "Rice Krispies, mutha fucks!" he'd yelled. "Snap, crackle'n pop, Rice Krispies!" The vision of his enemy—useless weapons, tattered clothing, empty bellies swollen from starvation—had given him more satisfaction than a hundred dead bodies.

Sweet, sweet revenge. Revenge had to be savored, not gobbled down. Old man Bronar was now on Freddy's menu, but the Marine wanted what was inside the shop, not the back of the old man's head.

He waited another ten minutes in the shadows, then approached the padlocked alley door. On his second day on the job he'd *borrowed* Bronar's key and had duplicates made. The padlock now sprung open easily and the door closed behind him before anyone passing out in the street could be the wiser. Smooth as spit.

Except for a few pale spears of streetlight coming through the front windows, the shop was dark. No problem; he knew the shop's layout like the palm of his hand; he'd swept every inch of the place for two months and—

The empty tin cans sounded like a barage of Blooper rounds as Claybourne's feet sent them scattering. The sole of one of his shoes lost all traction when it came in contact with something slippery, and for a fraction of a second he was airborne. He landed squarely on his spine.

Pain shot up his back and he gritted his teeth against the scream ballooning in his chest. Key-rist! What was goin down? Felt like he'd been run over by a fuckin' train!

Awkwardly, he rolled over onto his stomach, aware that along with his broken back there was a wet gooiness on his face. "*Oh, Lord! Don't let that be my brains!* The vision of the NVA soldier, minus the top of his head, came to mind and Claybourne gagged at the thought of loose gray matter seeping down over his lips and chin. Funny though, stuff tasted like . . . well, a little bit like Guard Shack coffee, kind of oily and—

Claybourne spat disgustedly. Transmission fluid. It was all over the deck. He could feel its wetness soaking through his shirt and pants.

Relieved that his skull wasn't leaking, he listened for shouts or the sound of footsteps. Nothing. Maybe someone had heard, but there weren't many folks in this part of town who gave a damn about what went on behind darkened doors.

Tentatively, he got to his feet, discovering that his back wasn't broken after all; he just had some badly pulled muscles. He was forced to limp through the mess on the floor. Thank Jesus there were no more booby traps. Had the old man left the oil cans around on purpose? Maybe. Maybe not. The old fuck wasn't always as stupid as he looked.

Bronar's prized possession was just where Freddy remembered it would be, on a shelf next to the old man's desk in the back office. It was a lot heavier than he'd figured, but then, Bronar had always bragged that his shortwave radio was the biggest and best rig in the Keys. "Yessir," Freddy had heard him brag to more than one impatient customer, "Ah gut the finest base station in the Keys. Fanon 8-80, solid state transceiver, IC circuit, not ta mention a Shure power mike and a co-linear antenna with a foot warmer for high gear. Gives me a bodacious signal, Bubba. Lets me know what-all's happening, if ya git my meanin'."

"Yeah, well, you gonna have yourself a bodacious surprise in the mornin', mutha fuck," Freddy muttered as he ripped away the cables connecting the radio transceiver to all Bronar's extra little gadgets. "If ya get my meanin'."

Cackling like Zamora's gramma did after she'd put a curse on Screamin' Don's GTO, Freddy hugged the transceiver under one arm and carefully made his way back out to the front of the shop.

The weight of the radio made him feel good—better than good, "triumphant" maybe. He knew he was taking more from the old man than just a hobby. While shuffling around with his broom back when he worked in the shop, he'd heard Bronar rappin' away in the office, usually to boats at sea. The messages were in some kinda code, but it didn't take a genius to figure out that the old Conch was heavily into runnin' dope from the islands and points south. The expensive radio equipment allowed the mutha fucka to keep track of the authorities, and the illegal power booster on the transmitter gave him the range to keep the smugglers' boats informed while still outside U.S. waters.

How much bread the man was getting out of the deal, Claybourne could only guess, but Bronar drove a brand new cream-colored Continental and wore enough gold and diamond flash to open his own jewelry store. He wasn't getting that kinda scratch fixing transmissions, that was for damn straight.

Freddy slipped out the alley door. After re-locking the padlock, he stepped out onto the sidewalk and began limping toward the center of town, the transceiver still under his arm, his clothes dripping transmission fluid. Felt pretty damn good to be alive.

The Mellow Lemon advertised itself as a "natural" food restaurant. It was in fact a hole-in-the-wall Duval Street joint where kids paid outrageous prices for sunflower seed salads, little glasses of canned pineapple juice, and Lipton tea favored with a dash of A&P nutmeg. At night there was almost always a gaunt guitar player singing anti-war or anti-government or anti-something songs, the simplistic free verse of the runaways, dropouts and dopers, nodding through the chemical haze of their rainbow world.

Watered down guava juice and herbal salads did not pay the Mellow Lemon's bills, but a thriving drug business did. Uppers, downers, smack, acid, mescaline, pot—anything wanted or needed to keep reality off the doorstep—it was all there, available for a price. The flower children had come to Key West to escape, to stare into the setting sun, thinking they had abandoned a world out of control, leaving behind on the mainland all the shit handed down by well-meaning parents and a society that saw everything in black and white. They had come to Key West seeking Utopia, finding instead the Mellow Lemon, where a few dollars made the world a candygram.

Claybourne went around back where the kitchen exited onto an alley, and rapped gently on a flimsy screen door. Inside he saw a girl working next to a mound of vegetables, chopping a carrot with slow, deliberate strokes. In answer to his knock, she turned her head toward the door, a wide, goofy smile on her face, eyes glassy. He did not wait for an invitation to come in; his arm was about to fall off, and the transceiver was slippery with sweat. He came into the kitchen and dumped the radio on the counter next to the sink. The girl watched without moving or changing her expression. Just what he needed, he thought, a zoned-out white bitch.

"Manallo around?" he finally asked.

She blinked. Her sacklike yellow muu-muu did little to hide the fact that she was very overweight. Her hair was long and ratty, a sweat-soaked bandana held the light brown strands away from her fleshy fat face. She spoke in a misty, faraway voice.

"Ebony."

"Say what?"

"Ebony. So rich, so dark, so full of secrets."

"Don't jive me, girl. Where's Manallo?"

"Have a carrot, black brother." She held out a piece of unpeeled carrot to him.

"Don't want no fuckin' carrot. Where's Manallo?" Freddy rubbed at the small of his back and looked for a chair.

"If only we could all share your blackness," the girl said, "the dignity and courage. I think the whip lashes of white slave masters should be shared by all of us with the stigma of pale skin. Only when we too have felt the boot heels of the oppressor can we share your nobility." Her eyes seemed to focus somewhere halfway up the Keys.

"Onliest whip lash you gonna feel is ma dick whompin' your head 'less you get Manallo for me," Claybourne snarled, deciding it was time to go into his hardass Panther routine. He didn't have time to waste on some white cow spaced to the gills.

"I dig your anger, soul brother. It's totally cool."

"Well, you gonna *feel* ma anger kickin' your butt inside out 'less you move your fat ass and get me the man. Can you dig that, bitch?"

"This is really far out, man," the girl said, smiling. "I mean, I can really get into this. I mean, like, I can feel the burden shift, ya know? A guilt trip is what I need for my Karma. Abuse me, use me, lay your hatred at my feet."

The girl paused for a moment, then changed channels. "Want some coleslaw? I made the mayonnaise myself from scratch. It was a beautiful experience, I mean, like, I always thought mayonnaise came from a jar, ya know? Really blew my mind when Eddie told me it came from eggs!" The girl's eyes rolled, then locked on a large bowl of wet coleslaw that was going brown around the edges.

She was saved from a possible severe ass-kicking as the bulky shape of Hector Manallo entered the kitchen, a Budweiser bottle in one hand, an unlit cigarette dangling from his lip. The sight of Claybourne sitting there next to the sink brought him up short, then an expression of recognition spread across his face. Freddy was about to speak when Hector silenced him with a raised hand.

"Hey dair, Bluebird," he said to the girl. "Eddie says he wants jou to change the celery on the tables."

The girl nodded, and after grabbing a bunch of fresh celery, left the kitchen. Hector watched her sway out into the dining area through a doorway filled with strings of small bells, then looked back at Freddy. His wandering eye was off in leftfield someplace, but the good one didn't blink.

"She don't wear no underwear, jou know that? But her brains be fried plantains. Only we don't take no chances, 'kay? So, what's happenin', Clayburg? Jou got some business with me?"

Claybourne pointed at the transceiver. "Yeah, got some goods for you ta move for me, man."

Hector spotted the transceiver. "Hay-zus Cristo!" he shouted as the beer bottle clattered into the sink. Frantically he began searching through the pile of vegetables on the sideboard—cauliflower, cabbage, carrots, and celery going every which way.

His frenzied search at last produced two burlap bags which he quickly threw over the transceiver. After piling some of the spilled vegetables on top of it, he turned to Freddy, throwing his unlit cigarette against the wall in what looked like an act of frustration.

"What the fuck! Jou crazy? 'er somethin'?" the wall-eyed brown man screamed. "Why don't jou just put up a big sign sayin' stolen goods for sale here. Jou know who be out front? The fuckin' sheriff, that's who!"

Claybourne pulled a toothpick out of his shirt pocket and rolled it into the side of his mouth. The ultimate cool. "Listen, man, keep your skivvies dry. Nobody seen me, Jack. I keep a low profile, you dig?"

Manallo answered by kicking hard at the baseboard under

the sink. "Shit! Jou cannot be walkin' around with hot goods in broad daylight. Just take one asshole ta put both of us away. An' who jou telling to keep his underpants dry? Looks ta me like jou pissed jou own pants."

"Just some transmission fluid, dude," Freddy grumbled. "And it's the fuckin' middle of the night out there, man, where the fuck you been? 'Sides, nobody in this enda town gives a shit what I'm carryin'. Look, dude, you interested in movin' my goods or not? 'Cause if you ain't, I'll take my business ta somebody else."

Freddy pulled the toothpick out of his mouth and began examining the tip like a surgeon with a freshly extracted biopsy.

"Jou fulla shit, Clayburg. Who else jou gonna go to, huh? Jou tell me that. Who else in this town jou gonna go to with hot stuff?"

"Fuck you, Manallo. Don't think I don't know you been rippin' people off." Freddy gestured at the other man with the toothpick. "Word on the street is you got a cee for them rings the brutha gave you, man. Seems like all you gave the Sandman was a twenty."

"That be bullshit, man. Who jou gonna believe, dat old drunk or Hector?"

Freddy got to his feet. "Gotta go with the brutha, you want it straight. But tell ya what, I let you handle my goods. Only, since this is the first time we're workin' together, I wanna be there when the deal goes down, you dig? Make sure I'm gettin' my due that way."

Hector shrugged. "OK with me, Bubba. Jou a fool, but OK with me. Sixty-forty split."

"Yeah, that's cool. Gotta protect my assets, that's all." Claybourne flicked away the toothpick and began heading for the back door. "So I'll be seein' you, Hector."

"Yeah, sure," the other man answered.

Freddy felt his foot hit a wet pile of cauliflower and cabbage, and for the second time that night found himself sliding across a floor. Flailing his arms, this time he managed to stay on his feet. He slammed out the flimsy screen door and came to a stop in the alley. Trying to recapture some lost cool, he pointed his finger back through the screen and growled out a warning.

"And I'm tellin' you, dude, you fuck with me an' I be lookin' for your ass. You dig?"

Manallo scratched his bulging belly through the fabric of his stained tee shirt, stared at Freddy through the screen for a while with the one good eye, then grinned his twenty-four karat grin.

"Jou people sure know how to dance," he said.

CHAPTER EIGHT

EVEN at one in the morning the tropical breath of August was hot and suffocating. Nothing like the daytime, though, when it sucked away a man's energy like a vampire at the jugular. In this climate Dracula did his feeding in broad daylight; the night was left to other creatures.

The branches of the scrub pines above him rustled gently, and Slater felt another rivulet of sweat trickle down across the burnt cork he'd rubbed on his forehead and cheekbones. The sky was clear; a quarter moon shed just enough light to throw shadows. From where he sat in the trees, Slater searched for a sign of his enemy.

He kept his eyes moving constantly, concentrating on the edge of his vision, never staring straight ahead. He had learned that the night played tricks on those who stared too long and hard into its depths. Sight was not a primary sense in the dark anyway; sometimes it could even work against you. So you had to compensate, had to allow some ancient part of your brain to take over, sharpening other senses so that the slightest change in pressure, temperature, texture, and odor were picked up and tucked away. The snapping of a twig, the intake of a breath, the smallest movement around your mental perimeter—all were fed to some place way back in there and stored for when you needed to rock'n roll for real.

"Melican Marine! Tonight you die!"

The enemy's scream came from Slater's left, maybe twenty meters away. It was followed by the crashing of brush and Slater's own swift movement as he rolled to his right, realigning his body to the direction of the noise. He waited a few seconds as he pinpointed the sound, then estimated where his enemy would be located. Slowly, ever so slowly, he got to his feet and began circling his prey, the only sounds a barely heard crunching of pine needles under his boots and the faraway thump of his heart doing double-time.

He had covered maybe thirty paces when he caught a whiff of something sweet, perfumey, and totally alien. Right away he understood that his enemy had made a serious mistake. The scent would lead him through the darkness like a flashing beacon.

He moved upwind, following the fragrance like a blood-hound.

The smell grew stronger and he thought he recognized it. Somewhere in his head a tiny warning light flickered; this odor was not in keeping with the traits and habits of the enemy he knew so well. Something here wasn't right.

The warning was overridden when he saw the shape in front of him. It was a man, standing in a small clearing, his back turned. Without a second thought, Slater reached for the bayonet scabbard at his belt, then lowered his shoulder and launched himself through the trees as a blood-curdling howl from the Stone Age rose to his lips. He hit the man in full stride and they both went down.

It was like wrestling with smoke. There appeared to be substance there, but in reality there was nothing. Too late, Slater discovered his arms were wrapped around an empty utility shirt reeking of Aqua Velva. As he spat out pine needles and coral dust, he guessed he was done for, fooled again by an enemy almost supernatural in cunning.

He guessed right. A scream came from behind him a split second before the creature was on his back. "Babe Luth eatah shit!" a voice roared in his ear. "You die now, yankee pig!"

Slater felt the scabbard of a bayonet drawn roughly across his throat. Once again he was dead.

As quickly as it had come, the weight on his back lifted.

Slater rolled over and propped himself up on his forearms. Above him the moonlight glinted off the bare chest of the man who had killed him, a smile slashing the face masked with camouflage greasepaint. The man threw back his head and gave out a half-assed Tarzan yell while beating his breast with clenched fists.

The Dutchman, Slater knew, was counting another coup.

Half-heartedly, he aimed a kick at Van Groot's groin. The blow was neatly parried, and the little man with the skinned head began dancing around the clearing, singing the "Marine Corps Hymn" to the tune of a song called "Little White Dove." Despite his recent death, Slater couldn't help laughing. Leaping around in the moonlight half naked like that, the Dutchman looked like an elf on speed. A real headcase. Guy was definitely from another planet.

The laughter only encouraged the little turd to become more frenzied in his dance, and by the end of the third verse he collapsed next to his victim, dripping sweat and gasping for breath.

"Gotja with the horse piss, didn't I, AJ?"

An answering grunt was all Slater could come up with as he put his head back and let the night sky lay it on him. He thought maybe he was beginning to enjoy the night again, like when he was a kid in his backyard trying to figure out what infinity meant. Nam had taught him to hate the night, the roll of manmade thunder, the shadows of ghosts, the lead weight of fear in the pit of his stomach. Now that he was back, though, the black shroud was gradually being replaced by a warm blanket again. He did not miss the irony; it was the same sky.

"Come on, man," the Dutchman finally said after catching his breath. "Better we dee-dee back to the phone an' check in. Never know when some asshole might come lookin' for us."

Van Groot was on his feet, shaking the pine needles and dust out of his utility shirt, then slipping it on. Slater mentally kicked himself for not paying attention to the warning signal in his brain when he'd caught the first whiff of Aqua Velva. No man who showered—at the most—twice a month would smell so sweet. No doubt about it, the Dutchman was one slick sucker.

The two men went and got their rifles from the tree fork where they'd stashed them before starting the game, the game the Dutchman called *Silent Kill*. Slater checked his magazine for dust, reinserted it, then swung the M-14 by the sling over his shoulder. The Dutchman was already ahead of him on the dirt road leading back to the shed and the Post Eleven telephone. He jogged to catch up.

"Hey, Dutch!" he called. "Slow down, damn it. I'm rubbin' my crotch raw."

Van Groot pivoted and continued at the same pace, now walking backward. "I told ya a hundred times, AJ, don't have 'em starch your utilities no more."

"Easy for you to say," Slater said as he came up next to the other man. "They don't make you stand inspection. I show up at Guard Mount in softies and it'll be my young butt."

"Hell, man," Van Groot said, "most you'd get would be an ass chewin' or a little probational bust. I been busted twice. A probe-bust ain't diddly squat. Yer still cherry till ya got a probe-bust around here."

Slater grumbled something and the Dutchman did a parade-ground-perfect "To the rear, march" so both men were finally facing the same direction.

"All I'm saying, AJ," the little man continued, "if ya want to avoid discomfort to your family jewels there, quit starchin' yer uts. It's supposed to be a fuckin' *work* uniform, ain't it? Just cause some fat-assed generals are fucked up in the head don't mean you gotta be too." The Dutchman spit from a load of tobacco he'd stuffed in his cheek.

"Tell that to Screamin' Don," Slater said.

"Fuck Brule. The man's had a hardon for the last hundred and fifty years. Screamin' asshole."

"Like I said," Slater continued, "easy for you ta say. You don't have ta stand any inspections. That guy reamed me out for ten minutes the other day just cause I had a zit on the end of my nose."

Van Groot chuckled. "That's cause you wash too damn much. Naw, AJ, the reason I don't gotta stand those chickenshit inspections is 'cause I made myself 'invaluable in other areas,' as the gunny would say. Them trucks need constant attention and tender lovin' care."

"Bullshit. Tollster filled me in a long time ago, you fuckin' skate. The gunny just got sick of hearing you get your ass chewed so he made sure there was always work to be done on those junkers before every Guard Mount."

There was no response for the next ten paces or so, then the Dutchman finally answered, trying a little too hard to sound insulted. "I'm beginning to understand. Yeah. Now I'm beginnin' ta understand, AJ. You wrecked my beauty last week on purpose, didn't ya? In a jealous rage. Pissed ya off she was always so nice ta me, stallin' out on you. Decided if you couldn't have her, no man would, so you wrecked her, you slimy sonuvabitch!"

Van Groot pulled his K-bar from its leather scabbard, the blackened blade only a dull dark shape in his hand. He held it up in front of his face, turned it one way, then the other, then tested its sharpness with the pad of his thumb.

"Gaw damn I'm hungry!" he said. "What say we get us some goosta, in honor of yer last night out here?"

"Only if we cook the goddamn thing," Slater grumbled. "I'm not eating that crap raw again, man, no way."

He hadn't even blinked at the Dutchman's show with the knife; after more than a month of serving duty with the crazy asshole, he'd pretty much gotten used to the little man's John Wayne routine.

"Damn it, AJ, no fires at night," Van Groot lectured. "How many fuckin' times I gotta tell ya? Fuckin' smugglers can see it for miles." He spit again and Slater heard a dull, sloppy sound over to his left. "Goddamn, how the hell did you get ta be a sergeant anyway?"

Slater didn't bother to answer. Smugglers? Who was Dutch kidding? But there wasn't anything the little man could say or do now that would've surprised him. Just like Claybourne, Tollster, and the rest of them had warned, he'd found out real quick why the other Marines at the Barracks were so gun-shy about standing duty with Eric Van Groot.

He *did* eat bugs, and a lot of other things besides—snakes, frogs, and grubs were all on the menu, always tailbone raw. He'd also rigged homemade booby traps all over the island and seemed to get his jollies leading Slater into each and every goddamn one of them. (They weren't all that dangerous, only painful, as Slater found out the first time he stumbled over a trip wire and got a mouthful of pine branch snapped in his face.)

Naw, the booby traps weren't so dangerous . . . . but the Dutchman's so-called "airborne operations" were. You got a Gray Ghost going fast enough and you could jump ammo bunkers, those rolling, dirt-covered humpback shapes divided in two by the access road. Hit one of those suckers at just the right speed and it was like hitting a ramp; you could launch the pickup truck out over and across to the top of the opposite bunker, just like some fuckin' circus act.

The Dutchman liked to practice blindfolded.

Last week, Slater had been talked into taking a crack at a jump on his own—the reason the two of them were now on foot. The Gray Ghost he'd been driving was over in the shop having a broken oil pan and tie-rod replaced and getting its front end realigned. The Dutchman had taken the damage done to the truck personally, and hadn't spoken for three days. When he did, he'd started calling Slater "AJ."

Fun and games were about over, though, Slater told himself. Tonight had been his last chance to collect the fifty bucks Van Groot had offered to any man at the Barracks who could get the drop on him playing *Silent Kill*. Earlier in the week Slater had been told by Gunny Brownell that he was getting moved to Post Ten. A step up, sure, but in some ways he was kinda sad to be going off Fleming. For all the little dude's craziness, Slater had come to think of Van Groot as his best friend.

"Gonna hate to see ya go, m'man," the Dutchman said as though reading his mind. "From what I hear, Dornato's a fuckin' basket case since the gunny told him he'd be replacin' you out here." They continued to straggle up the access road.

"The two of you oughta get along real good then," Slater offered.

"Fuck you. Just a sore loser, that's all you are." The Dutchman spat another stream of tobacco juice.

"Suck wind, Dutch!" Slater laughed. "Another two weeks and I'd be handin' you your ass."

"Who you kiddin', man? Give you two *years* and you'd still be shittin' yer pants every other night tryin' ta find my shadow. Face it, dude, you just ain't RECON material."

"Oh, and you are, huh?"

"Damn straight. Hell, I been practicin' my techniques out here for almost eighteen months now. Wouldn't be surprised if I could do ninety percent of *them guys* right now."

Slater glanced over at the sweaty, little-boy face of his friend. "Let me ask you somethin', Dutch. What the hell you know about RECON anyway? In the Nam you were a goddamn bulk fuel driver, right?"

Van Groot didn't miss a beat. "Didn't you ever read *Stars and Stripes,* AJ?"

"Sometimes. What the hell's that gotta do with anything?"

Van Groot grunted as if he'd decided Slater was as dense as cold pig iron. "Listen, man, every week almost they had a story about RECON in that rag. Them guys was always blowin' away a whole company a gooks or somethin'. Shit. While you was runnin' sweeps through a skivvy house and I was drivin' around a load of fuckin' diesel, them fuckers was doin' some heavy shit. I heard they was wastin' Zips in

Laos, man. Hey, one guy even got him a tiger! Brought the damn thing back on a chopper and had a coat made for his wife. Killed the thing with his knife, man, with his fuckin' knife!"

"Dutch," Slater said, "I hate to bust your bubble, man, but all that shit was pure propaganda. Them guys are just like every grunt you ever met. No worse, no better."

"That's bullshit!" Van Groot bristled. "Let me tell ya, I seen a squad of 'em comin' back in one day up at division when I was droppin' off a load of gas at Motor T. Talk about your tough lookin'dudes! These guys were mean muthas, no doubt about it. And yours truly is gonna be one of 'em."

"You really gonna re-up?" Slater tried hard not to make the question sound like a joke.

"Sure, why not?"

"'Cause you're certifiable, that's why not."

The Dutchman didn't answer. The crunch of their boots in the gravel was the only sound. Slater wondered if he hadn't overdone it.

The dim light from the shed came into sight, and the Dutchman went inside without a word to call in the hourly report. Slater leaned back on the corrugated tin siding, still warm from the day's heat, and pulled a letter out of his breast pocket. In the pale glow of the standing light, cloudy with bloodthirsty mosquitoes and fist-sized moths, he read the letter from home for the twentieth time. It was from his mother.

His brother and dad were fighting again, she wrote. This time because Marty had been busted at an off-campus anti-war demonstration. She was asking—begging almost—for him to write to Marty and try to patch things up, for the good of the family.

The neat, delicate handwriting blurred. He looked out into the darkness and tried to focus things. There were only wispy images, though, with no substance or clearly defined shape. No answers.

"Screamin' Don Brule catches you readin' on post, man,

you'll be shittin' out yer ears." The Dutchman's voice came as a welcome interruption. Slater carefully refolded the letter and returned it to his pocket, then pushed himself away from the wall.

"That's one thing he'll never nail you on, Van Groot."

"I can read with the best of 'em, smart ass."

"Yeah, skin books and comics maybe."

"Readin' is readin', AJ. I got me a classic I'm workin' on right now, called 'Nympho Gold.' All about this ice skater who lays all the judges at this big dog show."

"Dog show? What's that got ta do with ice skating?"

"Shit! How should I know? I ain't finished it yet. . . . But dig this, Norwick just told me on the landline that Slicks Johnson is gettin' married."

"No kiddin'?" Slater laughed. "I thought he already was."

Slicks Johnson was a black corporal in the section who'd been dating a girl in town named Moany. The standing joke around the Barracks was that Slicks was so pussy whipped that he already showed all the signs of being hitched.

"When's the big event?" Slater asked as he watched the Dutchman digging for nose nuggets.

The answer sounded a little nasal. "All Norwick said is it's the last liberty weekend next month. Slicks is invitin' the whole damn section. Sonuvabitch! And I really liked old Slicks; he was an OK dude." Van Groot sounded sad.

"Jeez, you talk like he was dead or something."

"Same as," the Dutchman explained. "Come on, pardner, Norwick says the CDO is out like a light and the SOG is entertainin' some squid's wife over in base housing. Let's get us some chow."

A glistening chunk of raw lobster, stuck on the tip of Van Groot's K-bar, was held up in front of Slater's nose.

"Care for a gobble, AJ?" the little man asked.

"You gotta be kidding," Slater groaned.

"OK, but don't say I never offered you nothin'." Van

Groot sucked the "langousta" meat off the tip of the blade and dug in for more.

The two of them were sitting with their backs against a row of pilings that formed part of the bulkhead of the cove. The "goosta" thrived on the rocky shelf off Fleming, and since the waters around the Key were restricted, the local lobstermen and sportsmen couldn't get at them. So the rock lobsters were left to Van Groot and his own personal lobster pot; he only had to share his catch with the gunnery chief on the day watch to ensure the safety of the trap. The Dutchman had come to think of Fleming Cove as his own private goosta hole.

Van Groot scraped away the last bit of meat and tossed the empty tail shell into the water. He began cleaning the knife by poking it into the sand at his feet as he let out a string of burps and sucked pieces from between his teeth.

Slater hadn't said anything about the feast, knowing that any reaction to the Dutchman's eating habits would only encourage greater and grosser things from the little pecker.

"Weird," he finally mumbled.

"Fuck you. Don't knock it till ya try it." Van Groot wiped the knife against his trouser leg and returned it to its scabbard.

"Naw, I don't mean your chow, man. What I mean is . . . it's just fuckin' weird, is all. Been back in the World maybe two months and already Nam is like a dream. It's like I went ta sleep on the bird going over and woke up back here in the States, and all the in-between stuff never happened. Then I start wondering if *this* ain't the dream, that maybe I'm still over there, all fucked up in a hospital, maybe even dead. You ever get that kinda feeling?"

Slater looked over at the other man who had pulled his utility cover down over his eyes. The Dutchman's answer came like it was trying to low crawl through barbed wire.

"Hell, AJ, maybe, I dunno. Never gave it a whole lotta thought. But yeah, sometimes I get feelin' like I didn't come back to the same place I left, dig? Aw, everything looks the same, same names, same faces, same smells, same everything, 'cept it's different. Then I get to thinkin' about Twilight Zone shit—ya know, like this is the wrong what-you-call-it dimension, or some such bullshit. Maybe, like, the Crotch fucked up and I get sent back ta the wrong place."

Slater cleared his throat. "Yeah. When I was back home it was just like that, just didn't fit. Ya know, 'bout my third night home I went out for some brews with my old high school buddies. Jesus, Dutch, it was like they were talkin' in a foreign language, man! Felt like I'd never even known 'em!"

Slater flipped a handful of sand out into the darkness. "Got down here, thought everything would change, being back with the Crotch and all. And it did, a little. But, you know, like the gunny called me in and told me about going on Post Ten. How it was time I took more responsibility and all that gung-ho crap. Well, shit, I know what they expect, but all of a sudden I just don't give a flying fuck, just wanna be left alone."

The Dutchman made an evil little laughing sound. "Guess you're just fucked up, AJ.

"Or maybe you ain't," Van Groot said slowly, continuing his train of thought (whatever *that* was). "Maybe it's them that's fucked up, the whole fuckin' country. Maybe we're the only ones got our shit together." His smile reflected whitely in the moonlight. "Hey, how'd we get on such heavy stuff? That letter you was readin' a 'Dear John'? Thought you said that cunt shafted you back when you was in WestPac?"

"Naw, just somethin' from home. My brother got busted at a demonstration and my ma wants me to talk to him."

"So talk to him, what's the big deal?"

"That's just it, man. Me and Marty don't speak the same language anymore. He don't understand me, and I sure as hell don't understand him. Last time I saw him he was going out the door, right after I tried ta give him some bread for his tuition. Said he didn't want my blood money."

"I got called somethin like that once," Van Groot said. "Comin' back off leave. Philly bus station. I was in my greens, and this cute little twat with braids and feathers in her hair and some nasty lookin' clothes comes up to me and spits on my sleeve. Calls me a baby burner."

"Whatja do?"

"Only thing I could do. Punched her fuckin' lights out. Missed my bus, but it was worth it . . . I need some chew." The Dutchman fumbled for his tobacco pouch. "See, that's the great thing about bein' in the wrong dimension, AJ. You can do the things you really feel like doin' without worryin' about no consequences. Course now, when I re-enlist for RECON then I gotta clean up my act. Those guys are *always* in the Twilight Zone, man!"

Van Groot snickered. There was a pause as he loaded the inside of his cheek with tobacco. "Tell ya one thing," he mumbled, "I'd go outta my fuckin' tree if it wasn't for spendin' nights out here. All that Mickey Mouse shit over at the Barracks—inspections, field days, and red-ass monkey business—that's for 'boots,' man. I shit you not, Jack, I can't wait ta get back to the real Crotch."

"Dutch, you're full of shit, ya know that? *This* is the real Crotch."

"Watch it, boy. Just watch yer—"

Van Groot stopped talking and Slater could see him cock his head like a chicken listening for the silent pad of a fox. Then he heard it too, muffled and faraway, coming over the lapping water.

"A boat," Slater whispered.

"Yeah, other side of the cove." The Dutchman was on his feet, sniffing the air. He was whispering, too. "Let's go."

Quickly they moved back into the treeline, out of sight of the water. At a fast jog they silently hugged the coastline, making their way closer to the sound of the chugging outboard.

Slatter squeezed his M-14 at port arms. Its weight, a pain in the ass for the last few weeks, now was a part of him, an extra arm that felt almost like flesh. An excitement ripped through him like an electric current: He was back in it again, doing what he'd been trained to do, doing what had become second nature to him during those twelve months in the Nam. He felt as though he had awakened from a long sleep. As soundlessly as he could, he chambered a round.

The two Marines came out of the trees above a stone jetty standing between them and the sound of the puttering outboard. They carefully picked their way over huge chunks of granite until they could look into the cove and still be undercover. The sounds of the motor grew louder, but they could not spot the source.

Only inches from the Dutchman's ear, Slater's lips hardly moved. "What do ya think?"

"I'd guess smugglers. Maybe Cubans, I dunno." The Dutchman spit. It sounded like thunder.

"Sh-h-h. What would Cubans be doin' around here?"

"After the ammo. Small arms. For their invasion."

"Invasion? What the fuck are you talkin' about?"

The Dutchman spit again. "How should I know? Could be they wanna invade Cuba, or the United fuckin' States, or maybe they just wanna impress their old ladies."

Slater searched for alternatives. He was, after all, in charge by reason of rank. "Maybe they're refugees? I heard about that . . . refugees."

The Dutchman snorted. "Ain't no refugees in a boat like that. Take a look."

Slater could see it now—a white hull, low in the water, a sixteen-footer at least, built for speed. There was no doubt that it had violated restricted waters; it was way inside the cove. It seemed to be headed for an outcropping of rock jutting out of the water about twenty-five yards from where the two of them were crouched.

"See anybody?" Slater eased the M-14 off safe. The adrenaline sent a hit through his body.

"Too dark." The Dutchman could not hide the excitement in his voice. "But I'll tell ya one thing, they're up ta no fuckin' good. No runnin' lights and they're workin' that engine so low its gotta be muffled with somethin'. Ain't no pleasure cruise, that's for damn straight." There was an almost inaudible click as Van Groot thumbed off his own safety.

Slater put his hand on the other man's shoulder, then pointed. "Look, you work yourself around towards those rocks. Any shit and we'll have 'em in a crossfire."

"Gotcha, AJ. Damn good thinkin' for a 'boot.'" The Dutchman was gone, melting into the darkness without another sound.

The boat's motor coughed, then stopped, and Slater watched the white hull glide to a stop. He thought he heard whispers, then the clank of metal followed by a splash. The boat lay midway between the rocks where Van Groot had headed and his own position. Whoever was out there had slipped into their trap.

The Dutchman's voice exploded across the water just as Slater thought he spotted two black shapes slipping over the side of the boat.

"Awright, assholes, advance and be recognized, and do it goddamn quick."

Slater cringed. No, no, you crazy shit. "Halt, who goes there," that's what you're supposed to—

"And let me hear the fuckin' password while yer at it."

Password? What password?

There was a long ten seconds of silence, then the Dutchman yelled again, this time his voice filled with a scary calmness.

"OK, muthas, have it yer way."

Slater saw the muzzle flash at the same instant he heard the crack. It was followed by three more. The streak of a red tracer round marked bullet number five. In the back of his mind something told him that things had gone too far. Yet even as he debated within himself, he felt the comfort of the M-14 butt in his shoulder, saw the white hull loom in his sights. Fuck it.

The rifle's buck was a long missed friend, the trigger squeeze as familiar as an old baseball glove. The heavy 7.62 NATO tracer rounds, burning with cheery Fourth-of-July luminescence, tore into the hull; chunks of wood and fiberglass danced in the air. Suddenly the target turned into a ball of flame, lighting up the cove in a cherry glow that felt warm on Slater's face even as bits of debris began falling on his position, forcing him to hunker down. He smelled the powder and smoke, then smiled. It was like the first taste of steak after three months of hamburger.

CHAPTER NINE

THE creature in black rose up out of the water in front of him like something from a bad horror flick. Slater wanted to turn tail and run but his thighs had turned to jelly doughnuts. The M-14 in his hands felt heavy now, a hundred-pound barbell smelling of hot oil and gunpowder. Fear tasted like old brass, Slater decided, like sucking on an empty bullet shell.

The thing in black made a horrible coughing sound, then reached up and tore part of its own face off and threw it up on the beach. It began to come toward him then, lurching through the shallows with a strange awkward stride. Inhuman. Slater saw the foot of a giant frog—silhouetted by the light of the still burning wreck—lift out of the water and then disappear. It was followed by another webbed foot.

The beast from beneath the sea reached the shore, gave out one gurgling cry, and collapsed onto the rocks.

"Help," Slater thought it said. So it was a man after all. Uh-oh.

"Keep yer hands out where I can see 'em," he heard the crazy bastard Van Groot saying to the man. The muzzle of the Dutchman's rifle was only an inch or two from the guy's head.

After the boat exploded, he and Van Groot had waited for a few minutes to see what developed. When no enemy fire came in, they met halfway between their two positions and tried to figure out just what had gone down. The next thing Slater knew, the dark shape was staggering out of the cove in their direction. Van Groot had gone down to meet it, but something about the explosion and the sight of a shape rising from the water had taken all the fight out of Slater, left him weighed down and worried, and yeah, scared shitless. What had they done? What *had* they done?

"Hey, AJ," Van Groot called, "you wanna give me a hand here?"

Slater didn't answer, didn't move. He felt paralyzed. The taste of old brass grew stronger. Something about this situation was way too familiar. Something bad had happened.

"Shit on a shingle, AJ!" the Dutchman yelled impatiently. "Come on, will ya? Cover this asshole while I frisk 'im."

He forced himself to move, to forget. Whatever crap they were into now, it was just part of the dream. Didn't mean a thing.

The man in the black rubber wetsuit was coughing and gagging up sea water when Slater got up close enough to see there wasn't any fight left in him either. A diver. The mask and snorkel were gone but the guy was still wearing his flippers.

While Slater pretended to keep the diver covered, Van Groot went through the motions of checking for weapons. When the little crazy found a knife in a scabbard strapped to the man's calf, he sounded like he'd caught the dude with an AK.

"Well, lookee here, AJ! Goddamn puke was fixin' ta waste our butts! I think we nailed ourselves a real honest-to-God infiltrator! Habla Español, pal? You speakee Cuban?"

The man in the wetsuit got very agitated, started flopping around like a landed steelhead. He was still spitting and coughing sea water so his words were hard to understand. From where Slater stood, they sounded like the ravings of a madman.

"Admiral!" the man spurted. "Concussion. Looked for him. No use. Get help!"

"Ain't in the mood for no fairy tales, Jose," Van Groot said, nudging the guy with the toe of his boot. "Caught ya red-handed here. Better come clean else I'll sic my buddy on your ass. He's a mental. Where's the rest of yer troops?"

"Couldn't find him!" the man gasped. "Too dark. My head. Get help!"

Slater's utility shirt was soaked through with sweat. His eyes burned. He felt a chill shake him from the top down. Something was badly screwed up here. This guy was no Cuban, no matter how much Van Groot wanted him to be.

"Give it a rest, Fidel," the Dutchman snarled. "You got one minute to—"

"Stow it, Van Groot!" Slater finally yelled, dropping his rifle and falling to his knees next to the diver. Gently, he rolled the man over onto his back. "What is it?" he asked. "What're you talking about, man? Who's out there?"

In the flickering light of the burning boat, which was slowly drifting in closer to shore, Slater watched the man's eyes open, and for a second they were filled with the look of somebody who'd just crawled out of a bunker that'd taken a hit from a CHICOM rocket. The diver's eyes focused on him, a cold hand grabbed the front of his shirt.

"Admiral Bledsoe!" the man choked. "Couldn't find him!"

Slater turned his head and looked out into the cove. All he could see was the black mirror of water reflecting the sputtering flames of the drifting wreck.

"Oh, fuck," he heard the Dutchman say.

Slater spun. "What?"

"Bledsoe," Van Groot sounded hoarse. "Commanding Officer of the whole damn shootin' match. AJ, we are fucked."

No time to think about it, had to act. He ripped at the laces of his boots, kicked them off, then began peeling away his shirt and trousers. The jagged rocks on the beach tore at his feet as he ran to the water and hit the surface, already wind-milling his arms in the half-assed crawl he'd learned one summer on Walled Lake.

He was out of breath in no time and began swallowing sea water. It tasted a little like gasoline, probably from the boat. Not enough to catch, he hoped, otherwise he'd be fried. Spitting and sputtering, he switched to the breast stroke. Wasn't sure what he was looking for; if the admiral was on the bottom, it was all over anyway. No way he could dive down and search. Too damn deep. Too damn dark.

"See anything out there, AJ?" he heard a worried Van Groot calling from shore. He didn't bother answering. Didn't have enough spare air. Shit! Felt like he'd been swimming around for an hour. God damn! They had really screwed up! The admiral, for Christ's sakes! What did the Crotch do to you for blowin' away an admiral? A thousand years in Portsmouth.

Slater's ears began to ring; his arms and legs felt like over-cooked spaghetti. He was going to have to call it quits soon or else the Coast Guard would be fishing a second dead man out of the cove the next morning. Maybe he should've called in to the Barracks for help first instead of jumping right in. Help would've already been on the way. Goddamn, Dutch! Go call in for some help 'stead of standing around on the beach with your thumb up your—

He swam head-on into a big piece of driftwood. Only driftwood didn't feel like rubber, wasn't shaped like a big link of sausage either, didn't wear a diver's mask or grow hair that looked like white seaweed. And a piece of driftwood sure as hell didn't groan or wheez either, even real softlike so that you could hardly hear it.

"Hey, AJ!" the Dutchman yelled out again, sounding very goddamn far away. "Forgot ta warn ya. Keep an eye out for barracuda, man! Some very vicious fuckers. Guy last year got a hand took off by one of them bastards. Be careful!"

Even dragging the large semi-conscious body of Admiral Bledsoe behind him, Jack Slater made it back to shore in record shattering time.

"And then I started artificial resuscitation on the admiral, sir," Slater said softly, "while Corporal Van Groot went up to Post Eleven to call in for help. By the time Gunny

Brownell and the Reaction squad got out there, the man was sitting up, breathing on his own. About five minutes later, the ambulance got there and took both of 'em out to the hospital. That's, ah, all I know, sir."

Slater and Van Groot were standing tall, locked at attention in front of Captain Brule's desk. Lieutenant Kargo stood off to the left while Screamin' Don just sat there and glared up at them like he was fixing to hose them down with a flame thrower. Everybody looked like shit—tired and rumpled and on edge. It was just after three in the A.M.

"You got anything to add to that, shit-for-brains?" Brule shifted his attention over to Van Groot. The soft indirect lighting of the office danced off the XO's glasses making it look as though his eyes were flashing strobes. Probably were.

Screamin' Don had been waiting for them when the Command Duty Officer's truck finally brought them back in to the Barracks. By the time Lieutenant Kargo arrived from the hospital, the XO had rousted Delkirt out of the rack and had the charges already typed up. Screamin' Don didn't even want to wait until daylight—the Office Hours would go down immediately.

"No, sir," the Dutchman sang out. "What the sergeant says is pretty much as if I said it myself. Them two came inta restricted waters an' failed to answer a challenge. So we blew 'em up. It's that simple."

"Well, it's *not* that simple, you half-wit cretin!" Brule roared. "In case you mighta missed it, Navy admirals get extremely pissed when their boats get shot out from under 'em. I'm talkin' pissed beyond belief." Screamin' Don leaned way back in his swivel chair and propped a big black corfam dress shoe up on the desk in front of him. "What did the aide have to say, Stan?" he asked Kargo.

The lieutenant cleared his throat. His voice still held the deep sleep he'd probably been enjoying back in quarters when his phone jangled and told him his men were shooting admirals. "He told me Mrs. Bledsoe was planning a dinner party for some junketing Congressmen next week. Admiral wanted to serve 'em all lobster he'd caught with his own hands. So they took the Flag's Boston Whaler and headed for Fleming Cove. Figured since those were restricted waters they could catch their limit in no time. They entered Fleming Cove, dropped anchor, then went over the side. Next thing the aide knew, there was an explosion and he was on queer street. Lost track of the admiral. Said if it hadn't been for Slater here, the—"

"Yeah, yeah, yeah," Brule broke in, "he's a big hero. But that was after the fact, wasn't it, Slater?" The points of light on Screamin' Don's glasses danced again and zeroed in on Slater. "*After* you put forty rounds of ball and tracer into the admiral's barge. *After* you and this dildo over here tried to start World War III in a goddamn *ammo dump*! *After* you sank and nearly killed a *fucking two star flag officer of the United States Navy*! If you think you're gonna get a medal for this night's work, Sergeant, you're even crazier'n your nut-cracker pal here."

Screamin' Don uncoiled out of his seat like he was following assembly instructions—lift part A to part B, swing parts A and B up to lock, repeat steps for parts C and D. It took him a few seconds, but suddenly he was at full height, sweeping out around the desk and coming at Slater from the side so that when he spoke, the words went directly in Slater's left ear.

"Now hear this, you trigger-happy turd," Brule bellowed. "You fired on a Navy admiral tonight, an admiral who just happens to be the Commanding Officer of this goddamn base! Do you know whose ass is gonna be in a sling over that? Do you? Not yours, hot-shot. Not your brain-damaged buddy over there, either. No. I'm the one who's gonna swing! Me, the acting CO of this looney bin! *My* record is gonna have the black mark. *My* dick is gonna get slammed in the car door! *My* life is gonna be pure hell for the next who-knows-how-long."

Slater could feel little particles of spit hitting the side of his head. Screamin' Don was really working himself into a lather. So far, everything the captain had said was true. Wasn't much he could do about it now except stand there and take it.

Brule paused to catch his breath, and at the same time side-stepped around so that he was standing directly in front of Slater, so close that when he spoke again his chin almost brushed the top of Slater's head.

"You know what I really want to do, Sergeant?" the captain asked, fairly quietly compared to the way he'd been shouting moments before. "I want to fucking kill you."

The muscles across Slater's back twitched and tightened. A hot wave of anger rolled up from below; he could feel his face start to burn. Brule had no right.

"You don't think I'd do it, do ya, stud?" the captain continued. "Well, I would. In a second. Tear your head off with my bare hands. What do ya say to that?"

"Try it."

The words were out before he thought; a natural gut reaction almost the same as the one that had grabbed him out on Fleming just before he began cranking off the rounds. He just said it, couldn't take it back, wouldn't have even if he could, even if it would've prevented Screamin' Don from going berserk.

The captain stepped back, his eyes wide behind the lens, his mouth trembling with rage. He growled, then slammed both hands into Slater's chest and grabbed hold of his utility shirt, pulling the sergeant in close against him as he stuck his chin into the other man's face.

"You fuckin' garbage! You threaten me? You threaten an officer of·the United States Marine Corps? I'm gonna rip your fuckin' guts out!"

Brule's breath was rank. Slater could see a piece of last night's dinner stuck between the front teeth. He figured it was time. His hands tightened into fists.

"Don! Let him go!" Kargo was forcing his way between the two of them, breaking Brule's hold on the shirt, pushing the big captain back. "What the hell's the matter with you?"

Brule shoved Kargo backward and the lieutenant staggered. "Let's go, Slater," the captain shouted, closing in again, this time with an index finger pointed at Slater's nose. "You wanna get down? Well, let's go to it, stud. I'm ready."

Although a crossed wire somewhere was urging him to wade into the officer, he remained standing at attention—tense and ready—but still at attention.

Kargo was immediately back in the captain's face. He planted his feet and leaned against Screamin' Don's chest, stopping the wild man's forward charge.

"Goddamn it, Don!" Kargo yelled. "Simmer down! Get a hold of yourself! Jesus! Look what you're doing. Are you crazy?"

Brule could've been snorting fire. His breath came in great gasps. He looked down at Kargo, took another deep breath, then easily shoved the lieutenant away.

"Don't you ever touch me again, Lieutenant," he snarled. "Not ever."

Brule pivoted and in three long strides went back behind the desk where he stood over the two open SRBs in front of him. Still looking down at record books, he finally spoke.

"You know something, Kargo, by all rights you should be up on charges, too."

"Now just a goddamn minute, *Captain*," Kargo began, his own anger suddenly flaring like a pop-up illum. "We can take care of—"

"You just can't seem to control your herd," Brule went on. "Oh, don't think I haven't seen it. The Great Slack is eating away the Guard while you play candy-ass big brother. If you'd open your eyes, you'd see it. You baby these pukes and they step all over ya. Well, that's gonna come to a screamin' halt, right now! You don't want to step on toes, then I will. You two give me your stripes."

Brule looked across at them and held out his hand. There

was a long, long moment of silence. "You heard me, give 'em over."

"Sir?" Van Groot croaked.

"Give me your stripes," Brule snapped.

Slater felt his knees buckle. His legs began to shake, almost with a will of their own. He understood what the captain wanted. He reached up and unpinned the metal chevrons on his utility shirt collar, then shuffled forward and placed them in Brule's outstretched hand. The Dutchman did the same. Brule leaned over his desk and hurled the rank insignia in the shitcan next to the desk.

"The only reason I'm not busting you both to buck private," Brule said evenly, "is because the UCMJ doesn't give me the authority to; I can only take one stripe at a time. Tell ya what I'd like to do, and that's give you both a court-martial. The way the squids work, though, they'd probably throw the case out and write you up for meritorious promotion. Now get outta my sight."

Slater took a shaky step backward, did an about-face, and left the office. Van Groot was right behind him. As they stormed off down the passageway, they could hear muffled shouts coming from behind the closed door. Kargo and Brule going at it.

"Goddamn," the Dutchman rattled, "Screamin' Don sure is on the rag, ain't he? Wonder what brought that on."

Slater found it very hard to speak; maybe he was in some kind of shock. He'd never seen anything like it, not even in boot camp. Not only had the captain threatened him, but had put his hands on him, shoved him, challenged him to a duke-out. He'd never seen a Marine Corps officer flip out so completely. Never seen such anger. And he'd never seen one officer ream out another with enlisted around either. Just wasn't done.

"Ya know, AJ," Van Groot went on, "you could probably write that asshole up for what he done ta you in there. They got some rule about officers grabbin' enlisted personnel like that. And you got witnesses."

"No sweat," Slater muttered. He knew damn well how pissing matches between enlisted poags and officers turned out.

"You hungry?" the Dutchman asked. "Still time ta grab some mid-rats over to the messhall. What ya say?"

Slater reached up to his collar and felt the empty pin holes where his sergeant's stripes had been. "Sure, why not," he said.

Out in the company street, Zamora's uncle howled at the moon while under the table in the Guard Shack Private Jiggs killed spiders in his sleep. As the Dutchman led the way out the Barracks and into the night, Jack Slater knew that the little dude had been right; they were definitely, positively living in the Twilight Zone. No fuckin' doubt about it.

CHAPTER TEN

SLICKS Johnson's wedding went down on the third Saturday in September in a building on Duval that the Justice of the Peace used for large ceremonies. Twenty bucks an hour and all the humidity you could handle.

Sitting in the back row of folding chairs, Slater took an open bottle of beer held out to him by the Dutchman and gulped a swallow. He'd missed the bachelor party at the Bamboo Room the night before and now Van Groot was trying to help him catch up.

"Do you, Hugo T. Johnson, take this woman, Monita, to be your lawfully wedded wife, promising to love, honor, and keep her in sickness and in health, forsaking all others as long as you both shall live?" The Honorable Alfredo Cardoza paused to search the yellowed bloodshot eyes of the groom standing in front of him.

For a long time the room was quiet except for the creaking ceiling fan. Cardoza leaned over to whisper in Johnson's ear, but Slater and everyone else in the room could hear what he said.

"Say, 'I do,' please."

The groom sagged at the knees and turned his head toward Benjamin, his Best Man, who stood behind him, holding him up by the back of his belt. The two Marines were the only grunts in uniform; everybody else was decked out in jeans and tee shirts. Slicks swayed unsteadily; the better part of a fifth of Old Granddad (breakfast, Slater had heard) lay in his gut.

"He talkin' ta me, bro?" Slicks asked.

Benjamin nodded and Slicks mimicked him, bringing a

round of titters from Moany's girlfriends in the front row. Slicks let his eyes roll back to Cardoza.

"I do-o-o, please!" he bellowed.

This time the laughter came from the other part of the audience, the Marines in the Starboard Section who could still walk. They'd closed the Bamboo around four A.M.

The Justice of the Peace, wilting in his heavy black robes, continued to drone on. "And do you, Monita Gelphin, take this man . . ."

"I tell ya, man, she was a knockout," the Dutchman whispered loudly in Slater's ear. "Goddamn hair hanging down to her ass an' a bod that would not quit. Fuckin' movie star, I shit you not. Never believe she was the Crack's niece."

Slater tried to ignore the little pest. Van Groot had been talking nothing else but the girl since rolling him out of the rack that morning. Only half listening, he watched Slicks reach out and pat his bride-to-be on the behind. She answered with a swat to his arm, bringing another round of laughter from the audience. Slater winced. Moany looked like she could hold her own in a pier brawl. He had the feeling that Slicks Johnson was in a world of shit.

"I'm in love, AJ," Van Groot plowed on. "I swear ta God I'm in love. Nice firm little boobies with nips that follow ya around the room. Jeez! Almost creamed my jeans when she started—Damnation! What died?"

An invisible cloud of riot gas had drifted across the back of the room; it smelled like rotten eggs. First one man, then another moved away from the assault and staggered down the aisle, looking for a seat closer to the ceremony and away from the sleeping Private Jiggs who was tied to a water pipe running along the back wall.

"What the fuck did you do to him last night?" Slater choked as he and Van Groot found seats down in the third row.

"Nothin', man, he's just got rotten guts, that's all."

"Bullshit," Bone Tollster murmured from behind them.

"Fed that fucker a bucket of hard boiled eggs. Saw him do it. Used up the Crack's whole night supply. Tryin' to impress that new chick. Showin' her Jiggs' trick." Tollster reached out and snapped the Dutchman's ear with his finger.

"Knock that off, dickhead!" Van Groot spat. Tollster was one of few Marines who could pull the Dutchman's chain . . . but only so far.

"Hey, hold it down," Slater chuckled. "You're sick, Dutch. Hard boiled eggs to a dog?"

"Yeah, but it backfired on him," Tollster whispered. "The chick took one look at Jiggs' hardon and took off."

"You show me any other dog gets a boner over chow, A-hole. Dog's got talent." The Dutchman flipped the bird at the man behind him.

"Fartin' in church is a real talent, man. Maybe you can get him on the Johnny Carson show."

"This ain't no church, butt breath, it's a fuckin' Justice of the—EEEOOWWW!" One of Tollster's fingers had been sharply rammed at the Dutchman's backside, catching the little man by surprise.

The yowl took Slicks Johnson's attention away from the very firm and well-rounded backside of Moany's bridesmaid, and a low collective groan came from the audience as two horribly maimed eyeballs rolled in the Dutchman's direction.

"What's happenin', ma man?" Slicks roared.

Moany's fist caught the groom just below the rib cage and he would have gone down if Benjamin hadn't been there. The Honorable Alfredo Cardoza gasped; Slicks only smiled and once again locked his sights on the bridesmaid's rear end, a rear end wrapped in a tight fitting black sheath that ended just below the swell of her butt.

"The man's definitely in a world of shit," Tollster said.

Slicks Johnson wasn't the only Marine interested in Moany's bridesmaid. Freddy Claybourne couldn't keep his eyes off her either, partly because of the skin-tight dress, but mostly because he was afraid she'd turn and spot him.

Earlier, the sight of her walking down the aisle had caused the knife scar on his side to twinge, and he worried that she might try to finish the job she'd started back in July out on Post Six. Whether or not she knew he was there, he didn't know, but he'd found a safe seat close to the door, just in case. Keep a low profile, man, and be ready to book.

"By the powers vested in me by the State of Florida, I now pronounce you man and wife!" The Justice of the Peace, now sweating as much as any half-drunk Marine, slammed shut his book and nodded at his wife, who sat next to an old record player off to his right. Smiling, he looked over at the groom. "You may now kiss the bride, Mister . . . ah, Mister . . ."

Benjamin shook Johnson awake, then whispered in the groom's ear. Slicks grinned, then lunged at the new Mrs. Johnson and tried to plant a kiss on her lips. She shoved him away and lifted the pink veil that was over her face.

A horrible hiss and crack came from the old record player, followed by the traditional wedding recessional, as though played in a blizzard by a band of fairies.

More noise—a different kind—erupted from the back of the room. Slater looked over his shoulder. The sound of the steel needle bouncing on a worn record had brought Jiggs back to life. The dog strained at his leash, croaking at the ceiling with his gravelly bark. Slater guessed that if Jiggs picked up the scent of sweating female, it was all over.

"Mister *Johnson*!" Cardoza shouted, finally remembering the groom's name.

The sound of his own name distracted Slicks from his unsuccessful attempt to find Moany's mouth.

"What you want?" he asked, confused.

"You may kiss the bride, Mister Johnson," Cardoza said.

"I'm tryin', man, I'm tryin'. She won't stay still."

There was a long scratching scream from the record player as Mrs. Cardoza switched from 78 to 33 rpm, and a slower, more familiar wedding recessional pumped into the room.

The wet smack of a kiss came from the podium and a cheer rose from the audience. Instamatic flashes popped in the front row. Benjamin let go of the groom's belt and the newlyweds lurched down the aisle, showered as they passed with handfuls of rice, black-eyed peas, and government-issue toilet paper.

While the section hooted and clapped, and while the girls in the front row tearfully hugged each other, the brides-maid's eyes flashed bolts at the man standing near the door.

Oh shit, she's seen me, Claybourne realized with a shudder. Didn't look like she had a weapon, but who could tell with that bitch? Knowing Shandy, she could have another bait knife stashed in the flowers she held.

He tried to avoid looking at her; each time his eyes met hers his insides trembled, yet again and again he was drawn back to her, like a kid cringing under a seat at the Saturday matinee.

Come on, man, he told himself, get your ass out of here before she—wait a second here, maybe he was seeing things, but it seemed as though Shandy was softening a little. Yeah! Well, shit! She was smiling nice and friendly now. Butter melting in the pan. She's come to her senses, bro, the legend lives! Be cool now, be cool and she'll dance to your music again.

Claybourne dared a wink and Shandy winked back as she led the rest of the girls down the aisle, moving her body in sensual time to the music.

Yes, sir, Freddy, you're inta that for sure. Hot Damn!

Slicks and Moany were already outside the door and the girls were weeping and laughing, chattering among themselves as they passed the back of the room. Suddenly there was a screeching crash of wrenched metal and falling plaster, followed by female screams and the gurgling, guttural cough of Jiggs on the rampage.

The dog had ripped the water pipe from the wall. Luckily for his intended victims, the lead pipe was heavy enough to slow his charge, and the girls made it out to the sidewalk before any of them were assaulted.

Sensing, maybe, that the girls were out of his reach, the now crazed dog sniffed the air and rolled his eyes toward the still-seated Mrs. Cardoza. The trailing pipe bumped down the aisle.

"Get some!" the Dutchman yelled.

Mrs. Cardoza made a clean getaway through a side door, and the dog sadly flopped in the middle of the floor and went back to sleep.

"Horny son of a bitch," Tollster growled.

"Fuckin' pre-vert," LeFey added.

"Lookit that thing!" Van Groot joyfully pointed out. "Jiggs got a hardon as big as Screamin' Don. How'd ya like to be hung like that, huh, AJ?"

Before he could think of a good answer Slater heard someone shouting at them from the doorway.

"What ya'll waitin for?" Moany's bridesmaid called. "The happy couple be waitin' for their send-off out here in the hot sun while you play games. Ain't gonna wait much longer."

One by one, the hungover Marines went onto the sidewalk, whimpering as bright sunlight hit their eyes like hot buckshot. The girls clustered around Moany's '67 Chevy, decorated with paper flowers and crepe paper streamers, plus a *Just Married* message written in artificial snow across the trunk.

The girls all giggled at something in the car. As the men staggered toward them, trying not to trip over weed-filled cracks in the sidewalk, the girls opened a path leading to the passenger door.

Through the open window Slater saw Moany behind the wheel, her eyes locked straight ahead, her pink wedding dress hiked up around her thighs. The only visible part of Slicks was the top of his head, jammed between the door and the top of the seat. Tollster leaned down and cupped his hands to his mouth.

"Incoming!" he yelled. Slicks didn't budge. Tollster turned to the rest of the onlookers and shrugged. "The man is definitely not feelin' any pain."

"Throw the bouquet, Moany, you got ta throw the bouquet!" One of the girls jumped up and down on the sidewalk, clapping her hands and screeching through the passenger window. "Can't leave before you throw the bouquet, girl!"

The new Mrs. Johnson looked down at the bundle of pink roses and angel's breath on the seat beside her, then seemed to scan the group of well wishers. Like she was looking for something . . .

Shandy leaned on the Chevy's right front fender, Freddy beside her.

"Sure, baby, it hurt like hell, still hurts," Freddy said softly. "But I know I had it comin'. Layin' in the hospital all them weeks got me thinkin'. Said to myself—that Shandy's a real tiger, boy. You gotta make up ta that girl real quick 'cause she's the best thing you come across in your whole life."

Somewhere between the building and the car, Claybourne had put on his wrap-around shades and had undone two more buttons on his sequined green silk shirt. As he spoke to Shandy he nonchalantly caressed his bare sternum with his fingertips.

"That's sweet, Freddy, it really is. I been so upset since I stuck you, thought you'd never forgive me." Shandy spoke while looking over her shoulder at the car's windshield. He figured she was too shy to speak face to face with the legend she had so brutally assaulted.

"Ooooo, lookit!" Shandy squealed. "Moany's gonna throw her bouquet! Won't come to me though. Maebell read my leaves an' she say I'm gonna be an old maid."

"Shoot, girl, no way. You too foxy lookin' for that. Be some lucky dude gets you."

Claybourne was too preoccupied with his change in fortune to notice the almost imperceptible movement of Shandy's hand. A high-pitched shriek from the rest of the girls startled him for a moment. He looked up in time to see a bouquet of flowers on a downward arch through the air, coming in his direction. Shandy stretched high and caught the flowers above her head. The black dress pulled even more tightly across her body.

While her friends cheered her good luck, Shandy jumped up and down in excitement, the bouquet still above her head. Freddy whimpered as he watched her body move.

The Chevy pulled away from the curb with a clatter of tin cans, a belch of smoke, and a squawk of rubber. There was a gasp as Slicks' head bounced off the dashboard, then relieved laughter as the groom was spotted looking back at them through the rear window. He looked surprised, but not hurt. Old Granddad had apparently prevented serious whiplash. As the car hung a left and roared in the direction of the Block, Slicks was last seen folding over onto the seat next to his beloved.

As they prepared to follow the couple to the reception, there was not a single member of the section who doubted for a second that Slicks Johnson was in a world of shit.

CHAPTER ELEVEN

AN hour later and the wedding reception was in full swing underneath a huge chestnut tree that stood on the edge of Moany's backyard and a vacant lot. Her house, a weathered Victorian with peeling gingerbread trim and a sagging back porch, was in a part of town known as "The Block," Key West's Harlem.

"Here's ta Slicks Johns'n. May he res'n peesh."

From a safe and sane forty yards away, Slater watched the Dutchman tip a bottle of Boone's Farm over his head and guzzle the last few drops. The little man's slurred toast to the groom had almost been drowned out by the thunder of Pink Floyd from the speakers in LeFey's top-down Olds. Van Groot was standing in the back seat, a crocked homecoming queen badly in need of a shave.

The car sat in the middle of the vacant lot, its doors standing open so nothing could muffle the sounds throbbing through the tape deck. LeFey had as much bread sunk in the sound system as he did in the car itself, and when it came to a choice between an oil change and a new tape, C-C-R or The Chambers Brothers always won over 10W-40.

Slater's eyes followed the empty green wine bottle as it sailed lazily through the air from the back seat of this jukebox on wheels. The bottle bounced once, twice, then lost itself in the knee-high weeds.

Pink Floyd was suddenly sliced off in mid-riff by the tribal guitar of Jimi Hendrix. The Dutchman began lurching around the back seat in time with the new music, stroking an invisible Fender Deluxe, his eyes glassy from bouts with a half a pint of vodka, a six pack, and the apple wine.

Get some yourself, Dutch.

Slater reached down absent-mindedly and scratched Jiggs behind the ears. The dog groaned but didn't move; he'd passed out in the dust under the shade of the picnic table soon after arriving in Moany's backyard. Even in a semi-coma, the animal's bowels worked on those eggs, which was the reason this particular picnic table had been abandoned for ones farther from the tree. But Slater had stayed; he needed time to munch on things.

Since the night of the shooting on Fleming Key, life had started to suck. Hard to forget the insane scene in the CO's office and the loss of his stripes, but what the hell, he could handle that. The day after, Kargo sat him down and warned him he'd better walk tall for a while, because he was now on Brule's shit list and would stay there until someone else took his place. Hell, he could handle *that* too.

Or could he? The last three weeks Brule had been constantly on his back, busting his chops every chance he got, hitting him with every petty regulation in the book. Sometimes he could taste the anger, bubbling up from his gut like hot puke, but it never got as far as it had in the XO's office that night. But who the hell knew? You could only be pushed so far, man. It scared him.

The news from home hadn't been all that hot either. The letter he'd written to Marty had come back stamped "return to sender." The asshole was refusing to acknowledge he even *had* a brother. Not that the letter had been all that brilliant. He'd found it difficult to put his thoughts into words, and the letter had sounded like sentimental garbage. Fuck it.

The puttering of a motor scooter distracted him. He looked up to see Rose McCracken guide a little red Lambretta into Moany's backyard, around a faded Quik-Trik Bar-B-Que sign and a ratty-looking armchair in which Earl Norwick snoozed, and into the crowd of Marines.

Sitting behind Rose was a young woman, almost hidden

by the Crack's wide body. Must be the girl the Dutchman has been slobbering about, the Crack's niece.

Rose steered the scooter to a stack of cinder blocks supporting one end of the uneven back porch. She wore a pair of electric blue stretch pants that showed off the size of her rear end, especially while she still sat on the scooter's seat. Slater was reminded of forty gallons of blueberry muffin mix oozing from a messhall mixing bowl.

While the Crack lifted cardboard buckets of fried chicken from the scooter's basket and plunged into the crowd of hungry grunts, her passenger remained standing near the tilting porch, a sour look on what looked to be a nice face. Finally, she followed Rose to the picnic table, where Moany sat like the Queen of Sheba, surrounded by her attendants.

The Crack's niece, Slater thought. Hard to see any family resemblance, though. The girl was everything Rose was not—young, thin, a real movie star, just like the Dutchman had said. Long brown hair—streaked with sunlight— danced as she walked, and compared to the peg-legged gait of her aunt, she moved with the grace of a fancy dancer on a TV variety show. So what if he couldn't see her face? With that bod, who the hell cared?

Her uniform was radical cool: bell bottom jeans nicely faded and tight as a second skin, fringed leather shirt, sleeveless, laced up the front with thongs so you could see what a nice tan she had underneath. On her feet were expensive leather sandals. She wore an Indian headband decorated with beadwork and bits and pieces of down and feathers.

Probably made in Korea, he thought cynically.

The girl joined Rose at the picnic table, and after an introduction to the bride, moved off to stand away from the crowd. Slater saw Bone Tollster approach her, say something, then back away quickly as though she'd nailed him with a hard shot to the breadbasket.

He didn't think any more about her until a few minutes later when he felt someone sit down at his table. Wondering who else would have the balls to get so close to Jiggs, he turned and saw her seated opposite him at the other end, staring out at the vacant lot.

Slater studied her for a few moments, at least he studied her profile, and realized she was the most beautiful girl he had ever seen. Beautiful, even though her jaw was set tight and her brow creased with the wrinkles of a nasty frown. She was about his age, around nineteen or twenty. Butterflies began to slam against the walls of his stomach.

Two things he could do, he decided. He could ignore her and maybe lose the chance of a lifetime; or speak to her and risk a put-down that would shatter the self-confidence he'd been trying to rebuild since the day he'd gotten the "Dear John" from Sandy. Almost a year ago now.

After he thought about it a while, he decided to keep his mouth shut.

The picnic table shook again, harder this time.

"Come on, honey," he heard Rose whisper to the girl. "You need ta meet some people, get back inta the swing of things."

"Please, Rose," the girl quietly pleaded, "drop me off back at the apartment. This just isn't going to work."

"Oh, shit. Sure it will. Give it a chance."

"But . . . but they're all so *weird*. And if I see that little creep with his kinky dog again I'll . . . I don't think I can get into this scene, Rose, really."

"Dutch didn't mean no harm. I keep tellin' you, these are good people!"

"Look like losers to me," the girl answered.

Losers? Slater bristled. Had she said losers? They were talking so low and the music was so loud that he couldn't be sure. He glanced over at them out of the corner of his eye. The girl stared at the Olds and the two legs sticking out of the back seat.

"Won't that ruin the battery or something?" he heard her ask. "Playing the stereo like that?"

Rose laughed. "It will unless LeFey stays sober and

remembers ta turn the engine over once in a while. Otherwise, he'll come back tomorrow and get a jump start. Happens all the time. The boys call it the 'Jarhead System.' "

"I kind of expected the 'Ballad of the Green Berets' or something. Not Jimi Hendrix."

Rose caught him looking. "Well, hi there, Jack Slater!" she boomed. "What ya doin' over here all alone?"

He did his best to act surprised. "Hey, how ya doin', Rose? When'd you get here?"

" 'Bout ten minutes ago. Seen Slicks?"

"He's hammered, probably sleeping it off somewhere." Slater forced himself to smile. He looked straight into the girl's eyes. What he saw was not pretty.

"Sorry you missed the party last night," Rose said, nervously tugging at her ear. "Least it saved ya the hangover. Heard Screamin' Don had you on extra duty." Her chuckle was forced. "But say, you ain't met my niece yet. Come in on Southeast Air just yesterday mornin'. Carolyn, say hello to Jack."

"Charmed, I'm sure," the girl mumbled.

"Howdy," Slater answered cheerfully. The girl didn't have anything else to say. She turned her head toward the other tables where someone had just screamed in pain.

"Carolyn's visiting for a while," Rose said. "She goes ta college, ya know."

"Oh yeah? What school?"

"Maryland," the girl finally said, shooting daggers at her aunt.

Slater remembered the day he'd had a wisdom tooth pulled. "Still on vacation?" he asked.

She looked over at him with a quick scornful glance. "I quit," she snapped.

"Hey, Rose!" someone shouted over the general roar of grab-ass on the other side of the yard. "Better get some chow before Tollster eats everything you brung!"

Rose seemed relieved to have an excuse to leave her

niece. "Honey, I'll be back in a sec. You want some chicken'n slaw?"

"No thanks." It was the first halfway civil thing he'd heard her say.

"Now you watch out for this handsome Marine," Rose cautioned, smiling at Slater. "They can sweep a girl right off her feet in nothin' flat."

"I'll bet," the girl mumbled again.

"I'll make sure they save ya some grub, Jack. You take care of my sister's little girl. Don't do nothin' ungentleman-like."

"Don't worry about me, Rosie," Slater said. Besides, he thought, I left my steel cutting gear back at the Barracks.

He watched Rose huff and puff her way to the party, huge butt rolling under tight fabric. Her limp was hardly notice-able. He had no idea what was eating on her niece, but he could live without finding out.

Other people's problems were not high on his list. He thought about Brule, and Marty, and a dozen other pin-pricks of worry. Wasn't any room for some broad with a wild hair up her ass, no matter how fall-down mouth-watering bitchin' she looked. If she didn't want to talk, that was OK with him.

Minutes went by; he had no idea how many. He'd almost dozed off when a roar of men's voices shook him from sleepy daydreams. He was kind of surprised to find that the girl was still sitting there.

"Do your friends always act like animals, or just at wedding receptions?" Her voice had a husky quality; it would have been sexy if it hadn't been for the bite in her words.

Slater saw what she was talking about. Over at the other tables a chicken bone fight had broken out—standard procedure at a section party. Moany and the other girls broke for cover as the Marines fired thigh and leg bones at each other from pointblank range.

"Aw, this is just a tune up before we rape and pillage," he said, smiling.

What he got back was contempt. "I believe it. But that's what the army pays you to do, isn't it? Bet you've had a lot of practice."

Her eyes were gray, with little flecks of black that flashed and made his pulse beat faster. He would've liked them more if the slap in her words hadn't hit him in the kisser.

"Say, you gotta problem, princess?"

"No, I don't have any problem, do you?"

"Didn't 'til a few seconds ago."

"Well, excuse me for breathing." She turned away, but she'd ticked him off and he wasn't about to call a truce.

"Let's put it this way," he said. "In the first place, what those guys are doin' is none a your business. In the second place, you're blowin' a lot of smoke about something you don't know shit about."

"What's that supposed to mean?" she answered, looking off at the battle. "Chicken bone fights the 'in' thing now, is that it?"

"We're Marines, lady, not army," he said. "Only pin-head civilians and dumbass chicks who think they're Apaches or somethin' get the two confused. What's that make you?"

"Frankly, Mister Wise-ass, it makes me see it was a mistake to sit down at this table in the first place."

Her words slashed him like a whip, and as she pushed herself to her feet and started to walk away, he felt the steam running out of his system.

"Hey!" he shouted. "I'm sorry."

She stopped and faced him. "So who cares?" she spat.

She might just as well have kicked him in the teeth. His hurt came out sounding mean again. "Yeah, right. So do me a favor, OK? Go piss up a rope."

"And you go screw yourself, soldier boy." She gave him the finger, then walked away toward Moany's back porch.

Nice job, Slater, he told himself. Had her eating out of

the palm of your hand. Oh yeah, and check for fangs in your ass when you get back to the Barracks.

Leaving Jiggs in a muddy puddle of drool, he got up and wandered toward the Olds where the Dutchman had passed out. He was worried that the little douche-kit might get sunstroke.

Even before he got to the car he could hear the munching sound, followed by the soft tearing of cloth. Only took one look inside to see what was going on. There was the Dutchman, sprawled out like some kind of sheik-of-the-burning-sands, chewing up LeFey's back seat. Cotton wadding hung from his mouth and there were teeth marks in the vinyl. Not sure what else to do, Slater reached in and slapped the top of the Dutchman's head.

"What the hell are you doing, numbnuts?" he yelled between laughs. "LeFey is gonna kill ya for this!"

Van Groot drunkenly pushed himself up to a sitting position, spitting out cotton.

"Whaja say, AJ?" he slobbered, a dumb grin lighting his face.

Slater was laughing so hard he could hardly get the words out. "I said—what are you doing, shit-for-brains? Eatin' a goddamn car?"

The Dutchman's head wobbled as he inspected his meal. This was enough to make him topple onto his back. Still chewing contentedly, like a milk cow with a mouthful of alfalfa, he offered Slater his totally logical explanation.

"First rule a par-tee-in', man. Never drink on a empty stomach."

Inside Moany's house all was cool and quiet except for the groans coming from the couch in the living room.

"Freddy, you stop that now," Shandy whispered as she pushed Claybourne's hands away from her leg. "What if somebody catches us?"

"Come on, baby, ain't nobody gonna come in here. They outside partyin'."

A sudden loud roar of voices came from outside.

"See, I told ya."

Freddy lunged forward and crushed her mouth with his. She tasted sweet. He pushed her down into the seat cushion, his hands roaming up and down her body in a frantic search for the zipper on her dress. She responded by thrusting her lower body hard into his pelvis, her knee sliding between his legs.

Where was that damn zipper? Couldn't find it. Had to break away from the kiss and make a visual recon while Shandy gasped, either for air or in pleasure—he couldn't tell which.

"Hurry, Freddy, hurry. I need you bad. You so good, Freddy, you so good. Love me good, baby. Lemme feel your magic."

"Right, baby, right—where's that gawdamn zipper anyway—gonna take you flyin', baby, flyin' high—baby, you gotta roll over a little so I can reach that thing. That's it."

"Be gentle, baby. Want it to be good, baby, but be gentle—Owwww! Be careful, sugar! You're catchin' my skin in the zipper!"

Shandy twisted away from the pain, throwing him into an awkward position. With their legs all tangled, and one of his arms suddenly trapped under her body while the other worked on the stubborn zipper, he went face down into the sofa cushion and couldn't lift himself out. He struggled to breathe, got only a mouthful of dust for his trouble. Sucking as much air as he could through the cushion, he gave the zipper one more hard yank.

The back door slammed and Shandy bucked, the two events coming almost at the same time. Her knee struck hard between his legs, sending a white hot pain through his groin. He screamed, the sound muffled by the rough fabric of the seat cushion.

The girl squirmed out from under him, unaware of the damage she had done to his "love housing." While he remained paralyzed in blood-pissin' agony, she rolled to her knees and looked back over the top of the couch, back down the long hallway connecting the kitchen with the front of the house, back from where the sounds of female laughter and chatter now drifted.

Shandy strained to hear why her friends had suddenly come into the house, but all she picked up were a few words that made no sense—something about chicken bones.

Her natural inquisitiveness had caused her to momentarily forget Freddy. When a low moan came from the floor in front of the sofa, she turned to see her would-be lover curled up in a ball, his eyes shut tightly, his face full of pain. With motherly concern she climbed down beside him.

"What's wrong, baby? What's the matter?" She began stroking his brow as she had seen done on numerous TV soaps, even though it was plain that the man's problem was a good deal lower on his body. "What's happened to ma lova man?"

Freddy answered with another moan. He was sure his nuts were crushed to mutha fuckin' pulp. The pain was bad, but the thought of a foreshortened love life was more frightening. Positive he would never ride again, he gingerly put his hands over his crotch and wished he were dead.

A few minutes later, though, when he finally managed to open his eyes, a minor medical miracle occurred. The sight of Shandy's body so close to his was like a soothing salve on his parts, drawing the dull lingering pain out of him like a great soft sponge. He was gonna be all right. His hand found the soft flesh of her inner thigh. Yes, he was gonna be just fine . . . better'n fine. Out-fuckin'-standing.

Shandy whimpered and grabbed the hand but didn't push it away. "Not here, baby, not here. One of them girls might see." Her voice was as hot as her skin.

"Aw, baby," Freddy begged, "I gotta have ya. And you gotta have me."

"Not here, baby, not here." Shandy squeezed his hand between her legs and looked around the room. Her eyes fell on the staircase. "Let's go upstairs. Nobody be comin' up there." She jumped to her feet and tugged him toward the steps.

He stumbled up the stairs behind her, mesmerized by her bottom swaying in front of him. If she'd been any slower, he would've dragged her down under him and fulfilled his dreams right there on the stairway. But it was all he could do to keep up with her. She really wants it bad, he thought, and while he knew he was supposed to be ultra-cool at this point, he found it impossible. By the time they reached the second floor, he'd ripped three buttons off his shirt and torn a fingernail trying to get his belt unbuckled.

Shandy pulled him down the hallway, stopping in front of the first closed door. She turned and threw herself into his arms, pressing her body against him, plunging her tongue into his ear. Before he could react, she tore herself away and opened the door.

Loud snores from the bed stopped her in her tracks, and Claybourne almost tripped trying to follow her inside. Slicks Johnson lay spread-eagled on the bare mattress, dead to the world, dressed only in his khaki uniform shirt and undershorts. Shandy put her hand over her mouth and giggled while Claybourne wondered if there was room on the bed for three. Hell! He'd damn well *make* room!

Didn't have to, though. Shandy turned. Holding him by the dangling belt buckle, she pulled him out of the room and back into the hallway. For a moment he wondered if her passion wasn't going to be too great even for him to handle. No damn way. The woman hadn't been born who could outdo the Mighty Hog. Soon Shandy would find it difficult to remember her own name.

He was panting by the time they fell into the next room, partly because of what he knew was coming, but mostly because of the physical exertion required to walk the hallway with his pants down around his ankles. As Shandy moved toward the bed, Freddy called up one last shred of patience and hesitated long enough to shut the door and throw the lock. When he turned and saw what was waiting for him, he couldn't help loosing his breath.

She had already freed the zipper and the top of her black dress hung down loosely over her hips. Sunlight from the grimy window fell across her bare breasts. Her eyes were shut, her mouth open and inviting, her head tilted back as though she was having a hard time breathing too. He heard himself making a funny gurgling sound as she hooked her thumbs in the waistband of her panties and began gently tugging downward.

"Do me, baby," she moaned, "do me good."

"Oh, Lordy," he croaked as he ripped off what was left of his shirt and tried desperately to kick off his shoes. Once done, he began moving for her, unable to tear his eyes from her body. He was within inches of her when her sweet-pudding voice brought him to an unwilling stop.

"Freddy, honey, get me the extra pillow from the closet, baby. With all that 'man' you got, I'm gonna need it."

Reluctant as hell, he staggered back to the closet door. His hand felt numb as he fumbled with the knob. The door wouldn't budge.

"Hurry, baby," she cried from behind him, "please hurry!"

Her words, pleading and sultry, pumped strength to his muscles. Bracing himself with a knee against the wall, he jerked the door open, the battle won in a screech of warped wood.

The first thing that registered as he looked into the closet was the pair of scissors aimed at his throat.

The second thing that registered was the face, the face attached to the body attached to the arm that held the pair of scissors aimed at his throat. The face was full of rage—brown eyes smoldering, nostrils flaring, teeth clenched. The growl of a meat-eating jungle animal came out at him.

The third and last thing that registered was that he was in a world of shit.

"Carlene!" he screamed, jumping back, his arms held out

in front of him to block the attack. "Carlene!" The scissors slashed the air as he ducked out of reach. "Carlene! Thought you was up north!" The words came out as a plea, as though this was all a nightmare and she was, in fact, still up north visiting her sick, goddamn mutha fuckin' aunt.

Deliberately, she began stalking him, blocking any escape through the bedroom door. There was blood in her eyes and Claybourne desperately turned to Shandy for help.

"Shandy, baby, help me for—Oh shit!"

Still half naked, Shandy now held a butcher's knife in her right hand, testing the sharpness of the point with the tip of her middle finger. The passion in her eyes had disappeared, replaced with an angry burn. She spoke to the other woman in guttural sounds, but her furious glare never left his face.

"Didn't I tell ya, Carlene? Your lova boy here's been two-timin' ya, cheatin' on your love while you was away."

"Ain't so, Carlene, ain't so!" Claybourne gasped as he continued to inch his way backward. "This gal caught me when I was liquored up, throwin' herself at me when my defenses was down!"

"Talk funny, don't he?" Carlene snarled in her deep baritone.

"Real funny," Shandy answered. "Almost as funny as he look."

"He be lookin' *more* funny, though." There was no missing the murder in Carlene's voice.

"Rye-on!" Shandy replied.

"Be *soundin'* more funny too, soon's we whop off his joy-boy."

"Rye-on!"

"His cheatin' days'll be over when we get done."

"Rye-on!"

"Won't be cheatin' nobody no more."

Like a punch-drunk tennis fan, Freddy could do nothing but look from scissors to butcher knife and back again as he retreated across the room. He suddenly got the bright idea that the two girls were bluffing. He decided to call their hand.

"Shit. Ain't you two a pair." He tried to laugh. "But listen here, there be plenty here ta go around for two. You put down them pig stickers 'fore I get mad and make you beg for it."

The tip of Carlene's scissors missed his nose by the width of a baby's hair. The whiffling sound it made cutting through the air, along with the breeze it blew on his face, caused him to reevaluate the bitches' determination. Wasn't no more doubt, Freddy figured, they meant to slice and dice all his favorite parts.

And given such circumstances, he did the only thing left for him to do. With his trousers still down around his ankles, he turned and ran . . . straight out the closed bedroom window.

CHAPTER TWELVE

MONDAY morning after Slicks Johnson's wedding, Slater sat in the second squad's cubicle, spit-shining his inspection shoes. He sat on his footlocker, only half listening to the Dutchman rag Claybourne about the broken arm.

"I said, ain't that right, AJ?" Van Groot shouted.

Slater heard his neck snap like a knuckle when he looked up. "Huh? You talkin' to me, Dutch?" Sometimes spit-shining could hypnotize you.

Van Groot sprawled across from him on another foot-locker. "Hell, yes, boy, what's the matter, you dreamin'?"

"Who you callin' *boy*, mutha fuck!" Claybourne yelled from his bottom rack where he lay with his head propped on two pillows.

"Sure ain't you, lip-shit," Van Groot said. "You hear the name chiclet-dick and you know I'm talkin' ta you."

"Suck ma pole, muff-sniffer. I be thinkin' about gettin' up and messin' your face . . . thinkin' about fuckin' you up bad."

"Yeah, right," Van Groot answered. "And maybe you be thinkin' about how ta dig your balls outta the back of your throat if ya try it." Van Groot shifted his eyes and the conversation from Claybourne back to Slater.

"Listen, Jack, old flyin fuck over there says he won't be standin' no more duty till he gets out of the Crotch, all 'cause he's got that pansy cast on his arm. That's bullshit, ain't it?"

"I'm so short I gotta climb a twelve-foot ladder ta take a shit," Claybourne shouted happily. "One hundred sixteen days, man, then I kiss this mutha fuckin' green

Weenie good-bye. Doc Hippy says I can keep this cast for least three months, man. Compoun' fracture. three mutha fuckin' months, mutha fucka! By then, man, ain't nobody round here even gonna recognize my name. Come January, I will be a free dude. Dig that!" Freddy's eyes closed and he smiled.

"See what I'm sayin', Jack?" Van Groot almost whined. "He can't do that, can he? Hell, guy I knew once only got a week's no-duty when a Six-by run over him. Mean ta say this sandbaggin' asshole is gonna get three whole months off?" The Dutchman looked like a man who'd just been told horseshit could fly.

Slater stopped working and put the diamond-glazed shoes down next to the side of the footlocker where no one would trip over them and wipe out a good hour's work.

"What it is, man," he said. "Don't know why you're getting all worked up about it. No skin off your butt if Freddy slides. Shit, only wish I was as lucky."

"You tell him, Slats, you tell him." Claybourne giggled, enjoying the unexpected support.

"Aw, shut yer A-hole, Fred," Van Groot growled. "You ain't considerin' the rami-fuck-ations of this situation, AJ. Sure as shit, without that sack of snot ta fill the guard roster, gunny and Kargo are gonna cut Fleming to a one-man post. Bad enough I gotta put up with that thumb-sucker Dornato, who don't know his pecker from a stackin' swivel. Now I gotta ride alone? Shit, how'm I gonna get in my trainin'? Tell me that! Know what's gonna happen? I'm gonna get rusty, that's what. When I get to RECON them guys'll eat me alive. All 'cause this pussy can't stand no duty with a piddly ass busted arm. Torks me off, man!"

"Aww, break ma heart, little man," Claybourne chortled from his pillow. "But you and this mutha fuckin' green machine just gonna have ta live without me."

"Yer damn lucky, ya know that, Fred?" the Dutchman went on. "If the major hadn't a gotten back over the weekend, Screamin' Don'd still be actin' CO. He woulda had your ass up on charges."

"Sure, sure," Claybourne grunted.

"Am I right or what, Jack?" Van Groot asked.

"Hell if I know," Slater said. He'd only gotten a quick look at Major Brocksneider that morning at Guard Mount. The major looked kinda like the actor who used to play "Maverick" on the tube. Didn't have any way of knowing one way or the other how the man would be as a CO. All he could go on was what the other Marines said about him—Brocksneider was fair and didn't dick with ya. Good enough. Anything would be better than Screamin' Don.

The door at the end of the squad bay rattled open and a voice shouted over the hum of radio music and conversation going on all over the deck. "Hey, Claybourne! Telephone!"

"Who is it, man?" Freddy yelled, making no move to leave his comfortable position.

"How the hell should I know?" the voice came back. "Just get your ass down to the Guard Shack and answer it ASAP or I'm gonna hang the fucker up."

The door crashed shut. Freddy lazily rolled to a sitting position and began pulling on a pair of utility trousers with one hand.

"Hey, Fred, how bout grabbin' some poggy-bait while you're down there. I ain't eaten since breakfast." Van Groot began digging down into one of the baggy pockets on his trousers.

"You buyin', chump?" Claybourne asked as he held out an open palm.

"Yeah. Get me a Pay Day. What you want, AJ?"

Slater reached for a can of Brasso. "Bag a peanuts."

The Dutchman carefully counted out his silver and handed it to Claybourne, "I got fifteen cents comin' in change, stud."

Claybourne squeezed the money and grinned. "We see, little man, we see." He turned and shuffled out into the aisle.

The bay door slammed closed. Slater shined brass while the Dutchman lovingly traced the outline of the eagle, globe, and anchor tattooed on his left bicep. When he tired of that, he looked over at the other man.

"So tell me more about the Crack's niece, man. Tollster says she's a real freeze-out."

"Nothin' ta tell," Slater answered. "Only talked with her for a minute."

"I said she was choice, didn't I"

"Yeah."

"Wish I hadn'ta passed out. Coulda put some moves on." Van Groot got a dreamy look in his eyes as he leaned back on his elbows. "Don't know what happened. Just passed out, man. Next thing I knowed, Security was wakin' me up. Still don't know how I got that squid fire truck started. Hey! How come Nar-vel's so pissed at me?"

Slater chuckled. "You chewed up the back seat of his car something fierce, man. Took him three rolls of duct tape just to patch the holes."

"Hell, I musta been dreamin' about that honey's cute little pie. Did she notice me, ya think?"

"Got me." Slater poured another dollop of brass cleaner onto his rag. "Tell ya one thing, though, wouldn't waste any time tryin' ta get into her skivvies. She's one of those chicks with a constant rag-on for us bloodthirsty killers. Typical fucked up chick who thinks she's savin' the world by not shaving her armpits."

"Hairy pits, huh? Gross me out!" The Dutchman wrinkled his nose.

"Naw, not that I could see," Slater answered. "Just her mental attitude is all. Really sucked. Like I said, typical shit-for-brains college chick."

"Sorry ta hear that, man. Just when I was sure I was in love too. But that's women for ya, make ya fall in love with 'em, then drop ya like a hot wazoo."

"Fuck it," Slater mumbled, rubbing away at the tarnish on his Guard buckle.

Van Groot pointed to Slater's work. "Don't know why you're sweatin' it so much, AJ. With the maj back, Screamin' Don's gonna have other things ta do 'sides keepin' track a you."

"Just tryin' to avoid getting shit on, Dutch."

"My ass. You just lost track of yer balls is all."

Van Groot said it good-naturedly, but Slater braced. He set aside the brass belt plate and, as he screwed the top back on the can of acrid-smelling liquid polish, let some of his anger out.

"Haven't lost track of nothin', man. If you ever came ta formation or bothered ta look at the training schedule once in a while, you'd know the section's got a dress rehearsal for an Honor Guard detail comin' up next week."

"Shit. Starboard Section gets the shaft again."

"What the hell you bitchin' about? You don't have to stand it."

"It's the principle of the thing, Jack. We're always gettin' stuck with the shit details while Port Section coasts."

"Port had burial detail last week."

"Big deal. What's it take ta plant somebody, twenty minutes? Fuckin' Honor Guard takes ya half the day the way the squids do things. Port Section always coasts."

Van Groot suddenly rolled off his perch on the footlocker and stomped around the cubicle. "Speaking of those Port pukes," he said. "You hear about Mopes?"

"Who?"

"Shithouse Mopes. Buck private. Stands Post Six for Port Section. Been down here a year. Started as a sergeant. Been busted four times."

"What about him?"

"Fucker was on dutes the other day an' loafed his lumber to some woman driving a Conch school bus."

"You're shittin' me!"

"Nope. It's a fact. Delkirt heard Screamin' Don tap dancin' on Shithouse's head. Poor bitch pulls up ta Six, ya know, ta come aboard and pick up the Navy rug-rats. Ol'

Shithouse asks her if she's seen the elephant. She says no. Shithouse pro-ceeds ta turn out the front pockets on his trop trou, then hauls out his pud. 'Well,' says Shithouse ta the woman, 'ya seen it now.'"

"Goddamn," Slater groaned, "now that takes balls!"

"You got *that* right! Course, the lady goes ape-shit. She an' her old man show up in Hollihan's office this mornin' yellin' and screamin' about lawsuits and revenge. While sergeant major's gettin' their story in writin', Screamin' Don's gettin' Delkirt to cut Mopes some orders. Straight up to Lejeune and Second Mar Div."

"You mean he got transferred?"

"Leaves tonight."

"Christ. Some guys got all the luck."

"Me, I woulda left ol' Shithouse on duty. Let ol' Shithouse and the gal's husband get at it . . . ta the death!"

Slater sighed. Just wasn't any way to stay pissed at Van Groot. "You and Screamin' Don make a pair, ya know that?"

The Dutchman laughed. "Pair a what? Jack, your trouble is ya got this fucked-up outfit confused with the real Crotch. What you need is some action. Ought ta think about goin' inta RECON with me. Man, we'd make one hell of a team." His eyes seemed to light up at the thought. "Dig it. AJ and the Dutchman. We could really show them hot dogs some shit!"

"Right, Dutch, right."

"Come on, I seen a lotta guys come and go out on Fleming, man. I know for a fact that you was gettin' off on my trainin'. So don't hand me any of this 'squared-away' horseshit. You was dragged off that post kickin' and screamin'."

"Just a game, Dutch. It's over now. Man, all I wanna do is get in my time and stay out of the brig."

"Aw hell, boy, you ain't thinkin' straight," Van Groot lectured. "RECON ain't like this place."

"Listen, man, you're dreamin'. The Crotch is the Crotch, no matter how you slice it. There are Screamin' Dons all over. . . . And in case you missed it, pal, the war is over."

"Always be a war, AJ," the Dutchman said quietly. He paused and then stretched.

Slater could only stare in wonder. Finally, he shrugged and reached for his spit-shined shoes. One of them was gone.

"Hey! Where the hell's my other shoe?"

"What's that, AJ?"

"My other shoe? Where'd it go?"

"You mean that shoe you been shinin' all mornin'?"

"Goddamn it, Van Groot, quit screwin' around!"

Slater stopped searching around the footlocker and looked up. Van Groot was pointing at something over near the windows on the other side of the cubicle.

Wishing he didn't have to look, Slater slowly turned his head, then let out a groan. Over where the sunlight was making a nice comfortable warm spot on the deck, Private Jiggs lay flat out on his belly, chewing on a big piece of black leather.

Claybourne entered the Guard Shack munching a candy bar. The Corporal of the Guard was busy making a log entry, and through the adjoining door Freddy could see Gunny Brownell bullshitting with Sergeant Benjamin. The lieutenant wasn't in.

The receiver lay off the hook on the counter. He hoped the call was from Shandy or Carlene, or both, apologizing. They sure as hell hadn't shown a lot of compassion when he was lying in the dust of Moany's backyard, waiting for the ambulance. Lucky thing the roof of the toolshed had cushioned his fall or he might've broken more than his arm. Maybe one of them women had come to her senses and wanted to make up. Well, it wouldn't be that easy.

"Claybourne," he said into the mouthpiece.

"Hey there, Bubba, what's shakin'?" Hector Manallo.

He hadn't seen Manallo since the night at the Mellow Lemon when he'd dropped off Bronar's transceiver. He'd talked to him a few times since over the phone, but all Manallo had to say was he hadn't been able to turn a buyer. Over the weeks, Freddy had pretty much lost interest in the deal. The bread had never meant much to him; his reward had come with daydreams of the old redneck finding a mutha fuckin' monkey wrench in his drug smuggling operation. The image of Bronar choking on a chunk of raw meat shoved down his throat by his former "nigger" employee had given Claybourne fine moments.

"So what you want, Conkman?" Claybourne asked impatiently.

"Jou be happy to hear ol' Hector finally find a customer fer jou goods. Why don't jou come by the Lemon tonight, man, say 'round ten. We can make us a little deal. How's that sound to jou?"

"Sucks, man. Had me a accident. Can't pull no libs at all for a while. Chumps over here won't let me out."

"Shit," Hector groaned. "How the hell jou expect to do business like that, man? Here I bust my ass for jou—what jou want me ta tell the customer, man? Mebbe he take his business some place else."

"Tell him ta get fucked with a mule's dick, I don't care," Freddy said. "He wants it bad enough, he can wait."

Hector lowered his voice, as if telling a secret. "Listen, Bubba, dis customer ain't no bum, know what I mean? He's pretty important dude, big shot, jou know? I don't think he's gonna like being told ta come back some other time. Right now, I think, we can make a pretty big score. He really wants the goods bad."

"Yeah?" Freddy reconsidered his options. His lost interest in the transceiver had quickly returned with visions of greenbacks. "Real bad, huh? Tell ya what. You go ahead and make the deal, man."

"Thought jou said jou want ta be here when it go down?" Manallo actually sounded disappointed.

"You can't hear so good, Hector? I said go ahead. I know you gonna be straight with me, know that for a fact. Ain't that right?"

"Sure, sure. But I made a deal with jou, Bubba. Hector Manallo always keeps his word, man. That's how I keep my best customers."

Claybourne was puzzled by the tone of Manallo's voice. The man sounded on edge. And why was Hector suddenly so righteous with him? He'd already made up his mind, though, and was getting bored. "What's the matter with you, Conkman, you deaf? I say go ahead with it, man, and don't bother me no more. I be lookin' you up when I get me some liberty. Now, can you handle that, Hec-tor?"

There was a pause at the other end of the line, then muffled voices. Manallo came back on. "OK, Bubba, if that's the way jou want it. Jou get in touch with me before jou come down here, right? This time a year I get real busy."

"I hear ya, Conkman. . . . And dig this—I *know* you gonna be straight with me. I *know* it. I can feel it in my fist."

Claybourne hung up, satisfied that he'd put just the right amount of danger in his voice. Manallo would not dare double-cross him. With a Pay Day candy bar and a bag of peanuts (but no change) in his pocket, he headed back topside.

Manallo pulled one last drag on the quarter-inch of Pall Mall between his lips then dropped the butt in his coffee. The butt sizzled as he studied its slow disintegration in the cold liquid.

"That bastard," he hissed under his breath.

"Now Ah know why Ah never cut you in on any of my action, Hector. Ya'll sure are one in-competent sonofa-bitch." The man sitting on the other side of the table spoke softly, but there was no missing the contempt in his voice.

Manallo felt a stab of fear in his scrotum and shoved the

coffee cup away. The two men were tucked in a corner of the empty Mellow Lemon's main room. Hector was real uncomfortable, had been since the night before, when old man Bronar had busted through the door, pissed.

"He prob'ly gonna come in next week," Manallo whined. "No problem, Mr. Bronar."

"Next week? Now ain't that just flat-damn-dandy. Only Ah got me some business up ta Miami next week so that don't do me any damn good. Ah got me a powerful anger here, Hector, and Ah am about ta take it out on *you*."

"Aw, jou don't wanna do that, Mr. Bronar. Jou got jou radio back. What else jou want from me?"

Bronar's fist crashed on the table, splashing coffee and bits of soggy tobacco on Hector's tee shirt. "Ah want that nigga's ass, that's what Ah want. No shinola spook steals nothin' from Belview Bronar without gettin' what's due his black ass!"

Manallo nervously wiped the back of his hand across his mouth. "Just a radio, Mr. Bronar. Why jou gettin so—"

"Just a radio! You gawl damned peckerhead spic! You got any idea how much losin' that radio has cost me? That piece of shit Ah got ta replace it ain't got half the balls as my Fanon. Two months now—more'n that maybe—Ah been listenin' ta static an' spic talk while all along *you* was settin' on my gear. If Buddy hadn't heard the talk from them long-hairs, my butt'd still be on the griddle."

The old man's boney finger pointed straight at Hector's nose and it didn't take much imagination to transform it into the muzzle of a .38. Hector squirmed and tried to will away the chill that Bronar's watery blue eyes produced in his crotch.

"Ah don't care how you do it, Hector, but Ah want that boy set up. Ah wanna be there ta see him wet his pants before Ah cut off his head. You best come up with something, else you'll be eatin' through a straw and pissin' blood. Understand me?"

Manallo had only to glance across the table at the pinched

face, the cruel bloodless mouth, to know there would be no talking his way out. If it was going to take the jarhead's ass to save his own, then so be it. He nodded his head and reached for another cigarette.

"Trust me, Mister Bronar," Hector said, "that nigger be as good as jours. Jou wait an' see."

CHAPTER THIRTEEN

TEN days later and the dawn came up like blossoming napalm. Street litter danced as a gale force wind put white caps on the waves. By mid-afternoon the wind slacked off but the sky was an ominous gray. Over in the Barracks parking lot Gramma Zamora shook her tambourine at the heavens, chanting ancient mumbo-jumbo, while Uncle and other members of the family hovered around a burning can of sterno.

Claybourne sat on a folding chair next to the pay phone on the second deck veranda, the receiver clamped between a shoulder and his chin. He played with three stacks of quarters with the fingers of his left hand, fingers sticking out from the plaster-of-paris cast now covered with a week's worth of ink doodlings, dirt, and designs painted in Day-Glo orange and red.

"Mama, I keep tellin' ya, everything's cool."

"Now Freddy, you be truthful with your Mama. You sure that arm's all right? Gotta be careful with them broken bones else they mend all crooked. You ain't tryin' ta play no basketball or somethin' with it? Tell me the truth. That's how you broke it in the first place. No sense temptin' any fates again before it mends. You get that lotion I sent ya? Miss Onate say it just the thing for broken bones."

"Sure, Mama, I got it. Workin' just dandy. Arm be good as new in no time. You don't worry about it, hear?"

He had no trouble seeing her though many miles separated him from the crumbling walk-up in southeast DC. A tiny woman, not even five feet tall, skinny as a rail, yet the strongest person he had ever known. Thursday, he knew, was her day off from the bakery, the one day besides Sunday when her hands were not covered with flour, her body not smelling sweetly of bread dough. Sure, he'd grown up dirt poor, but there had always been cakes and pastries. So what if they were a little stale? When he looked back at his boyhood, his best recollection in a sea of bad memories was the sight of his mama coming through the door with those cardboard boxes full of two-day-old goodies.

He could see the apartment too. Spotless, neat and clean despite the peeling paint and water stains on the ceiling. He had fallen asleep to the sound of her scrubbing or washing or sweeping those two rooms. Right now, she would be sitting in the tattered armchair next to the phone, an electric floor heater near her feet, the television blinking one of her quiz shows. The color TV was the newest piece of furniture—his gift to her on coming back from the Nam. She'd cried when he'd given it to her.

On top of the set was the photograph he'd had taken his first liberty after boot camp. There was a different man in that photo, a boy really, bustin' with pride in a set of dress blues borrowed from the photographer's coat racks. He'd been on top of the world when the clicking shutter captured him, proud and cocky, nineteen years old and ready to whip the world. In six months he would be in Nam and the picture would become that of a stranger.

But his mama had cherished it; she saw it as proof that her counseling had been right and correct. He would never have joined up if it hadn't been for her. Show the white man wrong, she'd said, show him we're willing to fight for this country too. Show him black folks ain't just looking for a free ride, burning and looting and talking big. Only one way to prove you're as good as he is, she'd said, and that's to fight when the call came to fight.

He'd fought all right, and along the way he'd seen how wrong his mama was.

"Are ya comin' home for Christmas, Freddy?" He could

hear the water pipe thumping over the line. Thumping was good; it meant the hot water was working.

"Don't think so, Mama. Be gettin' out, ya know, come January. Got me about a week's leave on the books. Figure ta sell it back to 'em. Be worth a hundred bucks or so."

"That don't sound right, sellin' your leave time. I never heard of such a thing. Won't get you in no trouble now, will it?"

"No, Mama, won't get me in no trouble. Just give me a few extra dollars ta get my best girl somethin' special."

She giggled. "Your best girl be mighty lucky."

"That's right. What you think she'd like?"

"Maybe like ta see her son." She began to laugh. "Course, she might could use one of them electric blankets. Man says it's gonna be a cold winter. You probably forgot what a cold winter's like, livin' in all that sunshine."

"I ain't forgot, Mama."

"Be good ta have ya home. Been so long."

"Yeah. Well, it's gonna be good ta get there."

There was a pause in the conversation. When his mother spoke again, there was worry in her voice.

"Freddy, I been havin' that 'dream' again."

"Now, Mama, I'm safe here. Never been more safe. Dreams is just dreams."

"I still worry. Promise me you'll be real careful. Don't be doin' nothin' dangerous."

"I promise. . . . Listen, I gotta go, gunny be callin' everybody. You take care of yourself, hear? Don't be workin' too hard."

"I'll send you some sweets. You be lookin' for 'em." Her voice began to crack, and he answered by trying to sound upbeat.

"You be lookin' for *me* come January, OK?"

"I sure will. Good-bye, honey. The Lord loves ya and so do I."

"Bye, Mama."

He waited until he heard the click at the other end, then

hung up. He knew she was sad that he'd miss another Christmas with her—the third in a row—but there was no way around it. Ever since the month's leave he'd taken after coming back from Nam, he'd sworn to himself that he'd never again go back to the neighborhood while still a Marine.

First leave home after the Nam, the bloods on the street had laughed at him when he'd shown up in uniform. Thought it was funnier'n shit that he'd let the Man use his ass while lily white butts filled college seats instead of the ranks.

There were other vets around, maybe a lot of them, but no one advertised that fact. He'd rapped guardedly with a brother named Quick for two hours one night at a blind-pig before he'd found out that the guy had been with the American and had seen some shit. Two days later, he'd heard Quick had been busted for possession and he'd felt obligated to go the dude's bail. Never saw Quick again.

There's been another man, name of Sales. He and Sales had played some ball down at the playground; wasn't till a week before his leave was up that he learned Sales had been with the squids in a swift boat squadron out of Saigon.

Quick had been bitter; he'd blamed the war for all his problems—busted marriage, trouble with the law, a fifty-dollar-a-day habit. Sales, on the other hand, just wanted to forget. For him Nam had been closed out as simply an experience in his life—nothing lost, nothing gained.

"Takin' it one day at a time, bro," Sales had said, "livin' every day like it was the last. And dig this, Freddy ma man, that paper sayin' 'Honorable Discharge' don't mean jack. You go lookin' for a job, the Man just wanna see some diploma."

With a couple of years left on his four-year enlistment, Freddy had come to Key West with only two things on his mind: to get his tour over and done with, and—always remembering the advice from Sales—to live every day like it was the last.

"Live every day like it was the last" had come to mean only one thing: if there was anything more important in life than getting laid, he hadn't found it. Course, there was no way to get any lovin' with a broken arm and the major's policy of no liberty on a no-duty status. Freddy figured it was time to remedy that situation. He sauntered off toward the Guard Office, hoping he could catch Lieutenant Kargo alone and fine-talk his way into some liberty. . . .

Out on post, men tightened their field jackets and hoped the rains would hold off for one more relief.

CHAPTER FOURTEEN

THE sand between Slater's toes was cold, wet and heavy like fresh cement. He wormed his feet deeper, anchoring himself against the next rush from the waveline breaking a few yards in front of him. The waves were small but angry, and in retreat each sucked a little bit of Smather's Beach into the Atlantic. Sucked at him, too.

He liked the sense of confrontation the waves gave him, something he could see and feel and strike back at. He bent over and picked up a smooth stone, threw it at the breaker line, then cupped his hands and yelled at the ocean. The wind tore the words away like confetti in a gale.

He stayed where he was standing for a few more minutes, hands in his pockets, looking out to sea. The water and the sky were as dark and confusing as his own thoughts. Nothing new, same old crap . . . except for those damn dreams that kept changing all the time. Last night's had been a real doozy.

They were in a ville, the whole squad—Banana Dick and Hunchback, Frankie and Dirt, all of them, even Choo Choo. A smoke break, everybody crapped-out in the dust. He saw Choo float into a hooch and come out with a big basket of something. Like magic, he right away knew what the "something" was—betel nut leaves. Choo started handing it out, big smile on his face. OK, well hell, zips chewed the stuff all the time; let's see what the rush is like, see what the deal is with this crap. Buzz time. Go for the gusto. So they all started packing it in, chewing and spitting and grinning like a bunch of goddamn kids sneaking smokes out in back of the Ag shed. Pretty soon they looked like those hundred-year-old mamasans squatting by the road, selling blackmarket Coca-Cola and Salems, mouths and teeth and lips and gums stained reddish-black, like antique furniture.

Then Choo started to laugh, an evil laugh, not his usual laugh at all. "Yo, Choo," Banana Dick says, "How come you didn't try none of this shit yer ownself? Not that bad once you get by the shitty taste, kind of a two-beer high. How come you didn't try none, Choo? You handed it out, right? So how come, man, how come you ain't—"

The blackish shit dribbling out of Banana Dick's mouth turned bright red. Slater right away knew what it was. Holy God! Blood! Rivers of the stuff. Fucking rivers! Then all of them, blood. From the mouth and eyes and ears and nose, like it was coming out of a two-inch firehose! Sweet Christ!

And Choo Choo laughed even harder, laughed as the flesh on his face melted away, laughed as his guts came slipping out of the bottom of his shirt, laughed and laughed and laughed as they all bled to death, the stinking dust soaking it up like it hadn't had a drink in a thousand years. . . .

Dreams were getting kind a scary. Did that mean something? Choo was dead. He could handle that, could *handle* it. Fuckin' dreams were weird, but that's all they are, Jack, just dreams. You can handle dreams too.

Finally he turned away from the sea and began walking the shoreline, parallel to the water but out of reach of its cold clutching fingers.

The beach was deserted. Not surprising given the weather. Even the snowbirds had kissed this one off. There was a storm brewing and only a fool or a madman would walk the beach today. Slater figured he felt like a little of both.

At least he was alone.

At least he'd thought he was alone. He spotted the dark shape of someone sitting in the sand far up the beach. Interesting—another crazy person. Could've turned and walked in the opposite direction, but he felt himself being pulled toward the stranger by curiosity and a stubborn refusal not to change his path. For once he wanted to follow a direction he'd picked himself, not one he'd been ordered to take. . . .

The other nutcase sat halfway between the line of dried seaweed that marked high water and the low concrete wall built to keep the beach's sand from drifting across Roosevelt Boulevard. Slater angled out of the surf on a line that would bring him up on the stranger's flank, let him check out the other dude before his own presence was revealed.

The crusty sand under his feet crunched, almost like rotten ice on a puddle. He felt it, but didn't hear a thing. The noise of wind and sea carried away the sound before it could get to his ears.

As he got closer, the dark shape took form, a slight figure in a dark blue sweatshirt, the hood pulled up over the head. The stranger was staring out to sea. Must be catching, Slater thought.

He closed to within a few yards, then, still unnoticed, stopped. He had seen the stranger's hands, slim, delicate, and pale, the hands of a woman.

"It's supposed to get worse," he said, loud enough to be heard over the wind.

His voice startled her. Her body tightened violently and she gave a little yelp before turning in his direction. She studied him for a moment, then spoke.

"I hope you're wrong."

The hood had thrown him, but there was no missing those black-flecked gray eyes or the sound of her voice. He stared at her for a few heartbeats, then jammed his hands into his pockets and turned to the ocean so that any barbs fired at him would only be glancing blows.

"Sorry," he mumbled, "didn't know it was you."

"You're the guy from the party," she said. It was a statement, not a question, spoken not for his benefit but hers.

He muttered a reply anyway. "Yeah, I'm the guy." He felt as though he was confessing a crime.

"I can't understand a word you're saying," she said loudly. "The wind."

He took a deep breath and turned to face her. "I said, sorry I bothered you!" He didn't know whether to walk away or stay for another reaming.

"Oh." It was her turn to look out at the waves.

For long agonizing seconds neither of them said anything more. Slater was about to leave when she surprised him.

"That's OK. You didn't bother me. I was getting ready to go anyway." She stood up and faced him, brushing the sand from the seat of her jeans. "If you don't mind my asking, what are you doing out here?"

Maybe it was the wind playing tricks, but the tone of her voice had changed from the one he remembered at the party. The hard bitchiness was gone, replaced by sort of a fragile sound. Or maybe his imagination was working overtime.

"I dunno," he said, not sure of the answer himself.

She nodded.

"What about you?" he asked. "Not exactly a great day to soak rays."

"Nothing else to do. Just looking for a few answers, I suppose."

"Any luck?"

"No," she answered softly.

A large heavy raindrop slammed into his nose. He hardly noticed it. "Hey, ah, listen . . . " Awkwardly he searched for the right words. "I . . . I owe you an apology for what I said before, ya know, at the party. I was kind of a bastard. I'm sorry."

She did not respond right away, only studied his face, trying maybe to see if his words were sincere or just due to the circumstances.

"Well, that makes two of us," she finally said.

Slater found himself with nothing to say. He had dropped his guard, half expecting her to sucker-punch him again.

Suddenly she had become a different woman, or at least he was seeing a different side of her, a side he liked a lot more than the hard-nosed chick he'd spoken to at the picnic table.

He stood there gawking at her, not sure of what to do next. There was no beach crowd to disappear into, no convenient exit. The long emptiness of the beach seemed to hold them together.

Scattered raindrops warned that the storm was getting closer.

"Ah, how'd ya get out here?" he blurted. Somebody had to say something or they'd be in for a drenching. Smather's Beach was a good two miles from the Bamboo.

"Walked," she said, following his eyes to the ugly black thunderheads rolling across the horizon in their direction. "Looks like a storm's coming."

"Want a ride?"

She looked back at him. "Yeah, do you mind?"

"Heck no. Come on, I'm parked down at the end of the beach."

Self-consciously he reached out as if to take her hand, then thought better of it and only motioned for her to follow.

For a while they walked with Slater a few steps in front of her. Both of them seemed to realize how foolish this was and without a word he slowed down and she sped up, and pretty soon they were walking side by side, their pace quickened by the ever increasing raindrops.

"That's it, way down there." He pointed at the Olds, the only car on the boulevard.

"Looks familiar," she laughed.

He had no idea what she meant. "Belongs to a friend of mine. I borrowed it. He thought I was nuts when I told him I was coming out here. Jeez! I forgot! The top's down. I think we'd better run for it. Narvel will have my ass if anything—"

The sky dropped. A curtain of water descended on them, a blinding torrent that came not by the drop but in a hundred thousand threadlike streams hammering the beach.

As she began sprinting out ahead of him, all Slater could think of was that the Dutchman had been right about one thing—she did have a cute little fanny. . . .

No contest. By the time they reached the car they were both drenched. LeFey's Olds hadn't done any better; there was already standing water on the floorboards.

The two of them tugged and pulled the rag top out of its well and into place. Despite the holes and tears in the sunrotted fabric, getting under its cover was a relief; it was not a warm rain.

While Carolyn—her name, he remembered—sat with her bare feet held out of the pool of water on the floor, Slater pumped the half-submerged accelerator and cranked the engine over. It sputtered, then held. He kept giving it little squirts of gas until he was sure it could survive on its own, then glanced over at his passenger. She was eyeballing the torn back seat, still decorated with the Dutchman's teeth-marks.

"You OK?" he asked.

She shivered. "I'm freezing!"

"I'll hit the heater in a minute. Better try to make yourself comfortable. We can't go anyplace in this mess—no wipers." He reached over and turned a switch to demonstrate what he meant. An abrasive scratching sound came from the windshield where two rubberless metal wiper blades scraped across the glass. He turned them off. "LeFey don't waste any money on non-essentials." His grin was answered with a quivering bottom lip and eyes that seemed to be asking for help. He coughed and turned on the heater, feeling useless but not sure what else he could do.

She hugged herself tightly and stared out the window. Her teeth chattered as she spoke. "I've never seen rain like this before. God, it's like being inside a waterfall."

"Think this is bad, you should see the monsoons in Nam. Can't hardly see the hand in front of your face." He tried to laugh but she had turned to face him and her blank expression gave him the idea that maybe she hadn't heard a word. Her lips were turning blue and the heater was still blowing cold air.

There was no conscious thought about what he did next; there just seemed to be no alternative. All of a sudden he was sliding across the seat, slipping an arm around her shoulders, pulling her close to him. She resisted for a moment, then buried her head on his chest. He could feel her quaking; whether it was from the cold or something else, he could not know.

It was strange at first; he hadn't held anyone like this for a very long time. He felt clumsy, unsure of himself, like the first time he'd played spin-the-bottle and found himself trying to figure out how to kiss a mouthful of braces. Then the closeness of her body produced a warmth that seemed to melt away the strangeness and cold thoughts. As the downpour continued, he wished it would rain for the rest of his life.

He felt her shudder and was sure she would push herself away. Instead, she reached out and pulled him closer. He glanced down but all he could see was the top of her head, still covered with the sweatshirt's hood.

He raised his freezing feet out of the pool of dirty rainwater on the floorboard and held them under the heater vent. The air from it was beginning to warm up.

She smelled of salt and sweat and perfume, all mingled together to produce a scent so completely feminine that he felt a rush of heat in his loins. He was embarrassed and immediately tried to will away the growing tightness in his groin, but he had no control. Goddamn, Slater, he thought, you're worse than Jiggs when he smells his chow.

Whether she noticed or not, he couldn't tell. Maybe it was the warming effect of the heater, or just the cramped position they were in. Whatever the reason, she finally pushed herself away from him and fell back on her side of the car. She glanced out the window, then back in his direction.

"Thanks. You're a good warmer-upper." Her voice was steady and he could see some color in her cheeks.

"Anytime." He tried to sound cool but felt like he was blushing. Blushing, for Christ sakes. It was his turn to look out the window. "I think it's lettin' up a little."

"I really am sorry, you know."

"Hey, no sweat. You can use me for a warmer anytime you want."

"No. I mean at that party. I was a real bitch. I'm sorry."

"Shoot. I wasn't exactly Mr. Clean myself. Me and my buddies are pretty thin-skinned when it comes to dealing with outsiders. Tendency is to jump down throats. Everybody seems to want to blame the whole thing on us." He fumbled for a tape in a bin LeFey had installed under the dash. "How about some sounds?"

"Sure. What was it like?"

"What was what like?"

"Vietnam."

"I dunno. . . . There's about a hundred guys over at the Barracks, everyone of 'em would give you a different answer. I guess I'm lucky. Lotta guys saw worse. . . ." He stopped. "Ya know, you're the first person who's asked. I don't know what the hell to say."

Elton John exploded out of the speakers. Slater quickly turned down the volume while Carolyn pushed her head back against the seat and shut her eyes. He was glad the subject had been dropped.

The music and the rain were hypnotic, and both of them just sat and listened for a while. Finally Carolyn arched her back and reached into the sweatshirt's pocket.

"God, I need a joint," she said. "Oh, shit!" She pulled her hand out of the shirt. Her palm was full of a small heap of wet grass and bits of soggy-looking paper.

Slater chuckled. "You can check the glove compartment, but I don't think you'll find anything. Pay day ain't until tomorrow. Besides, LeFey don't smoke weed too often.

Navy's got narcs everywhere. I think there's a pint a Jack Daniel's in the trunk if ya want."

She was rolling down the window. "No thanks," she said. She brushed the mess in her hand off into the gutter now filled with a rushing stream. "Rain's stopped," she pointed out. "Think you could take me home? I could use a nice hot bath."

"Sure. No sweat."

Sorry that the moment had to pass, Slater slipped the Olds into drive and hung a U-turn. The car responded like a battleship doing two knots.

He dropped her off in front of the Bamboo Room, the car backfiring, belching oil-soaked black clouds. From the sidewalk she said something to him through the open window. He couldn't hear her. She leaned through the opening, a curious smile on her face.

"What was your name again?" she asked.

"Jack. Jack Slater."

"Thanks for the ride, Jack." She waved and turned as if to leave. Then for some reason she turned in her tracks again. This time there was a teasing sound to her voice as she leaned down and spoke.

"What were you *really* doing out on that beach?"

"Picking up girls, what else?" He grinned.

Her laughter reminded him of the sleigh bells his old man hung up on the door every year at Christmas. "Rose was right," she said. "You guys *are* hornier than hell."

He shrugged. She waved again, turned, and walked away.

He watched until she'd disappeared up the outside stairway, glad she hadn't gone into the bar where he knew the Dutchman and some of the others were running up their tabs. He didn't want to share that final smile of hers with anybody.

It was only after he'd driven three blocks on his way back to the Barracks that he noticed his shit-eating grin in the rearview mirror.

Chapter Fifteen

HECTOR Manallo walked into the Dun-Rite transmission shop, smiling. He finally had some good news to give the old man.

Bronar's brother-in-law, Buddy, picked his nose with a grease-blackened thumb, reading an underground comic book as Manallo made his way through the debris of transmission parts, tools, and rags that littered the oil-smeared floor. An old Chevy with its guts hanging out was on the lift; rock music blasted from a cheap transistor radio hanging from the car's rear bumper.

"Hey there, Buddy, how's my man?" Manallo said as he scratched an armpit.

"Good," Buddy said without looking up. He began to giggle. "Lookit them tits, Hector." He held the comic up for Manallo's inspection, his eyes wide and childlike. "Golly, they look so good I could eat 'em." Buddy ripped the page out of the comic, stuffed the cheap newsprint into his mouth, and chewed.

"Hey, that be cool, Bubba. I bet they pretty tasty, huh?" It was common knowledge around town that Buddy had more than a few loose wires in his fuse box.

Buddy held the comic out to Manallo. "Want some?" He was still munching so the words were garbled.

"No thanks, man, I just ate, jou know? Say, is Mr. Bronar back in the back?"

"A-huh," Buddy grunted. He pointed the comic at the raised Chevy. "I'm workin' on that car there."

Hector looked up at the wreckage. "Jou doin' a damn

good job, too. Catch jou later, OK, Bubba? Maybe we eat some more tit together."

Buddy giggled again.

Hector waited to shudder until he'd turned his back on the man. Maybe Buddy was chldlike in some things, but he had a reputation for mind-blowin' violence too. Rumor was ol' Buddy once tried to tear a man's throat out with his teeth. The victim had complained about faulty transmission work.

The old man was sitting in front of the Fanon transceiver, fiddling with the dials, when Hector strolled into the office. Bronar did not look up.

"What you want, Manallo? Whatever it is, make it gawl damn short cause Ah got business ta tend."

"Hey! How jou know it was me, Mr. Bronar?"

"Smelled ya comin', beaner. Now say what you come here ta say else Ah'll git Buddy on yer ass." The old man turned a page in a little black notebook on the counter in front of him.

Hector leaned back against the doorframe. "Got good news. Talked with Clayborg on the phone 'bout a hour ago. He's comin' to see me this afternoon, after he goes see his doctor."

Bronar didn't say anything right away, and when he did, Hector was a little surprised.

"So, what the hellnation is a clay borg?" the old man asked.

"Clayborg, Mr. Bronar. Jou remember. He be the splib that ripped off jou radio there. Jou said jou wanted his ass. 'Member? Last month, when jou got jou goods back."

"Oh yeah," the old man mumbled. "This afternoon ya say? Too bad. Me and Buddy got some fishin' ta do." The radio crackled with a burst of static and Bronar whacked it with the flat of his hand. "That is, if Ah can get this here piece a shit ta work. Ain't worked right since Ah got it back from you. Maybe 'cause its innards was full a vegetables."

Manallo got a picture of the transceiver sitting under a pile of vegetables in the Mellow Lemon's storeroom and cringed. "Yeah, well, don't know nothin' about no vegetables, Mr. Bronar. Maybe . . . probably the splib—"

He was cut off by a squawk from the radio followed by the sound of a human voice, jumbled and faint. Hector thought he heard the word "firelight" which seemed to galvanize the old man into action. Bronar grabbed the mike and held down the transmit button.

"Firelight, Firelight, this here's Neptune, ovah." Bronar glanced over his shoulder, spectacles hanging from the tip of his nose like some kindly old grandfather. His words didn't fit the look, though. "Git the fuck outta here, Manallo, less you want Buddy ta rip out yer tongue."

"Sure, Mr. Bronar. Ah . . . what jou want me to do with Clayborg?"

"You have old Sambo at the Lemon around eleven tonight. Me and Buddy'll be back by then. An' you best have him waitin', ya hear? No fuck-ups this time, Hector, else Buddy out there's gonna play jump-rope with yer internal organs." The old man grinned evilly and licked his lips. "Yes, sir, tonight this ol' boy is gonna have him some black balls and rice for a midnight snack."

Jesus, Hector thought, whole damn family was inta eatin' strange shit.

The radio crackled again, the words louder and clearer this time. "Neptune, Neptune, this is Firelight. Do you copy, over?"

Bronar pointed at the door and turned to grab the mike. "You'd best haul ass now, Hector," he said. "Buddy likes ta cut chum after he eats tit."

"Well, Mister Claybourne," the skinny Navy doctor said as he studied the X-ray one last time. "The arm appears to be mending, slowly but surely. Another six weeks and it will be almost as good as new. I think you'll find that new cast I put on will be a lot easier to handle." The young man known as "Doc Hippy" around the Barracks winked at Freddy, who sat on the other side of the desk. "We'll just keep you on no-duty for a while longer, all right? Don't want to tempt anybody, do we?" The doctor motioned with his head in the general direction of the west wall of the office. Claybourne wondered what the eye chart had to do with a broken arm.

"Ain't gonna wear no glasses, man," he growled.

A baffled look crept across Doc Hippy's face. He had made a concerted effort throughout his eighteen months in the Navy to lean over backward for the oppressed black serviceman. From their own lips he had heard stories of torture, mental abuse, and injustice, and felt it his duty to do all he could to ease their burden. Yet the doctor hadn't the slightest idea what the man was talking about. He'd made a simple gesture in the direction of the Marine Barracks and somehow his patient had interpreted that as a prescription for eyeglasses.

"Ah, well, yes. I wouldn't worry about that," Doc Hippy floundered. "Your eyes are fine. It's the *arm* I'm concerned with."

Freddy sighed in relief. Regulation glasses were as uncool as shit kicker music. "Dig that, doc," he said. "Only problem is that no-duty chit. No-duty chit, that's not so cool. No town liberty with a no-duty chit. Maybe you could change it to light duty. See, with light duty I can take care of my business in town."

Doc Hippy frowned. "Yes, and it will also allow you to be forced to perform menial tasks. I detect the hand of your executive officer in this. What's his name? Captain *Brute* is it? If he has threatened or coerced you into making this request, I want to know about it. I've had enough of his meddling in medical affairs."

"No, sir! Capt'n Brule got nothin' ta do with it. CO just don't allow no town libs with no-duty chits." Freddy furrowed his brow as though deep in thought. "Now, maybe if you could make a note on that no-duty chit that I can have some town liberty, then—"

The doctor shook his head. "I'm sorry, but the granting of liberty is beyond my purview."

"Well, if you ain't got any preview, just give me a light-duty chit. See, my momma's comin' down for a visit. If I don't get any town libs, ain't gonna be able to see much of her. And bein' in a wheelchair and all like she is, she ain't gonna be able ta get around much."

Doc Hippy's eyes blinked behind his amber-tinted granny glasses. He rubbed his chin, then began writing on a blank chit. He finished up his work with a scrawling signature, handed it across to his patient. "There you are, Mister Claybourne. Light duty. If you run into any difficulties," the man arched his eyebrows, "let me know about it immediately. I'll see you again in two weeks."

Freddy folded the chit and rose. "Thanks, Doc. I 'preciate you helpin' me out like this."

"Think nothing of it. And say hello to your mother for me."

Freddy stared blankly at the doctor's smiling face for a moment, then caught himself. "Yeah . . . oh yeah, I'll do that. Only, I'll have ta do it with sign. Momma's been deaf for three years now."

"Oh, I'm so sorry to hear that," Doc Hippy said quietly. His patient was almost to the door when the doctor spoke again. "And, Mr. Claybourne . . ."

Freddy looked back.

"Power to the People!" Doc Hippy held up a clenched "power" fist.

Claybourne returned it. "Yeah, right on, man," he said.

Some chuck dudes were dumber'n fly shit, Claybourne thought as he glided down the steps of the dispensary out into the sunshine of midday.

He decided to take his time getting back to the Barracks. Liberty call wouldn't be until 1300, almost half an hour away. He knew the section was busy field-daying the squad bay and he didn't want to test the limits of his new light-duty status. Cast or no cast, Brownell would sure as shit hand him a broom and tell him to get at it. No way.

He killed some time rapping with a couple of bloods from the *Gilmore* out in front of the dispensary. Then he flagged down the geedunk wagon and grabbed a lunch of corn chips and a Coke. He was tempted to wander over to the PX, but somebody might spot him there, maybe even Brule, and then his ass would be shit out of luck. It was better to look like he was heading for the Barracks. That could take all day if he wanted it to.

Sorry, Gunny, the doc gave me some some kinda pill for the pain, felt like I was gonna pass out, had ta stop and rest now and then. Feel OK now, though. Liberty call go yet? Yeah, well, I be seein' you tomorrow mornin', Gunny. See, I got me that light-duty chit you been bustin' my ass about gettin' for the last couple weeks. That was the deal, right? I get Doc Hippy to put me on light dutes so I can stand a super, and you let me take some libs? Yeah. So like I said, be seein' ya. Got me some business out in town.

Definitely had some business in town. First, a quick stop at the Mellow Lemon to collect from Manallo (who'd been buggin' his ass to come in, seemed forever). Then maybe a new shirt, then a couple beers, then a shady spot on the Block to wait for school to let out. Maybe blow a little weed out back of the rib shack, mellow out before putting the moves on little Shandy. Girl should be ready by now, ought to be dripping like warm honey. Damn!

Visions of Shandy danced in his head as he lazily continued the long walk around the perimeter of the softball field standing between him and the Barracks. He could almost feel warm flesh surrounding him, drawing him down, washing away all the bullshit. Living every day like it was the last—so fine.

WHHH-HAM.

The explosion rocked him, almost knocked him down. For a split second he was sure he was back in Nam, taking incoming. Close. The shock wave and the boom had come at the same time. He stumbled, looking for a hole to dive into, a slit trench, a bunker, three sandbags, hell, *anything* to get into or under or behind. Nothing there, though. Only an empty softball field on one side of the street, a few Navy maintenance shops and repair sheds on the other.

Wasn't any chance to be afraid, except for that first sliver of something shootin' right up your ass into your guts while every goddamn muscle in your body jumps and tightens and your balls feel like they're about sucked right up into your throat. No chance to really be afraid, though. Too much going on; too much to figure.

Down the street a ways, off to his left, he saw a set of double doors on one of the maintenance buildings fly open. In a cloud of thick white smoke, a sailor in dungarees staggered outside, bent double and coughing like a sonofa-bitch. The sailor got maybe ten yards then collapsed on all fours, gagging and puking and pretty much acting fucked-up.

WHHH-HAMM.

A second explosion. A second shock wave and pop of eardrums. A second E-tool pick right up the poop chute, just not so deep this time. Damn!

He *saw* it this time, though—all in a swallow. The front of the same small building bulged, two whole sets of windows disintegrated outward, a small fireball rolled out the open doors and licked skyward followed by more dense smoke that changed from white to muddy yellow.

For one crazy breath he thought RPG attack. Shook that idea off quick, though. He'd been back in the World for pretty near two years now, enough time to quit thinking every loud fart was an enemy round. But there was definitely some bad shit goin' down across the street there.

Freddy looked around, thinking maybe he'd spot a big fleet of fire trucks and ambulances and a hundred squids rushing to the shed. Nobody. Street was deserted, and except for the one sailor still coughing and clawing at his throat, wasn't another soul in sight. That pretty much made him obligated maybe to go lend a hand, help the dude back down to the dispensary.

He took a couple of regular-sized steps in the direction of the smoking building, then a couple more—faster this time—then all of a sudden he was jogging, the new cast swinging loosely and easily, brushing his thigh.

Fifty yards maybe. Made it without losing his breath even. The sick squid had managed to pull himself all the way across the street from the smoking building. He was rolled over on his back, still coughing, but moanin' sorta too, rubbing at his eyes. Funny smell in the air. Chemical smell. Couldn't place it. Felt like it wanted to sting.

Freddy went down on one knee beside the hurting squid. "Hey, man," he said, "be still now. Help's on the way. Gonna be all right."

The sailor tried to say something, went into a coughing fit. Dude was in bad shape, but still reached out and managed to grab a handful of Claybourne's utility shirt. Like a man drowning, he struggled to pull Freddy down with him.

"Two," the man gagged out, "two inside!"

Freddy looked across the street at the bowed-out front of the building. Well, we all gotta go sometime, he thought to himself. Two dudes inside that mess probably already caught the Earlybird Special. Smoke was really pouring out of the doorway and empty windows now, dark brown stuff, rolling in big clouds, easy for somebody to spot. Fire trucks should be there pretty quick. He thought he could hear a siren someplace, not too close.

"Get help!" the sailor tried again. "Inside! Welbern! Ski!"

The man rolled over onto his belly and began spitting up a lotta bad looking crap that Freddy didn't want to see. Didn't want to think about what he ought to be doing either, but he did.

The first squid was easy to find. He was only a few steps inside the building's main doors, doors fuckin' *blown* off their hinges. Freddy didn't see the squid, fell over him instead. Smoke was too thick to *see* anything. And even if there wasn't any smoke, he still woulda kept his eyes shut 'cause that chemical shit was real real bad. Hurt his lungs, made his skin prickle and sting, really did a number on his eyes.

He felt around blind till he found the body he'd tripped over. Felt it with his good hand, found the back of the dude's shirt collar, then pulled him out of the smoky hell-hole and halfway across the street. Didn't know if the dude was alive or not, wasn't his worry right now.

Where was the mutha fuckin' fire trucks? Freddy blinked and rubbed at his burning eyes, looking up and down the street for some sign of help. Nobody. Nothing. Not a mutha fuckin' thing! Sheee-it.

This time when he headed back into the building, he spotted the sign out front. The sign was scorched but he could read it: BATTERY SHOP. What the hell. Coulda been worse; coulda read mutha fuckin' A-BOMB SHOP.

The smoke looked like it was easing off a little. Once he got inside he could make out dim shapes through the stuff. Still stung like a mutha fuck, though. He jammed his utility cap over his mouth and nose and tried to use it like a handkerchief. Didn't do much good. He could breathe, but had to pay a price. The air burned going down.

There were some flames over in a far corner, near a work bench. Big hole in the wall too, sucking off a lot of the smoke. Freddy thought he saw a pair of feet sticking out from under a pile of junk. Bare feet. Explosion must've blown the dude's shoes off. That bad. Dude was probably meeting angels.

Freddy stumbled over to the mess, began pulling away heavy hunks of metal and plastic, pieces of machinery and wood. Getting real hard to breathe now. He was coughing, spitting up. Uncovered enough of the body to see that the squid was in one piece. That'd make the family real happy.

One huge piece of stuff sitting on the dude wouldn't

budge—plastic casing, it looked like. He used his cast like a crowbar, jamming it under a corner of the heavy black junk and prying up with it.

The piece of junk moved, shifted, rolled back a little off the dude with no shoes, then shifted again, back down on the cast. Freddy heard something crack, felt a tear, then a pain like he'd never felt before rocketed up his arm—the bad arm—from his wrist to his shoulder. He screamed, heard himself scream, fell back flat on his butt.

He tried to lift the cast to check it out. Couldn't. Now *he* was trapped under that big piece of black shit. Pain everywhere. Hurt just being. Better do something, Freddy, or you gonna eat it.

Managed to wedge his shoulder behind the hunk of junk. Pushed. It shifted. Pushed again. Good Christ! Pain was blowing the top of his head off. Come on, come on, come on. Move, you mutha fuck! The junk rolled. Rolled back. Caught him again. Pinned the cast to the deck. Oh, God, such pain!

He yelled, sucked in a big lungful of that chemical shit. Anger took over from the hurt. With one mind blowin' heave, he ripped the broken cast out from under the huge heavy piece of junk. Get the fuck outta here, man! He pivoted on his knees, looking for a way out of the shed. Saw the big hole in the wall, started crawling for it, coughing and gagging as bad as that first sailor had back before the world was a giant red ball of ass-kicking hurt.

Remembered what he'd come for then. Didn't want to, but crawled back over to the body of the squid, grabbed a foot and started to pull, one handed, pushing his own body with his feet, half sitting, crabbing across the concrete deck, shifting his butt left and right, straining to hold on to the squid's bare foot.

Getting dizzy, fuzzy-like, couldn't seem to breathe at all anymore. Thought maybe he heard a lot of banging, then shouts. The hole in the wall, far away. Get out, you mutha fuck, get outta this. He could feel chunks of the cast dragging along with him. Pain was so bad. Never felt pain like that before. The cast bumped something. GOOD LORD GOD! He screamed again, couldn't stop it, even with the burning and gagging and coughing—he screamed.

"Over here!" he heard Mister Death holler.

He wanted to cuss out Mister Death, couldn't get a breath. Throat was full of hot sand.

Mister Death grabbed him under the armpits. Pulled him, lifted him, took him away. Wanted to fight, didn't have the strength. Momma Momma Momma. I love you, Momma. Looked up into the face of Mister D. Evil dude was wearin' a gas mask.

"Fuck you," Freddy said, just before he passed out.

The air was sweet in heaven. He opened his eyes to blue skies. Mister Death had been kicked out by the face of God. Just like he always figured, though, God was a honky.

"Rest easy, son," God said. (God had bad teeth too, and a funny hat—looked like a fireman's helmet.) "You're gonna be fine. Ambulance'll be along soon. Damn good job you did there, Marine. Damn splendid good job."

Hell, Freddy thought, glad somebody finally noticed.

CHAPTER SIXTEEN

BY ten o'clock the annual Officers Club Halloween Party was in full swing. The sounds of canned big band music, drunken laughter, even the tinkling of ice cubes against glass, were carried on the mild onshore breeze from the "O" Club terrace across United Street into the sentry shack of Post Ten where Jack Slater was standing the eight-to-midnight.

Anyone passing through the Fort Taylor Gate would have seen only a businesslike Marine sentry, armed with a .45 automatic and a tight jaw—not a man to mess with or push.

"Swear to God, you jerk-off," Slater growled out of the corner of his mouth, "I almost busted a cap on you!"

"Aw, piss off, man. It's Halloween. Give it a rest." The loud voice came from the dark shadows and thick tropical foliage in back of the shack.

"Cool it, turd," Slater whispered. "You want ta get us busted again?"

"Jesus, AJ, you sure have gone pussy on me. Ain't nobody around except those squid officers and their twats. They're all so shit-faced by now they couldn't tell the difference between a B-52 strike and a asshole whistlin' Dixie."

Slater adjusted his stance in the shack's doorway. "Where the hell'd you get that costume?"

"Souvenir, man. Smuggled it back in my seabag. . . . Hey, you are grindin' my jaw, know that? Here I go and leave one supreme party ta come and keep my buddy company and all you do is shit on my head."

"You shouldn't a sneaked up on me, specially dressed

like that. You're damn lucky I didn't blow you away. Wait one."

Coming from the direction of town, an old black and gold Dodge with a blue officer's sticker on its bumper rolled to a stop beside the floodlit shack. The driver was a pimply faced boy, no more than sixteen, in cut-off jeans, no shirt, and a ponytail. Slater had no problem spotting the six-pack on the seat beside the driver or the open beer can stuck between the boy's legs.

Ignoring the sneer on the kid's face, Slater snapped off a salute and waved the vehicle on base. The boy was in violation of at least a half dozen regulations, but one of the first things he'd learned out here on Ten was the unwritten rule that officers' cars were untouchable; they were not to be detained under penalty of a pissing match with Base Security, a match that the sentry could not win.

The car burned rubber and Slater resumed his position at an easy parade rest.

"I woulda had that punk for breakfast," the Dutchman announced from the darkness.

"Yeah, and his old man would've been all over you like shit on a shingle. . . . So tell me, Dutch, how's the party?"

"It's cool. Only it's supposed ta be a damn Hallo-fuckin'-ween thing, right? Yeah, but I was the only one ta show up in costume, except for some faggot friend of Rose's who came in dressed up like a fuckin' stripper. Fucker gave me the creeps. Garter belt, high heels, and one of them bras with the nipples cut out. Guy was a real flamer."

"Sounds gross."

"You got that—"

A high-pitched female squeal came from the direction of the "O" Club. "Damn, AJ! Hear that? Sounds like she got a bar stool up her chute!"

Slater laughed. "You hear about Freddy?"

"He finally die?"

"You're sick, man. Naw, heard the lieutenant was putting him in for a medal."

The Dutchman snorted. "Oughta give a medal to them corpsmen out at the hospital. They're the ones gotta put up with all his bullshit. Poor little pansy—just 'cause his arm's in traction thinks the world's gotta wait on him twenty-four hours a day. Freddy's gonna play that game for the rest of his tour, man. Tell you fact, Jack, when he comes back to the Barracks, I'm gonna be in his shit on a constant basis. Very fuckin' convenient, ya ask me, he keeps breakin' the same fuckin' arm. A medal, huh?"

"That's what I heard. For pullin' those squids outta the fire."

"Well, hell. Guess you gotta give even his sandbaggin' ass credit. Me, I woulda let 'em fry."

At one time or another everybody at the Barracks had been out to see Claybourne at the hospital. Hadn't looked all that good when Slater dropped in, seemed like he was in a lot of pain. He hadn't talked with Freddy much, some girl from town was there—Moany's bridesmaid—and she was taking up most of Freddy's attention. Word was Claybourne wouldn't even be back to the Barracks for a good four or five weeks. Some guys had it made.

"Level with me, Jack," Van Groot said, sounding serious all of a sudden. "You ain't goin' limp-wristed on me, are ya? Like Rose's friend?"

"What the hell are you talkin' about now?"

"You been actin' strange lately, man. Like you was in a trance or somethin'. Grinnin' all the damn time, not talkin' ta nobody, not pullin' no libs with your buddies, stinkin' like a French whore. Beginnin' ta think Key fuckin' West has got to ya."

"Don't know what you're talkin' about."

"So what're you doin' standin' dutes tonight for? Section's got libs and a party, and you're standin' Hollenback's duty. You got me very worried, AJ. Ain't no room in RECON for Juicy Fruits."

"Van Groot," Slater answered slowly, "I'm startin' ta think people are right about you, man. You *are* crazier than hammered dog dork. You think I'm standing Hollenback's duty for the jollies? Asshole's charging me twenty-five bucks. Come Saturday night, though, while you're eating jellyfish out on Fleming, I'm gonna be out on the town— with a woman. Get that, you sorry sack of shit? A woman."

There. It was out. Felt good, but he knew damn well he was in for it now.

"She white?"

"Damn it! What kind of question is that?"

"Hey! Just askin'. Hate ta see ya get hassled in every joint in town. She a Conch?"

"You gotta know? OK. It's the Crack's niece, man. Satisfied?"

The Dutchman's started to howl, an old hound dog crying to the moon. Slater looked up and down the street, afraid somebody would hear the strange sad noise and come to investigate. "Shut up, Dutch! You'll have the dog catcher on us."

"You sonofabitch!" Van Groot whimpered. "Steal your best buddy's girl, right from under his nose? Thought you said she was fucked up? Huh? Ain't that what you told me?"

"I was wrong. How's that grab ya?" If Van Groot really felt betrayed he would've already been kicking and swinging.

"So what the hell you been doin' the last couple of weeks?" Dutch wanted to know. "Besides douchin' in after shave five times a day."

"None a your business."

"Aw, come on, man. You can leave out the dirty parts . . . for now anyways."

"Damn, Dutch, does everything have to be a fuck book with you?"

"Just tell me where you been hidin' out. Nobody's seen you on libs with her. You got a room someplace?"

"Man, you've got a one-track mind. Hell, we just hang around Mallory Square is all . . . watch the sunset."

"Watch the what?"

"The sunset, asshole," Slater answered defensively. "You oughta try it sometime. Puts . . . puts things into whatdaya call it—*perspective.*"

"Horse pucky. You mean ta tell me, a piece of ass like that and you just been watchin' the goddamn sun go down? You better forget RECON, man. You goin' *hippie* on me!" The Dutchman spit a gob of Red Man and Slater imagined that by now the ground behind the shack looked like a sewer leak.

"I'm findin' this hard ta believe, Jack," Van Groot continued. "You been messin' with this incredible split-tail for two-three whole weeks and all you done is watch the fuckin' sun go down?"

"Do me a favor. Lay off."

There was some anger in Slater's voice and the Dutchman was not deaf. "Yeah, sure, AJ. Don't get uptight. I mean, you wanna watch the sun go down 'stead of drinkin' and whorin' and havin' fun with your buddies, that's your business. Now, if I was you, I'd—"

"Dutch," Slater interrupted, "you're gonna be missed at the Bamboo. If it's such a shit-hot party, why don't you go on back?"

"Well, I'd like ta do that, Jack. Trouble is, I'm tapped out. Rose cut off my credit again. Tab's only a hundred and thirty bucks. Geez, you'd think she'd want ta please her best customer."

Slater stepped down from the door of the shack and slipped around the corner. He reached into his trouser pocket, then extended a folded five dollar bill to the darkness. "Here, have one on me."

There was a rustling of bushes, then a hand appeared from out of the leaves and snatched the bill from Slater's grasp. "Hey, thanks, AJ! You're all right. I don't care what

Screamin' Don says. Listen, I'll pay ya back payday, OK? No lie."

"Sure, sure. Don't sweat it, man."

The Dutchman moved out into the light. He was dressed in black silk pajamas, sandals, and a conical reed hat that concealed most of his face. Only someone as crazy as Van Groot, Slater thought, would have the balls to go to a grunt Halloween party dressed as "Charlie."

Five bucks richer, the Dutchman walked back toward town. Suddenly he turned. "Hey, listen. Sorry about raggin' ya, man. Sunsets are cool. . . . And if I see that chick, I'll tell her you just shipped out ta Okinawa. Hey! Did I tell ya? Bone and LeFey rented themselves a crib down on Petronia. We're all goin' over there later. Think she'd like ta go?"

"Up yers, Dutch," Slater called to the disappearing figure.

"Ya mean up *hers*, don't ya, AJ?" Van Groot made a loud kissing sound, waved, and then was gone.

Slater went back to the doorway of the shack and let the night close in around him. Things had been going his way lately. Had been since the stormy day at Smather's Beach. . . .

At first, he admitted to himself, he'd been afraid to see her again. The girl he'd sat in the rain with at Smather's versus the bitch he'd gone toe to toe with in Moany's backyard were two different people. Which one was the real one? If she turned out to be the bitch-goddess, then that would pretty much wipe out the good feeling he'd been having ever since that stormy afternoon, the feeling that he was finally getting his shit together.

For two or three days he slammed around the Barracks like somebody poppin' speed. All hours of the day and night he'd find himself standing in the Guard Shack, fiddling with the phone, even dialing a few digits of the Bamboo's phone number. Forget it, man. Don't need the grief.

He couldn't get her out of his mind, though. Started moping around the squad bay, only went through the motions of standing duty. Nothing had any importance. Not even Screamin' Don writing him up for wearing "improper civilian attire"—to wit, a tie-dyed tee shirt—got his motor going. So who gives a shit? Bust me to private if you want, but just leave me alone. (The charge hadn't gone very far; Major Brocksneider dismissed it out of hand.)

He began to feel trapped. Every other night the guys in the section would take off on liberty, usually heading for the Bamboo. He wouldn't—couldn't—go along. What if he saw *her* there? What would he say? To be shot down in front of his buddies would be even worse than getting the shaft over the phone. He wound up watching many hours of green-tinted pablum on the Barracks TV.

One evening when he couldn't stand the smell of floor wax, dirty feet, and stale Cheetos any longer, or watch another minute of network bullshit, he threw on his jeans and a sweatshirt and headed for town, not for Duval Street and the bars, but north to Mallory Square.

Mallory Square, the town dock. By day it was a tourist trap, shops and restaurants catering to snowbirds searching for a taste of Caribbean color, thrilled to the saggy bottoms of their Bermuda shorts to buy a few yards of hand-painted fabric or a box of hand-rolled cigars or battle a platter of spicy handmade *bollos* that left the guts burning and the breath reeking of garlic.

In the early evening, though, Mallory Square became a flower-power Mecca for sun freaks. An hour before sunset they would begin arriving—the flower children, bikers, gays, drifters and beach bums, even a few straight snowbirds not sidelined from seasickness or second degree sunburn. All one big happy family.

You looked close, though, you saw some family secrets. Lotta glassy doped-up eyes, goofball smiles, tubercular coughs and phlegm-filled rattles. Place reeked of burning hemp and cocoa-butter suntan oil and banana-flavored feminine deodorant—a real chemical factory. For a price, brutha, anything you wanted was on sale. Six uniformed cops kept the "family" from ripping each other off.

Slater wandered the length of the dock that evening, sucking up the sounds and smells and sights. This was supposed to be part of what he had gone to war for, part of what men had died for, part of what his uniform was supposed to represent and protect. Piss on 'em, he thought, buncha assholes. He was in that kind of mood.

She sat with her back against a pylon, alone, looking out at the sun god balanced on the waves like a twenty-dollar gold piece. For a long time he just stood there watching her. When he finally got up the guts to approach her (armed with two snow cones he'd grabbed from a vendor), it was mostly out of a need to break the tension in his stomach and slow down the hammering of his pulse. Get it over with, one way or the other.

Even then a side of him wondered how the hell she could stare at the ocean so much; it didn't seem healthy.

"Strawberry or root beer?" his opening line went. She turned to face him, hard lines quickly softening as she recognized him. She even smiled when she saw the cones of red and brown ice held out to her.

"Yecch!" she said, reaching for the strawberry.

He took a seat on the seawall beside her and they talked into darkness, finally shooed away by a cop who told them the dock area was closing. Slater walked her to the Bamboo and then floated back to the Barracks.

Mallory Square at sunset had been their time together after that. No words were spoken nailing this down, no date was ever made for the next meeting. On evenings when the section pulled liberty he would walk to the dock and she'd be there, in the same spot, almost like she was waiting for him. And they'd talk.

Gotta be honest; the conversations weren't all that terrific. Pretty much one-sided. She seemed sad, so he tried to make her laugh. Sometimes he succeeded, sometimes she only looked at him with puzzled eyes. Couldn't blame her. Who the hell in his right mind could believe the stories about the Dutchman or Screamin' Don or Zamora's People or any of the other craziness of the Crotch? Have to be fuckin' insane to believe such stuff.

They'd gone on meeting like that for almost two weeks before he finally got up the courage to ask her out on a real date. She said yes, fine, what took you so long? Blew his mind.

With a duty weekend staring him in the face, he'd made the costly deal with a Marine in the Port Section named Hollenback. Twenty-five bucks to trade a Thursday for a Saturday duty. If Hollenback had only known the way things were in Slater's head, he could've gotten triple the price.

CHAPTER SEVENTEEN

"WHERE'RE my pens!" The old man next door to Freddy Claybourne's hospital bed glared with distant, demonic eyes, the cords of his scrawny neck straining to hold his head away from the pillow. "What ya done with my pens!"

"Already told ya, ain't got your pens, man! Leave me alone!" Claybourne wanted to roll his back to the old man's bed but the pulleys and wires holding his arm in traction didn't allow it. He groaned and tried to block out the old man's voice. What a way to spend a Saturday night.

"Want my pens! Gimme my pens! Somebody stole my pens!" Wheezing horribly, the old man began to thrash under his sheets. The first few times this had happened Freddy had been alarmed; now it was almost routine.

"Be cool, old dude. You gonna rip all them needles out again. Shit! Man can't get no rest around here. How they 'spect me ta heal if—" The old man started choking. "Aw, man, why you have ta be such a dumb old fuck?"

The ring of hollow metal hitting the deck and the slosh of liquid told Claybourne that the old man had emptied his own bedpan again. For such a skinny old mutha fuckin' bag of bones, the old dude could sure raise some hell.

"Corpsman!" Claybourne yelled. "Corpsman!"

A man in tropical whites stuck his head out of the TV room at the far end of the ward. "What ya want, Claybourne?"

"Better get your ass down here, man. This crazy ol' man be at it again."

"Be right there." The corpsman turned his back, drawn by a wave of laughter coming from the darkened TV room.

The old man's throat rattled like the last dregs of a milkshake being sucked through a straw.

"Groat!" Claybourne howled. "God damn it, Groat, you get your buns down here, man. Right now! I ain't puttin' up with anymore of your jive, boy. Right now, Groat, you hear?"

Slowly, the corpsman named Groat backed out of the TV room. Claybourne heard a tearing of adhesive tape and knew the old man had freed himself from the IV needle in his arm. Same ol' shit, every damn time.

Groat took his own sweet time walking the length of the ward. By the time he reached the two occupied beds, Claybourne was ready to kill.

"Man, Claybourne," Groat grinned, "you're missing a great show. That Gilligan's a real crack up. See, he was tryin' ta build a radio out of some—"

"Don't be jivin' me about no mutha fuckin' Gilligum, Jack. Just take care of this old fuck like you suppose to. Goddamn! Piss and blood all over, man. And listen to him, man! Listen! Dude is dyin', man, and all you be doin' is shuckin' me about some mutha fuckin' TV show!"

No way to be spending a Saturday night. No way.

Groat laughed. "All this rest and relaxation is gettin' to you, Claybourne. Be cool, bro. Another week and you'll be ambulatory. Then you can watch the tube too, right along with the rest of the ward."

The old man went into a gagging fit that sounded to Claybourne like the man's insides were coming apart. The corpsman finally seemed to realize that the old man was there.

"Well, good evening, Mr. Piplin. What seems to be the problem? You missed a good meal tonight. Saturday night is steak night, ya know. Bet they never served steak back when you were a sailor, did they?"

The old man croaked something between coughs and continued to thrash at his sheets. Groat gently but firmly pushed the man's shoulders back down, then felt for the man's pulse.

"Pulse is a little fast there, Walter. Shouldn't be overexerting yourself like this. Oh-oh. Looks like you've pulled your IV out again." Groat held up the needle under the old man's nose. "How are you going to get better if you keep tearing out your IV? I'm going to have to get the nurse. You be a good boy, OK? If you need anything just ask Claybourne here. He'll help you."

Freddy blinked in disbelief as Groat wandered off the ward in the direction of the nurses' lounge. He made a mental note to look Groat up with a baseball bat as soon as the arm healed.

This hospital shit was driving him crazy.

The first few days had been great; having a hero on the ward had been a novelty and the whole staff, from the orthopedic surgeon on down had treated him with respect. The lieutenant and the gunny had paid a visit, telling him about the meritorious promotion to corporal and the recommendation for the medal.

The guys from the section had come to see him too. Slicks had brought some homemade fried chicken, and the crazy-assed Dutchman smuggled in a bottle of cherry brandy. Tasted like shit but what the hell.

The biggest surprise of all though came when Shandy swayed in. Man! He'd figured it was all over at that point; the way he was trussed up she could slice him before anyone was the wiser. He expected a snarling tiger but got something else instead. She held his hand for half an hour, and even though it was hard to forget how she'd suckered him at the wedding reception, this time it really seemed like she meant it when she asked his forgiveness. Even with pain killers in his body dribbling marshmallows in his brain, he felt things hardenin' up. When she leaned over to kiss him good-bye, dragging her breasts across his chest, he'd groaned and drew his knees up to keep folks from seein' how she'd gotten to him.

His hospital honeymoon had ended after he'd been in the bed for about a week. Oh, he remembered it real good. It was the night they brought in the old wino, stinking and nearly dead, and dumped him in the bed next to his. The old man had been found on the beach, three breaths from qualifying for a VA financed hole in the ground. Things had been downhill for Freddy ever since.

Fewer and fewer visitors showed up. Suddenly Freddy Claybourne the hero became Freddy Claybourne the jarhead next to the old wino. The hospital staff seemed to lump the two of them together, maybe 'cause they were the only two patients on the ward who had to stay in bed.

"Please gimme back my pens. Gotta have my pens!" the old man groaned softly.

Freddy did a slow burn. In a few moments, he knew, the old dude would go ape again, and the corpsman and nurse were still nowhere to be seen.

"Gimme my pens!" The old man began to gurgle.

"Shit, mutha fuck," Freddy snarled. "Old man, you go dinky-dow on me, I'm gonna shove this cast up your ass." He managed to reach over to the bed table next to him and fumbled through the open drawer. "Here, you old shit, here's a goddamn pen!"

The black government-issue ballpoint landed on the sheet over the old man's chest. The gurgling stopped and Claybourne watched twisted fingers lovingly caress the plastic barrel. The old man rolled his eyes in Freddy's direction; there was a glimmer of thanks there.

Freddy reached for his radio. A fucking medal, he thought. About time he got some recog from the Crotch. The Green Machine owed him a damn medal, had since that day on the ridgeline. . . .

The company had been digging in when he got hit. Funny, he's always wondered what it would be like to get shot, but the real thing was nothing like he'd imagined. One second he was shoveling out his hole, bitching about something or other; an instant later he was sitting on his butt. He hadn't heard the shot, in fact, the first thing he'd thought of was that the company gunny had decked him for mouthing off. Goddamn! Felt like he'd been side-swiped by a truck. He remembered sitting there waiting for the gunny to start yelling at him, but all he could hear was a ringing that sent vibrations through his body. It was like maybe sitting inside an empty dumpster while someone pounded on the outside with a sledgehammer.

Then, through the ringing, he'd heard Hemphill yelling for a corpsman. Somebody must've gotten hurt. He wanted to get up and see what the fuss was about but he was too tired, his muscles didn't want to work anymore and his shoulder . . . his shoulder felt numb, as though not a part of him at all. Hemphill would just have to finish the hole on his own.

Suddenly the gunny was staring into his eyes. The man's lips were moving, but he couldn't understand the words; he was still inside the dumpster. The gunny looked worried. Well, shit, he shouldn't be going around punching the grunts so damn hard, just for a little bitching.

Then he'd felt gentle hands pulling at his utility shirt, undressing him. He'd looked around, looked down at his shoulder. Bright blood oozed from a quarter-sized hole. In him? No, had to be somebody else. No way Freddy Claybourne could get shot, no way. He was too cool to get shot.

The surgeon at China Beach told him he'd been lucky. The bullet had gone through clean. Couple of weeks and he was good as new, and back with the company.

He'd gone up to battalion S-1 looking for his Heart. The battalion's Awards and Decorations Officer, a fish belly lieutenant with no time in the field, told him there would be no medal. Well, why the fuck was that, he wanted to know. Because there was no evidence that it was an enemy bullet that had hit him. Might have been a friendly, lot of ARVN working the same area. Might have been another Marine. Couldn't be awarded a Purple Heart without evidence. Why, if the battalion wasn't careful, they'd be faced with troops demanding Purple Hearts for getting in fist fights or cutting themselves on C-ration cans. Had to control these things or the medal would be worthless.

He'd thought about the still-fresh hole in his flesh, thought about the first sergeant over in Kilo Company who'd gotten a Heart for tripping over a tent peg and skinning his knee, thought about the lieutenant in India who'd gotten one for a dog bite, then called the S-1 a no-good, mutha fuckin', ass-lickin' cocksucker. So instead of the medal, all he'd gotten was a bust to buck private. The Crotch owed him, no doubt about it.

"Mr. Piplin, are we going to have to tie you down? Claybourne, turn down that radio. Groat, get a mop and clean this up." The duty nurse had arrived.

Freddy turned and watched her poke the old man with a new IV needle. It was not easy; the old fuck was about out of veins.

"Can't you move him someplace else?" Claybourne whined. "Man can't get no rest with that dude goin' crazy all the time. Put him down the other end of the ward. Ain't nobody down there."

"Don't tell us how to do our jobs, Claybourne," the horse-faced woman answered. "He's here so he can be closer to the nurse's station." Her sharp-angled figure was all wrapped in a heavily starched uniform that crinkled everytime she moved. "Besides," she continued, "Mr. Piplin will be leaving us shortly for a VA hospital in Miami. Do you hear that, Walter? You're going to be leaving us soon. But you can't go until you get some strength back, and you can't do that if you keep pulling out your IV."

The old man fingered his pen and said nothing.

The nurse finished patching up her patient, and after insuring that Groat was cleaning up the bedpan spill, she left the ward. Moments later, Freddy was getting in a little needle of his own.

"Hey, Groat," he snickered, "how you like moppin' up piss?"

"Shut up, Claybourne. Next week or so, you'll be doing it."

"My ass. You ain't puttin' me ta work like these other dudes, man. Freddy Claybourne don't do no janitor work."

"That's what you think," the corpsman chuckled as he rung out the mop in a bucket of water. "Ambulatory patients have to participate in field days, that's hospital policy."

"Yeah? What you gonna do if I don't?"

"Nurse will call your XO and tell him you're not obeying a direct order. Could get you a Captain's Mast."

Freddy was about to challenge the Navy's right to put him to work sweeping floors and cleaning toilets while his arm was in a cast, when the double doors at the entrance to the ward opened and another corpsman came in leading a patient decked out in pajamas and robe and those faggoty little slippers they made you wear whenever you got outta bed.

The two of them were passing the foot of Claybourne's bed when the patient stopped and stared at him. The man's face seemed sorta familiar, a young guy with a scraggly-assed beard and a faraway look in his eyes like he'd been hypnotized or drugged. Freddy nervously watched as the patient began to come toward him with a strange stiff-legged shuffle. The dude's hands were outstretched and formed into claws, as if reaching for Claybourne's face. The man was almost to the side of the bed when Groat finally noticed him.

"Hey, Smitty," Groat yelled to the second corpsman. "You forgot something."

The second corpsman jogged back and grabbed the patient by the collar of his blue and white hospital robe. The man was led away to the TV room.

"What's with him?" Freddy asked Groat. "Man, dude looked crazier'n hell. Be comin' at me like he knowed me."

Groat rested his chin on the mop handle. "Yeah, poor shit's psycho, or at least he was. Came back from noon chow one day and went after his petty officer with a chisel. Been under lock and key on Ward D since July." He pointed at the ceiling. "They bring him down from the Funny Farm Saturday nights to see McHale's Navy. Doc says its good therapy."

"Yeah, well, better keep him away from me, man. Looked like he wanted ta mess me up."

"Who? Crabtree you mean?" Groat laughed. "He's so drugged up he can't hold his own fork. Anyways, you've got nothing to worry about. Pretty soon he'll be going back to duty. You'll never see him again."

With the slop of the mop, Groat got back to his clean up. The old wino had fallen asleep, the pen clutched tightly in his hands, his snores loud and regular. Freddy turned up his radio and munched on some cookies Shandy had brought him the day before. Yeah, he thought, Crotch definitely owed him a medal, if only for surviving crazy shits, stray bullets, and four mutha fuckin' years of bullshit. From now on, though, he was going to coast on home.

CHAPTER EIGHTEEN

A few miles from where Freddy lay in a Navy hospital bed soaking up the sounds of a Miami soul station, the door to the long narrow hole in the wall that was Angelo's Cafe was tied open, an informal invitation to anybody passing by on Duval to come in off the sidewalk for a drink and (if the sign in the big bay window was to be believed) to welcome "The One and Only" Boots Sugarbush back to Key West.

By Saturday night standards it was still fairly early when Slater and Carolyn walked into Angelo's. Though most of the bar stools up front around the piano and small bandstand were occupied, they found an empty table close to the action. The juke played softly and the candle in the red glass hurricane lamp on the table flickered in the gentle breeze coming in off the street. Slater figured somebody sharp could've made it into a movie—it was that good.

"Can you see OK?" he asked.

"Twenty-twenty last time I had them checked," she answered.

"Very funny. I meant the piano."

"I can see a lot of heads. Who is this guy supposed to be, Ray Charles?"

"Almost, at least in this town. You'll dig him, I guarantee it. I heard him play before he went up north to cut a record. Guy is definitely smooth."

A waitress, peroxide blonde pushing a hard thirty-five, interrupted, "What'll ya'll have?" she asked the wall.

Slater tried to sound casual. "Ah, bring me whatever you've got on draft, and—what do you want, Carolyn?"

"A Cuba libre."

"Ya'll got some ID?" the waitress asked, glancing out in the street at two men holding hands while dodging traffic. She shook her head and took the driver's license Carolyn had pulled from a hip pocket.

"OK, honey," the waitress said after a quick look. "How about you, handsome?"

Slater patted his pockets and pretended surprise, "Hell," he said, "must've left it back on base. Gee, I'm sorry lady, but don't worry, I'm legal."

"Can't serve ya without no ID." The waitress sounded bored. She watched the two men reach the sidewalk safely and begin to skip arm and arm toward the middle of town.

"Hey, come on, give me a break," Slater said. "I left it in my other pants." He slipped a five dollar bill onto the table and nudged it towards the waitress. "I sure would hate ta waste a lotta time goin' back ta get it."

The waitress's fingers flicked out and snatched the bill away. "That's a draft and a Cuba libre coming right up," she said.

Relieved, Slater eased back in his chair and watched the woman make her way to the bar. When he looked over at Carolyn, she seemed amused.

"Don't you have any fake ID?" she whispered.

"Never needed one. About the only place we go drinking is the Bamboo, and your aunt don't give a damn if we're twenty-one or not."

"Thought you said you heard this Boots character play here before?"

"Yeah. We sat out there on the curb. Me and Dutch. Heard a whole set before the cops chased us away. How's the job hunt going?"

Carolyn frowned. "Great, if I wanted to sell my body to shrimp boat crews and sailors. Otherwise there's not much available."

"So what are you going to do?"

"I don't know. Just keep drawing unemployment, I guess."

"Nice work if you can get it."

Carolyn's eyes narrowed. "You know something? You're a real smart-ass sometimes."

Slater laughed. "Smart enough ta know better'n ta get into it with you. Sorry, guess maybe I'm a little jealous."

"Of what?"

"You know, that *Easy Rider* stuff. Bein' able to live on the move, no problems, go where you want ta go and get Uncle Sam ta pay the bills."

"He doesn't pay much."

"You're telling me. I'm a corporal, remember? Garbage men make more than I do."

She looked at him real hard. "So why don't you quit?"

"Oh yeah, I wish. Naw, see, I got what you might call an ironclad contract with 'em."

"So? Contracts can be broken."

"Not this kind. Not unless I wanna play hide and seek with the FBI for the rest of my life. Nope, eighteen months left, and I'm stuck with it."

"God, that's so unfair!" She sounded angry. "Shit, you've already been to Vietnam for them. What more do they want?"

"Hey, don't blow your gourd over it—just the way it is."

Civilians would never understand, Slater thought, how different the world was in the Corps—no retreat, no compromise, no quarter given or expected.

"Gonna have ta leave," a voice like splitting granite said.

Three hundred pounds of beef on the hoof was suddenly standing next to the table. Slater looked up at a face that could stop clocks, maybe even freight locomotives with no engineer. He wondered how a human nose could be so fucked-up and still function.

Without much hope of success, he tried to ignore the monster. "Yeah, you're gonna like old Boots Sugarbush, Carolyn. Puts on a real good show."

"I said you gonna have ta leave."

The monster's hand, all twenty-five pounds of it, spread

out on the table. There was a tattoo of a black widow spider that was kinda neat, but Slater kept his eyes on Carolyn. He felt the beginnings of something rolling deep inside him.

"The lady ain't interested in buyin' any art work tonight, pal," he said. "Take a hike."

"I don't care what the lady is interested in, burrhead, *you* gotta go." The giant's voice alone, Slater decided, could strain ligaments. "Come on and be a sweety. Angelo he don't like no rough stuff in his place."

The black widow left the table and Slater followed it up to a thick chrome-studded black belt that went around a belly as big as Yellowstone. The buckle was a silver skull with eyes of ruby glass. Slater spoke to the skull, not all that keyed to look at the guy's face again.

"Some kinda problem?" he asked.

"No ID, no drink. No drink, no show."

"I got an ID."

"LuEllen says ya don't."

"Left it in the pocket of my other pants. I told her that."

"Well, you go on home ta mama and git it then. The tail here can save your seat till ya get back."

"You asshole," Carolyn snapped. "You big ugly asshole!"

The table seemed to lift off the floor by itself. It floated along horizontally for a few feet, then came down as gently as it had risen.

"That's it," the monster growled. "Both of yas, git yer butts outta here now."

Carolyn was ready to stay and fight. "Screw you!" she said, pretty damn loudly.

Slater could see the evening going down the tubes. "Come on, Carolyn," he said, "let's split. It's not worth the hassle."

"That's right, lady. Take your filthy mouth somewheres else."

"Fascist pig!"

"Who you callin' a pig, cunt? Get your ass outta here."
Guy sounded like he was reciting weather statistics.

"Watch your mouth, pal," Slater said. A nice solid hit of
adrenaline had dried out his tongue; his voice was a croak.

"Ugly asshole," Carolyn continued. Slater wondered if
she had a death wish. "Bet he tears the heads off chickens
for his kicks!" Her eyes were flashing pure hate.

"Goddamn hippie bitch," the goon complained, his voice
rising. "I oughta kick your ass."

"Knock it off!" Slater pushed his chair back and stood
up. All he could see was about five hundred miles of chest.
"We're going, don't sweat it."

The face looked down at him and Slater noticed a
mean-looking scar that went from the corner of the guy's
mouth all the way down to the third chin.

"I don't sweat nothin', peckerhead," the cruel face
warned. "You an' yer twat better get outta here before I bust
up both of ya."

"If your mother commits suicide, I don't blame her!"
Carolyn yelled.

The bouncer's growl was prehistoric. He made a lunge at
her, had her wrist in his grasp and a fist cocked for airmail
delivery when the hurricane lamp from the table was
rammed into his face. His growl was replaced by a scream
of horrible agony as broken glass sliced flesh and melted
candle was splattered into nooks and crannies and folds of
skin, there to slowly solidify as nerve endings and tissue
absorbed its heat. The monster fell to his knees, his fingers
clawing at the bloody wax.

Slater looked down at the remains of the hurricane lamp
in his hand, then tossed it aside. He'd cut himself; couldn't
tell how badly but there was no pain, only a warm iciness.
What the hell. He pivoted and slammed a fist into the
bouncer's kisser, felt teeth and meat breaking, then stepped
back and kicked the guy full force in the nuts, about like
going for a fifty yard field goal—more than enough height
and distance.

The huge man crumpled to the deck like his bones had all turned to gelatin, then lay whimpering in a growing pool of his own blood.

Slater caught a glimpse of Carolyn's face as he was dragged away by half a dozen rough hands toward the door. Her mouth was open in astonishment, her eyes riveted on the sobbing monster. Well what the hell did she expect, a nice bloodless fist fight between Roy Rogers and Black Bart?

"Come on, Carolyn," he heard himself say, "this place sucks."

For a moment he was being launched into free flight, then the sidewalk came up to greet him in an explosion of pain. He blacked out for a second, came to in the gutter, his nose inches from a soggy cigar butt.

"Better get him out of here, lady," he heard a voice say, "before Waldo gets his shit together. Waldo's real funny when it comes to his face."

"Jack, are you all right?" He felt gentle fingers touch his back. She helped him sit up.

The street spun a little but her arms held him steady. For a second he couldn't remember where he was. Her voice came through the fog, close to his ear.

"God, look at your hand! It's bleeding! We'd better get you to a doctor."

"I'll be OK," he managed. "No sweat."

"Here ya go, gyrene, use this." A handkerchief appeared in front of Slater's face. He took it, awkwardly wrapped it around the hand, then looked up at a chubby, olive-skinned, balding man wearing a bib apron and one gold loop earring. Guy looked concerned.

"Much as I'd like to serve you, kid," the man said, "I'd lose my license in a minute. There's two state undercover badges in there right now, just watering at the mouth to catch me serving a minor."

"Yeah, I can understand that," Slater said, feeling very logical all at once despite the cobwebs.

"Your bouncer's a real goon," Carolyn said to the man as she tied a knot in the handkerchief.

"He's not my bouncer, hon. Waldo likes to throw his weight around. Thinks it'll land him a job somewheres. He's too damn mean, though; nobody in their right mind will hire him. Listen kid, you and your lady come back when the season's done. Have one on the house."

Slater slowly got to his feet. "Thanks. Maybe we'll do that."

"Just ask for Angelo. That's me. Try ta remember me the next time I pass through your gate. I cater a lot of functions out there, and sometimes I lose my pass, know what I mean? Last time you made me go all the way back to the Main Gate to get another one."

"Didn't mean to start nothin' in there, man," Slater said. "Just that guy was going after—"

A blast from a car horn interrupted him, and he shifted around to see a long white stretch Cadillac pulling up to the curb. Angelo wiped his hands on his apron and headed back into the bar, jabbering to himself the whole way.

"Well, what do ya know," he mumbled, "only forty-five minutes late. Wasn't expecting his holiness till at least midnight."

Two young black men in turquoise tuxedos climbed out of the front seat of the limo and began unrolling a red carpet from the car across the sidewalk and into the bar. Both of them returned to the car and stood on either side of the passenger door. The door opened and a striking young black woman with long blond hair climbed out, followed by a roly-poly black man done up in a silk brocade dinner jacket and a long black cape. In one hand he held a walking stick, in the other a pair of gray velvet gloves. He paused to look up and down the sidewalk, let his eyes dance over Slater and Carolyn as if they weren't there, then, as the two men in turquoise bowed deeply, strode into the bar with the blonde on his arm. A round of applause greeted him, and

Slater caught a glimpse of swirling cape just as Carolyn poked him in the ribs.

"Who is *that*?" she asked. "The King of Nigeria?"

He tried to laugh; a sharp pain from his ribs held it in. "That's Boots Sugarbush. Sure knows how to make an entrance, don't he?"

"You'd think he'd won the Nobel prize or something."

"Nope. Only cut a record up in Miami. He's just a hometown boy back from the wars."

The applause and whistles that had errupted from inside the bar as soon as the musician had crossed the threshold were replaced by the plinking of piano notes in a burst of energetic high registry that reminded Slater of a cross between Jerry Lee Lewis and Little Richard. He watched Carolyn's face for some sign that yeah, it'd all been worth it.

"What do you think?" he finally asked, nodding toward the bar.

"I've heard better."

Just what he wanted to hear. "Want to go?" Standing on the curb just out of reach of the heavy traffic on Duval suddenly seemed pretty dumb.

"Not unless you do," she answered.

"You worried about Waldo?"

Her head snapped in his direction and she gave him a long, penetrating stare. "No. You're the one I'm worried about."

"What? This?" He held up the bandaged hand. "I'll be just fine."

"I don't mean that. It's just . . ." She paused for a moment. "I can't believe what you did to that guy. You could've killed him."

He shrugged. What was he supposed to say?

She shook her head as though she was not getting through to him. She was frowning but he could only think of how goddamn attractive she was. He studied the hair on her arm, golden fuzz, angel's hair.

"I'm sorry," he said. "Come on, I'll buy you a cup of coffee. Don't have to be twenty-one for that."

She dusted off the seat of her tight jeans. He could not tear his eyes away from the smooth curves the jeans formed and was forced to take a deep breath as he imagined what the fabric was hiding.

"I've got a better idea," she whispered, slipping her hand into his and leading him down the sidewalk. "Let's go back to the apartment."

He answered with a gulp.

Boots Sugarbush's music serenaded them for the next three blocks. Slater didn't hear a note.

The noise from downstairs was muffled but still seeped through open windows and thin wooden floorboards. Saturday night at the Bamboo Room crescendoed about two A.M. and the beginning of the long slide toward dawn began. Carolyn took another hit from her joint, passed it over to Slater, then leaned back into the couch. A bottle of vodka sat on the coffee table in front of her. All was right with the world.

"My dad works hard," she heard him say. "Ain't easy running a gas station. Ain't easy at all."

He had been going on and on about his family for hours—months—years. She sighed, knowing he would be back to his brother in a moment, continuing a pattern that had become all too easy to follow.

"Marty don't understand that, ya know? How come he don't understand that, Carolyn? How come he's gotta give the old man such grief?"

"I don't know," she said, suspecting he was probably not interested in an answer. He was just mumbling in his beard. Only he didn't have a beard; didn't have much hair anywhere. She laughed.

"What?" he asked.

Hair didn't matter. She liked him. Why did she like him? He was nice, that was it. At first she hadn't thought he was so nice, but he'd been nice at the beach and later down at the dock, and he liked sunsets. He hadn't been so nice in the bar tonight, though—God, not nice at all! How did he know she loved snow cones?

"Why did you go?" she heard herself asking.

"Why did I go where?"

"Vietnam. Steve says any fool could get out of the draft."

"Wasn't drafted; I enlisted. . . . Who's Steve?"

"You mean you volunteered? Why would you do that?"

"Because it was what I *had* ta do. Who's Steve?"

"A creep. A real goddamned creep. Thought he was God's gift to women just because he could play the guitar and had nice teeth. You've got nice teeth too, did you know that? Are you God's gift to women?"

"Not that I ever noticed. Tried to learn guitar once, though. Couldn't do it. Marty—my brother—he plays. He's good. I taught him to play baseball, ya know? We used ta play catch all night in the summer, under the streetlights. He hates me now. Why ya think he hates me?"

"Maybe because you went," she offered.

"I went 'cause I had to; went so he wouldn't."

"Spare me the propaganda."

"Sure," he giggled, "anything you say."

"Did you like it?" she asked cautiously, imagining Waldo's face after the lamp had crashed into it.

"Hell no! Are you crazy? It sucked, really sucked. Nobody over here knows how much it sucked, never will."

"Some of us do," she said, feeling very noble. "We marched and demonstrated. Some even went to jail—"

"Excuse me," he interrupted. "Six hours in the local lockup. Big fuckin' deal. Try strappin' it on for twelve months." He waved a hand listlessly, as if to dismiss the subject.

"You don't know what you're talking about," she said, feeling a little insulted as well as angry that she was letting another man get under her skin.

He looked at her; there was pain in his eyes. "Everybody thinks we're dirt, dummies, scum. You blame *us*! How come?"

"You're sick," she said, surprised at the hurt in his voice, "really sick."

"So what else is new?" Suddenly he was smiling.

She decided she didn't want to talk about the war anymore. It was perfectly obvious how he felt. Well, come to think of it, not perfectly obvious at all, quite the opposite.

What *was* perfectly obvious was that the joint was gone, burned away in enlightening smoke. He was still nice, she decided, even though he was screwed up.

"Rose warned me not to go out with you." It was her turn to giggle.

He seemed startled. "Why not? I thought she liked me."

"She likes you fine. She just said not to get involved with you—with any of you."

"Marines, ya mean?"

"I guess."

"Why?"

"She didn't say why."

"That's weird," he said. "She treats us all like a den mother, for Christ's sake. Man, I thought she was in love with the Crotch."

"The Crotch?" She giggled again.

"Crotch is what we call the Corps. How come you're here?"

"Here?" She glanced around the room, confused by his question. "This is where I live."

"No, no, why are you in this boonie town?"

She hesitated before answering. Why was she here? Because Mom had died? Because school had left her feeling empty and alone? Because Steve had dropped her for a pig with big jugs? She was here, she realized, because there was no place else to go.

"Because it's the end of the world," she whispered.

He has a nice face, she thought. Nice—was that the best

she could do? She was supposed to be an English major. "Nice" was all she could come up with? Hell of a vocabulary. Nice, nice, everything was nice.

"Can I kiss you?" he asked.

"That'd be nice." She laughed hard at that, roared in fact. Everything was nice.

His lips were dry. The first brush of a kiss felt like sandpaper. There was no pressure, only a touching. She opened her eyes and stared at the end of his nose. He broke away from her.

He kissed her again. This time it was better. She reached out to him and pulled him close; her long lost teddy bear had been returned. Breath, hot and warm, music through the floor, a tongue caressing her teeth. Even through the fabric of her clothes, skin sensitive to his touch. So nice.

Falling, falling, down, smelling her own sleep in the pillow. Tingling. Her breasts now bare, tingling. Arch in her back, up to meet him. Was she purring? Was that why a cat purred? Little electric shocks all traversing her body, coming together between her legs where the sea rolled. It should never end.

Steve, you son of a bitch, never like this with you. He's so gentle, body so pale, so pleasant to touch. You were nothing, Steve, all grunts and groans, a pig.

She sensed a gentle tug at her hips; a breeze tickled her bare legs—cool, stimulating, a thousand tiny fingers busily coaxing her skin to vibrate. Muscles stretched taut, relaxed, then stretched again in response to sensory pleasure while pastel colors swirled behind her eyes, a moving flow of abstract shapes, all wet and warm.

The touch of his lips gone; her only contact with him gone. She opened her eyes and raised her head, fearful he had left her. Then she heard a rustle of clothing and saw him between her knees, naked as she was, glowing somehow in a halo of light. She extended a foot; her toes touched his hardness and she heard him gasp. Tit for tat, she thought.

He moved slightly and her eyes hurt. The lamp behind him was blinding her.

"Turn out the light," she whispered.

And he did.

The walk back to the base had never been so short. He'd wanted to stay with her all night, to rest forever with his head on her breast, her heartbeats close to his ear, a lullaby. But hell, Rose lived there too. He'd had to get out before she closed downstairs. Damn funny what Carolyn had said about Rose, about her not wanting Carolyn to let things get too serious with him, with any of them. No way to figure it.

He turned up Southard for the Main Gate.

"Well, what do ya know," Bone Tollster said as Slater approached the sentry post, "here's Kool Dude with a shit eatin' grin on his face at zero dark thirty in the mornin'. Come take a look, Slicks, look at this dude. His tongue's hangin' out for shit's sake. Least I think it's his tongue."

"Ain't he somethin'," Johnson said, peering out around the corner of the shack. "Whang bang doodly screw, do that thing till it turn dark blue."

"What's with you guys?" Slater couldn't keep the grin off his face.

"How you like this dude?" Slicks said to Tollster. "His buddies are standin' watch while he's out with the ladies."

"Was it worth it, Slats?" Tollster asked.

"Worth what?" Slater put one foot up on the island.

"The twenty-five bucks you paid Hollenback to change duties with ya."

"How'd you know about that?"

"Little VC told us," Slicks chuckled.

"What else did he tell you?"

"Nothing much," Tollster answered slyly. "Course, couple of guys from Port Section passed through here a while ago. Said they saw you holdin' hands with the Crack's niece tonight. Out on Duval."

"Woo-wee! Get some, Jack!" Johnson slapped his knee.

"You guys are full of it."

"How come you're smilin' then?"

"I'm not smilin'," Slater laughed.

"Man, chow hall food gonna taste mighty bland after tonight, Slats. Once you tasted home-cooked chicken, ya know, messhall meat loaf don't make it no more." Slicks began making obscene slurping sounds with his lips.

"I gotta get outta here," Slater moaned, "before the little men in white coats come and take you guys away."

"Hey? Where ya going, man?" Tollster called as Slater stepped off the island and walked to the sidewalk across the street.

"Barracks," Slater answered. "Hollenback only took Saturday night for me. I got the eight to twelve today. Gotta get some sleep."

"Ain't you gonna tell your buddies what happened?"

"Yeah," Slicks jumped in, "and don't leave out none a the sloppy little details, boy!"

"What's the matter, Slicks, not gettin' enough at home?"

"Never too old ta learn somethin' new, man," Slicks teased. "So when you gonna go public with this lady a yours?"

"Next week at the Birthday Ball," Slater shouted over his shoulder, already headed for home. "Goodnight, girls. We can shoot the shit again in the morning."

He knew if he hung around any longer he'd be tempted to tell stories . . . and that would ruin everything.

CHAPTER NINETEEN

UNREAL, Dutch. Definitely unreal.

Slater watched Van Groot stagger halfway across the crowded dance floor, juggling three drinks and growling like Yosemite Sam with a hardon at anyone who got in his way. Guy was absolutely wasted, hammered, shit-faced. Hard to tell how he was still able to see.

Had to give the little dude credit, though; last guy in the world you'd expect to show up at the Crotch's birthday party in dress blues. Dress blue was the only uniform a Marine wasn't issued; a man had to buy dress blues out of his own pocket at almost two hundred bucks a pop. There wasn't ten men at the Barracks (except the "lifers") with dress blues, but here was the groadiest and grungiest of them all looking like he'd just stepped off a recruiting poster. The little nutcase had even spit-shined his shoes. So what if he'd been knocking back gin and tonics since four that afternoon?

Slater groaned as Van Groot sloshed one of the drinks on a fat woman in pink who was trying awfully hard to jitterbug to the thumping beat of "Proud Mary."

"Your friend's not doing too well," Carolyn said from beside him. She had to shout to be heard over the music coming from the Boots Sugarbush Combo up on the stage at the other end of the hall.

Slater saw Van Groot plunge into the crowd on the opposite side of the dance floor. Guy was lost . . . again. "He's doin' *too* well, that's the problem. Thanks ta Rose he was bombed three hours before he got here."

He glanced over at Carolyn who sat next to him at one of

fifty folding banquet tables set up for this shindig. For about the hundredth time that night, felt like he was going to melt down into a puddle of warm goo just looking at her.

You wanted to talk "fox," here it was, like one of those perfect airbrush jobs out of *Playboy*. Her dress, made on Rose's old Singer from a bolt of hand-printed fabric straight from the factory out on Simonton, was molded to her body like a sprayed-on bouquet of tropical flowers, and her hair hung to the middle of her back, golden highlights reflecting under the hall's overhead lights. He studied her ear, perfect and fragile; smelled the perfume and wished ta hell they were alone.

"It was just Rose's way of celebrating," she said, looking at him with those eyes that made his trousers feel three sizes too tight. "Told me she's always been too embarrassed to come to these things so she makes up for it with a party at the Bamboo."

"Yeah, but hard liquor at twenty-five cents a shot? That's like giving baby the whole candy store."

"Nobody forced him," she said, turning her attention to the blowout going on in front of them.

The bulkheads and overhead of the Mallory Square Community Hall had been decked out in red and yellow bunting for the Crotch's birthday celebration, but the decorations couldn't hide the cavernlike feel of the place. Even with all the shit the Barracks maintenance crew had hung, glued, tied, and nailed up, the joint still looked like a decorated airplane hangar. Hadn't stopped the partygoers, though. Place was packed to the gunwales.

The dance floor was choked with men in tuxedos or fancy Navy dress uniforms and women in formal gowns that went all the way from prom-queen ruffles and petticoats to state-of-the-art micro-mini. The Marines, most like Slater in tropical khaki uniforms, stood out in the crowd like dusty gate crashers.

"I still don't believe I'm here," Carolyn said, shaking her head. "This is a new low for me—a Nixon fund-raiser."

"Hey," Slater said, grinning so she'd know he was joking, "just like Dutch—nobody forced you."

"Nobody forced me like hell! You and Rose did a number on me, wiseguy. What else was I going to do, huh, after she stayed up three nights in a row making this dress? And the whole time you're telling me this was just going to be the guys getting together for a little party. Well, look what I got." She gestured out at the crowd with a sweep of an arm. "Prom night for Hitler."

He didn't know if she was serious or not, and decided he didn't much care. She was here, that was all that mattered, and he was enjoying himself. Damn! If she wasn't the best looking woman in the whole place, he'd—

Three half-empty plastic cocktail glasses were slammed down on the table, splashing booze and surprising the hell out of him. The Dutchman had returned.

"Wisht you people'd quit movin' around so much," Van Groot complained. "I been all over this dog'n pony show lookin' for ya."

"Swear we ain't moved an inch since you left," Slater answered, putting a hand over his mouth to hide the grin.

Van Groot slid into an empty chair on the other side of the table. It took a moment for his eyes to focus. He smiled at Carolyn.

"Havin' a good time, bitch?" he bellowed.

Carolyn ignored him, as she'd done all evening. She took a sip of her drink. Immediately her face bunched up.

"Good God!" she shouted across at the Dutchman. "What is this shit?"

"Just what ya ordered, baby," he answered, "Scotch'n Coke." Van Groot's smile remained fixed; his eyes closed in pride. They stayed closed for so long Slater was afraid the little shit had passed out.

Carolyn put her glass down and edged it across the table. "*Rum* and Coke, Eric. I wanted *rum* and Coke."

Van Groot's eyes popped open, wide. He reached over and took her glass. "Rum'n Coke?" he asked, sounding bewildered. "Rum'n Coke?" He stared at the dark liquid for a second or two, then chugged what was left, smacked his lips, and slammed the empty glass down so hard that the plastic split. "Yer right, little Crack, damn if it ain't rum'n Coke. I'll go get ya the right one." With that, the Dutchman was on his feet, heading back to the open bar.

"He's positively unreal," Carolyn finally managed.

"Ain't that the truth. Come on, let's dance."

They got up and walked to the dance floor, hand in hand.

On the other side of the hall, at another of the long banquet tables that'd taken most of the day to set up, Screamin' Don ran a finger inside the stiff white collar insert of his blues and tried to be inconspicuous as he checked his watch. Twenty-one forty. Another twenty minutes and the cake cutting ceremony would start. As soon as that business was over, he and Peg could take off. Babysitter was already costing him a goddamn arm and a leg.

A town councilman's wife (he couldn't remember her name) tugged at his sleeve. She was ripped pretty good and fading fast.

"Where's that darling wife of yours, Captain? I was gonna give her ma secret recipe for Key Lime pie."

"Indisposed at the moment, ma'am. In the powder room, I think."

"Oh." The woman took a long swallow from her glass. "Mebbe then I could give it to you," she said with a little mischief. "Would you like the secret to ma pie, Captain?"

Hell, he wasn't going to touch *that* with a ten-foot pole.

"Well, I'm gonna tell ya." She leaned over, almost fell off her chair. "Always make sure there's plenty ta go around," she whispered.

Sweet shit on Sunday! Brule felt a hand on his knee.

"Excuse me, won't you?" he said as he pushed back his chair and got up. "Have to check with the major. Ceremony is about to begin."

Goddamn civilians, Brule thought as he weaved his way

through the crowd. The Great Slack started with them, no doubt about it, and sometimes when they were all together like they were here, it made him want to puke. Soft and fat and completely worthless—all of 'em. What the hell were they doing celebrating with the Corps? This was a night for Marines, and Marines only. Why the hell the major had to invite all these goddamn civilians, he didn't know. Christ, they must be slopping down a few thousand dollars worth of booze alone. Goddamn fat-ass country club friends of Brocksneider would spend the night at a goddamn train wreck if the booze was free.

He made it to the head table where Major Brocksneider and his old lady sat like royalty between Admiral Bledsoe and Ernie Capaccino, who, Brule knew, was the major's bunghole buddy not to mention about the richest son of a bitch in the Keys. Brule also recognized the town mayor, the Monroe County Sheriff, and some poxy insurance salesman the major played golf with, all with their wives, girlfriends, or mistresses—who the hell knew, or cared.

The table was cluttered with a huge supply of glasses, ice, and bottles of the best liquor and mixers. While the open bar for the peons was mobbed three deep, the assholes sitting at this table only had to reach out for any drink their little hearts desired. The booze here had come out of the major's own pocket. By the looks of the labels on the bottles, he figured Brocksneider must've spent a small fortune impressing the Conch heavy hitters.

"Excuse me, sir," Brule said, leaning down so the major could hear him.

Brocksneider rolled his eyes and smiled. He was feeling no pain. "Hello, Don. Having a good time?"

"Yes, sir. Sorry to interrupt. The cake ceremony starts in about ten minutes. Did you want to get ready?"

The major blinked. "Hell, I thought we'd already done that. Haven't we already done that, Don?"

"No, sir."

"Joe Hollihan. Where's Joe Hollihan? Joe's the one in charge of the thing. He didn't get lost did he?"

"Sergeant major is outside, getting things organized. Do you want me to clear the decks?"

"Yeah! That's a good idea! Ten minutes, eh? Are you sure we didn't already do it?"

"Positive, sir."

"Okee Doak. Whatever you say . . . Oh, and Don, tell Joe to make damn sure that dog has relieved himself. I don't want what happened last year happening again." Brocksneider looked over at the mayor. "Damn mutt peed all over the dance floor."

The mayor chortled and pointed at his wife. "Lizabeth has the same problem, Tom."

Now how come I don't have any problem believing that, Screamin' Don thought to himself as he headed for the stage where he could announce it was time for everybody to sit down. Halfway there he had to duck and spin to get out of the way of some big tanned punk in a white tux who seemed to think the whole damn dance floor was a private spotlight. Goddamn civilians.

Slater was sweating like he'd just run a mile in a steambath when he got back to the table. Carolyn wasn't even breathing hard, dry as a C-rat cracker. How the hell did she do that? He reached for the beer Dutch had brought him. Damn. Hadn't boogied like that since high school.

The crisp clear notes of "Attention" sounded from a bugle and the whole crowd fell silent—more out of surprise, Slater figured, than understanding. Taking their cue from the head table, everyone got to their feet.

In a way, the sound of the bugle had also surprised most of the Marines. They were used to the off-key notes of their own Corporal Gurtzer. This bugler was definitely something else; Big League. Slater had met the kid, a PFC named Coolidge who'd arrived wtih four other "boots" aboard a Navy C-130 out at Boca Chica Air Station a few

days before. The word was the major had an asshole buddy
who was running the Drum and Bugle School up at Lejeune
and Brocksneider had talked his way into getting the
five-man contingent sent down to the Barracks on a week's
TAD, just in time for the November 10th birthday of the
United States Marine Corps.

The bugle call ended and the hall's lights were dimmed;
a spotlight popped on the closed double doors of the
entrance. A snare drum (played by another boot from
Lejeune) began a long steady roll.

"What's going on?" Carolyn whispered.

"Cake's comin'," Slater said.

"All this fuss for a cake?"

"Sh-h-h. Just watch. It's a birthday, right?"

The drumroll stopped. The double doors opened and
Lieutenant Kargo and Screamin' Don, drawn swords glittering in the light, walked briskly into the hall and down the
center aisle, their uniforms a glittering spectacle of polished
chrome and brass. They were followed by three other pairs
of men in dress blues, the Barracks Staff NCOs. At intervals
of about ten yards, each pair broke off right and left, came
to a stop, then faced inward. A guarded corridor leading
from the entrance to the stage was formed.

From up on the stage a slash of light reflected off the
bugle as the kid named Coolidge brought his horn to his lips
and began to play the "Marine Corps Hymn" in slow time.
A cold icy shiver ran up Slater's spine. That tune could do
a number on ya anytime, but now—played like that—down
right scary was what it was.

The spotlight danced back to the entrance where it fell on
Sergeant Major Hollihan and the dog. The crusty old
Marine stood at rigid attention, his dress blues looking snug
around the waist. The dog, panting heavily, was also still,
the leash from his collar hanging limp in Hollihan's hand.

The two of them began walking down the aisle, heading
for the base of the stage where the major waited on unsteady
legs. Hollihan walked slowly, in time with the haunting

music, while the dog kept up as best he could. As they passed his table, Slater saw that Jiggs was wearing his blues, complete with a gold lance corporal chevron and a National Defense Medal. He could also see the rainbow of color that covered the left chest of the sergeant major's blue uniform. He'd never seen Hollihan wearing his medals before—row after row of medals—and he was surprised at how many of them he couldn't recognize . . . wars and battles fought before he was even born.

"This is too much," Carolyn whispered in a tone he didn't like, didn't like one bit. What the hell! Did she think this was all some cheap trick, some bit off "Laugh-In"?

He turned and looked her straight in the eye. For a second he felt a powerful loathing, hot and deep. Then he softened. How was she supposed to know? How could any of them who'd never worn the uniform be expected to know?

Carolyn turned away; his look had sent a heavy message.

Hollihan and the dog arrived in front of Brocksneider. The sergeant major saluted, then took his post two steps to the right-rear of the major. Jiggs followed. All three faced the entrance of the hall as the cake was wheeled in.

The cart carrying the cake was escorted by four more Marines. While it rolled down the aisle, Slater looked across the table where the Dutchman stood.

Life is images, a hundred million images, most lost after the first exposure. Some, a very few, last for days, months, even years. And there are a handful—maybe less—that stay with a person forever. Such an image now burned its way into Slater's memory.

Despite all the booze he'd put away, Van Groot had hauled himself to attention, back straight, head back, chin in. Still, he looked almost like a little kid to Slater, even with the bulge of tobacco in his cheek and that fresh high-and-tight haircut. Maybe it was because of the tear trickling down the Dutchman's cheek.

Dutch understands, Slater thought. Semper Fi, Choo Choo. Semper Fi, my man.

• • •

Major Brocksneider dug his sword into the cake and hacked out a three-inch square. As per tradition, the first piece belonged to the oldest Marine present so Hollihan held out a paper plate. Unfortunately, too many highballs had flowed over the major's decks. As he turned with the piece of cake balanced on the blade of his sword, it slipped off and landed with a soft splat at his feet.

The sergeant major didn't miss a beat. "Eat it, you sonofabitch," he growled quietly.

Jiggs ambled over and after an inquisitive sniff, began lapping up his reward . . . a reward, maybe, for not pissing on the dance floor or going after the major's old lady.

Twenty minutes after the cake had been cut and divvied out, Slater and Carolyn were out on the dance floor, pretending to have a good time. He was still a little pissed at her, and she probably knew it. He wondered how the hell he could be counting the days till he was out of the Crotch, and still be so goddamn sensitive when it came to people criticizing it. He tried to catch her eyes, let her know he was holding no grudges. She wouldn't look at him.

The end of the formal ceremony (including the major slurring through a message from the Commandant) had been the signal for everybody left standing to let it all hang out. And that was kinda entertaining when you got right down to it, Slater decided. While Boots Sugarbush and his group were ripping out some hot rock licks, it was a kick watching people get down.

His eyes kept coming back to that civilian poag in the white tux. Couldn't miss him. He was gorking it up like he owned every square inch of the place. Big dude—almost as big as Screamin' Don only with a perfect body that looked like it'd been custom ordered from one of those ritzy stores that only rich people know about. Dude had a tan like mahogany stain and a fifty-dollar hairstyle. Young, maybe

mid-twenties, perfect teeth and a diamond pinkie ring that
flashed like a goddamn strobe-light.

But it was the dude's date that ripped the breath out of
your chest. Holy shit! Talk about your absolute wet-dream
fantasy—here it was, poured into a white mesh-linked
minidress that let you know everything she had was
absolutely real. A real bombshell, from the top of her
strawberry blond head to her curly foot-long false eyelashes
to her creamy pink lips to a tan that looked like it went *all*
the way up those incredible long legs.

Shit. You only saw perfect people like these two on
daytime soaps.

Somebody pushing forty, maybe the major, must've
asked Boots to slow it down a bit. The combo started
playing "Misty" and for a second Slater wasn't sure if
Carolyn was going to stomp back to the table or go along for
the ride. He was relieved when she stepped into his arms.
He forgot about the blonde in about a second.

"Check out the cowboy in white," she whispered in his
ear.

Good. She wasn't going to get on his case about the cake.
He wanted to pull her tight but he was dripping sweat like
a copper pipe on a hot day so kept some room between their
bodies.

"Yeah, I saw," he said. She smelled so good he wanted
to take a bite. "Real pretty, ain't he? His date don't seem to
be wearin' underwear."

"You noticed."

"Hard not to."

"They don't seem to be getting along too well."

"What do ya mean?"

Carolyn took the lead and pushed them into a half-turn so
he could see what she was talking about. The dude in the
white tux was standing a few feet away from the blonde,
shaking a finger at her. Guy was saying something; they
were too far away to hear what.

Not too far away to hear the slap, though. It cracked like a bullwhip over the music.

"Jesus!" Slater choked.

"What?" Carolyn pushed back so she could look at his face.

"He just belted her!"

She pulled away from him and turned around. The stud in the white tux was standing with his hands on his hips while the blonde held a hand over the right side of her face, her hairdo knocked out of shape and now hanging down over her eyes.

Carolyn spun around, her eyes flashing. "He . . . he just *hit* her? The bastard *hit* her?"

Before Slater could answer he saw Van Groot march across the floor and yank at the sleeve of the slick dude in white. The Dutchman came up to about the middle of the guy's chest. Hold on, you little pecker, don't—

Too late. Slater had taken maybe three steps in the direction of his friend when he saw the guy straight-arm Van Groot in the chest. The Dutchman went rolling head over heels through the crowd, scattering dancers who must've thought they were being attacked by a growling Tasmanian devil in a blue uniform.

More and more people were catching on that something was going down. The circle of stares around the couple in white was growing, like ripples in a pond. The dude didn't seem to mind. He went right back to yelling at the blonde, threatening her again with a raised hand.

Slater got to the Dutchman just as the little man was sitting up.

"Help me, AJ," he said, raising his arm. "I'm gonna clean that asshole's clock."

"Forget it, Dutch. Forget it."

"Forget it, nothin'! No asshole clobbers a broad at the Crotch birthday, man."

"Cool it," Slater said, pulling Van Groot to his feet. "Won't do any good startin' a brawl."

Slater felt something heavy and solid brush past his shoulder, then heard a familiar voice.

"That's all for you, mister. Pack your gear and lose yourself."

Slater felt a rush of pure hate. Brule. Why did the man have to be such a goddamn prick? Wasn't right. Maybe it was time ta do something about it.

He'd had this thing in his head, ever since the night of the shootout on Fleming, that someday when the time was right, he'd stand up to Brule and they'd see how far it went. Yeah, maybe it was time. Could get him some "bad" time, a court-martial probably, maybe even a . . . discharge? What the hell, though, Dutch had only been doing what should have been done. No need at all for Brule to jump in the little man's shit.

Not sure what he'd really do or how far he'd go, Slater turned to face the captain.

Well, shit. Screamin' Don was standing jaw to jaw with the guy in the white tuxedo.

"I said the party's over, stud," Slater heard the captain growl into that perfectly tanned face.

"Screw off, jarhead," the man said to Brule, a flash of brilliantly white teeth showing through an ugly smirk.

" Nobody sucker punches one of my men, mister," Brule answered evenly. "You're leaving, straight up or feet first. Take your pick." The captain stood with his hands hanging loosely at his sides.

"Fuck you," the stud snickered. "I don't take orders from bellhops. Get lost."

Slater's hatred dribbled away. All of a sudden he wanted to lead cheers. Goddamn, Captain! Wring the bastard out!

"I'll count to ten, wiseguy. Then I drop you." Brule spoke in a regular tone, just enough to be heard over a mean guitar riff coming from the stage. Slater felt lucky to have such a beautiful ringside seat.

"Bet you can't count that high, cueball," the stud replied.

Brule shrugged. "All right by me, sweetheart. You do the counting."

For the only time he could remember, Slater saw Brule smile. The smile came at about the exact same instant the stud in white wound up and swung a big roundhouse right that might've done some damage if the captain hadn't neatly blocked it.

Still grinning like a kid at Christmas, Screamin' Don snaked out a short left jab that caught the stud squarely on his perfect nose. Even from where he was standing, Slater could hear the smushing sound, sorta like whacking a piece of sirloin with a mallet. The dude's head snapped back, then came forward again in time to meet Brule's right hook. This time Slater heard a sharp crack as the dude seemed to lift off the deck about six inches, then come down hard, flat on his back.

"Yeah!" he heard the Dutchman shout. "Kick ass, Skipper!"

It was easy to see that the dude in white had danced his last dance of the evening. Dude was definitely bye-bye. Brule stood over the body for a few more seconds, like he was making sure, then pivoted smartly and marched— almost ran—through the gawkers and out toward the main entrance to the hall.

The music ran out of gas and Slater suddenly realized the whole hall had fallen silent. Then, slowly, a couple of people went over to check out the victim. Slater felt a hand on his shoulder and heard the Dutchman chuckling.

"So . . . how ya like *them* apples, AJ?"

Screamin' Don hauled a pack of Marlboros out of the top of a sock, lit up, then leaned back against the bollard. He was pretty much alone out there on the seawall. Zamora's uncle (there with the rest of the family on Brocksneider's invitation—get real) had tried to follow him when he left the Community Hall, but for once he'd been able to shake the guy.

A few couples from the dance had discovered that moonlight on the water and rustling palm trees were a real romantic turn-on, but Brule had found a spot on the seawall that was pretty much deserted. And that was just fine with him.

It was times like this that he always thought about the boy from Montana.

Jennings was the kid's name—how could he ever forget it? Second Lieutenant Don Brule's first duty assignment out of Basic School, a platoon of grunts, providing security for a firebase somewhere in the middle of the boonies. Two days in-country and he was in command, responsible suddenly for twenty-two lives besides his own, not to mention the safety of an arty battery—six guns and more than a hundred men.

First night he'd gone out to check posts and found the boy from Montana zonked out in front of his M-60. Hell, didn't want to come across to the troops as a hardass screamer. Just shook Jennings awake and warned him not to let it happen again. Nice, even-handed, understanding-human-being sort of approach. Sure, we're all exhausted, son, but you've got to stay awake on duty, the whole firebase depends on you.

Three nights later, he'd caught the kid nodding off again. Same deal. Don Brule wasn't going to be one of those gung-ho hardnosed martinets, no sir. He understood things better than that. All he had to do was explain to Jennings how very important it was that he stay alert (even though the firebase hadn't heard so much as an enemy fart in over six months) and the kid would respond. Good leadership meant that you didn't put people on report every time they screwed up. Better to work things out creatively. Maybe he'd make the trooper write out his General Orders a hundred times or something.

Goddamn you, Jennings. Shoulda had the gunny kick your ass, then written you up for a Special Court. Sleeping on post. You goddamn bastard.

Middle of the night, an explosion. Musty smells of wet earth. Darkness. Someone yelling "sapper." The oily steel of a .45 magically filling his hand. Out of the hooch in skivvies and jungle boots, scared shitless. The popping tear of automatic rifles. Another explosion. The blast tossed him into a wall of plastic sandbags. Knocked the dog crap out of him. Saw shadows flirting with the moonlight. An illum round popped—eerie haunting light from above. Over there, hugging the ground, a small brown man worming his way toward the gun pits while the face of the boy from Montana stares up with lifeless eyes. Fear, heart racing, not enough air, can't move. The boy from Montana was fucking dead. Dead dead dead, a bullet through the head. One step from going off the deep end, then a hit of adrenaline so heavy he could almost feel it shutting down everything he owned except the instinct to survive. The .45 bucks once, then again; the brown man a rag doll, flopping spastically, clutching at a fist-sized black hole in the center of his chest, his face a garish death mask painted by the artificial light.

Air hot from the blasts of explosives, stinking of powder and freshly turned mud. Voices everywhere, screaming, shouting, crying.

Another gook, naked except for a ragged loincloth, running toward the Battery Command bunker. Stop the fucker. Pointblank range, can't miss, pull the trigger over and over, no time to aim. An exploding skull, wet warm slime.

Another gook. Where did they come from? The .45 is empty. Throw rocks then, handfuls of dirt, feeling cheated when the enemy sapper is cut in two by a burst from an M-60. More! There must be more of them out there, beyond the wire. Kill ever goddamn one of them. Out there, in the dark, where they think they're safe. Come on, you fucking zipperheads! Come try me! Come try the great and terrible Brule!

Goddamn you, Jennings, Screamin' Don thought as he

flipped the filter of his cigarette into the harbor. Why didn't you listen? The Great Slack can kill.

Never again, though. No sir. Never again.

"Hey Don, you all right?

Kargo.

"Yeah, Stan, I'm all right." He pushed off the big iron bollard and straightened his tunic. "How's the punk?"

"Somebody said his jaw is broken. They just carted him off to the hospital. Major was looking for ya."

"I'll bet. His blood brother Capaccino must be having a shit-fit. Nothing like having your firstborn cold-cocked in front of the whole town."

Kargo chuckled. "Yeah. You coulda picked a better victim than Ernie's number one son. Figure you get an A for effort, but you might've flunked 'good judgment.' "

"Fuck him if he can't take a joke."

"Yeah. Fuck him."

Brule felt tired all of a sudden. "Saw him dump Van Groot. Damn. So pissed I couldn't see straight. Well, the major ain't going to forgive and forget on this one. I think I've screwed the pooch. Probably end up as the OIC of duck blinds out in Barstow."

Kargo put a foot up on the bollard. "Maybe. On the other hand, I heard old Ernie saying that it was about time somebody wised up his kid."

"No kidding? Wait till he sobers up. Different story."

"Who knows? Maybe you'll skate."

The two men just stood there for a while, listening to their own thoughts and the soft sounds of music drifting over from the dance.

Finally, Brule cleared his throat. "Knew I shoulda gone home after the cake came in. Peg wanted to dance, though." Screamin' Don flexed his right hand. The knuckles were starting to swell up. "Sitter's gonna cost me a bundle."

"Excuse us, sirs."

The two men turned. There, maybe ten feet away, stood Van Groot along with a couple dozen other Marines with faces as familiar as family. Nobody said anything, just shuffled around like they were waiting for something.

"Go on, Dutch," someone said, "we ain't got all night."

"Hold you water, Nar-vel," Van Groot whispered loudly. He stepped forward and held something out to Brule.

"Captain," he said, "we all got together and come up with a token for ya as a sign of our 'preciation for your fine work tonight. We figured maybe you could find some use for it. It's from all the men, sir, even the supply poags."

It was a bottle. Screamin' Don took it and examined the label. "Hmmmm, Chivas, the good stuff. Thanks. Thank you all . . . and happy birthday." He broke the seal and took a long pull. "Ahhhh. Excellent. My compliments on your good taste."

"Thanks . . . Skipper," Van Groot mumbled. He moved backward a few steps, then, with the rest of them, turned and walked back to the hall.

Kargo waited until he was sure they were out of range. "Chivas. The only place I saw any Chivas tonight was—"

"On the major's table." Brule chuckled, holding out the bottle. "Have one on me."

"Don't mind if I do."

As Kargo tipped the bottle and took a slug, Screamin' Don could only marvel. The Dutchman was absolutely, positively, fucking-A unreal.

Slater did most of the talking on the long walk back to the Bamboo. Maybe it was the booze or just the come-down from all the excitement, but he was babbling like he'd just discovered speech. Or maybe he was just trying to fill up all the empty air between them. Carolyn had hardly said anything since they'd left the party.

"See," he continued, "you'd be nuts ta buy a ride down here. All the salt air and everything, really screws up a car before you could even enjoy it. Most of the guys just save their bread till they get out or get transferred someplace where you don't have ta worry about . . ." He let it die. What the hell was he talking about?

"So," he said, "did you have a good time?"

"Marvelous."

That was it, a one word answer coming in that tone that he recognized as her pissed-off-about-something mode. It managed to shut him up pretty good.

When they got to the Bamboo, he followed her up the outside stairs to the landing. She pulled open the screen door and then looked over her shoulder.

"I'd ask you in, but Rose is sleeping and I'm pretty beat. Thanks for a nice time."

"Can't you, ah, stay outside here for a while?" For all the tension in the air, he still didn't want the night to end.

"Come on, Jack. It's almost four. I'll see you tomorrow."

"I got duty tomorrow."

"Then soon, OK? Thanks."

She leaned over and kissed him lightly on the mouth. He reached out for her, but she was already inside the door.

"Carolyn," he said, "somethin' wrong?"

She looked out through the screen. A light from inside kept him from seeing her face very well.

"Nothing's wrong," she said. "I'm just real whipped. Goodnight."

With that, she closed the door in his face and was gone.

CHAPTER TWENTY

IT wasn't until almost the end of November that the Navy released Freddy Claybourne from the hospital and sent him high-tailing it back to the Barracks where he could drive his own people crazy with his constant bitching and refusal to comply with standing orders. He still had a cast on his arm, but his days left in the Crotch were forty-one. He could almost smell the freedom. Now if he could only wangle some town libs, get out and git down with Shandy . . .

"The Secretary of the Navy takes great pleasure in awarding the Navy-Marine Corps Medal to Corporal Fredrick R. Claybourne, for heroic action as set forth in the following citation."

The khaki line extended down the company street, three ranks deep. Fredrick R. Claybourne stood facing the major while Captain Brule read from some official document. With a head full of daydreams, Freddy hardly heard a word Screamin' Don was saying.

"On October twenty-second, nineteen hundred and seventy-two, while serving at the Marine Barracks, U.S. Naval Base, Key West, Florida, then Lance Corporal Claybourne did, while in a no-duty status due to previous injuries and with complete disregard for his own safety, save the lives of two fellow members of the Naval Service. . . ."

Shandy Shandy Shandy. Brown Sugar. In the hospital. Told him the ambush at the reception got her even with Carlene. Now it was OK for her to be friends with Freddy. Carlene understood. He was Shandy's man now, fair and square. Did he like that? Shandy Shandy Shandy.

". . . Corporal Claybourne's bravery and devotion to duty was an inspiration to all hands, and was in keeping with the highest traditions of the Marine Corps and the Naval Service. Signed: the Honorable John H. Chafee, Secretary of the Navy. Delivered by my hand this twenty-sixth day of November, nineteen hundred and seventy-two, Thomas W. Brocksneider, USMC, Commanding."

Brule took his post and the major lifted the medal from its box, held out to him by the sergeant major. He pinned it to Freddy's chest, and after offering his own personal congratulations, stepped back and snapped to a hand salute. Claybourne returned it with his left arm as he'd been instructed by Hollihan before the ceremony. He'd finally gotten his medal.

A damn fine mutha fuckin' thing it was, too.

After the formation had been dismissed, and after he'd gotten some good-natured ragging from the section, Claybourne was headed for his rack and more zees when Brownell cornered him on the first deck veranda.

"Front and center, hero," the gunny commanded, pointing at a spot on the cement directly in front of him.

Claybourne ambled over. Brownell extended his hand.

"Congratulations, Marine."

"Ah . . . well, thanks, Gunny."

"How's it feel being a hero?" Brownell gestured at the heavy bronze medal on Claybourne's shirt.

"Freddy fingered the bit of colored ribbon and smiled. "Feels real good. Feel even better with some town libs."

"I'll bet. Sorry about that, though; you know the regs. No-duty status means no town libs."

"Damn, Gunny! We gonna go through all that shit again? Man, I ain't had no town libs in two months or somethin'. I got needs have to be tended to!"

"We've all got *needs*, Marine. Like maybe we *need* somebody from the Starboard Section who can stand supernumerary duty, even though that person may have certain temporary physical disabilities. And anyway, I got a feeling your *needs* are probably more like wants." Brownell laughed.

And so did Claybourne. Hell, the gunny was right. He wanted to see Shandy real bad. Her regular visits to him in the hospital had been promising. Now, decorated and almost mended, he was looking forward to being alone with her. Had some things he wanted to say.

"Tell you what," the gunny said. "You keep your nose clean for the next few days and I'll see if we can spring you next Saturday. I catch you sandbagging it around here and you can forget it, understand? But I'll almost bet, with your new medal there, the major might be willing to make an exception if the lieutenant and I can say you are bustin' your butt."

"Dig that! You just tell me what you want me to do!" Claybourne made a face and touched his damaged arm. "If I can, that is."

"Spoken like a real trooper, Fred. Now listen up. There's a photographer from the *Observer* coming over to take your picture this afternoon. Report to me at 1315 in the Guard Shack."

"Picture? What for?"

"Hometown news release. Plus they want to do a followup story on you for dissemination on the base here. You're a hero, Marine: Didn't you know that?"

"Shit. Why you gotta always be pullin' my chain for, Gunny?"

"Not pulling your chain. It's the truth. You're gonna have your picture plastered all over the front page . . . unless you break the camera with your ugliness."

Claybourne grinned. Might be just what he needed. A little recog like his picture in the paper would have Shandy making like sweet molasses in June.

"That'd be cool, Gunny, definitely cool."

The Bamboo Room was dark and cool, deserted except for Rose, who was bitching over the phone to her booze distributor. The smell of old beer, cigarette smoke, and mildew all got together and made the queasy stomach Slater had brought in with him worse. He sat at the bar, avoiding his own reflection in the wall mirror, waiting for Carolyn to come downstairs.

He'd taken off from the Barracks the second liberty call had sounded. The Dutchman had still been down in the Guard Office with the lieutenant on some special business, and though Slater felt a little guilty for running out on a friend, he was relieved. Van Groot wouldn't have understood wasting good liberty time worrying about a female.

But then the Dutchman wasn't in love with anybody or anything except maybe the goddamn Crotch.

What had happened? What the hell had gone wrong? The way he read it, things between him and Carolyn had started turning to shit right after the Birthday Ball, about the time she'd gotten the job as a cocktail waitress out at the Airport Lounge. Over the weeks since then they'd kinda been driftin' apart. Talked with her on the phone a few times, even went out to the airport once and hung around the lounge till they booted his ass out for bein' underage—but he hadn't had a date or been alone with her since the birthday. Something was wrong, and getting worse. Damn if he knew why.

Rose hung up the phone, then drew a mug of coffee from the big percolator near the cash register. She slid the full cup along the bar until it sat in front of him.

"There ya go, Jack. Fresh perked and guaranteed to put life in your bones and hair on your teeth. Want me ta cut it with a little Bacardi?"

"No thanks." He cradled the mug and sipped. The coffee was hot and bitter. He blew gently on its surface.

The front door opened and Slater held his breath. The bright light from outside blinded him but he could tell from the silhouette that it was Carolyn. His stomach felt queasier than ever.

"Well, hello there, hon," Rose bellowed, maybe a little

too cheerfully. "Look who's here bright and early ta see ya."

"Morning, Rose," Carolyn said as she approached them. "Hi, Jack." Her voice was groggy with sleep. "You off today?"

"Yeah. Training got canceled. Gunny Tolliver ran out of things to say about field hygiene."

It was supposed to be a joke, but maybe it was a little too inside for her. She stared at him blankly, then sat down on the stool next to him.

"How about some grub, hon?" Rose asked as she plopped another mug of coffee in front of her niece.

"Sounds good. I'm famished."

"Order of ham'n eggs, Bright!" Rose howled in the general direction of the kitchen. She waited, her eyes fixed on the swinging doors. "I know what he's gonna do," she mumbled. "He's gonna pretend he didn't hear me, just out of spite. Old reprobate." She cupped her hands to her mouth and yelled. "Come on, Bright! Hungry crowd out here! Shake a leg, damn your black heart!"

There was a clatter of pots and pans, the sound of a cupboard door opening and slamming shut, followed by the sight of the old black cook standing in the kitchen doorway, a prosthesis in one hand, a spatula in the other. He shook the artificial leg violently at Rose, his eyes blazing.

"Goddamn it, Bright!" Rose shrieked, "that ain't funny! That's my Sunday leg, you old son of an African whore!"

Bright opened his mouth and let out a deep ridiculing roar. Slater had heard the story a dozen times—Bright had no tongue; a woman bit it off during a fight back in '48.

"That does it," Rose said. "You and me gonna go round and round, old man. Right this minute!"

She stormed off toward the kitchen, armed with a plastic baseball bat she'd pulled out from under the bar. Cursing a blue streak, she plowed through the swinging doors. What came next was the rattling of pans, the crash of broken crockery, more cursing, and those funny sounds. One more big crash, then silence. A few moments later and the aroma of frying ham drifted out into the bar.

"Think she killed him?" Slater asked, still looking at the kitchen doorway.

"I doubt it," Carolyn answered. She yawned. "What are you doing here so early? Place doesn't start serving until noon, you know that."

"Haven't seen much of you lately. Thought we could— you know—talk maybe." Damn. Did she really think he'd come looking for an early brew?

"Gee, I don't know, Jack. I've got to get to work."

"Work? It ain't even noon yet. You don't start till eight."

"They're moving me up to hostess, and I've got to go over a lot of things with Ricky before I start. Longer hours but more money."

She sipped her coffee as his insides reached up and grabbed him. Longer hours? Shit.

"Ricky?" he said.

"The manager . . . Darn! it's freezing in here!" She began rubbing the goose bumps on her arms.

"That's kinda what I wanted to talk about," Slater said hesitantly.

"What? The temperature?"

"No. That new job of yours. Do ya have to work all night all the time? I never get to see you anymore." Don't whine, he told himself, don't whine.

"Well, I'm sorry," she said, sounding not sorry at all. "That's just the way things are. Really don't feel like partying at four in the morning after eight hours on my feet. You can understand that, can't you?"

"Sure. Listen, I was thinking. I got libs this Sunday. That's your day off, ain't it? Let's drive up to Bahia Honda. Have a picnic. I can get LeFey's car, I think, and we—"

"Can't. I've already made other plans."

Her words hit him hard. He could only stare at her, watch her rub at a wet spot on the bar. When he spoke he heard his voice crack.

"Carolyn . . . what's happenin' here? I thought you and me, we . . . ever since the dance and this new job, things have been kinda screwed up. You wanna tell me what the hell is going on?"

"Look, Jack," she said, "I don't want to hurt you. I've thought things through and decided I'm not ready for any relationship right now."

"Why?" he asked feebly.

"Why? I don't know why. I just decided, that's all. Ricky says you can't hide from things forever. You've got to face problems head-on. So I think I just have to get on with my life."

Ricky again. Maybe he'd like to introduce Ricky to a knuckle sandwich. See how much psycho mumbo-jumbo Ricky wanted to lay on his girl with a busted nose.

"But what did I do, Carolyn? Tell me that. You don't love somebody one minute and just decide not to the next."

She looked him straight in the eye. "I never said I loved you, Jack."

He knew his mouth was hanging open–like the big dead mounted sailfish on the wall—but no words came out. She was studying his face. There was something in her expression that made him feel like a stray dog about to be put to sleep.

"I like you, Jack, I like you a lot, but I don't love you. We can still go out together sometime, but I've decided I'm going to see and date other people. Besides," she tried to smile, "everytime I go out with you, somebody gets punched out."

"Oh bull! What kinda—"

"Jack, please! I don't want to argue with you. You'll just have to accept the fact that I don't want to be tied down again with a relationship. Do you understand?"

No, he didn't understand. And all he felt was anger and betrayal. "You're fulla shit, ya know that?"

He noticed her hands squeezing the plastic padding along

the front lip of the bar. Her knuckles stood out in pale bony relief. She seemed to shudder.

"I don't think I want to talk to you anymore," she said quietly, her eyes glancing up at the big Pabst Blue Ribbon clock over the bar.

"Fine by me." He pushed himself off the stool and paused for a moment in front of her, fighting the urge to pull her into his arms while at the same time finding it hard not to belt her.

There was a lump in his throat big as a goddamn football. "See ya around," he said.

He was carrying ten-pound weights in his tennies by the time he climbed the stairway to the second deck. The four-to-eight Relief had been posted; the regular work day at the Barracks had ended; the place was pretty well deserted.

Slater's belly felt as though it was full of broken glass.

He'd walked all over town since leaving the Bamboo, had walked away the afternoon trying to figure out some answers. No dice. Now he only wanted to find the Dutchman and get cross-eyed, commode-hugging blasted. Seemed the only righteous thing to do.

The squad bay was drenched with late afternoon sunlight slanting through the west windows. He could hear someone singing in the shower room, but except for some quiet talk coming from the newly relieved sentries in the next cubicle, and the snores of Freddy Claybourne, the whole deck was comfortably quiet. He supposed Van Groot was at chow so he rolled into an empty rack to wait, trying to block out the shittiest day he'd had in a long time.

"What's happenin', Slats?"

Slater looked over at Claybourne's rack. Freddy's face was half buried in his pillow. "Thought you were asleep, Fred," he said.

"Man can't sleep no twenty-four hours a day. What's goin' down out at the hospital?"

"I look that bad, huh?" Slater tried to laugh, couldn't quite pull it off. He caught sight of the medal pinned to Claybourne's pillowcase. "What's with the geedunk display? You afraid somebody's gonna rip you off?"

"Mean the medal, man? Why anybody want ta rip it off for? They'd still be a dollar short of a bottle a Ripple. Naw, I'm just gettin' the feel of the thing before I send it home." Claybourne's chuckle was muffled in the pillow. "My momma probably wear it to work. . . . How's the little shit doin'?"

"What little shit?"

Claybourne's eyes widened. "Dutchman, man. Gunny said it looked pretty bad."

When he was a kid, Slater had once owned a battered old Emerson radio. Somewhere along the line one of the plastic knobs had broken off leaving only a metal stub. Sometimes when he tuned the radio he'd feel a funny buzzing sensation run through his body. The same sensation hit him now.

"What the hell are you talking about?"

"Shit, man, you ain't heard?" Freddy sat up like a shot.

"Heard what, goddamn it?" The strange buzzing feeling wouldn't go away.

"The Dutchman, man! Stole a motorcycle out in town. Cops was chasin' him when he wiped out. Hell, thought you knew. Everybody thought you was—"

Somehow Slater had gotten to his feet. The look on his face made Claybourne get up too.

"Man, I thought you knew," Freddy whispered. "Dutch is messed up real fuckin' bad, man. They don't know if he's gonna make it."

CHAPTER TWENTY-ONE

THE "Emergency" waiting room at the naval hospital where Slater and Kargo were sitting was only a corridor with a few dinged-up chairs and two long wooden benches set up outside gray double doors. The two men sat across from each other at the end of the benches; nobody had said much since Kargo had ordered the rest of the section back to the Barracks.

"What time is it, Lieutenant?" Slater asked, lifting his eyes from the deck.

Kargo checked his watch. "Five minutes later than it was the last time you asked."

"What the hell's takin' so long?"

"Relax, he's in good hands."

Relax? Slater chewed on his lip like it was a hunk of Juicy Fruit. How could he relax? For all he knew Van Groot had already bought the farm. Not once since he'd come in had anyone on the hospital staff mentioned the Dutchman's condition. If it hadn't been for the lieutenant being there, he might've figured he was in the wrong place.

He kept seeing the dark smear on Roosevelt Boulevard. What had it been? Oil? Gas? Blood? Benjamin hadn't said anything when they passed the intersection in the SOG truck, but Slater saw that smear and knew—the Dutchman had really bitten off a big one this time. The bike was still there, off to the side of the road, a crumpled pile of rubber, chrome, and steel. A light blue Falcon sat nearby, its right side caved in. What the fuck had that little maniac been thinking—that he was still on Fleming Key jumping ammo bunkers? There were no red lights on Fleming, no little blue Falcons either, no cops in your rearview.

"Listen, I'm gonna look for some coffee," Kargo announced. "You want any?"

"No thanks." Slater felt his hands begin to shake again. He jammed them into his pockets. Let it out, he told himself, let it out before it blows your mind.

"Ya know, Lieutenant, I was supposed to pull libs with him today. Something else came up. If I'd been with him, this never woulda happened."

"Bullshit. You're not his mother. He's old enough to look after himself."

"But it ain't like him to *steal* anything. Dutch ain't a thief."

"He told the dealer he was taking the bike for a demo ride," Kargo said. "Nothing illegal about that. They'll have a hell of a time proving otherwise."

"What about the accident?"

"Doing eighty-five on North Roosevelt and running a red light *is* illegal, sorry about that."

Slater inhaled deeply and let his head fall back against the wall. "Wish I knew what the hell the little jerk was tryin' ta prove."

Kargo looked up. "He got kicked in the balls this morning. Maybe he just couldn't handle it."

Slater looked up sharply.

"I don't get it."

"Headquarters Marine Corps turned down his reenlistment."

So there it was, the Dutchman's one and only dream down the toilet. A reason maybe to forget about stoplights and speed limits and cop sirens . . . maybe even reason enough not to see little blue Falcons.

"The Green Machine strikes again, huh, Lieutenant?" Slater said angrily.

"They had their reasons."

"Sure. Don't they always?"

The look Kargo gave him warned him that he was treading on thin ice. But it didn't matter. He began to laugh; it was better than crying.

"What's so damn funny?" Kargo asked.

"It's all too much, Lieutenant. Here I got like almost two years ta do and want out, and here's poor ol' Dutch, who'd sell his mother for the same deal if he knew who she was. Now that's funny, don't ya think?"

The double doors opened and they both looked up. A teenage boy with a cast on his leg hobbled out on crutches alongside a big Navy chief who figured to be his old man. They didn't speak again until the boy and his father were well up the corridor.

"Say, Lieutenant," Slater said, "how about a trade? You know, like in the Majors. Dutch can have my two and I'll go home. How's that sound?"

"You know better than that."

"Yeah, but why not? Makes sense, don't it? I've had a belly full of the Crotch."

"Go outside if you're going to cry, Slater."

Kargo sounded pissed. Slater ignored the warning. "Know what the Crotch's done for me since I got back from fighting their little war? Lost me a brother. Lost me my girl. And now . . ." He paused and looked at the gray double doors. "And now maybe it's lost me my best buddy. Like I said, I've had a gut fulla the Green Machine, ya want ta know."

"Yeah, and I've had a gut full of you, Marine." The coldness in Kargo's voice surprised him. "You know what Van Groot's problem is?" the lieutenant continued. "His record makes the Corps think he's crazy, wacko, half a dozen tent pegs short of a full transport pack. And the Corps doesn't want—doesn't need—crazies anymore. The shooting is over. No more crazies. Do you understand what I'm saying, Slater? They do not want any more crazies!"

Slater looked away. What the hell did Kargo know? "Dutch ain't anymore crazy than I am," he muttered.

The double doors banged open again. A man in pastel green surgical coveralls stuck his head out and motioned them to join him.

"This man Van Groot one of yours?" the man in green asked as they got close.

"That's right," Kargo answered, "how's he doing?"

"He's one tough cookie, I'll tell you that. Commander Nesbit, Chief Surgeon."

"Is he gonna be all right, Doc?" Slater blurted. He didn't like the look on the doctor's face; it reminded him of someone who'd just lost a close game of pool with fifty bucks riding on the cushion.

"He just came out of surgery," the doctor said. "Had a hell of a time putting him under. Kept yelling he didn't want any anesthetic, wanted to watch." Nesbit managed a weak grin.

"Is he gonna be all right?" Slater raised his voice.

"He'll live," the doctor answered, examining Slater with a puzzled expression. "Mostly superficial cuts and abrasions. His face will look awful for a few weeks, but no real damage there. Thought there might be some internal bleeding—that's what took so long—but he's OK. Very lucky young man."

Slater felt relieved. The little shit had a charmed life, no doubt about it.

"Unfortunately," the doctor continued, running his fingers wearily through thick silver hair, "we couldn't do much with the knee; the damage was too extensive. We were forced to fuse what was left with nails and glue and baling wire. I won't bore you with the terminology, but I'm afraid he'll never be able to bend it again. His right patella—knee cap—was reduced to powder in the accident. Ten years ago he might have lost the leg." The doctor shook his head. "I've never seen anything like it. The pain must have been excruciating, and this man of yours was trying to cop a feel on the OR nurse. Unbelievable."

"Can I talk with him, Commander?" Kargo asked. "I'd

like to get some kind of statement. Line of Duty investigation."

"Don't see why not. He's in Recovery. Still a little groggy I'd imagine. We gave him enough gas to knock out a herd of water buffalo but he was coming out of it while we were still closing. Don't get him excited or he'll probably try to tap dance out of here on one leg."

Kargo looked over at Slater. "How about I take this man in too. He's Van Groot's best friend."

The doctor eyeballed Slater again. "Hmmmmm. I don't know. Policy is next of kin only until the patient gets on a ward."

"Dutch don't have any next of kin, sir," Slater said quietly. He noticed a reddish-brown stain on the surgeon's pants leg and remembered a similar stain on his own clothing back a long, long time ago. Choo Choo.

"You wouldn't be AJ by any chance?" the doctor asked. He didn't wait for an answer. "Before we finally knocked him out, he made me promise to see to it that AJ got his 'blues,' whatever that is." The doctor grinned at Kargo. "Also wanted to be buried at sea and have someone named 'Tiny' do a strip over his body. That name sound familiar?"

Kargo laughed. "Two hundred and eighty pounds of female who used to work downtown at the porno house. Van Groot dated her once."

The doctor laughed too, then glanced at Slater. "Don't stay too long, son. He needs some rest. And like I said, don't get him excited. Man's got enough thread holding him together to qualify for a garment union label. Just go through the doors and keep going to the end of the building. Hang a left and you'll be in Recovery. Anybody gives you any static, tell 'em I authorized it."

"Thank you, sir," Slater managed as the man turned away and headed up the corridor toward a room marked X-RAY.

"No problem," Nesbit said without turning. "You Marines are keeping me in business. I haven't had this much practice since Da Nang."

"Recovery" was a subterranean ice box, chilled and antiseptic, the pale beige walls and floor tiles clean enough to eat off. The nurse in charge, plainly PO'ed that the two of them had been granted visitation, made them put on surgical gowns and masks.

Van Groot was one of three patients recovering from surgery. Kargo and Slater recognized him only from the description of wounds and his name on the chart hanging at the foot of the bed. He was layered from head to toe in gauze and bandages, many oozing a dark yellowish-brown fluid. His right leg hung in a cast from the hip down; a fist-sized hole had been left in the plaster at the knee. Two drainage tubes curved out of the hole and down to a plastic jug. A bright red stain, about the size of a half dollar, gave a splotch of vivid color to the gauze-stuffed opening.

Slater couldn't tell if the Dutchman was conscious or not as he stepped closer to the head of the bed. The man's face was hidden behind the bandages; slits had been left for the eyes, nose, and mouth.

"What the fuck, over," a familiar voice croaked.

Slater looked over at Kargo who stood on the other side of the bed. The lieutenant grinned back at him.

"How ya doing, Dutch?" Kargo asked quietly.

"That you, Lieutenant?"

"What do ya say, asshole?" Slater added.

"Hey! AJ! Kiss my ass. How'd you get in here?"

"Doctor says you're gonna be OK," Kargo soothed. "You look like hell, but what else is new?"

"Yeah, and no more squat thrusts, ever! That's sure gonna break the gunny's heart." Van Groot tapped on the cast with a bandaged hand.

So he knows about the knee, Slater thought. Well, if it wasn't going to bother Dutch, it wasn't going to bother him. At least the little turd was alive.

"Hell, Dutch," Slater said, "What's a knee, anyway? Tolliver will requisition you a new one."

"Sure. In ten years he'll still be tellin' me it's on order."

"I'm going to need your version of what happened, Van Groot." Kargo paused and Slater sensed the lieutenant was very uncomfortable. "For the investigation. And, ah, for the record, before you say anything, I have to advise you of your rights. You have the right to remain silent—"

"That's OK, Lieutenant," Van Groot interrupted. "I heard it all before. No big deal. I was lookin' ta buy a bike for when I get out, ya know? Asked the dude if I could take a spin. Big mutha, seven-fifty cc, fuckin' hog. Goddamn throttle stuck on me out on Roosevelt. If I hadn't hit that car, I'd still be goin'. Nobody else was hurt, was they?"

"No," Kargo answered, "but the bike was totalled and there'll be one less Falcon for people to kick around. That's it, huh? Throttle stuck?"

"Yes, sir. That's what happened. Swear it on a stack of Bibles."

"That'll do it then," Kargo sighed. "I'll get Delkirt to type it up, clean up the language a little. Somebody'll bring it out for you to sign when you're feeling better. Anything I can get you, anything you need?"

"Nurse with big jugs would be nice."

"Van Groot," Kargo laughed, "you're incorrigible."

"No, sir. Just horny."

"Whatever. Listen, I'm gonna shove off before the hospital staff goes bananas. Besides, Slater here's been walking holes in his shoes waiting to chew you out. You take care, Dutch. I'm real sorry about that other thing this morning."

"Thanks, Lieutenant. No big deal."

"You want a ride back to the Barracks?" Kargo asked Slater.

"No thanks, sir. I'll thumb."

"See you tomorrow then." Kargo backed away from the

bed, took one more look at Van Groot's knee, scowled, then turned and walked to the exit.

Slater watched the clear liquid from the IV drip through the tube attached to the Dutchman's arm.

"You dumb shit," he finally whispered.

"Watch yer language, boy. I've killed men for less." Van Groot's chapped and crusted lips made the bandages near his mouth flutter.

"What the hell were you tryin' ta prove out there?"

"Wasn't tryin' ta prove nothin'. It was just like I said, damn throttle stuck on me."

"Right. Hey, man, you are crazy. Just 'cause the Crotch turned you down, no reason to pull your plug."

The Dutchman squirmed under his bandages, then coughed an indignant laugh. "Shit. You think I was tryin' ta grease my own ass? That's the stupidest thing I ever heard, AJ. Only havin' a little fun, is all. Hey! Where were you, man? Thought we was gonna pull libs together. Looked all over for ya. Guys said you'd already split."

"Just out getting my head handed to me."

"The broad, huh?"

"Yeah."

"Up hers. Anybody puts Coke in good Scotch is fucked up anyway." Van Groot's stomach seemed to heave. "Get me the barf bucket, man," he groaned.

The stainless steel pan was hooked on the side of the bed. Slater placed it gently on the pillow next to the Dutchman's mouth. "Want me to get the nurse?"

The Dutchman snorted. "That old ball bustin' bitch? Hell, no. She already threatened ta write me up for grabbin' her fat ass. Fuckin' squid."

"The rest of the guys were out here to see ya. Lieutenant made 'em clear out; they were raisin' too much hell in the waiting room. They'll be out the day after tomorrow, OK? Hey look." Slater fumbled with his guilt. "I'm sorry, ya know? If I'd been with ya maybe this wouldn't—"

"Cool it. I don't need no nursemaid. Anyways, it's all a

dream, remember? I ain't really here, you ain't really here, and my knee, it definitely ain't here."

Slater paused for a beat or two, then asked. "Where were you headed?"

Van Groot hesitated. "I dunno," he said softly. "Maybe Miami, maybe Canada, maybe the North Pole. Who's ta say? Just wanted to go—get away—know what I mean?"

The Dutchman gagged then turned his head and vomited into the pan. He tried to reach up to wipe his lips but found it too painful. Slater grabbed a corner of the sheet and wiped it for him.

The duty nurse scurried into Slater's line of sight. "I'm sorry, but you'll have to leave," she said officiously as she elbowed him out of the way and began attending her patient. "Doctor Nesbit shouldn't have allowed you in her in the first place."

"Give me another minute, will ya, Harriet?" the Dutchman asked hoarsely. "He's my main man."

"It's *Lieutenant* Mells, Marine, and I won't tell you again. All right, one more minute and then I call the corpsman." The nurse checked Van Groot's blood pressure and pulse. "Not one second more." She took the pan and moved off to another bed.

"You want my blues, asshole?" the Dutchman asked.

"What for, man? Only person they fit is a midget."

"You got near two more years, you prick. Plenty of time for you ta get into decent shape."

Slater moved closer to Van Groot's head, then past it so that he was almost touching the headboard. He could see the little man's eyes straining to look back at him through the slits in the bandages.

"Where ya goin', AJ? I can't see ya up there, man."

Slater reached under his sweatshirt and glanced around for the nurse. She was making notes on a clipboard on the far side of the room. An evil grin creased his face as he pulled the bayonet scabbard out of his belt. He held it out so Van Groot could see it.

The Dutchman's eyelashes began to blink furiously. "Hey wait a minute, buddy! No fair, man!" He arched his back, trying to squirm away from danger. "Harriet! Nurse! Help!"

"Only rule is there ain't no rules, Dutch." Slater reached out and drew the empty scabbard across the bandages around the Dutchman's neck. "Eat shit, yankee pig," he whispered, "and ya owe me fifty bucks."

The sky looked like melting raspberry sherbet when he walked out of the main entrance to the hospital. The waters of Cow Key Channel flowed swiftly in a blue-black moodiness, rolling the houseboats tied up along its near bank like bathtub toys. Slater breathed deeply of the salty air, ridding his lungs of the cloying smell of disinfectant and whatever else gave hospitals their distinct cloaks of odor.

For just a moment he thought about walking over to the Airport Lounge. It was closeby and she would be working by now. He dismissed the idea with hardly a second thought. He'd said all there was to be said that morning. So had she.

As he climbed down the steps into the circular drive, he decided to head back to town and the Bamboo Room for a couple of hooks. He suddenly had an overwhelming urge to be with his own kind.

CHAPTER TWENTY-TWO

THE first liberty Saturday in December and Freddy Clay-bourne was on the street again, first time since he'd gone through the window at Moany's. He wasn't surprised at how good it felt—how good *he* felt—strutting down Duval in his best silks and shades, catching his reflection in shop windows, breaking a light sweat in the warm mid-morning sun. The sight of the half-cast on his arm didn't bother him at all; it had become for him a badge of courage.

The Mellow Lemon's front doors were locked, blinds closed. Nothing strange about that. On Saturdays the place didn't get going until around four or five in the afternoon. Still, a mutha fuckin' hero shouldn't have ta go around back like the hired help. He started pounding on the bright yellow doors with his good hand, hard enough to make the glass rattle.

Took a while, but he finally got somebody up. For an instant the blinds behind the glass cracked open, then shut. He heard the click of a bolt being thrown. The doors opened far enough for him to get a glimpse of a puffy face and an eye blinking at the light.

"What ya want?" asked a woman's voice, heavy with sleep. "We're closed."

He remembered the fat hippie girl chopping vegetables on the night back in August when he'd ripped off old man Bronar. "Want to see Hector," he said, looking up and down the sidewalk with just enough show so it was plain his business didn't have nothin' ta do with a Jones for fresh-squeezed fruit juice.

222

"Just a minute," the girl said groggily. The door began to close.

"Ain't got a minute." He pushed his way in. Sonofa-bitch! Place was dark as the inside of a grave. Couldn't see a damn—

Freddy remembered his shades and slipped them off. Better. A lot better. He caught sight of a large white butt disappearing through the strings of bells hanging in the doorway to the kitchen. He followed.

Manallo sat at the table in a pair of imitation leopard skin bikini briefs, his heavy brown belly oozing out over the waistband. Hector was caught with a slice of toast halfway to his mouth dripping egg yolk. The full plate in front of the man reminded Claybourne of a bad head wound.

Out of the corner of his eye, Freddy caught a flash of female crotch surrounded by heavy marble-columned thighs, all quickly covered by a falling yellow muu-muu. He looked back at Manallo whose mouth still hung open in astonishment.

"Come for my money," Claybourne said, kinda fasci-nated by Manallo's breakfast. "What is that shit, man?" He pointed at the plate.

Manallo slowly put the toast down on the table and wiped the slimy yolk from his lips. "Black beans'n eggs, what jou think?"

Claybourne frowned. "Yeah, but what's all that red shit?"

"Some catsup, some tabasco, some peppers—hey! What the fuck jou doin' here, man. We ain't open jet."

"Like I said, I come for my money."

Manallo smacked his lips loudly. "Bluebird, get Clay-berg some breakfast. Sit down, man. How's the world a bee-bop?"

"Watch the mouth, mutha fuck."

Manallo grinned and reached for a bottle of rum. He poured a dollop into his coffee and offered the bottle to Claybourne. "Wanna drink?"

"No. Don't want no drink, don't want no breakfast. Just want my money."

"Hey! I seen jou picture in the *Mullet Wrapper*, man. Jou big hero, huh?"

Claybourne savored the recog but didn't show it. Instead, he put a cranberry colored patent leather boot up on the seat of an empty chair and leaned forward.

"Listen, dude. I come for my money. Ain't got time for no socializin' bullshit, you dig?"

"Hector," Claybourne heard the girl say, "I don't feel so good."

At the sound of her voice, Freddy turned and looked at her closely for the first time. She squatted in a corner, knees bunched up under the muu-muu. Her face looked pretty damn awful. The skin was drawn and gray, eyes sunken, without luster, rimmed with black rings that reminded him of old meat. She couldn't seem to stop licking her colorless lips.

With a dirty fingernail, Manallo removed some bean paste caught between his gold front teeth, then sucked the particle noisily into his mouth.

"Hector, it hurts!" she whimpered.

Poor bitch had a habit a mile long.

"Go upstairs and see Eddie," Manallo answered disgustedly. "Tell him I say ta fix jou up. Jou clean up out front jet?"

The girl struggled to her feet. She wobbled toward the back door, pushing her matted hair away from her face. Freddy caught sight of the track marks on her arm.

"I said, jou clean up jet?" Hector asked again—angrily this time.

She stopped at the screen door. "No," she whispered without turning around.

"Jou gettin' ta be a real pain in the ass there, Bluebird. Jou know that?"

"I'm sorry, Hector. I promise I'll—"

"Get lost." Manallo waved a newly dipped piece of toast

at her. She staggered out into the alley. Manallo worked a plastic spoon around in the mess in front of him, then greedily shoveled in another mouthful.

"What a pig," he said with his mouth crammed. "Hey, Clayberg, jou want a white girl ta take home with jou?"

"Shit. She got more tracks'n the Penn Central."

"Jou notice, huh? That's a problem. If jou notice, everybody notice. She got a real bad monkey. I think I gotta let her go. Too bad, she used ta be a good fuck. Maybe one of jou buddies like ta—"

"Hey, man," Claybourne interrupted, "didn't come here ta talk your family problems. Ain't gonna tell ya again. Want my money."

Manallo poured more catsup on top of his eggs and beans. "Jeah, I be hearin' jou, man. But jou gotta refresh my memory a little, 'cause I don't remember owin' jou no money." He looked up at Claybourne, his flashing gold teeth matching the crucifix around his neck.

Freddy nonchalantly examined a hangnail. "Hector, you the biggest mutha fuckin' mutha fuck I ever met. I got some bread comin', Jack, from a little transaction went down a few months ago. You dig, man? Or maybe I gotta freshen your memory with my foot up your ass."

With a fat forefinger Manallo rescued a trickle of egg yolk meandering down his belly. He licked the finger obscenely, then laughed. "Hell, Clayberg, I don't know what jou talkin' about. Maybe if jou come back tomorrow, then—"

Hector's words were cut off as a hand grabbed him by the hair on the back of his head and shoved his face down into the mess on the plate. As he gurgled and thrashed, he was aware of a voice next to his ear.

"Hear me good, bean fuck. My name is Clay-*bourne*, you got that? Clay-*bourne*. Ain't gonna listen ta no more of your bullshit, you dig? Nod your head if you dig. That's right. You gonna pay me my due, ain't ya? You be nice and polite."

Claybourne was enjoying himself. The sight and sound of Manallo drowning in his own breakfast reminded him of how good it felt to be on the street again, in charge of his own life. He gave a sharp tug on the handful of greasy hair, then stepped back. Didn't wanna kill the fuck, just scare him.

Manallo came up sputtering, gasping for breath, snorting out the bean paste packed in his nostrils, clawing at his eyes as the tabasco sauce dripped off his eyebrows. He jumped up and staggered blindly over to the sink where he stuck his head under the running water.

A few minutes later, after a lot of spitting and coughing and gagging, Hector turned on unsteady legs. He was still out of breath and had to hold onto the edge of the sink to keep from crumpling to the floor.

"Jou crazy, man!" he croaked.

"We all crazy, Conkman, didn't you know that?" Freddy twisted up a badass grin, then scowled. "Now that you finished eatin', get me my money!"

"Jeah, jeah, sure. Anything jou say." Manallo pushed himself away from the sink and lurched toward the strings of bells.

"Where you goin', mutha fuck?" Claybourne snarled. He made no move to block the other man's path.

"To get jou money. Other room. Cash register." Hector sounded like he was whipped.

"Yeah. Don't be long. I get nervous you be long."

The bells tinkled behind Manallo as he left the kitchen. Freddy yawned and sat down, then cursed quietly as he spotted a gob of food on one of his boots. Lazily he got up and searched the sink counter for a rag.

The thought came to him as he leaned over and wiped off the boot: What if Manallo had more balls than he figured? What if the mutha fuck was digging around out there right now for a piece, or rounding up some of the other assholes who worked in the restaurant? Yeah, well maybe Hector had left as a whipped dog, but a man'd be a pure fool to trust the tricky bastard. Pure mutha fuckin' fool.

Manallo forced his shaking fingers to dial the phone. He glanced back at the kitchen, making sure that the crazy nigger hadn't followed him. Crazy fucker was in for a big surprise. A voice at the other end of the line grabbed his attention. He cupped the receiver and spoke softly.

"Buddy, this is Hector . . . Hector Manallo . . . jeah. Let me speak to Mr. Bronar."

He waited impatiently as the line went silent, rubbed his burning eyes and tried to cough up a chunk of something caught in his throat. For just a second he thought he heard bells tinkle. When he looked over his shoulder at the kitchen doorway, though, he saw nothing. Must've been a breeze coming through the alley door.

The grinding of Bronar's voice over the phone brought him back to the business at hand.

"What the hell you want, Hector?"

"Mr. Bronar, how jou doin'? Got some pretty good news for jou."

"What's the matter with you, boy? Can't hardly hear you."

"Mr. Bronar, he's here right now. I got him all set up for jou."

"Who? Hector, you best be talkin' sense. Ah told you last time Ah'd do more'n have Buddy kick your ass if you dicked around with me again."

"It's him, Mr. Bronar. That nigger jou wanted. Claybourne. The one who ripped jou off. He's here, at the Lemon."

"You mean that spook that stoled ma radio?"

"Yes, sir. Thought maybe jou and Buddy could come over and take care of him right now. I got him hooked like a big fish."

"Hot damn, boy! Sounds mighty good. We'll be right—"

The line went dead. For a moment Manallo thought the

old man had hung up on him. But there was no dial tone, he realized, which meant . . . which meant . . . meant what? Furiously he rattled the disconnect button, groping for an answer.

He was still a little confused when he saw a piece of black telephone cord dangling in front of his face. Cord had a buncha little wires sticking out of it, like it'd been ripped—

Hector finally figured things out at about the same instant the voice spoke from behind him.

"Your ass is mine, mutha fuck."

It was as if a lighted match had been placed near the rear end of a great bullfrog. Manallo jumped three feet to his right, then scrambled in the direction of the kitchen.

Maybe if the light had been better or if his mind had been clearer or if the girl named Bluebird had done her morning cleanup like she'd been told, he would've gotten away. Trouble was, the tables and chairs were still scattered all over the place from the night before. A chair that wasn't supposed to be there tripped him and he went down hard.

Fear got him going again real quick, though. He scrambled on all fours toward the kitchen, panting now, only dimly aware of a throbbing pain in his shoulder. He was almost to the strings of bells when a hand grabbed the back of his imitation leopard skin bikini briefs and pulled him up short.

"Eddie!" he screamed, just before the lights went out.

From the end of the alley Claybourne looked back and saw a cream colored Continental come around the corner on two wheels. Definitely old man Bronar's ride, he warned himself. He'd gotten out of the Mellow Lemon at just the right time; another minute getting his revenge on the double-crossing Manallo would've meant curtains.

Which wasn't to say they wouldn't be hot on his trail as soon as they got Hector awake. Freddy started walking a little faster.

The streets of Key West were no longer safe for him, he

realized. The only safe place now was the Barracks. Thirty more days. If he could keep away from Bronar for thirty more days he'd be able to pocket his discharge and grab the first thing smoking north. Until then he'd have to watch it, stay outta town, almost restrict himself to the base. Might even have to volunteer for Fleming Key if push came to shove.

Shandy would understand. If there was one thing good about being a sentry it was that a man's friends didn't get hassled. Shandy would be able to come and go as she pleased, and if he just used his head, there were plenty of places on Base where a man could be alone with a woman.

He reached Southard and turned toward the Main Gate. Two more blocks and he'd be in the clear. He laughed out loud as he pictured what was going on back at the Mellow Lemon. In a way he was glad that Bronar now knew who had fucked up his operation for so long. The old man would go to his grave wishin' he'd never messed with Freddy Claybourne.

As for Hector Manallo . . . well, Hector was probably getting his ass kicked—again—right this minute. Besides . . .

Freddy shook the pocket of his slacks and something jingled with the loose change.

A loudspeaker over the door of the all-night laundromat signaled the coming birthday of Christ with the music of "Jingle Bells." As Claybourne passed by on the sidewalk, he spotted a gray-headed old woman through the window. She was reading a Bible to the fools who had chosen this Saturday to wash their clothes.

Freddy chuckled, not at the itchy-eyed bums getting a dose of fire and brimstone, but at the music. If you figured what had gone down back at the Mellow Lemon, when he and Manallo were alone, there was only one perfect song of the season, and it wasn't "Jingle Bells." No, seemed to him "All I Want For Christmas Is My Two Front Teeth" fit the bill a whole lot better.

CHAPTER TWENTY-THREE

WHEN the sergeant major walked into the Guard Office, Kargo and Brownell were going over the rough drafts of the Guard Roster for the upcoming holidays. Major Brocksneider's policy was that anyone with enough leave on the books could take either a week at Christmas or New Year, as long as no more than half the Barracks was gone at one time. The policy required implementation of a "running guard", in which every man not on leave would stand a six-hours-on—six-off duty schedule around the clock. It was a grinding routine, but most accepted it as an equitable solution.

"Gunnery Sergeant Brownell," Hollihan boomed, "I have got me a bitch."

The sergeant major stood in the doorway, ever present cigar clamped tightly in his teeth. The leash in his hand tightened and he hauled Jiggs into the office behind him.

"Better check your windage, Sergeant Major," Brownell pointed out. "That doesn't look like a bitch to me."

"Look at this asshole!" Hollihan roared, ignoring Brownell's joke. "Sonofabitch just got in. Thirty-six hours UA!"

Kargo could see that the dog was in bad shape. His coat was covered with burrs and dust, a pinkish stain slashed over one eye, the great head was bent, the long tongue hung nearly to the deck. Gasping for breath, the dog pulled back the corners of his jaws, producing something very close to a smile.

"Look at this fucker," Hollihan growled, "grinnin' like a goddamn boot just come from his first night in a cathouse.

This is gonna cost you a stripe, maggot ass," he warned the top of the dog's bowed head. "No canned meat for a week. All you get is dry chow, and I don't care if yer turds turn ta cannon shot. Got that?"

Without looking up, Jiggs collapsed in a heap at Hollihan's feet. Kargo fought to control his laughter.

"So what's this got to do with the Guard, Sergeant Major?" Brownell wheezed.

"He was out in town, Gunny. Conch dog catcher nailed him wanderin' down Truman Avenue. Only one way he coulda got out in town, and that's through one of our gates."

"The men're always taking him on liberty, Sergeant Major," Kargo said. "You know that. He's been out in town before."

"Yes, sir. Only this time he was alone, by hisself. Turd is startin' ta get mighty independent all of a sudden. I gotta feeling he caught a whiff and's decided ta pull libs on his own, deedee boppin' right off base anytime he feels the urge."

"Could be the men think he's got it coming," Kargo said.

"And that'd be a problem, sir. Much as they'd like him to be, this asshole ain't human. Fucker don't have the common sense ta keep a watch on his six o'clock."

"What do you want us to do?" Kargo knew that while Hollihan had come in addressing his complaint to Brownell, the timing had been well planned. Marine Corps sergeant majors were a crafty breed; they knew how to give orders to lieutenants.

"Like the gunny ta brief all the sentries, sir. Fucka-muga here don't leave the base on his own under no circumstances. The major agrees."

There it was. Hollihan was carrying an order from the major, and had presented it as a request from one NCO to another. Kargo figured Hollihan had missed his calling; he should have gone into politics.

"No problem, then," Kargo said cheerfully. "We'll start passing the word right away."

"Thank you, sir. Appreciate that."

Kargo got the feeling the sergeant major wanted to talk to Brownell in private. He got up from the desk and began unbuttoning his shirt while he headed for the door. "Think I'll get in a little roadwork while it's still cool."

Hollihan waited until the lieutenant was out of the office, then let the dog leash slip through his fingers. The dog was asleep. After ordering a cup of coffee from the Corporal of the Guard, the sergeant major went over to Kargo's desk and fell into the swivel chair.

"One of your men was in ta see me yesterday," he said to Brownell. "That kid Slater."

"I know," the gunny said. "I sent him."

"Think you might have a problem brewin' there, Ed. He's not a real happy Marine. Hell bent on getting out of the Corps. What's the poop? Thought he was pretty squared away."

"He was. Same old story. The duty's getting to him, the town's getting to him, for all I know this damn sunshine day in and day out is getting to him."

"I get the feelin' he's headed for a date with a brick wall. Might wanna keep an eye on him."

"I agree. Ya know, he tasted some pretty heady wine in Nam, Joe. Meritorious promotions, platoon sergeant for a while, running his own show. Garrison duty has got to be a real let down."

"Them's the breaks." Hollihan paused to take another look at the dog, still snoring on the deck. "How much time'd you have in before you made sergeant, Ed?"

"Five years," Brownell answered. "How about you?"

"Seven. If it hadn't been for the war, I'd still be a corporal. When we lost sixty percent of the platoon first day ashore, they *had* ta promote me. I was the only non-com left walkin' in the whole company."

Hollihan chuckled, but Brownell did not. The sergeant major's reference to "ashore" had been the beach at Tarawa. It was there he'd won the Navy Cross.

"Kids are getting promoted too fast these days," the gunny said, knowing it was what Hollihan wanted to hear. "Some of them just aren't cut out for the life. Anything you can do for him?"

"Nothin'." Hardrock picked a piece of tobacco off his tongue and studied it. "Hell, you know regs say he can't even put in for a transfer till he's got a year on station. By then, maybe he could qualify for an early out. Time bein', though, he'll just have ta tough it out. He put in for Christmas leave?"

"Negative. Said he couldn't take off with the Dutchman laid up in the hospital. Two of 'em are pretty good buddies. Might be more to it than that, though. Heard he's got a girlfriend in town."

"Well, like I said. Better keep an eye on him. I seen Horse Marines before. Ain't always a pretty sight."

The decorations on the big arched sign above the Main Gate rustled in a puff of warm wind. Plastic tinsel and a Santa Claus in short pants—Christmas in Key West. Slater still couldn't believe he hadn't put in for leave. He hoped the Old Man and Ma understood; he'd told them all about the Dutchman and the accident. He *hadn't* told them about Carolyn, though, or about the idea running in his head that he could still somehow get her back, make things the way they were just a few short weeks ago.

LeFey came out of the sentry shack licking his lips and the ends of his fingers. "Want me to take over for a while?" he asked. Slater had been checking vehicles alone while the other man took an unofficial break.

"Anymore doughnuts?"

LeFey grinned. "All gone," he said, rubbing his belly.

"Do me a favor. Don't accept anymore bribes."

"They ain't bribes, Slats," LeFey said. "I told ya, this time of year all the little old ladies will be dumpin' off goodies on us. Why'd you think I put in for leave at New Year? Come Christmas Eve, we'll be rolling in stuff. You watch. Last year I got about a thousand cookies, three Big Macs, two cakes, and twenty-five bucks in cash. Some little hippy chick even laid a lid on me. Man, I tell ya, we make out like bandits on the Main Gate."

"Goddamn, Nar-vel, that shit's gonna get you in big trouble one of these days."

"What, the grass? Come on, man. I ain't no dummy. I never take nothin' into the Barracks. Why'd you think Bone and me got that apartment? Speakin' of which, landlady just raised the rent on us. Goddamn ol' biddy. Wouldn't be so bad if she'd do something about her bugs."

"Landlady's got bugs?"

"Naw, the apartment. Huge suckers."

A white civilian panel truck pulled to a stop next to the island. LeFey stepped off the curb and approached the driver's window.

"What'ja got?" he asked.

"Delivery for the CPO Club," the driver answered. Slater recognized the man; it was Angelo, the guy with the earring, the owner of the club where he'd shoved the hurricane lamp into the face of the ugly bouncer.

"Got a pass?" LeFey wanted to know.

"No. Musta lost it."

"Well, you're gonna have ta park and apply for a tradesman's pass from Base Security. That's the building right over—"

"It's OK, LeFey," Slater called out. "He's cool. Let him on through."

LeFey shrugged—no skin off his nose—and waved the truck onboard. But Angelo didn't take off right away. Instead, he stuck his head out the window and shouted in Slater's direction.

"Thanks, Marine," he said. "When you gonna stop in for that drink? Things is pretty slow right now."

"Sounds good," Slater called back. "But in ninety days I'll be legal. Then none a us'll have ta sweat it."

Angelo laughed. "You bring that cute little girlfriend with you too, whenever she gets back in town."

"Oh, she's still around. Kinda busy though. Works nights out at the airport."

Angelo's eyebrows shot up. "Funny. Thought I seen her at the bus station 'bout twenty minutes ago. Her and her suitcase. I was droppin' off one of my waitresses going to Miami. Thought for sure I recognized her."

Slater felt a funny little tingle ripple up his scalp.

"Naw, couldn't a been her," he stammered.

"Coulda fooled me. She was talkin' with Rose Mc-Cracken so I didn't bother to say hello. They were huggin' and kissin' and bawlin'—you know the stuff. That's why I thought she was leavin' town."

"She was with Rose?" Slater's mouth went dry.

"Yup."

Slater turned his back on the truck and stumbled back into the shack. Angelo threw a curious glance at LeFey.

"Hey, I'm sorry, kid," he said. "Didn't mean to be droppin' bad news on your buddy."

LeFey looked in at Slater, then back to the driver. "Go on through. You're holding up traffic."

Slater didn't know Angelo had gone. And he didn't care that the line of vehicles waiting to pass onto the base was getting longer. His mind was jumbled. Nothing fit, nothing worked.

LeFey soon had his hands full. It was the end of the noon hour and everybody was coming back from lunch in town at the same time. The line of cars continued to grow.

"Hey, Slats," LeFey shouted. "Can you get the out-bound? They're starting to get pissed!"

Slater ignored the honking horns and the long line of backed up traffic. Without really knowing how it had gotten there, he held the phone in his hand.

"Guard Shack," a voice on the other end answered after four harsh buzzes.

"Bone, this is Slater. I've gotta be relieved. ASAP."

"What's the matter, Slats, Narvel's ugly face gettin' to ya?"

"Damn it, Tollster, I'm not fuckin' around! I'm leavin', with or without a fuckin' relief! You got that?"

Slater's voice was shrill and loud. LeFey had heard. He was looking into the shack, his mouth hanging open.

"Simmer down, man," Tollster answered, sounding worried. "Be back with you in one."

Car horns were blasting almost nonstop now, people getting angry as the line of cars waiting to get off-base grew. LeFey looked frantically at the line of traffic; there was no way he could handle both lanes.

"Slater!" he yelled. "For shit's sake!"

Slater just stared at him.

"This is Gunny Brownell," another voice suddenly crackled in Slater's ear. "What the hell's going on out there?"

"Gotta relieve me, Gunny," Slater whispered. "I've gotta get outta here."

"Keep your powder dry, Marine. What's going on? I just got a call from Base Security. They say there's a hellacious traffic jam out there."

"I don't give a shit about the traffic! Jesus Christ, Gunny, my girl is leaving town this goddamn minute! I gotta talk her out of it. Gunny, you gotta relieve me. Right goddamn now!"

"At ease there, Slater," Brownell said harshly. "We're not running the Dating Game. You know how we operate around here. Personal problems get handled on off-duty hours."

Slater rubbed a hand across his face. "I don't give a screamin' fuck, Gunny, don't ya understand?"

"You leave that post and it's a sure court-martial, you know that."

"Don't matter. What can they do ta me, anyway? Send me ta Nam?"

There was a long pause, then Brownell was talking again.

The gunny sounded real tired. "Slater, don't do anything foolish. Just hang on. I'll be out there in a few minutes. Try to get your shit together, will ya? Let me speak to LeFey."

"Don't think I can wait too long, Gunny."

"You damn well better!" Brownell shouted. "Put on LeFey."

Slater put the receiver down on the log book, then walked out to stand next to a sweating Narvel LeFey. While the other man hurried in to answer the phone, he started waving the traffic onboard with an unenthusiastic flip of his wrist. . . .

Five minutes later, the Barracks SOG truck pulled up at the gate in a screech of brake lining. Benjamin leaped out and made a beeline to the sentry shack. He touched Slater on the shoulder, motioned him to the truck, then took Slater's holster and .45 and strapped it on.

When Slater climbed into the truck, he found Gunny Brownell staring straight ahead with both hands locked on the wheel.

"Where is she?" the gunny snapped, sounding extremely pissed.

"Bus station."

"Be advised, Corporal," Brownell snapped as he popped the clutch and gunned the old gray pickup in the direction of town, "you've used up any slack you had coming from me or anybody else. I just hope she's worth it."

Slater squeezed the padded armrest and didn't say a thing.

CHAPTER TWENTY-FOUR

THEY got to the municipal parking lot just after the Greyhound pulled out in a belch of blue diesel exhaust. Brownell brought the Gray Ghost to a stop near the terminal building. Slater couldn't believe it.

"What the hell, Gunny!" he yelled. "The bus! Go after the bus!" He pounded the dash in frustration.

Brownell shoved the floor shift into neutral and turned off the ignition. The truck shook twice with engine knock, then died.

"Forget it, Marine. She's gone."

Slater growled and ripped at the truck's door handle. The chrome crank came off in his hand. Without wasting time thinking too much about it, he dived out the window, ignoring Brownell's shouted order to get back inside.

The bus was stopped at a red light a block away when he reached the edge of the parking lot and began running down the sidewalk. He yelled for the driver, waving his arms wildly.

The light changed.

He continued running for a few dozen more yards, gradually slowed, then stopped. The bus had disappeared from sight. He understood that the game—whatever game he'd been playing—was over. With a sickening drained feeling, he turned and walked back to the terminal.

Brownell was still sitting behind the wheel of the SOG truck. Rose McCracken stood next to the driver's door. She wore an ugly green shift and her usual ten pounds of cheap jewelry. Her face was puffy and when she spoke to him, her words were slurred; she'd been drinking.

"I'm sorry, Jack. But it's for the best."

"Why'd she do it?" he asked, searching Rose's face for secrets. "Not a word. Not even a goddamn phone call!" He turned his back on her and took a few steps toward the front of the truck. When he slammed his fist into the hood, his weight was behind it. He turned back to the woman. "Why?"

"I guess she just didn't have the nerve to face you," Rose said softly.

"But where'd she go? She told me you were all the family she had. Where'd she go?"

"Her daddy. Lives out in LA. She hasn't seen 'er heard from him in years. A few days ago she got a letter from him askin' her to come out. For Christmas."

For a second Slater saw a life vest being thrown to him. "Then she's coming back, right?"

"Aw, I'm sorry, Jack. Wish I could say that, but I don't think so." She watched his face cave in.

"Goddamn it, why not?"

Rose twisted her hands and wobbled a bit. "Well, her daddy promised her a new Mustang if she stayed."

"Are you shittin' me?"

"Oh, I know that sounds kinda shallow. But she had a lotta problems too, more'n she could handle. First her momma dyin', then some boy dropping her for another woman, then she started flunkin' school. Aw, Jack, Key West ain't no place to solve your problems."

He let his body fall back against the fender. He jammed his hands in the front pockets of his trops and stared down at the sun-baked blacktop.

"Don't be too hard on her," Rose offered. "It's partly my fault. She liked you an awful lot, but she was afraid."

"Afraid? Afraid of what?" A goddamn circus, he thought. Goddamn Barnum 'n' Bailey three ring circus.

"Afraid of you, Jack. Like I said, it was mostly my fault."

She took a deep breath, then let the air out slowly. When

she spoke again it was as if she were in another place, another time.

"More'n twenty years ago I came down here one summer and fell in love with the first Marine I ever met. Corporal R.J. Penderblast, stationed right over there in that very same Barracks. Rocky Penderblast. God I loved that man!"

Slater sulked. "She never told me about another guy," he said. Or had she? Somehow the name "Steve" popped into his head.

Rose went on as if she hadn't heard him. "Rocky and me was engaged. Carolyn's momma was coming for the ceremony." Her voice began to tremble. "Then came Korea."

For a moment Slater forgot his own troubles. Rose's face told him there would be no happy ending to her story.

"He shipped out ta Frisco. I was in love enough ta go out there with him. Even after his ship left, I stayed out there. Felt closer to him, somehow, doing that."

She paused to wipe away a tear. Slater felt uncomfortable enough to think about crawling under the truck. But he didn't.

"A few months later I got a letter from one of his buddies," she choked. "Said Rocky bought it in a mortar attack tryin' ta carry two wounded guys to a trench." She began to sob. "All they ever found was his dog tags! And this!"

Rose fumbled with a locket on a chain she'd pulled from under her shift. She held the open locket out for him to look at. He saw a heart-shaped photograph of a young Rose McCracken with her head touching a thin-faced young man who looked meaner than dog dirt.

Well hell, Slater thought, whatever turns ya on, I guess. "That's nice, Rose," he said.

"It's all I got to remember him by," she said between great racking sobs. "This, and a foot'n a half of hard oak." She rapped her knuckles on her wooden leg.

Slater glanced up at Brownell who had cradled his forehead between a thumb and forefinger and was staring down at the floorboard of the truck. Slater turned back to Rose, deciding that things were getting loonier by the second.

"When I finally figured Rock weren't comin' back," she said after blowing her nose on a frayed piece of Kleenex, "I just didn't want to live no more. My mind went—what you call it—blank. Walked all over Frisco in a daze. Walked right in front a one a them trolley cars. Cut my leg off cleaner'n a meat cleaver through Spam!"

Rose's description of her accident went right over Slater's head; something else was bouncing through his mind.

"Rose," he said, "did you tell this story to Carolyn?"

"I had to," she answered. "When I seen you and her was serious, I had to; I had ta warn her. Had ta warn her not to lose her heart to no Marine!" She turned a tear-streaked face up at him. "You people is always goin' off somewhere and gettin' kilt!"

Slater blinked. "Are you telling me she left because she was worried about losing body parts?"

"It's true!" she bawled. "That . . . an' a new Mustang, I suppose."

Whatever the reason, the damage had been done. Carolyn was gone. He wanted to laugh; he wanted to cry. He wanted to run; he wanted to lay down. Everything he wanted to do at that moment had an equal and opposite number. Finally, all he could do was bend over and put his cheek against the warm metal of the Gray Ghost's hood.

Rose squeezed his shoulder. "I think I know how you feel," she whispered near his ear. He could smell the booze on her. "I feel like that a lot too. There's a song I like ta sing when I feel that way. It helps a lot. Will you sing it with me?"

In a fog, Slater raised his head and stared at her. For now, right now, Rose was the ringmaster of this dog and pony show.

Seeing she had his attention, Rose stepped back, held her

arms wide, and began to sing "I Left My Heart In San Francisco."

Insane, he thought, everybody is insane. He turned away from her and walked to the other side of the truck. He climbed in next to Brownell.

"Gunny," he mumbled, "can we get the fuck outta here?"

Brownell started up and eased the truck away from Rose. She continued to sing to the bus terminal where two or three people, obviously bewildered, waited for a ride home.

"Did you hear what she said?" Slater asked as they pulled out of the lot.

"Couldn't help it." Brownell paused to shift gears. "Don't fool yourself, son," he said, almost kindly. "She left for the car."

Chapter Twenty-five

FOR his Christmas dinner, Slater scarfed down a can of Franco-American spaghetti, two Milky Ways, and a can of Coke, all compliments of the vending machines in the Barracks rec room.

The squids went all out for the men still on base Christmas Day; there had been a big feed going on most of the afternoon at the messhall—roast turkey with all the geedunk that went with it. Only a few Marines took the time, though; five days of a running guard had turned most of them into scratchy-eyed robots, staggering from post to bunk and back again. On a running guard it was impossible to get enough sleep. Luxuries like trips to the messhall— even on Christmas—were passed up for extra rack time.

Slater walked into the flickering electronic light of the TV room and listened to the snores of his own relief mingled with the sounds of a football game on the screen. The relief had come in almost a half-hour before; he was still awake because he'd been standing Corporal of the Guard and had been required to make a detailed inventory of weapons and gear before coming off-post.

For the sixth time in as many watches, his last entry in the log had been the same:

Properly relieved by Corporal Friendly. Lance Corporal Jiggs still reported UA. Respectfully, Corporal John Slater, USMC.

The dog had last been seen on the morning of the twenty-third, trotting out the Main Gate. The sentries on duty had reported him to the Corporal of the Guard, but by the time they'd gotten the OK to leave post and go after him, Jiggs had vanished.

The sergeant major had organized a search party right away—even Screamin' Don and Kargo had joined in—but all anybody had come up with was a pack of male dogs howling outside a fenced yard on Emma where a fuzzy poodle in heat was shaking her tail.

For a while after that the joke was that Jiggs had gotten his female smells mixed up and was probably out in Sigsbee trying to pork some squid's wife. The joke stopped after Hollihan talked to a little boy on the street where the poodle bitch lived. The kid said he'd seen a dog answering Jiggs' description get into a "big black car." The consensus of opinion was that some douche-bag snowbird had decided to take the bulldog back north as a souvenir. Many hoped Jiggs would tear out the bastard's throat, or at least make his life a living hell with timely blasts from his almighty bowels.

Thinking about the missing dog didn't help Slater's spirits, especially at seven P.M. on Christmas Day. He'd already talked to his folks; they'd both sounded kinda down. Marty wasn't home. He was spending his Christmas in an Ann Arbor commune.

Slater looked for an empty couch or armchair, spotted one near the back of the room, and collapsed into it. In a little more than five hours he'd have to wake everybody up and get them ready to go out again; until then there was time only for sleep.

"Hey, Slater," a voice whispered from behind him somewhere.

"Freddy? You still awake?"

"Yeah, man. Listen, wanna thank you for last night. Ain't had a chance."

"That's cool. Christmas Eve and all, I figured somebody oughta have some fun."

Claybourne—cast finally off—had been a supernumerary with him in the Guard Shack the night before on the midnight to six. When Shandy showed up, he let Freddy spend the rest of the relief out in the front seat of the SOG's Gray Ghost.

"Appreciate it, that's all," Claybourne said.

"No sweat."

Freddy cracked a sunflower seed between his teeth, then blew the shell onto the deck. He got up, came over and squatted next to Slater's chair.

"Think I know who got the dog, man."

Slater could smell the man's sweat. They were all getting a little ripe. There was enough light from the TV to see Freddy's face, and what Slater read there told him the man was not trying to jive him.

"What're you talking about, Fred?"

Claybourne whistled a sunflower seed back over his shoulder. "Out on Six this afternoon, while I was relievin' Sudlic so he could make a head call, this chick who works for a guy named Manallo stops by."

Slater had a vision of a cigarette bobbing between gold teeth. "Manallo? Cab driver? I know him!"

"Cab driver my ass. Dude is up ta his butt in every kinda shit you wanna talk about. I'll tell ya one thing, though, I had enough of his fuckin' around. Had enough of *all* of 'em."

"What makes you think he's got Jiggs? This chick tell you that?"

"Shit, this chick can't even say her own name, man. But she give me this note."

Claybourne pulled a piece of paper from his back pocket and handed it to Slater who unfolded it and tilted it towards the TV for enough light to read:

Clayborg
If you wanna see you dog agen, be at Stock Island in the junk yard at nine tanight. Come a lone.

Santa Claws

"You sure it's Manallo?" Slater asked as he glanced up.

"Damn right I'm sure. Mutha *still* ain't got my name right."

"What the hell's his problem?"

"He wants my ass, man. Him and another dude."

"And he thinks you're gonna walk out there alone and get a thumpin' just cause he grabbed Jiggs?"

"Hey, man, the dude never had no rep for brains." Claybourne hesitated for a moment. "So, you wanna come with me, man?"

Slater did a double take. "Where? The junkyard? You mean you're going out there? Shit, Fred, you just got through telling me it was a set-up!"

"Got any better ideas?"

"Call the fuckin' cops!"

"No way. This other dude, Bronar, is connected. No way the locals gonna bust him. You call the cops, man, and they probably gonna help him waste my ass."

"So let's get the gunny, or maybe the lieutenant, the sergeant major."

"Come on, Clyde. Those dudes way too straight for a gig like this. Besides, they probably wanna be askin' questions I don't wanna answer."

"Like what?"

"Like why them Conchs want my ass so bad in the first place."

"Which is none of my business, right?"

"If you gotta know, I'll tell ya."

"Forget it."

Claybourne grinned. "Could be some trouble," he said. "Tell you that up front."

"That dog saved my butt once. Figure I owe him." Slater watched another sunflower shell spin through the air. "What about you, Fred? What the hell does it matter ta you what happens ta Jiggs? Two more weeks and you're out, going home."

"I got my reasons," Claybourne answered. "Anyways, I *like* that dog, man. Ain't no cause for that mutha fuckin' Manallo ta mess with ol' Jiggs, man, no cause at all."

"Yeah. So . . . you got some plan?"

"Damn right I got a plan," Claybourne answered indignantly. "Think I spend four years in this jive-ass outfit for nothin'? Now pay attention, cause tonight we are righteously gonna kick some butt."

Claybourne watched the headlights come down the winding access road that led to the junkman's shed where he'd parked. He leaned back on the front fender of the top-down Olds and watched headlight beams play across the surrounding mountain range of rusting junk. Stacked skeletons of whole automobiles danced for an instant in the light, with the pitted carcasses of appliances and bones of creaky-looking bedsprings and waterlogged mattresses.

The big car pulled to a stop twenty yards away. Before the high beam flicked on, blinding him, Claybourne saw three men in the cream colored Continental. If nothing else, Bronar was predictable.

The Continental's engine shut down. The lights were left on. Car doors opened and closed and a few crunching footsteps sounded before Manallo's voice floated across the clearing.

"Jou come alone, Freddy?" Even in the harsh light, it was easy to spot the gap in Manallo's gums where his front teeth used to be.

"Damn right I come alone," Claybourne snapped. "Think I need a army ta protect me from *you*, man? Don't make me laugh. Where's the dog? I ain't got all night."

"Well now, if it ain't Uncle Sam's prize coon," a second voice broke in from the darkness behind the Continental's lights. "Ain't seen you in a while, boy. Where you been keepin' yourself?"

Freddy jumped away from the fender. "Who's that? That ain't Bronar? Damn you, Manallo! You double-crossin'—how many teeth I gotta knock outta your head before you learn!"

"Hush your mouth, boy," Bronar snarled. "Hector does what Ah tell him. So will you."

"Eat fuck, old man," Claybourne snapped back.

Bronar stepped forward, his face grotesquely backlit. "You made a fool a me, nigga toes. You cost me a lotta money too. No nigga does that ta Belview Bronar, not without payin' it back with interest."

Claybourne lazily leaned back against the fender. "Kiss my ass, white dick."

Bronar sucked in an audible breath, as if shocked by Claybourne's words. "You a mighty uppity black sonuvabitch," he snarled, then turned his head and spoke over his shoulder. "Buddy, bring me this boy's face."

A huge shape nearly blocked the beam from both headlights as Buddy lumbered out of the darkness and began moving in Claybourne's direction. Freddy jumped off the fender and took two steps backward, his arms outstretched in front of him. "Hold on, now," he said, fear in his voice. "No need for no violence!"

"Shoulda thought of that before, boy," Bronar giggled. "Ain't no stoppin' ol' Buddy, once he's got the scent."

The shape of Buddy came on, as slow and determined as a rising tide.

"Manallo, I'll get you for this!" Claybourne shouted.

"Sure, sure," Hector lisped through the empty space in his gums. "I be shakin' all like a leaf, Bubba."

Claybourne stopped long enough to reach down for a handful of gravel. He threw it at Buddy. "Stay away from me, mutha fucka!" Freddy shouted.

Buddy shrugged off the gravel and kept coming. By the time Claybourne had stumbled back past the rear fender of the Olds, Bronar's in-law was only a few feet away.

Slater waited. He was crouched low on the floor of the back seat. When he heard the crunch of Buddy's footsteps pass directly beside his position, both he and the riot shotgun came up at the same time; a round already in the chamber. He drew a bead on Buddy's jawbone.

"Better stop right there, asshole," he growled, "or your brains'll be in Miami before your shit hits the ground."

The sound of Slater's voice caused Buddy to freeze in his tracks. Slowly he turned his head, his beady pig eyes focusing on the muzzle pointed at his face. Right away Slater realized (with a twitch in his guts) that there would be no bluffing those eyes; there was no surprise there, no fear either, just blind acceptance of this new twist of events.

Buddy looked back at Bronar, maybe for new instructions, then took, a step in Slater's direction.

It was time to put up or shut up, Slater decided. Another second and the big man would be able to reach him. The "safety" in his head clicked "off" again, just like it had other times, with the cabby, the bouncer at Angelo's, with the admiral's boat. Time to git down and boogie.

He started putting pressure on the trigger. Bye-bye, bad-ass. Then he caught himself. Here they called it murder.

Almost as though it had a will of its own, the stock of the shotgun rotated out—a quick darting butt stroke that was over and done with so quickly that the only proof it had happened at all was Buddy, collapsing like big game brought down with an overdose of tranquilizer.

Bronar and Manallo froze at the sight of the indestructible Buddy so easily chopped down. They backed off toward the Continental.

Slater pivoted smoothly, the shotgun stock snapping back to its comfortable spot on his cheekbone. The muzzle jumped, first at Bronar, then Manallo, so each had a good look at the inky blackness of smooth-bore. Unlike Buddy, they recognized eternity when they saw it.

"One more step and I'll spatter you!" Slater screamed. The rush that had come with the butt stroke made his voice sound like some bug-fuck crazy, just the right amount of insanity.

"On your bellies!" Slater yelled again, trying to control the firecrackers popping all through his brain. Git down, git down, git down, YEAH!

Manallo couldn't get on his stomach fast enough; the old man only fell to his knees.

"Man said on your belly, mutha fucka," Claybourne screamed, running at Bronar with clenched fists. Bronar wobbled, then fell back on his rear end, his arms wearily raised to block Claybourne's blows.

But Freddy didn't hit him, didn't touch him. Humiliating the old conch would be much more satisfying than a beating.

He brought his face within inches of Bronar's ear and yelled. "Maggot! Mutha fuckin' scum! Think you're some kinda tough?" Freddy was riding high. "You ain't nothing' but worm shit. Old donkey jizz, that what you is, cock-sucka. Man said on your belly! You hear the man?"

Bronar didn't answer and Claybourne slapped him lightly across the mouth. "What's the matter with you, *boy*? You deaf? Goddamn redneck cracker mutha fucka! Know what I'm gonna do, ol' man? I'm gonna ram my dick up your skinny ass."

Claybourne sidestepped so he could look into Bronar's eyes. "My big *black* dick, right up your butt. Gonna get my buddy ta take some Polaroids too. Put 'em up all over town. How'd you like that?"

Bronar avoided Freddy's eyes. "Leave me be, nigga," he whined.

Slater touched Claybourne's shoulder. "Check him for a weapon, man. Look what the other asshole was carrying."

Freddy paused and glanced at a blue-black revolver hanging loosely from Slater's trigger finger. He cursed under his breath and released Bronar with a shrug, pushing the man flat on his face into coral dust as he methodically frisked him from head to toe. He found nothing.

Leaving the whimpering Bronar on his belly, the two Marines walked to where Manallo lay, face down. Claybourne squatted down next to Hector's head and twirled the revolver while Slater stood guard, the shotgun nestled casually in the crook of one arm.

"Fixin' ta smoke somebody, Hector?" Claybourne hissed.

"No way, Freddy." Manallo was scared; you could hear it. "It was for the rats, jou know? Place fulla rats."

Claybourne glanced up at Slater, saw a look of disgust, then turned back to the man on the ground. "You ain't wrong about that, shithead. Now where's the dog?"

"Keep your yap shut, Manallo," Bronar managed to gasp. "Don't tell these sonsabitches nothin'!"

Slater stepped back over to the old man. "Mister," he said evenly, "I don't know you, but my friend here is itchin' for an excuse ta do major surgery on your bod. Why don't you shut up so we can get this over with?"

The tone of Slater's voice must've lulled Bronar into a false sense of security. He raised his head and looked the Marine straight in the eye. "You boys is dead men, you know that? Ah own this town. When Ah put the word out, there ain't gonna be a hole big enough for you ta crawl inta. Not on the street, not on the base, not in that Barracks where you live. Believe me, boy, you gonna die regrettin' every second a this."

Slater rocked easily on his heels and grunted a laugh. "Hey, Fred, time for some company, don't ya think?"

"Yeah, man. Don't look like no more of these assholes comin'."

Slater stuck two fingers in his mouth and whistled.

They came from all sides, a constricting circle of dark phantom figures, soundlessly entering the periphery of the light thrown by the headlights, and the spotlight on the junkman's shed. Some wore jungle cammies, others faded standard-issue forest green. Their faces were masked with smudges of black, brown, and green camouflage grease, a new race of humanity. A few of them carried shotguns, others nightsticks or vicious weapons from the world of junk around them. They said nothing, and their faces—the little of them Bronar could see—showed no emotion.

"Take a look, old man," Slater said, "take a long look. You read the papers, watch TV. We are the dudes who've been doing the killin' for you. Only the secret is we *wasn't* doing it for you. Know why we did it? I'll tell ya, you bastard. Because the gooks fucked with us!"

As he spoke, Slater brought his face closer and closer to the old conch until he was only inches from the other man's sagging face. His voice caressed Bronar like a lover's breath. "I hope you understand what I'm sayin', old man. If you get out of here alive tonight, it's very important you understand. Anything happens to me or Freddy, then somebody from this Green Machine is gonna blow away your skinny ass like he was crushin' a cockroach. Look at these faces. See anybody you could recognize later? There are a hundred swinging dicks where we live, an' more from where that came from. You could spend the rest of your life runnin' and there'd still be somebody from the Crotch to grease your worthless ass."

Slater's voice dropped to a whisper. "See, Mister, nobody fucks with us. Nobody. It's what you might call . . . a tradition."

For a long moment the only sound was the old man's wheezing search for breath.

"Gettin' late," someone in the circle finally said. "Relief goes in less than two hours."

"Remember what I said, old man," Slater warned as he got to his feet. "Remember."

Manallo squirmed as Claybourne kicked him in the side. "Get up, Conkman. We got some business with you yet."

Manallo struggled to stand.

"Ain't gonna ask ya nice again, Conkman," Claybourne said, cocking the pistol in his hand. "Where's the dog?"

"I dunno, man," Manallo answered dully. "I swear to jou, I dunno."

Slater hissed. "Don't play games with us, man. Where's the fuckin' dog?"

"I dunno I tell jou!" Hector shrieked. "He got away maybe!"

Claybourne was about to slap the man's face when Slater pushed him aside and grabbed Manallo's chin, squeezing an opening big enough to insert the first inch and a half of shotgun barrel.

"Now you listen to me, you greasy son of a bitch," Slater spat into Manallo's face. "We don't have time for your shit. You're gonna tell us where that dog is or I'll splatter you. Now TALK!"

"Arbragwahumppp," Hector choked, finally figuring out there was only one way out of this mess. Slater slowly withdrew the shotgun and let the man slump to his knees.

"The frigidaire, man," Manallo whimpered. "The frigidaire."

Most of them had smelled death before; the cloying, putrid, faintly sweet odor was unmistakable, unforgettable, like no other smell on earth. As they gathered around the old refrigerator where they'd been led by the sweating man in the shit-fouled baggy trousers, they knew before the door was opened that Jiggs had taken his last dump on the sergeant major's rug.

He had died fighting. Even in the darkness it was easy to see the claw marks and teeth holes in the insulation. Dark blotches of dried blood stood out distinctly on his mottled brown and white coat; his massive jaws were locked open, still searching for one last breath of life.

For a long time they stood silently staring at him, then Rodriguez quietly said a prayer in Spanish. Slater handed the shotgun to Claybourne and lifted the dog's body into his arms. Without a word he turned and began walking back to the shed, staggering a little, surprised by the dog's weight and the heaviness in his own heart.

Tollster wanted to stuff the three prisoners into the airtight crypt of the refrigerator and call it a night. Slicks Johnson commented on how that wouldn't work unless they chopped up the bodies since the refrigerator was an old model and not big enough for five hundred pounds of raw meat. Benjamin (the proverbial "cooler head") said they had to draw the line at murder. It was left to the streetwise genius of Claybourne to come up with a revenge they could all live with.

CHAPTER TWENTY-SIX

JIGGS lay in state on the sheet-draped pool table, the body wrapped in Saran Wrap on Rose's orders. She was as sad as anybody, but she had to think of future business. Before hitting her private stock of Scotch, she brought a dozen scented candles and placed them around the table cushions. The flickering light and smell of incense made Slater think of a Buddhist shrine.

One by one the other Marines had taken off, some of them—like Slicks—to slide home for a few minutes with a wife or girlfriend, the rest back to the Barracks to get ready for another tour of duty. Only Claybourne and Slater stayed to finish one final pitcher of beer. By the time the last glass was poured, they had less than twenty minutes to get back to the base.

"Mutha fucka didn't deserve to die," Freddy said, looking over at Jiggs. The good feeling he'd felt watching the naked and hog-tied bodies of Bronar, Manallo, and Buddy dumped in the trunk of the Continental had faded. "Think maybe we shoulda wasted them dudes."

"Wouldn't change nothin'," Slater mumbled. He forced a grin. "Besides, your idea was a hell of a lot better. Daisy chaining those pukes was beautiful. I can still see 'em, squirmin' around in that trunk, nose to asshole. That old bastard's gonna be smelling Manallo's shit till the day he dies."

"Ain't that the truth," Claybourne chuckled. "Tell ya, though, I 'bout dropped my trou when Tollster started shootin' up that big bad Lincoln. Sheee-it! BOOM BOOM BOOM!"

"Yeah, instant Swiss cheese. We're lucky it's Christmas. Shotgun fire usually attracts some attention."

"Shit, wasn't nobody in miles of that place. Sign said the junkman won't be back till day after tomorrow. Man, is he gonna be surprised when he opens that trunk!"

Slater laughed; he could see it. "Tell ya one thing, time we got finished with it, that car was nothing' but scrap metal. Junkman oughta thank us." He drained half his glass with one long thirsty gulp. "Wish the Dutchman coulda been there," he said after wiping his mouth. "Stuff like that's right up his alley. I'm gonna have to go out there tomorrow and tell him all about it. He's gonna be frosted we didn't take him with us."

Claybourne rolled his beer glass between his palms. "Yeah, ol' Dutch woulda got off on it, that's for damn straight."

Slater held his hands up to his face. "Jesus! Would ya look at that! I'm still shaking."

"You comin' down from the high, man, that's all."

"Yeah. Just like the Nam. You too?"

"Shit, why you think I went out there tonight? Think I risk my ass just for that poor ol' dog, man? I figured ta get me one more of them mind-blowin' rushes before I went home." Freddy laughed. "Better'n speed, man."

Rose began singing a Christmas carol from her perch behind the bar. The bottle in front of her was almost empty. Slater looked around at limp decorations hung all over the room, wondered if Christmas would ever be the same. Last year he'd shivered in a bunker standing a radio watch; this year he was sitting at the wake of a dog. Next year? Who the hell knew?

"When're you going home, Fred?" Slater asked quietly.

"Week'n five days. Turnin' in my trops for some decent threads."

"Think you'll miss the Crotch?"

"Me? Miss the Machine? You shittin' me?"

"Know what I can't understand, Fred?" Slater asked the

ceiling (the beer was starting to do a number on his brain).
"Can't understand how the hell I can hate the Crotch so
much and still get the goosebumps when I hear that song."

"Shit. You mean that Hallsa Monte Zuma stuff? Shit.
Only time I get goosebumps lately be when Shandy looks at
me and her eyes tell me I'm in for some specials."

"*Specials* all right," Slater kidded. "A knife in the gut."

"Naw, man. Me and Shandy finally got an under-
standin'. Ain't no other woman can do for a man like she
can. . . . Tell you the truth, man, I think we might be
gettin' serious. Soon's she graduates in June she's comin'
up home ta meet my mama. Think I'll maybe be lookin' ta
get me a job in security or somethin'. DC's got a lotta need
for security. All them fat-cats in their million-dollar pads,
scared shitless of the niggers. They'll be lookin' for
somebody knows how to think on his feet."

Slater raised his glass. "Good luck to ya, man. You're all
right, Fred, ya know that? For all your bullshit, you're all
right. Merry Christmas, man."

Freddy grinned and lifted his glass in return. He emptied
it, then put it down with a thud. "Time we was gettin' back.
Screamin' Don might be showin' up."

"Hell, it's Christmas. He's home with his family."

"Don't mean nothin'. That man takes CDO serious."

"Come on, Don's mellowed out, man. Ain't really
screwed with anybody since the Birthday. He ain't gonna
pick Christmas Night ta start again. He told Benjamin not ta
call unless Castro invaded."

"Maybe. But I am one dude who's too short ta tempt fate
at this late date." Claybourne paused for a moment, proud
of his poetry. "Dig that, Jack. Ali ain't the only brutha
who's beautiful."

"You think that old man you whipped up on's gonna
cause us any trouble?" Slater asked.

"Bronar? Who you kiddin'? After that line a bullshit you
gave him about one of us killers 'round every corner?
Anyways, he knows if he messes with us he's gonna get the

whistle blowed on his little operation. Feds and state pig
will be on him like flies on his old lady's privates. Appear
ta me that—"

"Hey, what do ya mean—my line of bullshit?" Slate
interrupted. "I was serious!"

"You gotta be shittin' me."

"Hell if I am," Slater answered, feeling a little ticked off
"Anybody screws around with one of us has the rest to dea
with, just like in Nam."

Claybourne pushed back his chair and stood. "Slats, yo
dreamin', boy. Don't know what war you was fightin', bu
the way I seen it, it was every man for hisself. We was jus
countin' the days, man, countin' the days and hopin' i
wasn't your own butt blowed away. Ain't nobody gonna
look after your ass 'cept your own self."

Slater couldn't get his eyes to move. "You're wrong
Freddy," he mumbled. "You're wrong."

"No way, man. Ain't nothin' changed since the day I wa
born. And it never will." Claybourne checked the Pabs
clock over the bar. "Time ta dee-dee, man. Let's go."

Slater nodded wearily and stood up. "I'll settle up with
the Crack."

As Claybourne drifted over to the door where Bright th
cook sat snoring in a chair, Slater approached Rose. Sh
was humming softly; it sounded like "Silent Night."

"What do we owe ya, Rose?"

She looked up, wet and unfocused eyes roaming before
falling on him. "Oh, hi there, toots. Merry fucking Christ
mas." Her words were slurred and mushy.

"Same to ya," Slater said. "What do we owe ya?"

"Ferget it. On-a house for Marines tonight."

"Better not. Second relief'll be along in a while to say
good-bye to Jiggs. You could go broke."

"On-a house," she murmured. "Merry Christmas."

"Yeah, you said that."

"That fella find Claybourne yet?"

"What fella?"

"Fella's been lookin' for him around here all day. Says he's got some money for Freddy Claybourne. I told him Claybourne don't come in here so often, but this guy keeps hangin' around. Don't like that. Looks creepy. Bad for business."

Slater turned toward the door where Freddy waited. "Hey, Claybourne! Rose says some dude's been lookin' for ya. Says he's got some money for ya."

"Sure. Manallo. Owed me some bread. Come on, let's went."

"Carolyn says ta say hello," Rose said before Slater could take a step.

"You hear from her?" He couldn't keep the excitement out of his voice.

"Coupla days ago. Christmas card. Says she startin' school out there in LA. Next month. She'n her daddy gettin' along real nice since he got her the Mustang."

Slater thought he felt his pump jump. Ta-bump. A rim-shot. "She said hello, huh? Anything else?"

"No . . . it was kinda short."

"Just hello?"

"Just hello."

He scowled into the bar mirror. Claybourne's voice reached him in a fog.

"Move your butt, Slats. We gonna have ta run for it!"

"Rose, you got her address or something?"

She blinked at him for a few seconds, like the question was being translated at the United Nations. Finally she nodded. "Yeah. Suppose it's around here someplace. I'll look." She thumped down to the end of the bar and began rummaging through a box of receipts and papers.

"I ain't shitting you, man," Claybourne called from the door. "I'm bookin'. With or without you."

"Sure it's here someplace," Rose mumbled.

"Cool it, Fred," Slater answered as he made his way down the bar to stand beside Rose. "Somebody'll cover for us. I'll be there in a sec."

"Kiss my ass, man. I ain't riskin' no bad time for bein UA. I'm too short."

Rose cursed as the box full of papers slipped out of her hands, spilling the contents on the floor. She awkwardly went to her hands and knee and continued the search. Slater vaulted the bar and started to help her.

"Fuck you, Slater," Claybourne shouted. "I'm gone!"

Slater heard the door open then slam shut. He peeled a soggy scrap of paper from the floor and examined it. Somebody's IOU. He stuffed it back into the box.

He had a sinking feeling that he was burning his bridges, that he should've left with Claybourne. But Claybourne had more to lose than he did. Freddy was getting out, going home, couldn't hack the bad time. So what if this gig landed him in front of the major, cost him some time? Time he had plenty of. He wanted that address.

"Here it is!" Rose bellowed. She fell back on her rear end, her wooden leg smashing like a baseball bat into a cabinet. "Bren'wood. Bren'wood, California!"

He heard himself whoop for joy, like a little kid who'd just found a quarter on the sidewalk. He reached for the envelope. His fingers were only millimeters away when he heard the shots out on the street.

Maybe in a few years he would mistake those sounds for a truck backfire or cherry bombs in the still air of a summer's evening. But he was too soon back, too soon back from where small arms fire was a way of life.

His first reaction was to drop to his belly. Three more muffled cracks.

"Manallo!" he spat. "You son of a bitch!" How had the bastard gotten out of the Lincoln?

He forced himself to his feet, tasting old brass in his mouth, ignoring it as he followed Bright out the door. He low rolled out onto the asphalt, his mind blank except for the nagging voice telling him what a fool he was to come out here with no weapon.

It was dark in the alley, darker than the dimness inside the

Bamboo despite the streetlight on Duval. He caught sight of two men scuffling about ten yards away. One laughed hysterically; the other made no sound at all, except for strange tongueless grunts. Bright was kicking ass. But where was Claybourne?

He tried to get up. Something slippery took his feet out from under him. His hand came up in front of his face, wet, warm, and dark. Too dark to be water, a part of him calmly decided. Jesus Christ! Oh, Jesus fucking Christ!

He saw the body then, wedged in the angle of the Bamboo Room and the alley.

"Freddy!" he called. The body did not move.

Not again, dear God, not again. He crawled on hands and knees. Warm wetness was everywhere, pooling blackly around him. He pulled the body away from the wall, rolling Claybourne onto his back. He ripped off his shirt and used it to try to plug the holes. But there were too many, too many holes oozing life.

"Corpsman!" he heard himself screaming, "Corpsman!"

Freddy's mouth was full of blood; he could taste it as he covered cold lips with his own. He spat, then started again, blowing his breath into the body of a friend.

It was like trying to inflate an innertube with a bad leak. Each breath in was followed by a warm trickle out. Again and again he blew life in. Again and again it seeped out.

"Breathe, goddamn you, breathe!" he croaked in Claybourne's ear. Freddy did not answer, only stared back with unblinking eyes.

CHAPTER TWENTY-SEVEN

A Navy front loader with a backhoe (sent over by one of Hollihan's drinking buddies at the Chiefs' Club) had scooped out a deep six-by-three trench in the rocky soil out behind the Barracks maintenance shed. A small plywood coffin now rested on a couple of two-by-fours laid over the open hole.

The off-duty relief, the office poags, and a few men back off leave, stood in ranks on one side of the box, while the burial detail lined the other. Hollihan and the major stood side by side between the two groups, completing a rough "U" around the gravesite. They had come to say good-bye to Jiggs, the best way they knew how.

The sergeant major stepped forward. As far as he was concerned—as far as anybody in authority was concerned— Jiggs had been run over by a hit-and-run driver in town. Nobody above the rank of sergeant would ever know any different.

"Jiggs," Hollihan said gruffly, "you was as mean as a boot DI and as nasty as a San Diego whore with the clap, but ya stood yer duty like a Marine, and you was one of us. We'll miss you. May God watch over you, old friend."

If there was moisture in the sergeant major's eyes as he about-faced and took his post beside Brocksneider, no one dared see it.

On Benjamin's command, the burial detail aimed their rifles toward the sky and a volley from seven M-14s shattered the stillness of morning.

Three times the volley rolled, and each time Slater flinched; he'd about had his fill of gunfire.

For the three days since the murder he'd had little or no sleep, and the problem wasn't being on a running guard anymore. Kargo had taken him off the duty roster the day after the shooting so he'd had plenty of time—too much time maybe—to battle the reruns of Christmas night: the junkyard, the refrigerator, the dead dog, the horror at the Bamboo with the gunshots and blood and lifeless body of Freddy Claybourne. Slater could still hear the maniacal laughter of the kid with the scraggly beard as the cops dragged him away.

Scuttlebutt had it that the man's name was Crabtree, a tin-can sailor with a long history of mental illness. Word was that the man had done a stretch in the Navy's booby hatch for going after his captain with a crowbar. A big investigation was going on right now at the hospital to find out why this character had been released to return to duty.

But why had he gone after Freddy Claybourne? It didn't make any sense.

If Slater's hours awake had been a hell of doubts and questions, trying to sleep was worse. No sooner did his head hit the pillow than the nightmares began—in wide-screen technicolor.

Thought he'd destroyed the negatives to that hot day in the paddies near Duc Lom, but now parts of that horror played out for him again, just like they'd done before, right after Choo bought it. Bad enough seeing Choo Choo's shattered body lying in the muck, bad enough to make him scream and wake up with the cold sweats, but it got worse, a lot worse.

He would see himself opening that refrigerator door and Choo Choo—not Jiggs—would fall out, eyes wide and sightless, tongue black and swollen. Then he'd spot Claybourne, floating in knee-deep brown paddy water that looked like diarrhea, face contorted in a grin of death. And the nightmare would continue like that for as long as he slept—Jiggs, Freddy, and Choo Choo exchanging places and attitudes of death. Bad shit.

The clear notes of "Taps" came from the stand of palm trees on the opposite side of the Barracks grounds. Gurtzer played as he'd never played before; sadness and grief poured out in every lonely note. Slater felt a lump in his throat as the small coffin was lowered into the ground.

Major Brocksneider and Hollihan held a hand salute until the bugle's song drifted to an end, then the formation was dismissed. They all walked away except Slater, who stayed until he was alone. He walked to the open hole, stared into it for a minute, then took something out of his pocket and tossed it in.

He'd heard that another one of Hollihan's drinking buddies at the Chiefs' Club had promised a brass plaque to mount on the slab of stone that would eventually mark the grave. Slater had decided the plaque was not enough. Bright had found the gold teeth near the spot where Freddy had fallen. He'd turned them over to Slater who'd just put them where he was sure both Jiggs and Claybourne would have wanted them.

An hour later Slater trudged down Southard Street, a bulging laundry sack hanging over his shoulder, bouncing against his rump. Visiting hours at the hospital didn't start until fourteen hundred so he'd decided to kill some time washing his clothes and underwear. Kill some time, and get away from the Barracks where the grave reawakened visions. Dressed in jeans, shower thongs, and a Grateful Dead tee shirt, he headed out into no-man's-land.

Not much shaking on the street quiet except for the laundromat. He was half a block away when he heard singing—an old Baptist hymn. The words were garbled. One female voice, clear and distinct, rose above the clutter.

He knew the laundromat was a magnet for bums, winos, and anybody else in Key West down on his luck. It offered a roof, a few hard benches, and dry warmth on cool nights. Local cops seldom rousted the place; the laundromat kept drifters off the streets and away from cash-paying snow-birds.

This morning the bums were out in full force. As he claimed a washer and sorted his clothes, Slater noticed that the choir of vagrants and drunks (their song over) bunched up around an elderly woman with netted silver hair and a black wool cardigan. She handed out sandwiches and fruit, spouting Bible verse almost as fast as her congregation gobbled the chow.

Slater added soap to his load, shoved in a quarter, then settled on a bench.

"Got a quarter for the Lord?"

Slater turned to find a tin can held in front of his face by an almost toothless old man, with gray stubble and hollow, bottomless eyes full of white snot.

"Lord needs a drink that bad, does He?" Slater asked.

The old wino's eyes narrowed. "Don't blaspheme, sonny. You got enough sins ta send you ta hell already."

Slater sand-blasted the man with his glare. "I've been to hell, old man, and it ain't shit."

The wino shook his tin cup; a few lonely coins rattled loudly. "Save yourself, brother," he shouted, "before it's too late!" The man's eyebrows twitched weirdly.

"Get out of my sight, mister," Slater growled, "before I stuff ya in with the rinse cycle."

"What's all this, Brother Piplin?" The silver-haired lady faced the old wino, but Slater saw her give him the once-over.

"This boy's blasphemin', Sister Eunice," the bum whined. "Got no respect for the wrath of the Lord."

"Yes, yes. You let me handle it, all right? Why don't you go help Brother Ralph distribute the food?"

"If you say so, Sister," Piplin answered meekly. "You watch out. I seen his kind before; they're mean."

"Thank you, Walter. I'll be just fine."

Piplin muttered and shuffled toward the rest of the men.

Slater felt the woman's eyes on him as he watched the old bum slyly empty the tin cup into his pocket.

"Well . . ." The woman sat down beside him, her Bible held to her bosom. "You certainly got Brother Walter upset, young man. May I ask your name?"

"Jack Slater, ma'am, and I think you oughta know that your Mr. Piplin there is ripping you off."

"Yes, yes, I know. Old habits are hard to break. But he's trying to cleanse his soul for the day he stands in front of the Lord Almighty for judgment. Mr. Slater—may I call you Jack—Jack, have you ever considered how you would answer to God if this very day you died and found yourself in front of that heavenly throne and He asked you what kind of life you'd led?"

Behind the wire-rimmed glasses, pale blue eyes danced with an intensity Slater had seldom seen before. He felt those eyes peer inside his head, strip away flesh and bone, probing for weakness. He decided his best defense would be the wise-ass mode.

"I don't know, ma'am, but the way things have been going lately, I'd have plenty of time to think up something good waiting in line."

He could see she did not understand him and that she did not care for flippant answers even though her tight little smile didn't budge.

"Do you have any idea what eternal damnation is like, Jack?" she asked.

"I've eaten Navy chow," he said after thinking it over for a few seconds. "Figure that's pretty close."

For a brief moment she looked shocked, then quickly regained her composure, once again sweetness and light.

"A sense of humor is one of His gifts, but don't let it rob you of salvation."

"Why not? Life is supposed ta be a joke, ain't it?"

She held the Bible out to him. "There's not one joke in this book, and this book *is life*. In it are all the answers."

"Funny, that's what my DI said about the Marine Corps Guide."

"Then you have been led astray. Satan works in confusing ways. Sin is his calling card, lust is his middle name. Is Satan in your heart right now, Jack?"

"Not that I noticed. Sometimes he gets into the head of my pecker, though." He'd about had his fill of preaching, and he figured he'd bring it to a screeching halt. He felt ashamed, though. The old lady meant well; there was no need to get dirty.

Surprisingly, she didn't seem ready to quit. If anything, her eyes blazed even more intensely. She clicked her tongue.

"Tch, tch, tch. You young people today. Don't you know your life can be snatched from you at any time? No one is immortal. You are gambling with your soul, Jack, your *soul*. Do you want to die with an unclean heart?"

"Not anymore than I want to die with unclean skivvies, ma'am. That's why I'm here."

She reached out and touched his arm. "You may mock me, Jack," she said, "but don't mock the Lord. Repent your sins, accept Christ as your savior. Open your heart to Him and you will have everlasting life." She paused and looked up at the ceiling, as if God were somewhere in the cobwebs and fluorescent lighting. "He *died* for you, you know."

It came to him then, more real than it ever had before. He was back there, wading across the paddies from dike to dike, a routine patrol. It was hot. The sun was boiling. They were all dripping sweat, the only sounds heavy breathing and the wet sucking as muck clung to their boots, their feet thick squares of lead. It was his squad, his patrol, and he had taken the point, leading nine men on the familiar long walk that over months had become as routine as breathing. His eyes burned, his gut churned, his mouth too dry to swallow. Only a hammering in his head drove him on, a slow cadence—pick 'em up, put 'em down, left, right, left. He felt a hand grasp his arm. He stopped and turned

*tired eyes on the other man. Choo Choo. A brother, funny
dude, a cool dude, a take-no-shit dude who'd give a friend
his last drop of water or a sweet drink of syrup from C-rat
fruit cocktail. They had been together almost nine months.
Blood brothers, Choo Choo said.*

"Hey, man," Choo Choo grinned, "quit hoggin' all the
excitement. Go back to your radio, chump. The man is
callin'. You just let the Great Bazoo take the fuckin' point
for a while. You lookin' like shit."

"Screw you, Choo," he'd answered. "How come you
waited till we were only half a klick from home?"

*That was it—"half a klick from home"—the last words
he'd ever spoken to the man. Choo Choo slogged ahead
while he waited for Banana Dick and the radio.*

"Bravo 1-2, this is Bravo 1," the handset on the PRC-25
crackled. "Got a SITREP for me, over?"

*He was about to report an all clear when the booby trap
went off.*

"Are you all right, young man?" the woman asked.

Slater turned and stared at her. "You're right," he said,
"he *did* die for me!"

"Praise the Lord!" The woman clapped her hands.

*Slater dropped the handset and ran through the slop. It
was all a dream, something his fried brain had cooked up
moving through the paddy: the girl, the dog, Freddy,
Dutch, Key West—all a dream. Now he was on the edge of
waking up; he could feel it, just as he could feel the mud
sucking at him, slowing him, keeping him from reaching the
paddy dike.*

"I didn't ask him to!" he yelled.

"Of course, you didn't," the woman answered, awed.
"He didn't need to be asked."

*The mud wall of the paddy dike came away in his hands
as he clawed to climb it. He felt himself slipping back into
the muck. "Choo Choo!" he heard himself cry as he tore at
the mud. "Oh God, don't die, don't die." He began to cry.*

"Why him?" he asked the old lady in his dream. "Why him?"

"Because He loved you!" she exclaimed.

Through the tears he saw him then, what was left of him, face up in the muddy water, unmoving, an arm raised stiffly in a last good-bye. This was reality—the sight, the stink, the horror of reality. This was where it was at, the whole bloody ball of wax.

"He didn't have to die," he sobbed. "No reason for him to die."

"Brother Walter! The rest of you!" the woman shouted joyously. "Come quickly. Come pray with our new lamb. Jack, will you open your heart now? Will you open your heart and let Him in?"

"Yes," he answered the dream lady, coughing and choking on his own tears.

"Will you ask His forgiveness?"

"Yes, yes, just don't let him die."

"Then He isn't dead, dear boy. He lives!"

Slater raised his head, his tears burning hot on his skin. "He's alive?" It was too much to hope for.

"Yes, of course."

"Where? Where is he? I want to see him!"

"He's here! He's with us now!"

"No shit?" Slater didn't notice the old lady flinch; he was too busy searching the laundromat for that familiar face. All he saw was a lot of slack jaws, empty stares, hovering like hungry hyenas. He felt a moment of panic—what if the dream lady was lying to him? But no. Choo Choo, you son of a bitch. Just like Choo to make a joke, to hide from him. He jumped to his feet and shoved his way through the crowd of grizzled old men.

"Choo," he shouted, "when I find you, I'm gonna kick your young butt six ways from Sunday!"

He spotted the industrial dryers lined vertically on one side of the room, and immediately knew where Choo Choo was. He heard his own laughter as one by one he tore open the dryers. Someone pulled on his shirt, but he ignored it. It wasn't until he'd checked the last dryer in the row that he answered the insistent tug.

"Mr. Slater, Mr. Slater," a distraught-looking grandmother shouted at him. "You won't find Him there!"

"Where is he then? In a washer? Crazy fool!"

"Mr. Slater. Jesus does not hide in dryers or washers. In order to see Him you must ask Him into your heart."

He did a double take. How could she be so stupid. "I'm not lookin for *Jesus*, lady."

"Then who are you looking for?"

"Choo. Choo Choo Wilkes. My buddy."

"Well, he's not here as you can see!" she said, spreading her arms as if to reinforce the statement. "But perhaps he too could join us and be saved."

He felt something drain out of him then, like a suction hose pulling his insides through a strainer, leaving nothing but fatigue and frustration, and pain. He gagged.

"Goddamn you," he said to the woman, "He can't join us, lady! He's dead! Why have you been fucking with me?"

"Mr. Slater! Really! There is no need for such language." It was never going to end. He would never wake up, never *wanted* to wake up. Waking up would mean finding Choo Choo staring at him from the muck. Better to stay in the dream. But if this dream world was crazy, it was high time he joined the freakin' party.

Jack Slater began to peel off his clothes.

CHAPTER TWENTY-EIGHT

THE desk sergeant was matter-of-fact as he read out loud the arresting officer's report to the big Marine captain sitting across from him.

"According to eyewitnesses, the perpetrator, in a state of total undress, then followed Mrs. Eunice Howe out of the aforementioned Fister's Laundromat and onto the Southard Street sidewalk. He then proceeded to follow her northeast on Southard to Duval where Mrs. Howe's screams alerted other witnesses to her situation. With the perpetrator still in pursuit, Mrs. Howe then entered Maldonado's Cuban Sandwich Shop, 17 Duval Street, where she asked the counterman, one Alonzo Castro, to call the police. According to Mister Castro and a dozen other patrons of the shop, the perpetrator then entered through the front door and did then cause his male member to become erect and did perform masturbation upon same."

The desk sergeant paused and looked over the rim of his reading glasses. "This boy of yours been to Vietnam?"

"Yeah," Brule answered, his mind's eye trying to picture the scene in the sandwich shop.

"Figures," the officer said.

Screamin' Don felt a desire to reach out and grab the man by his tongue and shake until something gave. They were all such pompous assholes.

"It's this new generation, I guess," the sergeant sighed, "the one we're always hearing about. My war—the big one—we never had any of these kinds of problems. Did what we had ta do and forgot about it. My opinion, kids today had it too easy growing up."

Fuck you, Brule thought. He forced himself to swallow his anger; his words came out brittle but controlled. "Vietnam didn't cause this, Sergeant; coming home did."

The officer's mouth curved up in a contemptuous grin. "Yeah, sure . . . anyways," he focused again on the report. "To continue here, let's see—seeing that Mrs. Howe had taken cover behind the counter in the aforementioned establishment, the perpetrator exited the shop and began running in a southeasterly direction down the middle of Duval Street, becoming both a hazard to himself and to the orderly flow of traffic. No less than six motor vehicle operators reported finding it necessary to swerve to avoid causing injury. A vehicle owned and operated by the Conch Train Tours of Key West was forced to halt by a near riot among those passengers desirous of a photo opportunity and those seeking to avoid further view of the perpetrator's continued sexual behavior as previously described."

The desk sergeant made an up and down motion over his lap with a clenched fist, then continued.

"Due to the aforementioned traffic congestion, this officer was not able to close with said perpetrator until he had reached the vicinity of the Southern-Most Point. When I arrived on the scene, four separate vendors approached and informed me that the appearance of the perpetrator had caused panic among a large group of tourists, and had resulted in a substantial amount of damage to their property. I myself saw a great number of broken conch shells and other souvenir items scattered about the area.

"I then further followed the perpetrator on foot down to the water's edge where I successfully cornered him on an outcropping of rock. The perpetrator—white, male, five-ten, approximately one hundred and fifty pounds, short brown hair, no distinguishing body marks—ignored my verbal commands to surrender himself. This officer was forced to wade out to him to place him under arrest. I read him his Miranda rights and escorted him back to this station. He refused to make any statement. Subject was turned over to Sergeant Sylvester Markarn for subsequent booking. Signed: Officer Chester 'Chick' Cabrel. Key West Police Department."

The desk sergeant eased back in his chair and took off his glasses. "Ya know, this boy would still be a 'John Doe' if we hadn't found his ID in the trash at that laundromat. He clammed up on us like a nigra with lockjaw. We put him over to the county lock-up."

"What about his clothes and personal stuff?"

"Gone." The sergeant shrugged. "Winos took everything."

"I'll sign for him now," Brule said.

Brule came off the county jail's elevator and followed the turnkey through a heavy steel door and down the corridor outside the cells. He'd been to this zoo before, checking on other Marines who'd fucked up in Monroe County, but he'd never gotten used to the place, the cages full of fear and hate, the feeling that you'd fallen into a nest of vipers.

"Ya know, I can understand a man getting horny," the deputy offered, "but when it comes ta poundin' your pud in public . . . well, ya gotta draw the line somewhere. Here we are."

Screamin' Don saw the other men in the cell first—a big fat blubber ball in dirty briefs sucking his thumb, a skinny rat-faced kid sitting on a bunk and picking dead skin off the bottom of a foot, a couple of winos over in a corner sleeping off their sterno drunks in pools of their own barf. Against the back wall of the cage, Slater sat on the bare concrete, naked except for a blanket around his shoulders. There was a strange blank look on his face.

"Goddamn it to hell!" Brule exploded. "You put him in with this fuckin' sewage?" He whirled on the turnkey who took a couple of steps backward, his face reflecting surprise at the bark in the captain's voice.

"Hey, ease off there, Marine," the deputy blurted uneasily. "Look around for Christ sake. We're bustin' at the seams in here. Wasn't any other place to put him. Besides, it wasn't my idea in the first place."

"Why didn't you just flush him down the toilet and be done with it?" Brule hissed between clenched teeth. "Of all the fucking horseshit this two-bit tank town lays out, *this* takes the cake."

"Now hold on there," the deputy stammered. "You've got no authority here. You got any complaints, you see the sheriff. Don't take it out on me."

Brule looked back into the cage. The turnkey was right. Damn you, Slater, he thought. Why did you let them do this to you?

"Where are his clothes?"

"He don't have none," the relieved turnkey answered. "At least he didn't have none when they brought him in. We was all out of work duds. You can keep the blanket for a while. Just make sure it gets brung back. . . . Come ta think a it, better sign for it down at the desk."

The key rattled in the lock; the cell door opened with a crash. Screamin' Don took a step inside the cell, ignoring the other occupants.

"Slater?" he called.

The Marine looked at him for the first time.

"Time to go."

Neither of them spoke until they were seated in Brule's car and pulling out of the jail's parking lot. Slater stared straight ahead out the windshield, the blanket still loosely draped around his body.

"Sorry about all this, Captain," he finally said.

Brule glanced over, then returned his attention to traffic. "Just answer two questions, Slater," he said harshly. "Were you high on something? Pills? Weed?"

"No, sir."

"Drunk?"

"No, sir."

"Then why?"

"I don't know, sir. Just sorta flipped out." Slater paused. "Where we goin'?"

"To the Barracks. Get you a uniform."

"Then what?"

Brule downshifted as they approached the Main Gate. The sentry on duty was already snapping to attention.

"Then?" Brule thought things over one more time, then made his decision. "Then we're going to the hospital."

"You think I'm crazy, Captain?"

Screamin' Don looked over at the man and tried to smile. "Slater, you'd be crazy not to be."

EPILOGUE

Winter 199—

BRIEFCASE in hand, the dapper little man waited just outside the security area. The Miami airport's metal detection gear was powerful and the pins in his leg sometimes sent the buzzers and red lights into spasms. He could live without the hassle.

Suddenly a crowd of travelers with pale skin and clothing a little too heavy for South Florida temperatures came down the long corridor from the gates. Impatiently he scanned faces, realizing that there was a good chance he would not recognize the man he was looking for. It had been a while.

Slater followed the other passengers toward the main concourse. He wondered if he'd missed Van Groot at the gate when he passed the metal detectors and security guards.

"Hey, AJ! How they hanging?"

He saw him then, leaning on a cane and dressed in a rich-looking sportcoat and tailored slacks, shirt open at the collar. The changes were apparent but not startling: twenty extra pounds maybe, receding hairline, a few wrinkles, deep tan. There was no missing the grin, though, or the twinkle in the eyes. Besides, only one person had ever called him AJ. Feeling conspicuous in his off-the-rack Sears suit, he grinned back.

"Hello, Dutch," he said. "Good to see you."

The security guards were attracted for a moment by loud boisterous laughter. They carefully watched the two men hugging, then turned their attention back to their X-ray machines.

"What do you say we get a drink?" Van Groot said, still squeezing Slater's hand. "We've got plenty of time. Baggage handlers are on a slow-down strike."

"Whatever you say, Dutch. You're running the show."

Van Groot sipped a martini while Slater nursed a brew. The cocktail lounge was a cool dark place with piped-in music—a cocoon compared to the hustle outside. They spent half an hour talking old times, updating each other on their lives since the days at the Barracks, rehashing news that had been passed through occasional letters and telephone calls over the years. Slater was a card-carrying member of the middle class, had an associates degree in management, manager and owner of a Speedy Printing franchise, a wife and two kids, thank you, got some pictures right here in my wallet. Van Groot, on the other hand, was an American success story. He'd risen from assistant grease monkey to owner of a new car dealership, German Imports.

"Recession proof," the Dutchman chuckled. "The worse things get, the better my business. I tell ya, Jack, it's a gold mine."

"I can see that. You look good, Dutch. You really do . . . so tell me about this lady you're gonna marry. When do I get to meet her?"

"Tonight. At the rehearsal. Maria is a fox. Lot of class too. Her old man owns twenty miles of coastline."

Slater whistled. "Wow, sounds like you hit pay dirt."

"Yeah, only trouble is, the coastline's in Cuba." The Dutchman popped an olive into his mouth. "Now he runs a bakery down in Little Havana. They're good people. Two of her uncles bought wheels from me—cash on the barrelhead. I think they're gun runners, at least Raul is." He winked. "Maria can't wait to meet you, man, you and your missus. When's she getting here?"

"Saturday. Kids' winter break doesn't start till then. She'll drop 'em off at my brother's house, then fly on down."

"What's your brother doing these days?"

"Marty's a lawyer. Works for the Republican party. . . . Listen, Janet and I want to thank you for footing the tab for all this. I felt—still feel—a little guilty accepting."

"For Christ's sake, Jack, we've been through this already. You're my Best Man! And anyways, you're doing me a favor. Think I want to be the only 'gringo' at my own wedding? Besides, I owe ya."

"Bullshit. You paid me back that dough a long time ago."

"I can never pay you back, bro," Van Groot said deliberately.

"Bullshit," Slater mumbled this time. He felt embarrassed and looked away.

"I kid you not," the Dutchman continued. "Without that little nest egg, I don't know where I would've ended up. With it I had a chance to get my shit together."

"Well, you had it coming. After that shaft job the Crotch gave you, you had it coming."

"Shaft job?"

"You know, getting turned down for re-enlistment and all, for a few petty infractions."

Van Groot laughed. "Ya mean little things like blowin' a Navy admiral out of the water?"

"Yeah."

"Come on, AJ," the Dutchman said, throwing his arms wide. "They did me a favor, wouldn't you say?" He took another sip of his drink. "Otherwise, I'd probably still be out on Fleming Key, eating raw goosta. The joke is, *you're* the one they sent home for being dinky-dow."

They both laughed. How goddamn crazy it all was, Slater thought. Not so much what had happened to Van Groot as the whole mish-mash of events that shaped a man's life, events he had no control over.

"You ever hear from anybody—from the Barracks?"

"Naw, you're the only one I've kept in touch with really.

Sergeant Major Hollihan owns a bar down on the Keys. I drop in once in a while and bullshit with him."

"Wonder what happened to all those guys."

"Beats the hell out of me. Heard Benjamin—remember the little brother with the moustache? Yeah, he was killed in that Beirut bombing. And last spring I think Hollihan told me Lieutenant Kargo was a colonel or something, pushing papers up in DC. Anybody else, I dunno." Van Groot stretched, then checked his watch. It was a Rolex, Slater noted. He guessed he could have one just like it for half a year's pay. The Dutchman was definitely in the big time. "Listen, AJ, why don't you go get your bags? I'll get the car and meet you outside."

"Like I said, Dutch, this is your party."

Van Groot fumbled for something in his briefcase, then awkwardly stood, using the cane to maintain his balance. He placed a chamois-wrapped object in front of Slater.

"Little present for my Best Man," he said.

It was only brass, although under the bar lights it gleamed like gold. Slater read the inscription:

LANCE CORPORAL JIGGS

USMC

25 December 1972

HE DID HIS DUTY

"I figured if anybody deserved the thing, you did," Van Groot said.

"Where the hell did you get this, Dutch?" Slater felt a chill go through him as he ran his fingers over the cold metal.

"From his grave, where else?"

"But . . . why? It was supposed to stay there. He couldn't hide the exasperation in his voice.

"What for? So it could be buried when the bulldozers came? Things like this have to be remembered, Jack."

"Bulldozers?"

"It's what they usually use when a building has burned down," Van Groot said softly. "Bulldoze the whole area."

"The Barracks burned down? Thought it would've lasted another fifty years."

"Yeah, well, it needed some help from a guy named Willy-Peter."

Slater studied Van Groot's face for a moment, looking for a telltale smirk that would confirm a joke. The Dutchman's expression told him it wasn't.

"Why?" he finally asked, unable to find a reason in his own mind.

"I'll tell ya why, AJ. The Crotch has been out of there for years. Some fuckin' politicians wanted to turn it into a goddamn halfway house for junkies and scumbags."

They just stared at each other for a long while. Slater was not sure he understood, or that he ever would.

The Dutchman grinned. "Besides, I couldn't burn down a whole country, could I? Go get your bags, AJ."

Slater watched the little man turn and walk out of the lounge, rocking back and forth on the bad leg. When Van Groot had disappeared into the crowd, Slater looked back down at the grave plaque. He smiled.